AN ISLAND
PRINCESS
STARTS A
SCANDAL

Also by Adriana Herrera

Las Leonas

A Caribbean Heiress in Paris

Dating in Dallas

Here to Stay
On the Hustle

Sambrano Studios

One Week to Claim It All
Just for the Holidays…

Dreamers

American Dreamer
American Fairytale
American Love Story
American Sweethearts
American Christmas

Mangos and Mistletoe

Finding Joy
Caught Looking
Her Night with Santa
Monsieur X

For additional books by Adriana Herrera,
visit her website, adrianaherreraromance.com.

AN ISLAND PRINCESS STARTS A SCANDAL

ADRIANA HERRERA

CANARY STREET PRESS

CANARY
STREET
PRESS™

Recycling programs
for this product may
not exist in your area.

ISBN-13: 978-1-335-00634-9

An Island Princess Starts a Scandal

For questions and comments about the quality of this book, please contact us
at CustomerService@Harlequin.com.

Canary Street Press
22 Adelaide St. West, 41st Floor
Toronto, Ontario M5H 4E3, Canada
CanaryStPress.com

Printed in U.S.A.

To the OG Leonas, Nicole Cedeño and Indhira Santos, who have been happily letting me get them into trouble going on thirty years. Las amo, siempre.

Como diria Pedro… *Hay gente que hay que aguantar toda la vida.*

AN ISLAND
PRINCESS
STARTS A
SCANDAL

At the time, Sappho was reborn in Paris.

—Arsène Houssaye, *Confessions: Memoirs of a Half-Century, 1885*

One

Manuela del Carmen Caceres Galvan was a failure.

An absolute, unequivocal, dismal failure. It was the only title one could use for a person who, after three weeks in a city known the world over for its endless supply of debauchery, remained thoroughly undebauched.

And she was running out of time. In six weeks she would have to return to Venezuela to be married. With every minute that passed, the Parisian bacchanalia she'd fantasized about from the moment she'd agreed to enter into a loveless marriage slipped further away from her. Matters were truly arriving at a critical point, and she was determined to act.

It wasn't that Manuela was being forced into a union she reviled. On the contrary, she'd accepted Felix Bernard Kingsley's offer eagerly, as was her duty. It was true that Felix didn't possess much when it came to charm or family name. And he was not exactly an accomplished conversationalist or what one would call handsome or particularly interesting. But one attribute he did possess was the very one Manuela's parents valued above others: a very large fortune and no compunction whatsoever when it came to buying himself a beautiful bride with the right connections.

Marriage to a man who at the precise moment he'd asked for her hand informed her she should not expect fidelity was not exactly the stuff of fairy-tale endings. But twenty-eight years of witnessing her parents move through life as if consequences were merely abstract concepts had made Manuela a pragmatist and a realist. Pretty girls from families with unfortunate finances and very expensive tastes existed solely to secure advantageous attachments, after all.

She knew who she was.

Which was why when unexciting Felix with his perennially damp hands asked for hers in marriage, instead of dwelling on what she was giving up, Manuela smiled and nodded and thought about the injection of cash into her father's business. She imagined what colors she'd choose for the dozen gowns from the House of Worth Felix promised she could buy in Paris. She comforted herself with the knowledge that her parents could never again blame her for ruining the family.

In truth, considering her less-than-stellar options, she was quite content with her lot, and she still had a few weeks of freedom. Because despite the precariousness of her circumstances, before she'd allowed Felix to slide his gaudy ring on her finger, she'd made him promise to send her to Paris to procure her trousseau. It just so happened her two oldest and dearest friends from finishing school would be in Paris in their own pursuits. Luz Alana attempting to launch her rum Caña Brava into European markets, and Aurora endeavoring to forge some connections with other lady physicians. That two of Manuela's own paintings had been selected for the Exposition Universelle was the final sign that she was destined to enjoy her last months in the city of love before her impending nuptials.

Her parents, who'd never cared much for Manuela's artistic bent, were less receptive to her plan than Felix—who had been suspiciously eager to send her away for the summer—but Manuela had anticipated their protests. She sorted that minor hiccup by pointing out to Consuelo and Prospero Caceres that the best way to rub their restored financial glory in their peers' faces was to announce that their daughter would be embarking in a lavish, months-long Parisian shopping spree. She'd boarded a ship to Paris the following month. The first three weeks had involved a barrage of fittings at the modistes and conveying herself to what seemed like every housewares shop in the city to select from an ungodly number of curtains, rugs, wine goblets and tea sets, but now with that drudgery out of the way, she was finally free to enjoy herself.

An auspicious step in the right direction was finding herself at Le Bureau this evening. The notorious brothel, she'd been informed, offered among many other things meeting spaces for women seeking the company of other women. It took weeks of wheedling to convince her friends to accompany her on an exploratory mission, but the minute they'd walked in, Luz Alana had run off with Aurora in search of the owners of the pleasure palace, pursuing a business connection. Manuela understood her friend was under enormous pressure to secure some funds and had let her go, but she didn't have all night. They would have to return home eventually. Their cousin Amaranta had so far been the most lenient of chaperones during their time in Paris, but even she would take issue with them arriving home at dawn when they were supposed to be taking in an opera at the Théâtre Lyrique. Which was why she'd had to commandeer Antonio—Aurora's cousin who lived in Paris—for her expedition to the upper floor.

"You are sure there are entertainments to my specifications up here?" she asked her companion, who responded to her question by pointing at the red-papered walls. The lighting in Le Bureau was kept low enough that she had to put her face very close to the wall to make out the drawings, but once she did, she gasped with utter delight.

"Oh my," she said, the words rolling out of her like a purr while she ran her gloved hands over the black lines depicting couples engaged in a delightful array of erotic activities. One in particular displayed two women locked in a sensual embrace that made a shiver inch up her spine. It was so bold, so blatantly explicit, Manuela found herself a bit light-headed.

"Antonio, this is depraved," she whispered reverently, extending a finger to trace the lines of the sketch. Everything about this place was a fantasy, including the women etched in the paper: she knew this. But for a moment she allowed herself the luxury of wondering what it would be like to have that. A lover who would lay her on the grass for lazy, toe-curling kisses. A life and love that could live and breathe in the sun.

"No seas pendeja, Manuela," she muttered, giving herself a swift mental kick in her ample nalgas. She walked away from the idyllic lovers. Her musings, like the figures on the wall, were chimeras, but that didn't mean she couldn't find a very satisfactory way to spend this evening. No time for sentimentality when there was vice and perdition to chase down.

"Let's go, Antonio," she urged her friend, as she pulled her small watch from her bodice and winced. "We have less than an hour before Luz Alana and Aurora start looking for us." She should've never agreed to Aurora's request to reconvene at midnight. It was ridiculous to expect her to get anything truly outrageous done with this kind of time constraint. "How am I supposed to make any progress in my utter corruption if I am only allowed mere minutes?" It truly was the outside of enough.

"This is Paris, my dear." Antonio reassured her with a pat on her back. "You won't have to toil long to find at least a dozen ways in which to permanently stain your soul," Antonio quipped happily, which did amuse her.

"Then, enough dallying, Antonio. Lead me to sin!" She

clapped her hands with all the passion of a soldier rearing to be led into a battle as she ran up the stairs with her guide to the demimonde cackling behind her.

But this was no laughing matter. This was the city of sin, for goodness' sake, and the worst one she'd committed so far was accidentally exposing an ankle while avoiding a puddle. Tonight she would disgrace herself in some capacity, or there would be hell to pay.

"Here we are," Antonio informed her as they reached the landing of the second floor. There was not much to see. Once one reached the top of the stairs, the landing split in two directions, each leading to a different doorway. A red one on the right, and a black one on the left. The floors were made of black marble, and with the walls papered in the same tone, the message was quite clear: *you are entering a place of secrets.*

"That's the women's area," Antonio pointed to the doorway on the right. Above them, Manuela noted the crest of the Cisse-Kellys, the Irish-Senegalese twins who owned the establishment. The red double doors were open and flanked on either side by two very large men dressed in the burgundy and gold livery of Le Bureau. "There are open parlors with different offerings you can peek into," he winked, and anticipation fizzed under her skin like the bubbles of freshly poured champagne. The idea of room after room full of wicked offerings sent a delicious shiver through her as she faced down the doors. "A few wealthier clients have their own private rooms where they entertain, but those are usually closed."

Manuela nodded, ferociously curious about what kind of events one needed a closed door for at a *brothel*. "And you'll be in there." She lifted a finger to the black doorway.

"I could come with you," Antonio offered, likely hearing the nervousness in her voice. "They don't typically allow men in there, but I could explain you're only visiting Paris and—"

"Absolutely not," Manuela interrupted, swallowing down

the flicker of anxiety thrumming through her. This was not a place for girls too scared to be on their own. This was a place for women who knew what they wanted and were taking bold steps to obtain it. "I am offended at the mere suggestion I'd need assistance to get up to no good." She harrumphed for her friend's benefit, making Antonio dissolve into giggles.

"I suppose part of the thrill is getting to do this on your own." He leaned in to kiss her on the cheek as she practically levitated with the need to go in search of this long-awaited adventure.

It wasn't that she expected something magical to happen here or that she was foolish enough to believe someone beyond those doors would somehow change the course her life. She didn't need or want that. All she craved was to—for at least a few hours—freely be a version of herself she'd so far only imagined.

"I'll be perfectly fine."

"If you're sure…"

"I have never been more certain of anything," she affirmed, offering him a radiant grin for good measure. She didn't bother denying her nervousness, Antonio knew her well enough, but right beneath that there was the undeniable excitement at the possibility of being in a room with other women with her same inclinations.

"Go!" She shooed Antonio to his side of the floor, as she nodded at the two gentlemen at the red door. "I will not leave this place without at least one scandalous anecdote for the carriage ride home."

"I have no doubt you will…" Antonio began, but she was already on the prowl.

"I'll see you at midnight," she whispered over her shoulder before setting off.

Manuela's French had never been as good as she'd liked, and she wasn't quite sure what the guards told her about la dixième porte before she was allowed in the ladies' quarters. In any case, she set off down the long hallway, her pulse fluttering in her throat. It was a long, wide passage lined with sconces that kept the space illuminated enough not to trip on anything but not so much one could clearly see the faces of those passing by. Unless you were close enough to kiss, which was a very promising sign as far as Manuela was concerned. She supposed the most valuable attribute of any establishment offering the services Le Bureau boasted would be its ability to guarantee discretion.

It wasn't that Manuela was a complete ingenue. After her time at her Swiss finishing school ended, she'd managed to persuade her parents to allow her to remain in Paris for three glorious months studying at an arts seminary. While she was there, she'd heard rumors from other girls of places that catered exclusively to women looking for the company of other women. She would have probably mustered up the courage to venture to la Butte perched above the city where these establishments existed, had her time in Europe not been cut short.

Unfortunately, ten years later, the sum of her experiences with other women amounted to a few stolen kisses with Catalina Montero, the daughter of one of her father's business associates. Though things with them had ended abruptly—and disastrously—the questions she'd held so deeply buried about herself, about her nature, had been answered with the blare of a thousand trumpets with each heated kiss, each secret look, each furtive touch with Catalina. After, when she'd been told that acting on any urges of that nature would irreparably tarnish her soul, Manuela refused to believe it. How could something that felt so essential, that made her feel so gloriously alive, be wrong? She'd come back to Paris to find that feeling again, to at least temporarily revive those slumbering pieces of herself one last time.

As she reached one of the open doors, Manuela swept aside her musings about the dismal past—and future—and focused on the much more promising present. She stopped when she heard music spilling out of one of the rooms in the corridor. "Finally," she thought as she took a hesitant step toward the threshold, unsure of whether she was allowed inside.

It was a large room, and around it milled about a dozen women. Four were dancing in front of a string quartet set up in a corner. Women dancing together was not exactly scandalous, but these were not the demure ballroom-dancing lessons Manuela had taken at her finishing school. Not with the way these women were tangled in each other. Not with their bodies so close they seemed fused together. And their faces, hungry expressions, lust blazing in their eyes. It made her feel like an intruder; it made her ache.

A plump redhead who was much shorter than her partner had to bend her head far back to gaze upon her lover. She had her eyes wide open, beaming as the other woman curled a lock of fiery hair around her fingers. The gesture, their private, tender smiles unfurled a pang of longing Manuela hadn't felt in years. As she watched them move around the room, arms wrapped around each other, she wondered if these women had fiancés or husbands in some faraway place to go back to or if this truly was their life. If they came here whenever they pleased to dance cheek to cheek and kiss and touch.

"Mademoiselle, this is a private party."

She'd been so enthralled in watching the dancers the gentle rebuke caught her completely by surprise.

"Pardon," she apologized breathlessly, her heart leaping up her throat, as the woman politely—but firmly—closed the door in her face. "Well, that wasn't very nice," she muttered to herself as she started down the hallway again. She wished she'd asked Antonio more about how these rooms worked. He'd said she could go into the ones that were open, but clearly that wasn't true of all of them. Aurora would say it was just like her to go barreling in without considering what lay ahead.

In this moment, what lay ahead were additional closed doors.

All but one, at the very end of the hall. She noticed the number above the double doors was ten.

La dixième porte.

It was the only room the guards had mentioned, and now she wondered if they'd been advising it was the only room available to her. She supposed someone would let her know if she was not allowed, as they'd done in the previous one. She told herself she'd be careful as she stepped inside, but instantly became much too preoccupied with the room's decor and art to care much about permissions.

The room was quite large, and it was clearly for entertaining. There were a couple of sitting areas at both ends of the space and more settees and chaises placed in corners and along the walls. There was also a large sideboard which at the moment was empty but she assumed would be used to serve food and wine.

The decoration was not exactly masculine, but it was very dapper. The colors surprised her. The walls were a tea-rose pink with black accents, and the upholstery was of black velvet. She took in the bountiful flower arrangements around the room. Sprays of pink and black gladioli. It was a blend of the feminine and masculine Manuela found very intriguing. She also appreciated the departure from the ostentatious gilt and fringe which was the current preferred style in Paris. It was understated, and yet everything was indisputably sumptuous and expensive.

Whoever owned this room had no need to overtly display their wealth. One of the skills one gained after being raised in affluence only to lose it in adulthood was the ability to note when you arrived at a place where wealth was merely incidental.

The mistress of this place—another assumption based on this being the area reserved for ladies—had to be an art lover, judging by what was hanging on the walls. Manuela strolled around the periphery, sticking her nose right up to the pieces. There were at least a dozen different paintings, one more exquisite than the next. The styles differed, as did the sizes, but the theme was singular: women loving women. It was deliciously illicit to see this much carnal feminine pleasure. What kind of person, *what kind of woman*, was free enough to display her preferences so brazenly?

"One who probably knows all the secret places I am desperate to discover." She needed to stop talking to herself out loud, but there was too much happening inside her to not voice some of it! After circling the room she finally tipped her head up and had to clamp a hand over her mouth to keep from squealing.

"Oh my." She whispered reverently as she took in the magnificent ceiling. First there was the chandelier. Oval shaped at the base, with a black lacquer stem inlaid with mother-of-pearl flower petals. She counted sixteen large glass spheres jutting from gilded arms. It was impressive in size and craftsmanship, but what made her stumble was the fresco rendered all around it. The pastoral scene brought to mind Botticelli's *Primavera* with its dark background and vivid flora. But in this garden the graces were not whispering secrets to each other, they were making love. There were no absent looks to be found in their angelic countenances. Instead there was palpable carnality to the scene that stole her breath.

Manuela's eyes went back and forth over the figures on the ceiling. She caught sight of fingers digging into flesh, hands straining to touch a lush hip or arched back. Two of the graces had their mouths fused together while the third knelt before them in offering. The composition of it was vivid and languid… achingly sensual. Gooseflesh bloomed on her skin as she moved farther into the center of the room, needing a closer look.

She was transfixed in particular by the pair depicted at the very edge of the fresco. One was brown-skinned and lying on a rug, her back propped by pillows as she looked down at her lover who was suckling one of her breasts with aching tenderness. The sight of the two women in such an intimate embrace shook Manuela. She'd seen art with a sensual tone to it, of course— she'd secretly even tried her hand at some erotic art. But frescoes of this scale were typically done by men, and *this* could've only been done by a woman, of that Manuela was certain.

There was something about a man's perception of feminine beauty that always felt to her a bit warped, misunderstood. Manuela seldom encountered any true vulnerability in the lovely faces of the models. It seemed to her the scope of a man's gaze when it came to femininity was limited to that of the mother or the vixen. A woman could only be truly good if she was devoid of any sensuality, and if it was present in her, then it had to be taken—and afterward, succinctly punished. She'd always wondered if that was why the Madonna was such a compelling subject for men, because they could envision her beyond a thing to possess. That a woman's body could only truly be sacred when it served as a vessel. This painting subverted the very notion of that. For this artist the female form was made for pleasure.

She wondered if there was a signature somewhere but was too far away to tell.

"There must be something I can use to give me a boost," she muttered to herself as she scanned the room's opulent furnishings. Finally on the far side, below a particularly lusty rendering of Artemis and Callisto, she spotted a black velvet footstool and ran to fetch it. Her slippers made her slide ominously on the gleaming parquet floor, and it occurred to her that perhaps climbing onto the sleek surface of the sideboard with her shoes on might not be advisable. It was true that the sensible thing would be not to climb on it at all, but she could be sensible when she when was back in Venezuela.

"It will just be a quick look," she promised herself as she slid out of her velvet slippers, perfectly aware she was wasting precious depravity-seeking time, but she was only human. Who could resist taking a better look at such beauty? Manuela could never pass up the chance to feast her eyes on art that truly moved her. Some had a hard time stopping when it came to wine or chocolate. Just one sip or one bite was never enough when it came to things that were so pleasurable to consume. For Manuela, art was intoxicating.

With urgency she tossed her silk stockings beside the discarded shoes. The constriction of her corset proved to be a challenge when climbing the sideboard, but she persevered. The fresco was still about five feet above her head, but from her perch she had a perfect view of the pair lying on the rug. Her eyes kept coming back to the pained ecstasy on the face of the dark-skinned woman as her lover kissed her breasts. Her lids heavy with lust, hands clutching the pillows for purchase. She was absolutely riveted by the idea of being touched where anyone could see. The prospect of a lover who would never deny her a caress, would never hide their passion was no more than a silly dream, but that was what art did: it made fantasies tangible, painted the picture of your deepest desires.

"The Cisse-Kellys said we should expect amenities for the exposition, but this is excessive even for them."

The sultry voice coming from below—which sounded mildly amused, thank goodness—almost caused Manuela to stumble right off the sideboard.

She'd been caught. Why did she have to always go trampling around the world like a brown sprite and not thinking before she acted?

"You ought to keep that door closed," she said defiantly, in place of an apology. Dear God, what was wrong with her?

"It's my art's fault that you are climbing my furniture, princess?" There was still a hint of humor in the woman's voice. And did she just call her *princess*? *Please let this be the precursor to a torrid fantasy,* Manuela silently begged from her perch.

"Do you need a hand to come down?" It was more of an order than a question. But if she thought that would embarrass Manuela she was in for an unpleasant surprise.

"If you're worried about the furnishings, I made sure I took off my slippers, and my feet are very clean."

"You mean the feet that are currently on my Nero Portoro marble."

Goodness, that voice made coils of heat burn inside her. "If you don't want people climbing on your furniture, you should cover up that fresco—" It occurred to her that going on the offensive with exactly the kind of woman she was hoping to meet was not the wisest of choices, but Manuela had never been too wise. She leaned forward to offer a flirtatious apology but slipped on the sleek top of the sideboard instead. She promptly plummeted to the ground like the hopeless muppet she was, only to be caught by the most striking creature she'd ever seen.

"Oof," the Valkyrie groaned as she took the impact of Manuela's body crashing down on her. "You do make your presence known, princess," her savior whispered as she held her.

"I—" Manuela's words failed her, bewitched by those lavender feline eyes.

"Angels falling from the sky—the French have truly outdone themselves." For once, Manuela had no pithy comment our saucy remark to volley in return. This woman was as breathtaking as the art on her walls. Her strong embrace the most comforting thing Manuela had felt in much too long. Those arms, as slender as they were, could've been made from steel.

"Where did you come from, angel?"

"From the stairs," Manuela responded numbly, much too stunned by the vision in front of her to come up with an intelligent response. The woman was older—not that one could tell from her face, but because there were a few streaks of gray at her temples. The rest of her hair, which was pulled back in an elaborate crown of braids, was very black. Her remarkable eyes were swirls of gray and lavender, like cloudy amethyst. The color was so unusual it made Manuela wish for her watercolors.

"Did anyone tell you what happens on the second floor?" the goddess asked, still not letting go of Manuela. This was a blessing and a curse, because while she was absorbing every detail of that exquisite countenance, it was getting harder to refrain from doing something that would likely get her in more trouble than she already was.

Her skin tone was bronzed, which was an interesting juxtaposition to her refined English accent. And her face was not what one would call conventionally beautiful, but she exuded a certain kind of captivating arrogance. She was very serious, even though her eyes seemed to sparkle with humor. Her brows were thick and very long, giving her a forbidding air. The bridge of her nose was wide, as was her mouth. But while her lips were lush and full, her chin was small, delicate. It was a face full of contrasts and angles, and Manuela really should begin responding to her questions.

"I'm sorry," she apologized, and then instantly put her foot in her mouth, again. "Your face is distracting me." That lavish mouth tipped up, and something whooshed in Manuela's belly.

"Maybe you do know what happens up here." Her eyes twinkled with mischief.

"I know what happens," Manuela managed to say, her voice shaky. Why was she being so timid? She was here to meet women like this, beguiling and wicked. "You have excellent taste in art." Art? Was she truly talking about art? Despite her faux pas, when Manuela looked at the beauty, she was happy to find a hint of appreciation in her expression.

"Hm." The sound she made was of curiosity...which had to be a positive sign? Manuela's body certainly thought so, or at least she hoped that was the reason for the ball of fire spreading to her limbs. "So your interest in my fresco was not distaste, then."

"Distaste?" Manuela exclaimed, affronted as she pulled away from the embrace and immediately regretted it. "Absolutely not. It's glorious." She rubbed her hands over her arms which felt too bare now that they were no longer in contact with those strong hands.

"Glorious enough to make you discard your shoes to explore." She was being teased, she knew that, and her behavior had been quite gauche.

"My apologies for climbing on your furniture," she conceded, and a thick, black eyebrow rose suspiciously at her apology. Manuela considered her overture accepted, and after a sufficiently aggrieved pause, she continued. "I only wanted to look at it more closely. I tend to forget the rules of propriety when I happen upon an exciting piece of art."

In order to cement her contriteness, Manuela swept her glance downward and noticed that her companion was wearing trousers. But these were not ill-fitting men's trousers or the split skirts Aurora used. They had clearly been made just for her. The fabric looked like silk, and it was a very dark green. The fitted jacket, vest and tie were of precisely the same color. The only contrast was found in her crisp dark gray shirt. The effect, combined with the cut of the suit, accentuated her height instead of attempting to conceal it. This woman truly was every one of Manuela's fantasies come to life.

"You find art with women making love intriguing, then." That raspy, alluring voice was like a siren song to Manuela. There was heat in those lavender eyes, and Manuela ached to be scorched.

Be bold, Leona, she told herself, smiling at the nickname she and her friends had given themselves in finishing school. "It's intriguing, but I think *arousing* is a better word."

She was well-rewarded for her boldness, and in the next instant was back in those strong arms. Manuela was curvier than this sinewy, slender woman, but she'd never felt as cradled, as protected as she was in that moment.

"We are kindred spirits, then." Once again Manuela found herself tongue-tied, utterly dumbstruck by this Amazon. "Are you an artist?" Her eyes were focused on Manu's ungloved fingers which were perennially smudged with paint or charcoal.

She'd been fiddling with a drawing on the carriage ride over, and it seemed she had not properly wiped off the evidence.

"I didn't get it on anything, I promise." This was a lie, of course. She was always leaving traces of her curiosity over things, but the woman seemed to find this amusing.

"Tell me what you find beautiful about it."

Manuela squirmed, eyes trained on the slippers and stockings on the floor. This shyness was irritating. She was never like this. She strove to always be the boldest person in a room. But she was usually in rooms where people were shocked easily. There was no precedent for this place or this woman.

"Shouldn't I put my shoes on?"

"No." It wasn't a rebuke, not when it was delivered with such ease. This was a woman accustomed to having people heed her commands. Manuela had met generals with less poise. She raised an eyebrow in question when Manuela remained silent. Her lips were so full and plump, it was almost obscene. It was such a stark face in some ways, but that mouth was as inviting as perfectly ripe fruit. One could not look at it and not crave a bite. "Tell me about my fresco, princess."

Had the request been about anything other than her thoughts on a piece of art, Manuela would likely be too awestruck to come up with a sensible answer, but this was the one thing she never faltered on. And she was vain enough to want to make an impression on this mysterious woman who had quite literally swept her off her feet.

"It's the point of view," she declared and her companion turned her face up to the ceiling at the comment. The tip of one shiny burgundy boot tapped on the floor as she considered Manuela's words. "Simply from the effect it has on me, the places my eyes are drawn to. I know it was a woman who conceived it."

"Fascinating," she said, still looking up.

"It's the way they're looking at each other, you see," Manuela explained, pointing a finger at the ceiling. "It's so active. There's no flaccidity, no languidness to these women. These Graces are positively galvanized with each other. The desire is palpable." Another one of those curious sounds escaped her companion, encouraging her to go on. "They are in front of what they want and are free to reach for it, utterly unguarded in their desire. This artist understands that women are only mysterious to those who don't deserve their naked honesty." This earned Manuela a surprised look and an almost rueful smile.

"My friend Cassandra made it."

"Cassandra Aguzzi Durocher," Manuela guessed.

"Very good, princess."

Manuela's entire body lit up from the praise, paired with the very appreciative glance at her décolletage. She was wearing at least five layers of clothing, but this woman made her feel exposed, undefended. "I saw her work at the Biennale in Florence last year. I'd recognize her style anywhere. It's exquisite." Cassandra Aguzzi Durocher was a very well-known Brazilian landscape artist. She was quite gifted, but she was of particular interest to Manuela because a few years earlier she'd caused quite the scandal after fleeing to Paris with her lover—a Peruvian lady doctor.

"You are quite exquisite yourself." There was so much promise in those words, Manuela imagined her body electrified like Eiffel's tower in the evenings. More emboldened now, she challenged herself to press closer. Their heights differed by a few inches so the top of her breasts brushed against the woman's smaller chest. It was delicious friction, she almost whimpered at the thought of being naked with this languid, sultry creature. Of looking her fill, while her hands roamed the lines of her. Pressing their bodies together until their hills and valleys were meshed.

A fingernail softly dug into her chin, bringing her back to the moment as her face was lifted. Her throat went dry with aching need, her insides blooming again. Firm fingers now cupped her cheek.

"Have you ever been kissed by another woman?"

"Yes," she answered breathlessly. Lips tingling from the promise in those amethyst eyes.

"Did you like it?"

Manu attempted to answer, but when she parted her lips a nervous puff of air was all she could produce. She was confronted with a foxy, wily smile that weakened her knees.

"Is that why you came here tonight? To be kissed?"

Nothing she'd envisioned as she entered that hallway could've prepared her for what she'd actually found, however she was finally remembering what she'd come searching for.

"I wouldn't mind being kissed by you." Blood rushed to her temples at her boldness, but the corners of that ripe mouth tipped up with amusement.

"You look like an angel."

"And would you be the devil in disguise, poised to be my downfall?" Manuela probed flirtatiously, annoyed by the disappointment she felt at the woman's fixation with her looks. Wasn't this what she wanted? Why did that bother her?

Because that was the only thing people saw. Because it was the only thing they ever cared to see. What had she expected? This was a brothel. A place for anonymous trysts. Not a place to find love. Not that love had any place in the life Manuela has chosen for herself.

Still, she wanted the kiss more than her next breath. She stretched up eagerly and felt a hand at her lower back, bringing her closer. She strained for it, lifted herself farther. She closed her eyes, parting her lips expectantly, her mouth dry while her pulse fluttered frantically in her throat.

The jarring sound of a clock striking midnight broke them apart, sending Manuela stumbling back with a yelp.

Antonio.

"My friend," she said regretfully as she moved for the door, then remembered she was in her bare feet.

When she turned, the Amazon was standing behind her with her slippers in one hand, the other on her hip in a provocative stance.

"There is no Prince Charming here, Cinderella," she teased, handing over the slippers.

"I have no use for a Prince Charming," Manuela declared, her more brazen self finally making an appearance as she slid on her footwear. "The villains are always much more intriguing."

The other woman sent her a long, heated look but didn't move, and she was quite done with waiting. Impulsively she rushed forward, rose on the tips of her toes and stole a kiss from that tempting mouth. At first, it was a soft, tentative kiss, but soon she was being pulled closer and skilled lips were taking hers with dizzying skill. Yes, this was what she needed. She was floating, her legs, her body loosening to this seductive caress. Her body coming alive with every touch.

"Mademoiselle, a gentleman is looking for you," someone called from the door, wrenching her away again.

"Demonios," she practically cried, frustrated beyond belief. It was her own fault for dallying with the art. "I have to go. Perhaps I'll see you again?" she asked hopefully as she stepped away. But in return she only received another one of those burning stares and a disappointing shrug of a shoulder.

"Paris is like a village, princess, especially for women like us."

Two

———————————

"Don't look at me that way, Luz Alana Heith-Benzan. I am extremely cross with you," Manuela told one of her two best friends as their carriage navigated the streets of Paris on the way back to their rented town house on the Place des Vosges.

"What did I do now?" Luz Alana asked, wide-eyed as the three of them bounced around on the banquette on the bumpy ride from Le Bureau. The streets were crowded even at almost one in the morning. It was as though no one in Paris wanted to go home to sleep in the event they missed something. This city always had a marvelous amount of diversions, but the exposition had transformed it into something absolutely incandescent, and Manuela finally had experienced a tiny touch of that magic. Magic that she desperately wanted to experience again, though she had no idea how to go about it.

"You know exactly what you did, Miss All Business," Manuela huffed, while Luz Alana feigned innocence. "I cannot believe you kissed the Great Scot while I barely got to see anything of Le Bureau. *I*—" she dramatically poked her own chest for effect "—was the one who came here with the intention of being ravished in a dark corner by an exceedingly disreputable rake, or rakess in my case."

Which could've happened had you not prattled on about a fresco for an eternity.

"I didn't exactly plan to kiss the man, Manuela," Luz Alana protested. Her beautiful face flushed with pink at the memory of her tryst with the Scottish whisky maker. Manuela wasn't truly cross with her friend. Dutiful Luz Alana had been doggedly—and so far fruitlessly—attempting to find an ally since they'd arrived in Paris, and Evanston Sinclair so far was the only one to take her seriously. And it seemed obvious to everyone the man was interested in more than just a business venture with Manuela's best friend. It was welcome news, really. Luz Alana had been dealing with so much since the death of her father, she deserved a little indulgence, especially the kind that came in very large and handsome packages. "Besides, you met someone," Luz Alana shot out as the three of them descended onto the street as quietly as they could.

A smile tipped up her lips at the thought of her own dashing stranger at Le Bureau. "Oh, all right. I forgive you." She accompanied the verbal olive branch with a pat on her friend's arm. "She was beguiling," she admitted, thinking of the lush mouth and canny eyes. She only wished she'd had more time. "But I didn't even get a name. I have to return to find her."

"I am *not* going back to that place again," retorted Aurora, in that infuriatingly stubborn way of hers.

"That's easy for you to say. You already saw people making love five feet from you!" Manuela protested, while Aurora shuddered at the mention of the show her friends had unknowingly walked into at the brothel. "I will have to go back to experience it myself." Poor Aurora groaned.

"You should've seen her face, Manu." Luz Alana's words were strained as she tried her best not to laugh. Aurora had no such compunction.

"I will not dignify that filthy comment with an answer," Aurora huffed haughtily. "Could we please focus on getting into this house without announcing ourselves to the entire street?"

"Good point," retorted Luz Alana in an impressively controlled voice, while Manuela struggled to smother the laughter bubbling up in her chest. This was why she'd wanted to come with them to Paris. When the three of them were together, adventure always ensued. "How are we supposed to get inside without alerting Amaranta to the fact that we arrived hours past our curfew, smelling like whisky, tobacco and sex?"

Luz Alana's question returned Manuela to their current exploit, and she noticed the distressed set of Aurora's mouth. The last thing they needed was their friend going into a panic. "Luz, why would you say something that will only encourage Aurora's dramatics?"

"It's not dramatics, Manuela. I cannot be found walking around this city at all hours of the night reeking of sin and regret."

"I only wish I smelled like sin and regret," Manuela said wistfully, eliciting a fit of giggles from Luz Alana and an exasperated eye roll from Aurora.

Aurora sighed as she peeked through the small glass window on the town house's front door and reached for the door handle. "Don't bother, it won't open." Manuela whispered, to which Aurora responded with a very pugnacious raising of the eyebrows. "There's another door around the back," Manuela chided, hiking up her frothy skirts and signaling to the back of the house.

"Then, why didn't you say so?" Aurora cried.

"Because I was busy mentally berating myself for not getting my lady's name! Come over here." She waved a hand to the back of the house, and the others followed her with dark expressions. "I'm so cross with myself," she admitted, as the others stared at her in confusion. "I *had* her. She was exactly what I'd dreamed of when we arrived at Le Bureau, and I left with no means of finding her again."

"You will have more chances," Luz Alana assured her, with a soft pat on her shoulder. Even Aurora shot her a sympathetic look.

"Never mind." She knew her friends didn't understand her, but they wanted to see her happy regardless. That was their friendship in a nutshell: unconditional.

Once they got to the back of the house, Manuela pointed to the small door in the sunroom she'd commandeered as her art studio. "We only have to climb the ladder." She trembled remembering the climbing she'd done earlier that night. The memory of tumbling into the arms of that beautiful woman, of the way she'd called Manuela *princess*, sent a shiver through her body.

She should've kissed her sooner. She should've found out who she was. Antonio, who had stayed at Le Bureau after all, offered to investigate but couldn't promise he'd find out anything. The establishment was quite strict about keeping their patrons' anonymity, but she hoped what the beauty had said about Paris being a village was true. She couldn't shake the feeling she'd made a grave mistake by walking away.

As she, Luz Alana and Aurora climbed under the cover of darkness, she promised herself one thing: if she was granted another chance to kiss her mystery woman, she would not hesitate.

"Ouch, carajo! Manuela, open the door!"

Aurora's pained yelp snapped Manuela out of her musings, but she'd been so lost in her thoughts she had to get her bearings. "Here," she whispered, turning the handle. "I left it unlocked." She winced when the door creaked. The sound was like a gunshot in the silence that surrounded them.

"Careful with that, the paint is still fresh," she warned as Luz walked ominously close to the portrait of Clarita that she'd finished that day. Clarita, Luz's younger sister and Manuela's protégée—

and the only other person in their household who knew how to enjoy herself—would be livid when she found out Manuela had failed to recruit her as their lookout for the evening.

"Good grief, has this house's hallway always been so long?" Aurora whispered as the three of them attempted to reach the staircase leading to the bedrooms. She sounded so exasperated Manuela let out a laugh, which elicited a firm *Shhh* from Luz Alana. They were as quiet as a herd of elephants.

"Bandidas!"

Luz yelped, startled by Amaranta's reproach coming from somewhere in the dark expanse of the house.

"Diablos, we were so close!" Manuela cried with heartfelt regret. From behind her she could hear Aurora's curse and Luz Alana's guilty gasp. "Amaranta, querida, you didn't have to wait up for us!" She tried to infuse her words with as much guilelessness as one could while caught in the act of slinking back into a house after an evening of brothels and champagne...and kissing strangers.

"Not one of you is as sabia as you think you are," Amaranta scolded as she made her way to them, illuminating the space with the small gas lamp in her hand. "Manuela, wipe that smirk off your face. Your mother would have me skinned alive if she knew what I'm letting you get away with." Despite her threats, their chaperone looked more amused than disgruntled as she ushered them into the parlor where she'd apparently been holding vigil. There was a half-empty glass of port and Luz Alana's copy of *Blanca Sol* by Mercedes Cabello de Carbonera on the small table next to an armchair. Amaranta had only started the book that afternoon, and Manuela noticed she was almost halfway through. She'd clearly been there a while.

"Ay, prima, we were just celebrating Luz Alana's triumph at the judgment tonight. Her rum got a ribbon at the exposition." Luz Alana shot Manuela a pointed look as she arranged her gown on the settee. Her friend clearly didn't want to expound too much on her own adventures that evening.

"I tried to tell them, but you know how they are." Aurora didn't even attempt to provide an excuse and went over to the sideboard to pour herself some port.

"Aurora," both Manuela and Luz Alana chided. She had always been the weakest link, confessing to a crime before they were even suspected of it.

She sent them both a look that said *I can't live with the weight of these lies* and to Manuela's horror launched into her confession. "They dragged me to a live—"

"Ah, ah, ah!" Amaranta frantically held up her hand, shaking her head. "I do *not* want to know. That way I'll at least have some plausible deniability of your whereabouts. Besides, I'm waiting up for a different reason."

At that, Luz Alana looked concerned. "Did Clarita give you any trouble, prima?"

Amaranta sighed in feigned exasperation at the mention of their charge, but the indulgent look on her face told a different story. "She was very cross that Manuela left before they could do their daily boberia, or whatever it is they call it."

Manuela wished she could wake up the little fresca. Clarita and Luz Alana had lost their mother ten years earlier and their father only two years before. For Luz Alana, it had been devastating. For Clarita, who was only eleven, to lose both parents at such an early age had made her wise—and morbid—beyond her years. The child also possessed a streak of wildness that Manuela could connect to. That was why she'd devised their daily boberia. Each afternoon Clarita came up with something absolutely ridiculous for them to do which Manuela dutifully went along with. So far, they'd played various pranks on the very unamused porter, had attempted multiple magic tricks with varying degrees of success, and on one occasion spent a day creating an astonishingly lifelike papier-mâché mouse they'd left in Aurora's medical bag. It was the most fun she'd had in Paris, until tonight. "Ah, we will have to make sure to do two of them tomorrow," she declared, then took a seat across from Amaranta, who thankfully seemed more amused than upset by their sneaking around.

"I don't think you'll have much time for boberias tomorrow," their chaperone countered, pulling a small card from her dressing-gown pocket. "This came while you were at the opera, Manu." The pointed tone in which Amaranta said *opera* told Manuela their cousin knew they'd never planned to go to the theater.

"What's that?" Aurora asked, as she poured them glasses of port.

Manuela took the card from Amaranta. "I have agreed to have lunch with one of the people interested in purchasing Baluarte."

"Oh," Luz Alana said in surprise, as she reached for the small glass Aurora passed her. "I didn't know you'd reconsidered selling it."

"I haven't," Manuela retorted, awkwardly, not entirely sure why she'd agreed to this lunch. "But," she said and lifted a shoulder, focusing on reading over the note so that she didn't have to look at her friends' concerned faces, "it won't hurt to listen to their new offer, even if I don't accept it."

Baluarte was a piece of land in Puerto Cabello, on the western coast of Venezuela, that Manuela's grandfather had purchased shortly after arriving in the country seeking exile.

Twenty-five years earlier—when Manuela had only been three years old—her family had been forced to leave their native Dominican Republic for opposing the ruling government's plan to annex the country back to Spain. They'd managed to establish themselves well enough. Her paternal grandparents brought their knowledge in candle making to Venezuela and opened a factory that thrived under Ramon Prospero Caceres Santoro's leadership.

Ramon purchased Baluarte as a gift for Manuela's grandmother, Carmen Delia. The two hundred acres of seafront property were to be used to fulfill Carmen Delia's lifelong dream of opening an art colony where women from the Americas could come and learn. Once Manuela began to show interest and talent for the arts, her grandmother shared her dream with her granddaughter. For a long time, Manuela imagined her future self at the helm of a school that welcomed and nurtured promising women artists. But when the family's business began failing once Manuela's father took over the reins, they were forced to sell their holdings to keep the family afloat: including her beloved Baluarte.

To Manuela's—and her parents'—surprise, six months ago, almost two years after her grandmother's death, a solicitor appeared at their home to inform them the beachfront property once again belonged to the family. It appeared that when Carmen Delia sold Baluarte, she'd included a clause allowing for her to buy it back within five years of the sale. Without her son or daughter-in-law's knowledge, the matriarch had managed to cobble together the funds for the purchase and left the deed in Manuela's name. It had been her final attempt to not only keep that lifelong dream alive but to give her granddaughter a chance at some independence, though, by the time the land came to her, Manuela was engaged to be married, the dream of the art school long dead.

The solicitor had also brought with him the news that Baluarte was very valuable to a consortium who wanted the land to finish a South American railway. When the offer came, Manuela *had* considered it, but the sale, at the consortium's originally offered price, would barely cover what Felix had already given her family to pay off debts and restore their home to its former glory. It would not be enough to maintain her parents—and her own—lavish tastes for long. Still, her parents had insisted that she sell, claiming the land should've rightfully gone to Manuela's father. For once she'd set aside her guilt and sense of duty and stood firm.

Manuela thought of the letter from her grandmother the solicitor had given her. The elegant loopy writing and the familiar scent of the camphor oil she rubbed on her joints.

Use it for something that makes you happy. No paying off debts. Your parents have taken enough from you.

"I don't understand you, Manu," Aurora moaned, flopping down on one of the armchairs. "You could sell this land and get rid of that social-climbing blowhard you agreed to marry. You could finally have some independence."

Of course, Aurora, whose family was one of the biggest producers of vanilla in the world, thought that being independent was as simple as selling a piece of land. "I don't understand your wardrobe choices either, Aurora, but I still love you and willingly go out in public with you."

"Why would you get her started on that, Manuela?" cried Amaranta while Luz Alana clamped her mouth shut.

"I need to dress in a way in which I can do my work, and physicians are always on duty...and don't change the topic! I am serious about this."

"Tell me again, about your society," Manuela asked, very seriously while Amaranta threw herself on an overstuffed cushion and Luz Alana pretended to knock herself out with her fan. Manuela almost laughed at the ease with which Aurora could be distracted by simply dangling one of her causes in front of her nose. The evils of women's fashions as a hindrance to their ability to succeed in the workforce was at the very top of her list.

She was still wearing the same walking suit she'd left the house in that morning. Both Manuela and Luz Alana had changed into something more appropriate for their evening plans, but Aurora could not be bothered. Their friend was a devoted advocate of the Rational Dress Society which had been founded in London at the beginning of the decade and for years now had repudiated what they called *impractical clothing for modern women*. Aurora had even started her own chapter of the society in Veracruz with moderate success, to the horror of her father and three brothers. By the time Aurora was done with her lecture on the folly of bustles and corsets as subjugation devices, Manuela's land would be forgotten.

Unlike Manuela, who had never been strong enough to stand by her convictions if it meant losing her comforts, Aurora lived by her principles. As much as she relished giving Aurora a hard time, she admired her friend for that. Aurora did not back down from what she wanted. When she'd set out to become the first woman licensed to practice medicine in Mexico, her father had threatened to disinherit her, but she had persevered. Even now she was in the midst of a row with the man over her decision to use the inheritance she received from her mother building women's and children's clinics. When she informed her father of her plans, he promised to see her destitute before he'd ever allow her to do it. Instead of pleading her case, Aurora defied him by coming to Paris to organize the venture with other women physicians. She intended to test model clinics in Paris together before they took their findings back to their own countries. She would do it too, even if it cost her everything. There was nothing that Aurora was not willing to sacrifice for her work.

Manuela didn't have that kind of fortitude. She'd thought she did when she'd dreamed of the art school with her grandmother. But all those years when their family had to beg and borrow, the humiliations they had all endured to keep up appearances, had broken something in her. She didn't have the strength to give everything up for her convictions. To turn her back on position and a life of comfort to pursue a passion that even her parents dismissed as unimportant. She painted because it was like air to her, but was merely breathing truly living?

"Manuela del Carmen." Aurora's reproachful tone told her

that her friend had finally wised up to her tricks. "You are wicked—"

"I am," Manuela said, preening, but Aurora was not amused.

"Why are you not taking this chance to break free from your parents, Leona?" Had she used her typical haughty tone, Manuela could've returned with something cutting or even told her to mind her own business. But she could hear and see her friend's agony on her behalf.

"I am not like you, Aurora," Manuela told her friend, who sent her one of those pained expressions. They'd already had this conversation many times. In New York where they'd all met to embark on their voyage to Paris. On the steamer to France, and multiple times since their arrival in the city. Aurora still couldn't understand why Manuela would choose to marry a man who she could not love, when she technically had a way out.

"Don't you want to be free, Manuela?"

"What exactly does the word *free* mean to you, Aurora?" Manuela asked, suddenly irritated. "The sale of Baluarte is not going to support my family forever. What do we do when the money runs low again?" she demanded, her face hot with shame and indignation. Because it was true that Aurora had never backed down from what she wanted, but she'd also never had to see her own father on his knees begging lenders for mercy. She hadn't been the one keeping track of every penny as she watched her mother and father overextend the family to the brink of ruin.

"You are not responsible for your parents, Manuela," Aurora countered with the guileless fervor of the lavishly wealthy. And that wasn't fair either: her friends just wanted to help. "That's probably why your abuela didn't tell them she'd recovered the land. She knew they'd want to use it for themselves. You didn't tell them to go into debt. You didn't tell your father to make those unfortunate business decisions."

Manuela hadn't, that was true, but her actions *had* cost him an investor who could've saved them, and she had to atone for that. She had been for almost a decade now. She may not have caused their debt, but she had been the reason why their last chance at saving the business had fallen through. She simply could not walk away and leave her parents destitute, as much as she might like to.

"Aurora, I am not like you. I would not be content living in some squalid hovel here in Paris so that I could be an artist." She sounded angry, and Manuela made a point to never let that kind of emotion dominate her. Anger, resentment, regret were emotions that did not serve women in her position. They made one bitter, and bitterness was such a useless emotion. It required so much energy, almost as much as pretending did. Manuela could hardly muster up the reserves required for that. "I can't love Felix, that is true, but it's not as if I could marry a person I could fall in love with." She shut her eyes when the tall sinewy figure from Le Bureau flashed in her mind again. She wondered what it would be like to taste that mouth again, decided she'd make sure to find out.

"I *like* comfort. I like staying here in this beautiful town house and dining at Le Grand Véfour and buying dresses at the House of Worth." She could never love her husband, but she could be content in a life full of luxuries. She didn't think there was anything, other than giving up painting, that could tempt her to risk losing that. "I want my parents to be comfortable and something must be sacrificed in order for that to happen."

"Your happiness shouldn't be it," Aurora declared into the uncomfortable silence.

Manu shrugged and tipped back the glass of port. Her mind swirling with images of what she'd seen at Le Bureau. The women dancing in each other's arms, the open desire in their eyes. Happy, free, unafraid. Nothing that could keep a roof over her head, nothing she had any permanent use for.

"I am doing the best I can, Aurora. The art school was Abuela's dream. A silly dream." She lifted the port to her lips and drank again, telling herself that the ache in her chest was not coming from the words she'd just said.

"I loathe this for you, Manu," Aurora said in a strangled voice, her hard gaze on the gaudy ring Felix had placed on Manuela's finger.

"Don't. Be happy for me, because this is enough." It had to be. She would make sure that it was.

"You deserve more." Amaranta whispered in hushed indignation.

"Perhaps, but this is what I have, and I mean to make the most of the time I have left. No more letting Luz distract me with her business or you with your list of good deeds," she announced, making light of things by pinching Aurora on the cheek. "I will be the very picture of feminine licentiousness. Depravity and indulgence will be the only things I strive for." Aurora whimpered and Manuela laughed. Again, those bright lavender eyes appeared in her mind. "At least there's three of you to douse all the Parisian fires I mean to leave in my wake," she joked, making her friends wince.

After a moment, Aurora capitulated by raising her glass. "May God have mercy on the unsuspecting souls you decide to unleash the full force of the Manuela Caceres Galvan inferno on."

They drank in silence for a while and Manuela's mind once again drifted to her encounter at Le Bureau. She was still recalling the sensations of that kiss when Luz Alana spoke up.

"But why go to the meeting at all?" she asked, pointing to the note card in Manu's hand. Her business-minded friend was much too observant to allow Manuela to distract her from the matter at hand for too long.

"I am curious," she confessed, running her fingers over the embossed name on the creamy white card. *Cora Kempf Bristol, Duchess of Sundridge*. "How often can one boast of dining with a duchess?"

"What could you possibly have in common with a matronly

aristocrat who is probably being forced by the menfolk to bully you into selling them the land? Because one thing is certain, she is not likely to be the one calling the shots for these railway negotiations," Luz Alana asserted, with the derision of a woman who'd been turned away by every man she'd attempted to do business with since she'd arrived in Paris.

"I am sure we won't have many shared interests," Manuela conceded, then amused herself by imagining the duchess's horrified expression if she was to share the details of what she'd gotten up to that very evening. "But this old biddy has invited me to Au Rocher de Cancale and—" she lifted a finger in the air for emphasis "—I hear the oysters are excellent."

"I thought you were going to search for the mystery woman from the brothel tomorrow," Aurora pointed out, then winced as Amaranta shot them a very unhappy look.

"That will be *after* the oysters, Leona." Tomorrow she'd go to luncheon and enjoy her champagne and oysters. Then she'd apply herself to exploiting the last weeks of freedom she'd bought herself.

Three

"La duchesse arrive!"

Cora Kempf Bristol, Duchess of Sundridge, jumped in surprise at the loud thump on the side of her carriage. "For God's sake, Maggie, tell them to stop. They're going to alert the entire street that I'm here." She leaned out the window to look at the two young boys who shot off like tiny missiles in the direction of her offices, announcing her arrival at the top of their lungs.

"Of course, Your Grace," her secretary promptly replied before sticking her head out of the carriage window in order to quietly berate the footman for not suppressing the boys' enthusiasm.

This ruckus was no way of doing business, not when she was preparing herself for what was sure to be a trying meeting and her mind insisted on pondering the mysterious Cinderella she'd discovered in her rooms at Le Bureau. She'd been so taken by those impish eyes and smart mouth she'd forgotten to ask for a name. It was for the best, of course: she'd gone to the brothel on a whim, hoping to purge some of her nerves in anticipation of this morning's assembly. But after that encounter, she'd lost her appetite for one of her usual bedmates. Instead, she'd stood in the middle of the empty room, sipping brandy and examining with renewed interest a fresco she'd looked at a thousand times.

"You are aware it's your own fault? That you've caused the staff to pay these little street urchins to look out for you." The humor-laced voice of her Tia Osiris brought Cora's attention back to the present.

"How exactly did I do that, Aunt?" The older woman's mouth twitched while Maggie's own face turned a deep shade of red.

"By being an absolute tyrant! They are terrified of you arriving by surprise and catching them unawares." She laughed as she said it, but Cora knew her aunt wasn't completely jesting.

"They are perfectly aware I will be here today," Cora rebuffed. "Besides, they should *always* be ready for me. That is why I pay them the exorbitant sums I do." She wasn't put off by her aunt's words or by the suggestion her staff feared her. She had standards, and she liked things done a certain way. "When a man is exacting, he's called a fearless leader, fit to be a general. When a woman does the same, she is a harpy." She was being overly sensitive, but her nerves where on a razor's edge today.

"Querida, you know that is not my view of things." Her aunt who had fought ardently for women's rights in their native Chile and had been even jailed for her efforts would never think that. She would also never abstain from giving Cora a piece of her mind when she thought it necessary. "You amuse yourself by catching them by surprise. The last time you did that a footman lost a tooth." Tia Osiris was amusing *herself* now.

"How is it my fault the man tripped on a rug?"

"Because he was running to warn the cook you were arriving two hours early," her aunt shot back. Maggie, whose face was worryingly red, squirmed in her seat.

"I am not that bad," Cora said grudgingly.

"I think you underestimate how intimidating you can be, querida." Tia Osiris eased the barb with a pat on the hand.

It was true that she could be forbidding, but it was the only way to earn respect in the corner of the world in which she dealt. She prided herself on being a generous employer. She made sure the people who worked for her had everything they required. She didn't want anyone tending to *her* needs while their own families went lacking. But she was not amiable. In fact, the expectation that she be some kind of benevolent matron, only because she was a woman, never ceased to irritate her.

She—and her temperament—were so well-known in Paris society that it was rare these days to encounter anyone who didn't keep their distance from her. Which was why last night has been so surprising. No one who knew Cora would ever dare enter her Le Bureau rooms uninvited, much less think of trampling all over her furniture in their bare feet. But her little artist had done that very thing: she'd made herself at home in Cora's space, with her art, and made her see it all in a new light. She'd been left wanting more, and it had been a very long time since Cora had been plagued with that feeling when it came to a woman.

"Your Grace, how many more minutes shall I tell the coachman?" The urgency in Maggie's voice brought her out of her musings, and by the look on the girl's face she'd likely been trying to get Cora's attention for a while.

"You have your head in the clouds today, mi amor."

This, from Tia Osiris, stung. Not because there was any kind of chastisement in her voice but because other than her stepson Alfie, Tia Osiris was the only person in her life who could see right through the mask of perennial tediousness Cora worked so hard to maintain.

"Not in the clouds, Tia. In the boardroom I am about to walk into," Cora lied. "I have a long list of men to decimate, and I don't want to accidentally leave any of them off the hook." The quip was received with a rueful smile from her aunt, but she'd been right. Cora was being fanciful and that would absolutely not do today.

She had to focus on the task at hand. Diversions with pouty lips and generous bosoms were indulgences for men, not for the women attempting to beat them at their own game. The next hour could put within her grasp the leverage she'd been working toward for the last two years—the last decade, really—and she was much too close to let a pretty face to make her stumble. That she would never allow again.

"What time is it?" she asked, looking out the window.

"Two minutes before the convocation time," Maggie answered. She'd been sitting in the carriage for an hour now, waiting for the men she'd summoned to arrive at her building. With her carriage out of sight a few hundred yards from her door she could time her own arrival. There was very little left in her life that gave Cora as much joy as making a room full of men wait for her.

"Let's linger another five minutes and then go," she instructed and sat back just in time to watch Edouard Blanchet ascend the steps to her door. A smile tipped up her lips at the thought of the pompous, odious Blanchet fuming as he sat waiting for her. Men like him were accustomed to the world bending to their whims. They could not abide even the smallest discomforts, which was why Cora strove to ply him with as many as she could every time they met.

It was elemental for a woman playing the games of powerful men to cultivate a slight air of unpredictability. Men—spoiled, wealthy men, in particular—could be like children: one had to keep them just a mite untethered. She never overdid it with her lateness—when dealing with fragile prides, it never served one to indulge in hubris—she just took long enough to assert the fact that her time was more valuable than theirs. "Five minutes are up, Your Grace," Maggie voiced, her ever-present pocket watch in hand.

"I hope they're ready for me, because *I* am ready for them," she declared, coaxing an unsure smile from the young woman.

As the carriage began to move again, Cora turned her attention to her appearance. She ran the palm of her hand over the coiffure done to her specifications and the small hat by her favorite milliner. The trousers from the night before had been replaced with one of her business day suits. The luscious artist had not commented on Cora's attire, but she'd certainly appreciated it. Her eyes had widened, and an enticing flush had pinked her cheeks when she'd noticed the trousers and jacket. She'd been so deliciously expressive. Eyes large and dreamy when she'd stared up at Cora's mouth.

She should've kissed her properly. She should've taken her to the bedroom and peeled off all those layers of emerald silk. She'd been barely able to sleep, wondering how all that beautiful brown skin would look on her pristine satin sheets.

"Did you hear me, sobrina?" her aunt asked from the banquette across from hers.

"Sorry, Tia," she apologized with an internal wince, as she noticed her aunt's not-so-subtle examination of her face.

"You can't be nervous about the meeting? Or did one of those pretty girls you like to entertain at that den of iniquity you frequent finally snare you?" For a second Cora panicked, wondering if she'd been affected enough to give herself away, but then the older woman laughed and leaned to buss her on the cheek. "As if you'd ever let that distract you." She paired the woeful comment with a click of her tongue, as she reached for Cora's hand. "I wish you would find someone, but I know you. Too focused on business to make time for love."

Despite herself, the comment smarted. "I am sure you have not forgotten what happened the last time I made time for love, Tia." The older woman's smile flagged at her words, and Cora turned away, swallowing the bitter bile of those memories. She knew her aunt could not help it. Osiris was a romantic, with an ability to love and forgive that went beyond anything Cora could comprehend. But her aunt's grace did not live in Cora.

She was unforgiving, and she was ruthless with anyone who detracted her from getting what she wanted, even herself. Once before, love had almost cost her everything. She would not let that happen a second time.

Her aunt made one of those worried sounds of hers as Cora breathed through her nose, forcing down the bitter taste of her old shame and futile regrets. She had absolutely no time for dwelling on a past she could not change. Not when she had a room full of men to bend to her will. "Does this jacket look right, Tia?" she asked, smoothing a hand over the row of small buttons running down her chest and changing the subject.

"You look beautiful in anything you wear," her aunt said affectionately, the harsh words already forgotten.

Cora smiled and leaned in to kiss the familiar papery warm skin of her tia's cheek. Her mother's younger sister, and the only blood relation she willingly spent any time with, had never judged Cora's choices. Not when at seventeen in a fit of rage she'd shot the man her father informed her she'd be forced to marry. Not when her father shoved them together on a steamer to London with a trunk of money and told Osiris he'd kill them both himself if Cora was not married to a peer in six months' time. Not when Cora informed her she'd be marrying Benedict Bristol, the financially embattled Duke of Sundridge, after only knowing the man for a day.

Not even when she'd disgraced herself so thoroughly they'd had to leave London in the middle of the night mired in scandal.

The carriage jolting to a stop brought her attention back to her surroundings. She inhaled deeply, feeling the tight encasing around her torso and smiled at the constriction. A reminder that despite the many bindings placed around her, today she would win. It was a victory ten years in the making.

Despite not loving him in the way a wife should—and their almost twenty-year age difference—her marriage to Benedict had been a happy one. He'd been the first person to notice—

and encourage—her affinity for business. With his blessing she'd begun investing the fortune her father had given Benedict as her dowry in trade floors and other ventures, all of which paid off handsomely. Within a couple of years, she'd garnered notoriety among London society for her sharpness in investments. Largely due to Benedict's boasting of his duchess's talents and the exorbitant gains in the family fortunes.

For a short time, life seemed ideal. And then Benedict's illness took him. Cora almost lost herself. Grief-stricken at the loss of her best friend, she'd made terrible mistakes. Coped atrociously with the loss of a husband who had never been a lover, but who'd given her something she'd never had from anyone other than her aunt: unconditional love, friendship and respect.

Her behavior in the months after his death was appalling. She'd ignored the business interests she'd so carefully built, losing herself in a string of increasingly destructive affairs. The last one being particularly catastrophic. The entire episode left her embarrassed and plagued by the crushing shame of knowing she'd broken her promise to Benedict to be a good steward of his son's future. After that, all she'd cared about was wiping clean the stains of those mistakes. She'd ruthlessly—and at times unscrupulously—rebuilt her position and carefully cultivated a reputation that became synonymous with business acumen and unyielding ambition.

She'd been meticulous and patient.

Without Benedict's support she had to be more cautious. She'd quietly backed investments—incredibly risky ones in the beginning—that proved to be wildly lucrative. She made profitable alliances with common-born financiers hungry enough to do business with a peer that they were willing to overlook her gender.

When success came, she made sure her name was whispered in every well-heeled smoking room in Europe as the savviest of investors and a very good woman to know when one was looking to replenish their coffers. It took some doing and more than one door being slammed in her face, but eventually the rumors about her Midas touch landed in the right ears, and people—as they tended to do when money was in the mix—quickly forgot her past disgrace. She'd bet on the aristocracy's greed being stronger than their principles, and she'd been right.

After years of her investments and advice yielding them fortunes, they'd had to grudgingly admit she was far better at making money than they were. She'd made herself implacable and indispensable among the peerage and now the same men who once had laughed at the idea of doing business with a woman sat at her table and waited...for her.

She wasn't deluded enough to believe they respected her or that when she walked into a meeting they didn't resent her very presence. It was avarice, but she could work with avarice. As long as they knew their place, and hers.

"Shall we go and make grown men cry, Maggie?"

Maggie's slender back shot up like a soldier's at the question. "Yes, Your Grace." Tia Osiris smiled approvingly at the girl's eager reply while Cora ran a hand over her narrow dark green tie which matched her slim skirts and bespoke jacket. All of it made by the most exclusive tailor in London. Cora loved a Worth gown and wore them occasionally, but she made sure to walk into these meetings in the same armor the men did.

"I do love that shade on you, dear," Tia Osiris commented as Maggie handed Cora the papers she'd need to apprise her co-investors in South American Railways of her discoveries.

"Dark green *is* a hunting color," Cora retorted, eliciting a delighted laugh from her aunt.

Once she'd descended from the carriage, she looked up to find Osiris beaming down at her mischievously. "Hazlos sangrar, mi amor."

Cora pushed herself up to receive a kiss on the forehead. "It will be a bloodbath, Tia." Anyone walking by would witness the sweet older woman expressing her love to her niece and would never know Osiris Villanueva had just been instructing Cora to bleed the men she was about to meet dry.

"I'll have tea ready when you return, querida."

With a nod and a tap on the door of the carriage, Cora sent her aunt off and turned in the direction of her building's door.

She strode in with purpose. Her feet falling on the ground in the steady, forceful gait she'd perfected for moments like this. She didn't sway her hips femininely, she didn't tilt her shoulders just so in order to display her attributes to admirers. She moved like the men she dealt with moved, forcing everything in their path out of the way.

For years she'd observed how the men she did business with walked. She examined their footfalls, the length of their stride. The way they favorably tilted their heads when they saw an ally, how they sneered when they crossed a foe. She'd learned to emulate that arrogance, to embody the ostentatious confidence. When the Duchess of Sundridge walked into a room, men stood up—not out of deference but out of fear, and that was exactly how she preferred it.

"We're certain St. Michel's information is accurate?" she asked Maggie one more time. St. Michel was a scoundrel, but he had never brought her the wrong information. If he had this time, she'd make sure to bestow upon him a very unpleasant lesson on what happened to people who lied to her.

"Yes, ma'am. Collier also heard the same." After receiving the information from St. Michel, whose salary at the Ministry of Finance she supplemented in order to be apprised of any information she required, she'd deployed another of her less refined information gatherers who had his own ways of uncovering what she needed. "*Le Temps* will run it in the evening," Maggie confirmed just as they reached the door to the meeting room.

She handed the papers back to Maggie and gripped her walking cane in one hand. The other flew to the knot of her tie.

She fingered it, slid an index finger between her neck and the suffocatingly tight starched collar of her shirt. Ran a hand over the bodice, fortified in the knowledge that there was nothing at all about her appearance they could sneer at. Her skin prickled with erratic anticipation, thinking of the ace she would carry in with her today. She made herself wait another minute, glancing down at her boots to check for any imperfections or smudges from the street. Unbidden, an image of the lush beauty haunting her thoughts appeared in her mind. God, the hungry looks she'd given Cora. Those sweet little puffs of air when she'd leaned down for a kiss. It was not the time or place for those musings, but she allowed herself a second to remember the way those plump lips had parted eagerly for her, then she snuffed it out like a candle. Those desires could never walk into this room with her.

She arched her spine and breathed in as she took hold of the doorknob, listening for any discernible words in the chatter of the men on the other side of the door. It would be a performance, as it always was.

"Gentlemen," she said over the rustling of ten chairs sliding on her rugs at once. "No need to stand," she offered, as she made her way to her place at the head of the oval table, aware it was a futile request. They'd all rather be shot than have her standing over them for more than a second.

She took them in as she passed by, accepting greetings and kisses on the top of her gloved hand. It was comical, the way in which they insisted on observing this gentlemanly gesture. It made her think of them as lions attempting to have tea with their would-be prey. Unfortunately for them, there were no gazelles in this room.

"Brenton." She tipped her head in the direction of a stout man of about thirty-three who was sitting by the door. His beady gaze bitterly fixed on her tiepin. "How is your brother?" As expected, the man's face twisted grotesquely at her inquiry.

It was frivolous to provoke him, but she abhorred haughtiness and Brenton was an imperious little prick. The two brothers had inherited one of the biggest fortunes in Scotland and proceeded to squander a large portion of it in gambling hells. A few years ago they'd come to Cora with the last of if, begging her to help them make some investments to recover their losses. She'd been happy to, in exchange for their family's traders' box at the London Stock Exchange and Brenton's ruby pin, which he'd loved to boast had been a gift to his family from Queen Elizabeth. Cora and Brenton loathed each other, but her counsel had restored the brothers' fortune, and they'd proved themselves useful with their connections.

"Carroway, have you sorted that small issue I sent you a note about?" she asked, moving on to a decrepit baronet standing near the middle of the room. The *small issue* was granting a marriage annulment to the daughter of one of Tia Osiris's friends. His son was a violent bastard who had terrorized the girl during their honeymoon. She'd fled the country house they'd been in at the first opportunity and had been in hiding ever since. It had taken nearly hostile convincing on Cora's part and some very pointed reminders of how she'd helped him recover from near bankruptcy to keep them from hunting for the poor girl.

She watched the old man struggle to keep the fury from his face. When he finally spoke his tone was barely civil. "I'd prefer not discussing private family matters in public."

"I can come to your home and discuss it with you," she offered pleasantly. "But I become very peevish when I am forced to repeat myself." His chin trembled at her much harsher tone. "You won't like it if I lose my temper over this, and I promise neither will your son." Threatening Carroway before a meeting where she'd likely need his vote later was a risk, but she had other ways to convince the old man than reminders of how she'd saved his hide with a few investments.

"By the by, when will Lady Calliope be returning from Venice?" Carroway spluttered with barely restrained rage, but miraculously he managed to maintain control.

The baronet's much younger wife was a frequent guest at Cora's more licentious nocturnal gatherings. She was presently in the throes of a particularly passionate affaire de coeur with a voluptuous Argentinian soprano. The Carroways loved to present themselves as stalwarts of morality, and this would be the kind of news that would certainly be a blow to their name. Not the fact that their son was a violent oaf.

"If he signs, her family will say she's gone to a convent," she whispered giving him more grace than he deserved.

After a long moment he nodded. "I'll make sure Robert sends the papers this week," he told her before storming off to take his seat. She looked after him, swallowing down the bile in her throat. She knew every time she did something like this, she weakened her position in this room. That when she reminded them that her loyalties lay elsewhere she made herself vulnerable, but dammit, what had she garnered all this power for if every once in a while she couldn't wield it to set a woman free from a terrible situation?

"I appreciate you coming on such short notice," she finally said after a long pause, her hands braced on the edge of the table. "I know everyone is preoccupied with the exposition, but since we are all here in Paris, I thought I'd deliver the news in person." She relished the startled looks being volleyed around the room, the rustling of fabric indicating unease. "It is not the kind of development one wants going on a wire any clerk in the city can get a hold of." She made sure she injected an air of mystery into that last bit, her fingers gently tapping on the polished wood as the men around her murmured impatiently.

"We are all ears, Your Grace," Blanchet offered in a nasty tone. Cora tipped her head at the man, making sure to infuse her own distaste of his person into her expression.

"I will get on with it, then. We know Monsieur Blanchet is

a busy man." *Busy doing absolutely nothing,* that was. She reached for her leather folio and pulled the flap open for effect as she scanned the faces around the room. "It has come to my attention through one of my trusted sources that late last evening, an order was issued for the arrest of Ferdinand de Lesseps and his son for embezzlement." She sighed internally at the mix of vacant and confused stares trained in her direction and carried on. "This means that the Panama Canal Company will be forced to declare bankruptcy by the end of the week." Cora paused after delivering the news.

The constant scheming required to stay at the top of this heap had begun to wear on her as of late, but these moments still provided some enjoyment. She had to bite the side of her mouth to keep from grinning when her associates finally understood the significance of the news and began to all speak at once. It was, after all, information that made their joint endeavor a potential gold mine.

"And how did you hear about this?" Carroway asked, not even attempting to hide his doubts about the veracity of the information.

"One of my men was able to access the warrant," she said, pulling out the piece of paper St. Michel had delivered in combination with his oral report. She pushed the paper to Carroway. "See for yourself."

Carroway's thin mustache wiggled on his lip as he read. His eyes widened further the lower he got on the paper. When he was done, he slid it to the man waiting impatiently beside him and turned to Cora.

"The Colombian government has expelled the French," he exhaled, as the others looked at the paper intently. Cora merely struggled with the desire to puff up her chest and crow.

De Lesseps, who had successfully executed the construction of the Suez Canal, had spent the last eight years in Central America attempting to build a connector between the Pacific and Atlantic Oceans. But after thousands of workers' deaths from yellow fever and malaria, not to mention hundreds of millions of francs lost, it seemed he had finally run out of luck. Effectively making the railway Cora and the men in this room were on the cusp of finishing the only viable cargo route connecting the Atlantic to the Pacific that didn't involve a trip around the continent.

It had taken three years of work. Countless hours and an army of engineers and agents to devise a plan to lay down a railway that crossed five countries. Beginning in Chile and ending in the Caribbean coast of South America. The South American Railway could get two cargo ships' worth of steel from the mines in Cochabamba to Edinburgh in under two weeks. With the Panama Canal out of the picture, the next best option required a month at best.

"Once we finish *our* railroad, we will have the only transcontinental transport system in the Americas' southern hemisphere." She made sure to include the men in the room with that *our*. One had to be magnanimous in this kind of scenario. Besides, there was no need to remind them she'd been the one who brought the project to them. That she'd offered them shares for pennies. Not to mention taking on most of the responsibility of getting it off the ground. They knew that as well as she did.

"This will make us a fortune." An Italian aristocrat—and one of the very few people in the room she didn't openly despise—boasted with glee. Cora smiled internally, knowing what else she had up her sleeve.

"I hate to ruin the moment," Blanchet called from the other end of the table. His eyes narrowed in Cora's direction. "But we still don't have the land to finish the railroad. We have been stalled for a year now."

Cora mentally popped the recriminations and insults she could wield at the man like soap bubbles and soothed herself with the knowledge that she was about to assert her position in this pack.

"Thank you, Monsieur Blanchet, for reminding us that all

the attempts have been unfruitful in delivering us the remaining tract of coastal land needed to finalize our railway." It took every ounce of will she had to keep from pointing out that it was her efforts and connections that had secured the ninety percent of the railway that was already completed. But Blanchet's family had a lot of pull with the French Ministry of Foreign Affairs, and he had delivered when it came to requesting permits for construction at some of the more troublesome locations. And he was right: they were yet to secure the land they needed to finish the route they'd planned for.

They'd made offers on more than two dozen different pieces of land, to no avail. A year later and they were still stuck three-quarters of the way to the Venezuelan coast, but there was one slice of land that could solve all their problems.

"I may have a solution," she finally offered.

None of the men in the room seemed very reassured. "You've told us that very thing a few times already," Brenton declared in that voice that set her teeth on edge. "We've talked among ourselves—" They'd talked among themselves...without her.

"I thought we had agreed there would be no meetings without all members of the consortium present." She must've betrayed her impassiveness, because after one look at her face Brenton dissolved into a coughing fit. If she flew into a rage like she wanted to, they would use it against her. They'd tried it before. Blanchet and his cronies had practically staged a coup demanding that she relinquish her majority of shares because she'd been what they'd called an ineffective lead. But they had not gotten the best of her yet, and they wouldn't today.

Blanchet turned away from his loose-tongued comrade, focusing on Cora. He looked so pleased with himself she didn't bother asking who'd organized their little secret meeting. He'd pay for that, she'd make sure of it. "We gave you ample time to find a solution," he announced magnanimously. "And we've decided it would be best for a few of us to travel to South America this time. Given that your *connections* have not yielded results."

Cora gritted her teeth at his mocking tone. "My connections have yielded the very information that puts us at a great advantage to act," she reminded him, which he promptly waved off.

"I do believe it is still easier for *men* to do business in the less refined parts of the world." She had to bite her tongue not to remind the insolent little worm that the only person in the consortium who spoke Spanish was her.

"Oh, there will be no need to cross the Atlantic," she said with a breezy gesture. "Not that we have time for that. Announcing the railway as soon as possible is imperative. And like I said, I have a solution. It seems that the piece of land we looked at in Puerto Cabello has changed proprietors." Ten pairs of eyebrows rose almost in unison. "The current owner, a Señorita Caceres Galvan, is currently in Paris. And she's agreed to meet with me."

She made sure to use her mother's tongue as effectively as she could. These days she only ever spoke Spanish with her aunt, and in the almost-twenty years since she'd left her native Chile, she'd lost quite a lot of her fluency, but none of these men would know that. The effect of her words was exactly what she'd hoped. Throats were cleared nervously and more than one worried glance was shot in Blanchet and Brenton's direction.

"I told you I would deliver you the land, and I will do it." She leaned on the table, her posture bellicose. Her gaze daring one of these men to cross her again.

"Why can't we bring her here to talk to the consortium?" Blanchet countered, his tone less hostile, though his face remained flushed.

Cora tsked apologetically, hands in front of her in a helpless gesture. "I'm afraid that won't be possible. She has agreed to talk only to me, and I don't think it's advisable, or appropriate, to drag a young woman into a room full of men." That lowered the temperature in the room, but a few continued to eye her suspiciously. "I would've thought you'd be delighted that my being a woman has finally become useful." The barb landed. The unspoken rule of her being allowed in these rooms was that she never disturbed the facade they'd constructed which conveniently ignored the fact she was a foreigner, a woman—and one who loved women too. But on this occasion she was running out of patience.

"If this thing in Panama is really done, we need to announce an estimated completion of the railroad before all the business delegations leave Paris," Carroway put in, and she almost cried in relief at hearing someone be sensible for once.

"We can't announce anything without a deed to that girl's land," voiced one of the two Williamson brothers in the back. The two were American traders who didn't much like doing business with anyone who wasn't what they considered of their type but were too greedy to stay away.

Her aunt always teased her for the ways in which she prepared to come into these rooms, but it was the only way to survive these men and their nonsense.

"I will get you the deed," she assured them. "Miss Caceres Galvan responded very positively to the invitation." The little chit had done no such thing. It had taken more than a dozen notes to finally obtain a *yes* to her request for a luncheon meeting. Cora mused on the report sitting on her desk from her agent in Venezuela. In addition to procuring her a brief history of the land in question, he'd provided a history of the Caceres Galvans. They were a prosperous Dominican family who had migrated to Venezuela in the late 1860s and had operated a candle-making business with great success for twenty years. But it seemed Miss Caceres Galvan's father was not as good in the candle trade as his predecessors had been, and the family had been mired in debt for years. This explained the young heiress's engagement to Felix Kingsley, an American financier looking for some inroads into South American society and with the financial funds to buy his way into that goal.

"How do we know this new owner will sell?" countered Brenton, who was truly scraping at the very last of her nerves.

She knew from personal experience that some South American heiresses were easily swayed by a chance of mingling with European aristocracy, and a duchess was the next best thing to the queen. She didn't have much to go on when it came to Miss Caceres Galvan, but Cora fully intended to do and say whatever she needed to in order to part the young woman from her land, and once she did, she'd come back here and demand she be named chairwoman of South American Railways.

"I know because, as you are all well aware, I am very hard to say no to," she told them, standing up and grabbing her walking cane. "I will talk to the heiress and get us that deed. Then we can announce the completion of the railway at the reception at the Charost Palais next month." That elicited some excited chattering. The British ambassador would be hosting a reception for a group of European businessmen present in Paris for the exposition at his residence. Once the news about de Lesseps began making the rounds, their announcement of a new railway crossing South America would be a boon.

"*If* you get her to sell," Blanchet insisted, but Cora was growing bored of this.

"Now, if you gentlemen will excuse me," she said, collecting her papers. "I have an heiress to persuade." Cora headed toward the door, perfectly aware that if any of the pairs of eyes trained on the back of her head could transform into blades, she would not walk out of the room alive.

"She invited us here, and now she's leaving," protested Brenton as she reached the doorknob.

"I will keep you all abreast of how things proceed with Miss Caceres Galvan, but I anticipate that there will be plenty to toast next month." Cora practically thrummed with excitement at the idea of rubbing in the face of every major player in Paris that she'd delivered one of the biggest coups since the railways had begun. The only thing standing between her and the kind of power she desired was a mercurial heiress from the Caribbean. And she would make sure to do away with that bit of trouble in short order.

Four

"Are you certain you don't want one of us to come in with you? If this conversation turns into a serious offer, it might help to have someone there to talk it over." By Manuela's accounts this was the fifth time Luz Alana had asked to accompany her to the lunch since they'd left their town house.

"I will be fine," Manuela insisted, trying not to get annoyed. She understood that her friends meant well, but their overprotectiveness had begun to wear on her. "I think I can handle a conversation about selling a piece of land. I'm not that incompetent." Her sharp words seem to reverberate through the carriage, and she immediately regretted the outburst.

"I'm sorry," she apologized to her friend, who seemed more surprised than hurt by Manuela's unusual display of temper. "Baluarte is a sensitive subject."

"No, I am the one who is sorry," Luz Alana said contritely. Manuela's chest ached, seeing that mask of pain and grief shroud her friend's face. All three of them had experienced terrible loss in their lives, but Luz Alana's had been terrible and recent.

"Let's not fight, Leona," Manuela offered, clutching her friend's hands.

"I'm not sorry," Aurora retorted from the bench opposite them. "I'm worried about what this old battle-ax is going to try to talk you into, Manuela. You are much too nice, and you make decisions impulsively."

Manuela rolled her eyes, annoyed all over again. "I'm not going to just give the woman my land, Aurora!" She was interrupted by the carriage pulling to a stop in front of Au Rocher de Cancale, and immediately a nervous flutter began in her belly. "Now you've made me anxious," she complained, staring at the ornate door of the restaurant.

"We are being silly," Luz Alana, always the peacemaker, conceded. "You will be fine. If this last month has taught me anything, it's that society ladies detest any kind of conversation pertaining to money. She won't raise the subject." Manuela knew Luz Alana was probably saying this more for Aurora's benefit than anything, but she appreciated the effort regardless. "Enjoy your luncheon, Leona. When we see you at the Mexican soiree tonight, you can tell us all about the dowdy duchess." The last two words were said in a hilariously nasal and haughty tone, at which Manuela couldn't help but laugh. She opened the door to the conveyance herself and was met with a very finely dressed footman already waiting with a stepping ladder. Once she was on the sidewalk, she turned back to Aurora who was clearly considering whether to launch herself out of the carriage.

This was how they had always been: Aurora the defender, Luz Alana the planner, and Manuela the wild one of the bunch. Her Leonas, her pride. The ones she could always count on, even when they didn't understand why she did the things she did.

"I won't do anything outrageous, I promise." She leaned in to kiss them both on the cheek. "Besides, what could possibly be waiting for me in there that could make me change my mind?" Once she'd waved her friends off, she walked up to the door which was being held open by another comely gentleman.

How many footmen did this restaurant have?

As she stepped inside, once again that feeling of fluttery anticipation came over her, which was only enhanced by the realization that the establishment was completely empty. It was midday, and this being one of Paris's most fashionable restaurants, she'd expected to find a boisterous lunch service with garçons carrying trays of food fluttering about. The tables were finely set. Crisp white linens were set with gleaming silverware and crystal goblets, except there was not a diner to be seen.

Had she gotten the day wrong?

"Monsieur," she asked the footman who'd led her inside. "Le restaurant, est-il fermé?"

"Oui, mademoiselle," he said, vaguely, just as another man who had the air of someone in charge headed toward them.

"Bienvenue, Mademoiselle Caceres Galvan. Her Grace awaits you in our private salon upstairs." The man gestured to a set of stairs at the far end of the room. "If you will come with me, please."

She considered the situation, and the obvious effort to impress her. The duchess might not want to discuss money, but by closing a restaurant for their meeting, she was certainly making the point that she had plenty of it. It was obviously a ploy to dazzle her into selling them the land, but she wouldn't hold it against the woman. Manuela had absolutely no qualms with having some of the old lady's fortune lavished on her.

"Lead the way, monsieur," she answered amiably, before taking the stairs.

The walls leading up to the second floor were papered in a light blue that was similar to the design from Le Bureau. Unlike the very erotic pastoral scenes of the pleasure palace, Au Rocher de Cancale's featured an array of nautical ones. Fishermen and sea captains embellished the rooms, she supposed as a nod to the eatery's famous seafood dishes. And of course, recalling the decor of the brothel instantly brought her encounter to the forefront of her mind. That morning she'd woken up thinking of her mysterious woman. She'd barely opened her eyes when she had already reached for the sketchbook next to her bed. For hours she'd applied herself to capturing that wide mouth and those perfectly shaped lips. She'd even foregone breakfast and had instead sat in the sunroom dabbling with purples and grays on her palette until Aurora and Manuela had tempted her to the table with the promise of freshly brewed coffee.

"Mademoiselle, s'il vous plaît." The server's gentle but clearly urgent tone forced Manuela out of her daze. How long had she been standing at the top of the stairs? "I will make sure that the duchesse is ready for you." That was said with a bow and a very sharp click of the heels.

"Of course," she said apologetically, as her nerves began to get the best of her again. She made herself stand up straighter, making sure the curls around her face were framed properly. It was not every day one met a duchess, even if it was one who was only after her land.

If anything, she'd have a delectable meal and could use the news to appease her mother's many demands for information. Manuela winced as she thought of her mother's recent reminder not to do anything in Paris that would make Felix reconsider their marriage. Lunch with a duchess would give Consuelo Galvan de Caceres *exactly* what she wanted—something to brag about to the friends she was visiting in London.

The door finally opened, and the enthusiastic footman ushered her in. To Manuela's frustration, instead of finding the older woman, she was led down yet one more passage. The restaurant was like a maze.

As she made her way down the hall to where she hoped to finally meet this elusive duchess, Manuela began to regret accepting this invitation.

She didn't want to think about Baluarte or fill her mind with choices that didn't really exist. Even if she agreed to sell the land, she'd chosen her path. Her fate was sealed, and she was squandering her precious free time by agreeing to this meeting. She ought to be with Antonio doing a little sleuthing about her lady in trousers instead of traipsing through this building to have lunch with some stuffy old woman.

What if her beauty with the amethyst eyes was frantically searching Paris for her too? She could see her now with that tall, commanding way of hers, standing like a general in her silk trousers ordering an army of footmen to leave no stone unturned until they found Manuela. Her heart skipped at the image. She'd arrive at the Place des Vosges after her tedious lunch with the stodgy duchess and be set upon by two elegantly uniformed servants. They'd pluck her from the street and put her in an extravagantly decorated carriage. They'd diligently convey Manuela to a stately palace in the outskirts of Paris, where she'd marvel and gasp at the lush manicured gardens. Once inside, she'd be guided into a sumptuous parlor, and there her goddess would be, with her inky-black hair flowing around her shoulders, her arms wide open.

"Here we are," the footman said, rudely snatching her out of her glorious reverie. And for all that her friends didn't trust her self-control, Manuela exhibited an enormous amount of it when she resisted blurting out an exasperated *Finally*. She was so annoyed by all this pomp and circumstance that even if she had been considering selling this Duchess of Sundridge her land, she'd now turn her down out of pure spite.

Aurora always said that the trick to entering a room with confidence was to do it in a righteous rage, and Manuela found that in this instance it was very sound advice. When the door opened, she was much too irritated to be distracted by nerves and made her way inside at a clip. She might have to give this so-called *duchesse* a piece of her mind.

Manuela had worked herself into such a state that it took her a moment to locate the other woman. There was a circular table at the center of the room, but she was not sitting there. She stood by a large window looking at the street below. Her hair was very dark in the sunlight, and she was certainly not shaped like a matron. She was tall and slim with the body of an equestrian, Manuela thought. Her clothes were very austere. No bustle, ruffles or any of the fripperies that were the latest Parisian fashion. Her green morning suit was well cut and elegant, but nothing one could describe as ostentatious.

The duchess was probably one of those rich women who prided herself on her supposed frugality. Too restrained for lace or tulle, but happy enough to close down an entire restaurant on a whim.

Manuela took a few steps farther into the room until she was close enough to speak to her hostess without having to yell. This was tiresome, and Manuela would make sure to tell the high and mighty Duchess of Sundridge exactly that—if she ever deigned to turn around.

"Your Grace," she said curtly. The woman's back went up in surprise as though she'd been lost in thought. Something about the way she set her shoulders released a riot of hummingbirds inside Manuela. Her body tensed in anticipation and a funny tremor erupted throughout. She thought of something she'd read about animals sensing when an earthquake was approaching. That they could feel the vibrations of the incoming disaster long before humans did and would scurry away to find shelter. What was her body telling her? And why was this woman not turning around?

"I began to think you were going to leave all these oysters for me to eat, Señori—"

The duchess whirled to face her with the quickness of a woman much younger than what Manuela had imagined and froze midsentence. A blade of sunlight piercing through the window cast the duchess's countenance in shadow for just a second, but even before she stepped back into the light, Manuela knew. The proud set of that chin and the lines of her graceful, slender neck were burned into her memory.

This couldn't be real. She had never been this lucky. Perhaps she'd fallen asleep in the carriage. Or maybe Aurora's constant droning about rules had finally put her in a hypnotic state.

But for a mirage she was stunningly vivid. "Is it really you?" Manuela took a careful step forward, her heart slamming so violently in her chest she was having a hard time breathing. Of all the... "I thought you'd be a stuffy old lady!" she exclaimed giddily. The duchess did not seem delighted by this coincidence. Her face was pinched and drawn, that seductive mouth now flat. Manuela's true identity was clearly not a happy surprise for this woman.

"Miss Caceres Galvan," the duchess finally said, stepping toward her with an outstretched hand, her voice politely distant. "Thank you for coming to see me today." Was she supposed to pretend they didn't know each other?

You don't *know each other,* a voice that sounded a lot like Aurora told her. It took her a moment to get a hold of herself. Her mind was in chaos and her feelings hurt, which was ridiculous.

"Your Grace," she finally said reaching for the proffered hand. Just as it had been last night, the touch was shocking. How could this woman be so serious, so cold, when Manuela felt as though they were exchanging electricity through their palms?

"Take a seat, Miss Caceres Galvan." At the duchess's invitation, one of the footmen promptly pulled out a chair from the table for her to sit. The duchess remained standing on the other side, glancing at her with her ramrod-straight posture and such a shuttered expression most people would not notice the flutter in her jaw or the looks at Manuela's dress she kept stealing.

Most people wouldn't, but Manuela was an artist: she was trained in perceiving even the most minimal gestures, to capture any mannerisms hinting at a mood or that could assist in evoking a sentiment on the canvas. The duchess might be skilled in concealing emotions, but Manuela was just as talented in recognizing them. "No need to be so formal, Your Grace," Manuela said sweetly, as she lowered herself into a plush chair. "Please, call me Manuela. We had such a warm first meeting, I feel as though we already know each other." The minor flutter in the woman's jaw evolved into a moderate vibration as Manuela leaned back and beamed at her.

"Champagne, madame?" offered a very handsome young man to her right.

With one eye on the duchess, Manuela turned her attention to him. "I would love some," she chortled, like the prospect of a glass of the sparkling wine was the absolute highlight of her day. "You are quite good at that," she praised as he poured the wine into her cup. He blushed, and the duchess's mouth pursed forbiddingly. How had this same woman laughed delightedly at the sight of Manuela atop of her sideboard? "I do love the bubbles." She directed that remark at the duchess, who was still standing by her own chair.

"Leave us, please." The server was out of the room with impressive speed, which left them finally alone.

"Are we going to continue pretending last night didn't happen?" Manuela asked genially as her lunch companion took her seat at long last.

"Miss Caceres Galvan," she started, her tone dripping with condescension, and Manuela's temper got the best of her.

"Manuela," she requested in her sweetest voice, glancing into those lavender eyes, which were stormy with a mix of frustration and something far more volatile. She was sorely tempted to see what would happen if she tossed a match into that open flame.

"Manuela," the duchess conceded, her gaze locked somewhere between Manuela's shoulder and neck. "I invited you here because I'd like to buy your land in Puerto Cabello."

So much for Luz Alana's prediction that there would be no business talk. She sounded friendly enough, but the set of her mouth displayed her irritation at having her plans thwarted by Manuela's identity.

"Cora, can I call you Cora?" It wasn't a question, but the duchess nodded tightly and Manuela almost laughed in her face. Even when she knew she was in a bind the woman could not stand not being in command. It wasn't that she was irritated at the duchess—well, no, that wasn't true. She was supremely annoyed and also highly aroused, which was frankly rude. It was just that she'd built up such a grandiose reunion in her head, and it was such a disappointment to have *this* be the way in which she met this woman again. But Manuela had navigated much more treacherous waters with far less of an advantage, and she was finding it surprisingly invigorating to have some leverage for once. "Baluarte isn't for sale," Manuela finally replied, in a cloying tone that made one of the duchess's eyes twitch. She recovered quickly and leaned in again, and this time her voice was pure ice.

"Everything is for sale for the right price. Tell me yours."

Manuela took another sip from her coupe and took her time responding. She also noticed the way Cora's eyes slid from her mouth down to her bosom. She was not the only one here recalling their last tête-à-tête. "I have no need for money. My fiancé is one of the wealthiest men in South America. He can provide me with absolutely everything I could wish for."

Not everything, a nagging voice very similar to that of the woman sitting across from her resounded in Manuela's head.

"But this could be *your* money," the duchess cajoled. "I can arrange for it to be held in a place your new husband won't find it."

Manuela wasn't insulted by the suggestion that she might need a secret stash of money in case she needed to escape her marriage. It was the suggestion that this deal was supposed to be for her own benefit that angered her. It was the same way

Felix talked to her, with this facade of benevolence, as if his only concern was her well-being. But to Felix, to her parents, to this duchess, Manuela was just the means to them getting what *they* were after. Status, money, a railroad. She always gave in, went with the path of least resistance, convinced herself that if the result brought her some benefits it was not worth the trouble of fighting back. That she could be content with the outcome. She didn't feel like settling for resignation today.

"Like I said, I don't need money." Manuela infused her voice with as much bored indifference as she could manage.

"Everyone needs money, especially women who don't have a fortune of their own to fall back on. With the sale of Baluarte, you could have that." The duchess took a sip of her own wine, and Manuela's eyes followed every move. The way her strong, long fingers curled around the stem, the way she tipped her head slightly to drink. The tantalizing sight of a pink tongue as she lapped up a drop of wine from her lip.

"I'm not interested."

"We've already made you a very generous offer, and I am prepared to increase it." She waved a hand at whatever she saw in Manuela's face. "I know it can be so gauche to talk about money, particularly for women of our social realm."

"*Our* social realm." Manuela almost rolled her eyes at the false overture. Like a duchess would ever consider a Venezuelan heiress to be of her ilk. Manuela almost laughed, but she was becoming quite curious about how much more of this conviviality she could coax out of the duchess before her patience snapped.

"That's correct. I am certain we can reach an understanding today, woman to woman." It was on the tip of Manuela's tongue to tell the duchess she could think of far more interesting ways in which they could come together...woman to woman.

"The thing is, Your Grace, the understanding won't be about what the land is worth to me but what it is worth *to you*." Manuela leaned on the table at an angle that she knew placed her assets in their most favorable light. "When you sent your agent with an offer a few months ago, I didn't respond to you, but I did make some inquiries about your railway."

The Duchess of Sundridge was clearly not expecting that, and her relaxed posture quickly returned to one of heightened alert. She'd probably arrived here thinking she'd make quick work of Manuela. Bowl over the unrefined foreigner with champagne and an empty restaurant before she talked her out of her land. But just because Manuela didn't like to think about money didn't mean she didn't know how.

"I know how much your group is set to lose if you can't finish the railway, and I also know I am your last resort. Which means that the sum you suggested is about a quarter of what I expect to be paid. Are you prepared to increase your offer by that much?"

A small, impressed smile appeared on the older woman's lips, flushing Manuela with heat. Irritating negotiations or not, she was still very much feeling the echoes of that kiss.

"Very good, Manuela," the duchess said flatteringly, weakening Manuela's resolve ever so slightly. "I like a woman who drives a hard bargain." That comment went right to her core, and she had to turn away for a moment. It would not do to melt to the floor after a little bit of calculated praise. She reached for one of the oysters, then thought better of it and slid off her glove. She fluttered her gaze up to the duchess as she took one of the shells between her fingers and brought it to her mouth. If the duchess was going to use every piece of ammunition at her disposal, Manuela would do the same.

"I love oysters." Delicately she slid the tip of her tongue over the mollusk and had to hide a grin when Cora sucked in a breath. "It's the brine, the salty tang of it." She was being crass now, provocative in a way that was not at all appropriate, but she couldn't make herself care. "I adore the taste." She chucked back the chewy bite and moaned with pleasure, without taking her eyes off the duchess for a moment.

The air sizzled around them as she daintily dabbed the sides of her mouth with a napkin. The duchess licked her dry lips nervously, and Manuela finally felt like she had some footing in this conversation.

"What if I told you that my price isn't just money?" Manuela heard herself ask. The duchess arched a manicured eyebrow.

"Go on," she said, leaning back in her chair, her legs crossed, and that's when Manuela noticed that she wore split skirts like Aurora.

"I prefer you in trousers."

The duchess took the shot in stride, obviously resigned to the fact that Manuela would not let go their previous meeting. "And I prefer you in dresses that accentuate that wonderful bosom of yours." The wicked smile she sent in Manuela's direction was brimming with such promise her skin tightened. But just as quickly, the warmth drained from the woman's face, and her expression hardened. "I warn you, Manuela. If you think you can talk me into a higher price by holding my personal life over my head, it won't end well for you."

"Oh, I have no intention of doing that," Manuela assured her and decided she'd played this game long enough. She winced at the thought of what Aurora would say, but she was a little drunk on finally having a bargaining chip, and she'd use it to get exactly what she wanted. "You can buy my land, but it will cost you more than money." The duchess trained her canny eyes on Manuela, her gaze unwavering.

"I will make sure you get whatever it is you want," she said impatiently, but Manuela heard the trepidation in her voice. This woman did not like being at a disadvantage, and unfortunately for her, Manuela found that she very much enjoyed holding all the cards.

"I am very pleased to hear that, Your Grace. And I must admit you were right, everyone has a price, even me." She leaned back, crossed her own legs in a mirror image of the duchess's own pose, the stem of the coupe dangling between them. She stretched the moment out until her companion's demeanor was so strained Manuela thought she'd leap across the table, demanding she open her mouth. Finally she spoke. "My price is you."

Five

Throughout her life, Cora had prided herself in thinking on her feet. She'd endeavored to develop an ability to look at a problem and calmly consider the possible solutions. In fact, it was that set of skills which had earned her reputation among the men she did business with. While her associates raged and ranted, she could calmly assess her next move and discern the best option. More than once she'd heard them expound on her equanimity being one of the reasons they could tolerate doing business with a woman. She had what they considered the nerves of a man. But now, the only thing her mind seemed to offer up was the realization that she was still dying to kiss that mouth. Even when her indiscretion from the night before could quite possibly ruin her plans for the railway.

"You're going to have to explain things a little further, Manuela." The thrill of saying her name caught Cora by surprise. She wanted to say it again, slowly, huskily. Right up against her ear as Cora's fingers dipped into her… Dear God, what was happening to her?

Thankfully the heiress saved her from herself by expounding on her absurd demand. "My personal circumstances are about to change drastically in about two months," she began, and Cora could practically see the dark cloud settling over the younger woman at the mention of her future. Manuela Caceres Galvan could say whatever she liked about her impending marriage, but this was not a bride eagerly awaiting her walk down the aisle. "I have six weeks to do as I please here, and I'd like to spend it enjoying the liberties I'll have to leave behind when I depart Paris."

"And you want me to help?" She wasn't sure why she asked. It was clear that the girl intended to trap her into being her sapphic fairy godmother. And from her little speech about the railway, Cora knew it would not do to intimidate her. Ribbons and ruffles notwithstanding.

"Oh no, I want more than help. I want you to show me. I want to know the places where women like us can be free in this city." The earnestness in Manuela's voice called to something that Cora could simply not allow into this room. They were not kindred souls or any such rot. This little chit was *extorting* her, and it mattered very little that she shared the same preferences when it came to lovers. "I want to experience what I can of that life before I return home. But I need a guide."

Cora almost laughed. Of all the things she thought she'd be asked as payment, this was not anything she could've even remotely conjured up.

"That's all you require for the land?"

The imp shot her a look that clearly said *You should know better than that.*

"I'll need four times as much money as you initially offered, and we will have to redraw the lines of the portion that I'll sell. But yes, that is all." The traviesa fluttered her eyelashes at Cora before gulping down more champagne.

A flush of pure heat exploded in Cora. The sweet siren from Le Bureau had intrigued her, but this sly, bold woman was enthralling, and for a woman like Cora, this was the kind of lark that could prove catastrophic.

"Why me?" Cora heard herself ask.

Manuela smiled, but this time the brightness in her eyes shifted into something far less appealing. There was dread there, and resignation. But she when opened her mouth her voice was clear and unfaltering. "Because I can make you." Her lips tipped up wickedly. Cora swallowed nervously. "And I like how you kiss." She would not touch *that* comment with a ten-foot pole.

"Isn't it a bit impulsive to let go of your property for a few weeks of enjoyment?" She would cut out her own tongue before talking herself out of this deal, but she had a conscience.

"A person could live a lifetime in six weeks, Your Grace. Entire lives have been changed in less," the heiress told her, undaunted. She was clearly dead set on doing this.

"If I decide to do this, and I am not saying that I will—" Cora infused as much intimidation into her words as she could, but it seemed that the only person in Paris immune to her notoriously mighty temper was sitting at the table with her, sipping champagne. "—I will make you sign a contract. You will be bound to sell Baluarte." Cora spoke in the voice she typically reserved for moments when she had to remind her associates who they were speaking with. "There is no force on this earth that will keep me from that land once I've fulfilled my end of the agreement," she warned, meaning every word.

"I understand." Manuela was so infuriatingly calm, while Cora could scarcely keep track of the turns this conversation had taken.

"I just want to be clear on something, Señorita Caceres Galvan," she went on. "I don't advise that you attempt toying with me. I have absolutely no compunction when it comes to tearing down someone for going back on their word." Was she trying to get the girl to back out of the sale? What on earth was wrong with her?

"I have no intention of going back on my agreement, *if* you fulfill yours."

"I will have to think about this," Cora replied, astonishing herself. But this suddenly felt too risky. She needed to think this over. She needed a damned war council. "I don't have time to be your Paris guide."

"But you will find some time. *If* you want the land, that is," Manuela volleyed back, in that same airy tone she'd delivered every other of her conversational bombs. "All I require are a few invigorating evenings." She whirled her finger, one eyebrow raised coquettishly, and all the air in Cora's lungs escaped at once. "I am sure someone as impressive as you can discern a number of enjoyable escapades for a simple island girl like me." If the vixen knew just how close Cora was to foregoing all sense of decorum, she wouldn't have ended the statement with a saucy wink.

"I have no way of knowing what you consider enjoyable, Miss Caceres Galvan."

"Oh, I think you do, Your Grace," she shot back, that devilish grin fastened to her lips. "I'd even venture to say you know precisely what that is."

"Why are you amenable to sell this now when you didn't so much as respond to our previous offers?" Cora inquired in an attempt to derail this runaway train.

"I like these terms far better." That was delivered with a grin, before the heiress reached for her glass again. It was almost empty, and on impulse, Cora reached for the bottle submerged in the bucket of ice and leaned to pour her more.

"Are duchesses supposed to serve people beneath their station?" Manuela asked in that salacious way of hers.

"I think you know by now that I don't exactly abide by society's expectations of what a duchess ought to do." For that, Cora was rewarded with a sultry half-lidded look that almost made her swallow her tongue. This Caribbean siren with her chocolate eyes and luscious mouth could upend Cora's existence.

"I have a kinship with rule breakers, being one myself."

God but she wanted to devour her. "Your parents or your fiancé won't object to this?" Cora threw this out in a flailing attempt to douse the flames in those brown eyes. It worked, for a second, but anyone who underestimated Manuela Caceres Galvan's tenaciousness did it at their peril. There was steel under that very tempting package.

"They have no control over what I do with my land," she said, then laughed a little too loudly. "If they did, my parents would've sold it the minute it was passed to me."

For the first time Cora thought she was seeing the real Manuela. Behind all the vapid smiles and salaciousness, there was a brittleness that Cora recognized. The brittleness at the heart of any person who understood that if she dared show the world who she truly was, it would scorn them.

"Do we have a deal, Your Grace?" She extended a hand, and Cora braced herself for the jolt of electricity she knew would come at the contact.

"I don't have enough information to make a deal yet." It was exceedingly challenging to sound or appear formidable when the slightest contact set her on fire. "I will need a day to consider and draw up my own terms. I will call on you when I'm ready."

"The offer will expire if I don't hear from you tomorrow." Cora could only stare when her companion rose elegantly and gathered her reticule from the chair. "I'm afraid I must go." She sent a pitying look to the uneaten oysters before winking at Cora. "I am to pick up my dress on Rue de la Paix for an outing this evening. It's a shame, really," she lamented, extending a hand to Cora. "I've always wanted to seal a deal with a kiss..."

Cora almost laughed at how genuinely affronted she looked. Felt slightly hysterical at the irony of meticulously devising a plan only to see it demolished by a frilly princess. And it was her own fault for thinking too little of the heiress because she was beautiful and young. Maybe her stepson was right, and she had been spending too much time with rich old men. One thing was certain: Cora had been had today.

And even in defeat, she wanted her. "If you keep talking about my kisses, I might have to oblige."

Manuela froze in front of the door, the glove in her hand fluttering to the ground. Cora picked it up before taking a step forward. She should let her walk away. This was over. The deal was on the table. She should call the footman. Walk Manuela to the street and send her on her way. But it seemed today she couldn't keep from running into burning buildings.

Muddying the waters here was the worst thing she could do. But the need to taste that mouth again was driving her mad. She was shaking from it. She took another step so that Manuela was caught between Cora and the closed door.

"Déjà vu," Manuela whispered.

Cora's fingers traced the edge of the heiress's face, her skin tightening with every needy sound she made. "Such a gorgeous girl," she told her, and Manuela melted. She was so expressive, so mercurial. One minute she was a hellion making scandalous proposals, and the next she was all molten need. "I should've kissed you longer last night."

"You should kiss me now," Manuela protested, surprising a laugh from Cora. Resisting all this incandescent energy was going to be hell.

She caught that stubborn chin between her fingers and lifted that mouth to hers, coaxing a deliciously frustrated whimper from the intrepid beauty. This Cora was good at. The seduction. The unplucking. It had been years since she'd properly done it. Since the disaster with Sally, she much preferred cursory encounters involving no kind of emotional investment. Her passion went into her business and the people she cared about. She didn't trust herself with it anywhere else. And she didn't want to think about Sally Fraser and her deceit now.

Manuela grunted, circling her arms around Cora's neck. "You are very frustrating," she complained.

"So impatient, princess." She didn't make her wait for long.

Cora realized the magnitude of her mistake the moment their mouths met. She didn't stop, she didn't think she could if she tried. She licked into that hot mouth. Deepened the kiss with her tongue until she could taste the saltiness of the oysters, the sharpness of the champagne and something altogether more intoxicating.

A hand cupped the back of her neck, bringing her in, and then she was the one being kissed. She kissed like a gale, sweeping Cora right off her feet. Her hands skating over those wonderful curves. That sweet, clever tongue insinuating itself with unbridled enthusiasm.

To Cora's eternal shame, it was Manuela who broke away. She slid out of the embrace flushed. Her eyes glassy and her mouth so red and puffy Cora had to look away.

"For the record," she began, breathless and gloriously beautiful. "This is my definition of *enjoyable*." That was the splash of cold water Cora needed to get back in control. This could not be some six-week-long romp, this was business. Business that she would not endanger over a few kisses.

"This can't happen again," Cora declared and saw a flash of regret in the heiress's gaze, but it was quickly replaced with the bravado that Cora now recognized as armor.

"That's a pity," she said breezily, without looking at Cora. "You'll have to introduce me to some other ladies who will be open to engaging in that type of enjoyment with me, then."

Cora did not like that suggestion and found the reasons for her irritation even less appealing. She had to get her out of there. "I will come to you, and we will discuss the terms of this agreement, Manuela. Tomorrow."

"I'll be ready for you, Your Grace."

Only after she'd watched the heiress get in a carriage and disappear into the bustling Rue Montorgueil did she notice the heiress's glove was still in her hand.

Six

"Has the young heiress been properly decimated?" Cora's step-son Alfie asked as she walked into the study.

"Not quite," she responded shakily, making a beeline to the decanter by the fireplace and pouring herself a healthy serving of whisky. She needed fortification before delving into what had just occurred at that blasted luncheon.

"I had the mate ready for you," Alfie told her, pointing to the tea service on the low table by the hearth. The round, squat gourd sat with the bombilla, a silver straw, protruding from it. One of their family rituals was drinking the tea together in the afternoons. But today yerba mate would just not do.

"I need something stronger," she huffed, before tossing back a gulp of the scorching spirit.

"Imbibing before sundown," her stepson observed, unhelp-fully. "I take it Miss Caceres was not as malleable as you hoped."

Cora made an unhappy sound as she sat on the armchair across from Alfie, one finger massaging her temple. She was still reel-ing from that lunch—from that kiss—and wished she'd had a moment to digest what happened before having to explain it to anyone. But Cora kept her days full, every minute she was awake accounted for, and she'd foolishly assumed she'd make quick work of Miss Caceres Galvan and had agreed to tea with Alfred, Cassandra and Frederica. Her stepson and her two best friends were the last people she wanted to talk to right now.

"I thought you'd be delayed. Weren't you meeting with Grayson about the renovations?" she asked in an effort to divert his attention, but he knew all of Cora's tells.

"Good try, Mother," he retorted, seemingly delighted at her sad attempt to sway him in another direction. "Renovations are in order, and the house in Belgravia will be ready for us in six weeks. Now, tell me what has brought up this thirst for my single malt at barely half past two."

For the past year they'd been working on getting Bristol Park, the Duke of Sundridge's home in London, ready for Alfie's return. Since Cora's humiliating scandal, they'd stayed away from the city, but now at almost twenty-five, Alfie wished to assume his place in the House of Lords. Announcing the completion of the South American Railway was supposed to be Cora's final coup before their return.

It would do her well to remember that all of those plans could be undone if she didn't go along with Manuela Caceres Galvan's ludicrous proposition.

Nothing had gone as planned in that meeting. She shouldn't have kissed her. It would've been hard enough to keep her distance, but now that she'd properly savored that mouth, now that she knew there was a lot more to Manuela Galvan than flirtatious banter, it would be a test of endurance to keep from ruining everything. She should be in her office devising some other way to get that land away from her; instead, here she was fingering the glove she'd left behind and sulking.

"Has another foe been bested?" Cassandra asked, her pretty face split in a mischievous grin as she breezed into the room.

"She just arrived and, as of yet, has only groaned and guzzled whisky, which tells me perhaps things didn't go as planned," Alfie announced with irritating gusto, which of course delighted Cassie. Frederica, who had come in behind her beloved, sent Cora a commiserating look.

Cassie was as sunny and gregarious as Frederica was broody and serious. Upon meeting them, one would never think that two people who were so different could be so suited for each other, but they were a perfect match. Cassandra's emotional and vivacious nature was tempered by Frede's more analytical, sedate personality. Cora had introduced them years ago when she began her patronage of Cassandra. Frede, who came from a wealthy Peruvian-Austrian family, at that time had been embroiled in a legal battle with her medical school in Germany, demanding they allow her to attend her classes in trousers. Cora had invited the two of them to her country house in Champagne, and from the moment they'd set eyes on each other they'd been bonded. Cassie had gone back to Vienna with Frede a couple of months later and stayed there with her until she'd finished her medical studies. They'd been in Paris for a few years now, stronger than ever.

"Corazón Aymara, I am waiting," Cassie demanded, using her full name to emphasize her dwindling patience.

Cora had to be careful with what she said here. Cassie was an unrepentant romantic and for years now had been on a mission to couple Cora off. If she even sensed Cora was now up to her neck in extremely confusing and thoroughly lewd feelings toward Miss Caceres Galvan, she would get ideas. She opted for going on the offensive.

"That's why you came here today, to hear the gossip?" The chastisement had absolutely no effect on Cassie, who shot her a shameless grin as she sat on Frede's lap.

"Absolutely. You know I live to hear about your business exploits." Frede gave Cassie a baleful look even as she tightened an arm around her lover's waist and planted a kiss on her cheek.

Cassie immediately melted into the caress, and soon they were canoodling, all interest in Cora's troubles forgotten.

"Did I miss anything?" asked Tia Osiris when she sauntered into the room, followed by Martirio, her black cat.

"So far we've only gotten a few sighs in between gulps of whisky," Alfie reported, to which Tia Osiris responded with a raised eyebrow.

"Is there anyone else in this household that would like to come and hear about my lunch? Perhaps Cook or Maggie? The porter?" Cora rebuked.

"No seas malcriada, Corazón," Tia Osiris chided as she took a seat next to Alfie. "I assume things didn't go well. You are not one to hold back when there is something to gloat about."

She wasn't humble, that was true. But why would she be? She worked hard for all her victories, and no one ever criticized men for boasting about *their* wins.

"Things didn't go exactly as planned, no," she finally said, as her captive audience looked on. "Last night I found a woman in my rooms at Le Bureau. Specifically, I found a woman in my rooms at Le Bureau atop the sideboard, trying to get a better look at your fresco, Cassie."

Cassandra's eyes widened comically while the other three looked between them, puzzled expression on their faces. "She climbed on your furniture? Are you certain...that's the only climbing she did?"

"Yes," Cora bit out, mystified all over again by such an unfortunate coincidence.

"What does this have to do with the luncheon?" Frede asked with interest, probably guessing where things were headed.

"It seems that Miss Caceres Galvan, who owns the land I need, and the—" she almost said *nymph*, but Cassandra absolutely did not need any more encouragement when it came to her fantasies regarding Cora's romantic life "—woman who availed herself of my rooms are one and the same."

As she expected, her so-called loved ones exploded in laughter. "This is why I avoid Le Bureau and Montmartre when I am closing in on an important deal. Too many potential disasters."

Cassandra rolled her eyes.

"I don't understand why you're finding this so distressing, Cora. If the girl has certain interests in common with you, I would say it's absolutely serendipitous," Tia Osiris exclaimed.

"It is a nuisance and a complication." She did not like when her personal life interfered with her business.

"But you were intrigued by her," Cassandra prodded, jolting Cora out of her thoughts.

"Liebe, she might not want to be doing business with someone she's interested in in other ways," Frede told Cassie, who deflated.

"Might I remind all of us we still don't know what occurred at this luncheon," Alfie said, attempting to bring everyone back to the conversation. "Mother, other than the awkwardness of the situation, something else clearly went awry with the heiress. Won't you tell us?" She needed to share this with *someone*.

"The sum of it is that she will agree to selling me the land if, in addition to quadrupling the sum we offered, I personally show her Paris for women like us, as she put it, until she returns to South America."

The silence following that could only be called *charged*. Tia Osiris, who had been petting her cat, had her hand suspended in midair. Alfie seemed to be struggling mightily to keep from spraying a mouthful of whisky all over himself. Even Frede, who was typically better at maintaining an air of stoic composure, had developed an intense twitch around her mouth. Cassandra, the traitor, was laughing so hard she'd slid off Frede's lap and was now doubled over on the rug. "Your plan to steamroll the silly little heiress with your title and some champagne backfired mightily, sobrina," Tia Osiris grossly understated.

"Astronomically." The most distressing part of all this was that instead of wanting to hatch up a scheme to get out of the situation, Cora's mind kept serving up possibilities of places to take Manuela. An image of the two of them dancing at her friend Claudine's brasserie had taken residence in her head, and now it was all she could think of.

"I know surprises are not something that you enjoy," Alfie began, once he could speak again. "But perhaps this is a good thing." He held a hand up before Cora could protest. "You have this affinity. If she wants help finding that part of Paris, you could use the time together to ingratiate yourself to her."

"I don't like that," Cassandra offered, soberly. "If the girl is desperate to find women she can be her true self with, it is not right to use it against her."

"She's essentially bribing me, Cassandra," Cora reminded her friend, who sent her a disapproving look.

"Perhaps she was as impacted by your meeting as you were," Tia Osiris suggested. And that was exactly where she could not let herself return to. That first meeting. To the soft, sweet girl she'd had in her arms and of the way those big brown eyes had pierced her. How she hadn't seen anything as appealing in what felt like a lifetime. How that kiss had awakened something she'd thought was lost.

"She's an artist," Cora said quietly. Her inability to stop talking about Manuela was quickly becoming an additional problem. "She's got two pieces in the exposition." This she'd learned from the agent she hired to dig up information on Baluarte's owner.

"She's obviously brilliant," Cassie exclaimed.

"*You* have a piece at the exposition," Cora drawled, eliciting a smug grin from her friend.

"Exactly." She jumped up and clapped her hands while Cora tried to remain calm. "It means I am aware of the level of brilliance required to achieve such a feat."

Cora laughed, her gaze on Frede, who smiled indulgently at her beloved. "How do you put up with her?"

Frede, who conducted herself with icy aloofness regarding most things, smiled warmly at Cassandra, her blue eyes burning with such devotion, Cora's breath caught in her throat.

"She is my every delight." The slender, pale woman's passion for her lover was so clear in that moment it felt almost intrusive to be there. Cassandra's face was a reflection of Frede's affection as she bent to kiss her. They murmured something private and intense against each other's mouths and once again Cora's traitorous mind brought up the image of Manuela, those molten eyes and that soft, kissable mouth. The way it tempted Cora.

"You should bring her to Pasquale's tonight. Sarah Margaret and Fleur will be showing their work." With Cassie's pronouncement the truth of her situation finally sank in, and with it the realization that to get the land, she would have to introduce Manuela Caceres into the most intimate, most fiercely guarded areas of her life.

Tonight wouldn't do at all. What she needed was some distance from the heiress before going into battle again.

"I don't know if dinner is such a good idea," Cora equivocated. "And tonight won't work either," she told Cassie. "Alfie and I have the soiree at the Mexican pavilion," she reminded her stepson, who appeared even less excited than she was at the prospect of another evening dealing with peers and diplomats.

As far as Parisian evenings went, the Académie Pasquale was not exactly risqué. In fact, it was one of the most renowned and notorious art schools in Europe, famous for having trained many emerging stars of the art world. However, Cora's fondness for the institution was due to its founder Aristide Pasquale's dedication to training women artists.

Instinctively she knew that Manuela would love Pasquale. Would love even more to attend a show for one of the most prominent couples in the Paris art world. Sarah Margaret Dalton was a renowned landscape artist who made no secret of her love of women and flaunted her relationship with Fleur Bonneville, a fellow artist. Cora had no opinion on how people chose to conduct themselves in their affaires de coeur, but the last thing *she* needed was Manuela Caceres Galvan getting any ideas.

"Sarah Margaret and Fleur tend to be a bit too outrageous, and the last thing I need is to get caught up in a scandal a month before Alfie and I return to London."

"Mother, no one cares—" Alfie began to protest, but Cora held up a hand.

"Alfred, please, don't argue with me on this. I will not do anything to jeopardize your entry to the House of Lords. I've already done enough damage, without needing to remind everyone why you haven't been in London since you were in short trousers." That was met with a series of sighs, deep inhalations and a particularly strained *Not this again* from Tia Osiris.

"Yes, this very thing, again," Cora shot back, swallowing down the bile that typically accompanied this topic of discussion. "We have been planning Alfie's return to London for years. It is well past time for him to assume his place as Duke of Sundridge. I will not permit anything to do with my associations to interfere with that." She was finally on the cusp of repairing the injury she'd caused her stepson's family name. By orchestrating his return to Britain as one of the wealthiest men in Europe and a major shareholder of what was soon to be the most profitable railway project in the world. No one would dare snub a man with that kind of power, with that kind of influence. But for everything to go to plan, Cora could not let any whispers about her to resurface. Gallivanting around town with Manuela Caceres Galvan would almost certainly do it.

"I have no intention of giving Miss Caceres Galvan carte blanche over my life. I have to carefully assess the types of diversions I'd take her to and bringing her along to an exhibit featuring erotic renditions of Greek art merely hours after her proposing this demented scheme might give her the wrong impression."

"And what impression would that be?" Tia Osiris's inquiry was not at all innocent. She was clearly enjoying Cora's misery.

"The impression that this will be some sort of romp where I take her on the sapphic adventure of a lifetime, Aunt."

Alfie spluttered at that, then went into a coughing fit after inhaling some whisky. She moved to thump him on the back, even as she sent a dire glance in the direction of her best friend and her aunt. "I must keep very clear boundaries around what I do with Miss Caceres Galvan."

All of this infuriated her. If she was a man, she wouldn't have to consider any of this. She'd happily take Manuela for a roll in the hay with two or three trollops, and no one would blink.

"And when have you ever been against a romp?" Cassandra insisted. "Just last year you arranged a three-day bacchanalia for that government official you were buttering up about some kind of permit."

That had been tiresome. She'd arranged for a pleasure palace in the Loire Valley and filled a fountain with champagne for the man, who had proceeded to splash around in it in the nude for the benefit of the five girls from Le Bureau Cora had procured and paid for. It had not been pretty from what she'd heard, but in the end, she'd been able to build a bridge which cut the transportation time between her vineyard in Champagne and the bottling plant in half.

"Could it be you're developing a case of scruples, sobrina?"

Cora shuddered at Tia Osiris's suggestion. Scruples were for people with weak stomachs and lack of ambition. Scruples had nothing to do with it.

"There's always dinner with the gang tomorrow." Cassie, when she chose to, could be quite persistent.

The gang was an array of women artists from the Americas living in Paris who gathered monthly at Frede and Cassie's for the evening. Cora cherished those dinners and had never taken anyone along.

To her horror, the idea of bringing Manuela didn't seem off putting. This was all wrong. *All wrong.* Manuela Caceres Galvan was a means to an end. Certainly no one Cora could plunge into her private affairs.

"I have to consider how I will do things with Miss Caceres Galvan. She is—" She broke off, refusing to voice the words floating around her head.

Radiant, lush, much too tempting for her own good.

"She is a problem I mean to solve as far away from my personal life as possible."

Seven

"*That* is the old battle-ax?" Aurora inquired loudly, a finger directed at the Duchess and Duke of Sundridge who were at that very moment making their way down the marbled staircase of the Mexican pavilion. It took Manuela a second to react to her friend's astonished question, due to her own surprise.

"Good grief, Aurora, don't point!" Manuela whispered, as she pulled down her friend's finger and pressed one of her own to her lips.

"How is it that in the past five hours you've failed to inform us that the old biddy is very much not old? The woman looks like an Amazon!" She ignored Aurora's outburst, wincing internally at the thought of just how much she'd failed to share with her friends about her luncheon with the duchess.

She should've known she'd be here tonight. All evening the ushers had been announcing aristocrats from every corner of Europe. The Mexican delegation's soiree turned out to be a gathering of the highest echelons of Latin American society attending the Exposition Universelle. Not even her parents, who despite their financial troubles still had connections, could secure an invitation for her. But Aurora's family—one of the richest in Mexico—had made a hefty contribution to the construction of the pavilion the country built for the exposition, which made Manuela and friends guests of honor that evening. Not that one would think it by the way Aurora was dressed.

"Is that mud on your hem?" Manuela asked, truly horrified. Aurora waved her away and kept her gaze on the Duchess of Sundridge and her companion, the duke—her son according to Antonio—who were now doing a circuit around the room. It had not occurred to Manuela until she'd heard the duchess's title called in conjunction with the younger man's that there might have been a spouse and children. It could be quite a scandal to take up with this woman.

"Don't change the subject, Manuela." Aurora waved her off, her mouth set in a way that forecasted one of her lectures. Manuela was decidedly not in the mood for one of those, not when the duchess was in the room. Had she gotten even more beautiful in the hours since they'd parted?

She was dressed in a dark purple dress, almost black. Like the morning suit she'd had on earlier, it was very simple in its design and yet she still managed to stand out. There wasn't an eye in the room that didn't turn when she glided past. Her statuesque form commanded attention, which she disregarded in turn. The Duchess of Sundridge was the embodiment of aloof disinterest, but Manuela knew the storm hiding behind that mask. She ached to be consumed by it again.

Even in the midst of her lustful musings, Manuela could not help but admire the large room. The Mexican pavilion, or Aztec Palace, as it was named by the delegation, was built in a pre-Colombian style inspired by the Pirámide del Sol in Teotihuacán. The facade of the building resembled the stone walls of the ancient monument, with its twelve bronze bas-relief figures of Aztec kings and deities, which made for quite an impressive sight. The inside was just as magnificently decorated, illuminated by fully electrified chandeliers made of copper and adorned with Mexican green onyx. The balustrade the duchess's hand slid down as she entered the room was carved out of the famous zapote wood, which had an almost orange color. There was what seemed an army of servants walking around with trays laden with French champagne and Oaxacan mezcal. It was a lavish affair, even by Parisian standards.

"Manuela," Aurora cried, making her jump.

"Dios mio, Aurora!" she exclaimed, clutching her chest. "I didn't have time to tell you," Manuela demurred, even as she averted her eyes from her friend.

"You had time to pick up that...dress," Aurora observed, her eyes narrowing on Manuela's latest acquisition from Jeanne Paquin.

Manuela had been so unsteady after the very unexpected meeting with the duchess—and her own outrageous proposition— that she'd soothed herself by opting to wear the most outrageous of the dresses she'd ordered from Madame Paquin. The fabric of the skirts were a gauzy swirl of bright blue and yellows which gave it the appearance of two puddles of paint someone had swirled together with their fingers. The bodice was blue and adorned with shiny yellow beads along the sleeves and décolletage. It was certainly not the kind of gown one was meant to blend in with, but there had always been something reassuring to her about attracting the wrong kind of attention. She found a sort of comfort in seeing certain people react as badly to her presence as she expected them to, and the tongues were already wagging accordingly this evening.

A pair of young women in identical dresses done in complementary shades of pale green and pink walked by them, their heads together and mouths hidden behind their fans. Aurora hissed at them loudly, and they responded with satisfying squeals of horror before scurrying off.

"Really, Aurora, how unladylike." Her friends were true gems, even when Manuela wanted to throttle them.

"I hate these cabrones," Luz Alana lamented as she joined them again, her pretty face tight with frustration.

"No luck with the shippers?" Aurora asked, momentarily distracted from interrogating Manuela.

Luz huffed out a frustrated breath and snatched a glass of champagne from one of the servers. "No."

Before Manuela could even open her mouth, Aurora held up a hand. "This one is in the process of reporting about her luncheon with the duchess."

"I'm not sure why you are so preoccupied with what's happening with me, Aurora, when Luz Alana is the one who needs assistance." Manuela attempted to deflect, but her friend was not budging.

"Luz Alana is absolutely fine. That big Scot is besotted with her. I'd be surprised if the man doesn't buy all her rum before the week is out, just to get in her good graces." Despite herself, Manuela grinned at Aurora's bafflement at what had been unfolding between their friend and the Scottish distiller. She was much too independent, and contrary, to find a man's interference in her affairs—even if it was with the best intentions—as appealing as Luz Alana seemed to find the attention of Evanston Sinclair, who, they'd just learned, was also the Earl of Darnick.

"That may be the case, but I don't understand why you're harassing *me*." It was futile to delay the unavoidable, but she might as well enjoy herself by yanking Aurora's chain.

Manuela jutted her chin in the direction of the crowded dance floor. "Wasn't that Colombian heir sniffing around, after you danced with him?"

Aurora's eyes became slits of absolute loathing at the mention of the very handsome—and arrogant—gentleman who'd taken her out on the floor for one of the danzas. "That comemierda, he's lucky Amaranta made me take that scalpel out of my bag, or I would've done him some violence."

"Manuela, picking fights with Aurora will delay this only so far," Luz Alana chided. "Tell us what happened." Manuela knew her friends would not be happy that she'd done the exact opposite of what she'd promised. But that wasn't the reason she was stalling. She was usually more than happy to scandalize her loved ones with her antics. She didn't want to hear she'd made a grave mistake.

"Oh, all right," she said and sighed in feigned petulance, her heart racing with nerves. "But if I am going to tell you, we need a place more private, and it must be fast. I don't want to lose sight of the duchess." Aurora rolled her eyes, while Luz Alana shook her head. "Come on," she urged her friends. "There's an alcove I saw earlier where we can talk."

"In here," Luz Alana said, ushering them behind a curtain.

"Oh goodness, I'm utterly terrified of what is going to come out of your mouth," Aurora whimpered. Luz Alana straightened her back as if bracing for impact.

"You both look like you expect me to slap you across the face," Manuela protested. They were right to be worried, of course, but they could at least pretend to not consider her an absolute lost cause.

"I am growing roots, Manuela," Aurora pushed.

"So here is the thing," she began and was surprised to hear a quake in her voice. "Remember the night at Le Bureau?" she asked and was promptly lambasted with an exasperated *Yes* from Aurora and *You mean last night?* from Luz Alana.

"I told you I met a woman."

"The woman of your dreams, who you vowed to search all of Paris for." This was delivered deadpan by Aurora.

"Well…" She stretched out the word long enough to make Aurora turn a bright shade of red. Was she holding her breath? "It turns out I didn't have to look for very long." Manuela's laugh was a bit shrill, but at this point it was pointless to pretend this conversation was anything other than unhinged.

"Which means?" Luz Alana asked, whirling a hand in the air.

"Which means," Manuela echoed, feeling every muscle in her face tighten.

"Por el amor de Dios, Manuela!"

"She's the duchess," she finally blurted out, the words ricocheting around the small space like gunshots. Aurora actually reeled back from the revelation, while Luz Alana stared at her slack-jawed. "The Duchess of Sundridge wants to buy Baluarte. And I'm going to sell it to her." Into the resounding silence that followed, she added quietly, "I'm still marrying Felix. That's not changing."

"Is that woman trying to blackmail you?" Aurora, who was merely a couple of inches taller than Manuela, demanded with violence in her voice as she raised herself to her full height. "Because I don't care if she's a duchess. I will not allow it."

Across from her Luz Alana remained quiet, but Manuela knew she would echo the sentiment. Her two Leonas would have absolutely no issue confronting one of the richest, most powerful people in Europe if it meant protecting Manuela.

"No, boba," Manu laughed, bopping Aurora on the nose with her finger. "She's not blackmailing me." In truth, if anyone could be considered a blackmailer it was Manuela, but Aurora was too volatile for Manu to risk going into too much detail on how exactly things had transpired during their lunch. "The duchess made me a very good offer..." How could she say this without it resulting in one of her friends collapsing or worse? "And I countered with my own." Neither of her friends blinked. "I've asked that she sponsor me as I explore some social circles and venues in the city that cater to women with our same interests," she finally said.

Luz Alana pressed a palm to her forehead, a distressed noise escaping her lips.

"Are you truly giving up your only asset—your inheritance from your abuela—in exchange for a month and a half of parties?" She expected Aurora to say this, and Manuela couldn't exactly refute it.

She could tell her friends that she couldn't have stopped herself if she'd tried. That she'd walked into that room today, taken one look at Cora's hard mouth and those wounded violet eyes and had fallen a little in love, but they would probably find her reasoning lacking.

"I'm not giving it away. She will pay me for the land. The other part is what I consider a bonus. She offered to put the money in an account that Felix can't access." Her friends seemed slightly relieved by that, but Aurora's frown remained firmly in place.

"I want to be glad that you will have some money of your own, but I know what usually happens when you have very sudden, very radical changes of heart."

Aurora was that rare breed of woman who managed to break the rules while still observing as many of them as possible. She carried herself with a righteous zeal. Unflinching. Manuela, on the other hand, merely wanted to live loudly for a few weeks before she was silenced by a marriage and life she was not strong enough to escape.

"I know this is outrageous," she admitted, which only deepened the matching frowns directed at her. "I have my own reservations regarding it. But I am running out of time, and for this summer at least, I want to be happy much more than I want to be good." She hoped that they, of all people, would understand.

Manuela was accustomed to being the so-called wild friend, but it hurt when no one in her life seemed to be able to see past it. When no one could recognize her impetuousness for the desperation it was. How did she explain that today, sparring with the duchess, felt like the first time anyone had ever seen her as more than decoration? That seeing a glint of admiration in the duchess's eyes at Manuela's boldness—even when she looked ready to throttle her—had set free something in her she didn't know was captive?

"And you will be able to walk away once it's time to go home?" Luz Alana inquired after a long moment.

"I have it all sorted out. Don't worry about me," she insisted.

"What is it that you really want with this woman, Manu? Are you truly going to give away your last piece of security for a few nights of fun?"

Had the question come from Aurora, Manuela would've said something scathing just to start an argument. But Luz Alana rarely spoke out against Manuela's more impulsive antics. She suspected it was because deep down Luz Alana sometimes wished she had the freedom to be a bit foolish. That though she loved her younger sister and was deeply committed to her taking the family's rum to other markets, her obligations were too many.

Manuela wished she could tell her friend that sometimes being the person who no one trusted with anything beyond a modiste's recommendation could also be a curse. That when your only value to your family amounted to your marriage, you could be in a wretched place indeed.

"All I ask is that you support me like I have supported both of you." This was important to her and she needed them to see that. "I am aware of what this looks like, I am even aware I'll more than likely come to regret it at some point in the future, but right now this is what I want. *She* is what I want." Aurora pushed two fingers into her eye sockets so deeply Manuela worried her eyeballs might pop out. "I am not you, Aurora, I am not strong enough to stick to my principles even when I'm threatened with disownment."

"But you are strong, Leona," Luz Alana insisted, reaching for her hand. "You are strong, and you are brilliant. I am not saying you need to give up your comforts. I am not even asking you not to enjoy your freedom while you are here. I just wish you had something to fall back on. I want you to be all right."

"And I love you both for it," she said sincerely. She knew that unlike her parents, these two women truly only wanted what was best for her. "Right now all I need is for both of you to not judge me."

"Oh, all right. Why does everything with you two need to end in tears?" Aurora protested, reaching for Manuela's other hand. "I should know better than to think either of you will listen to any of my extremely reasonable advice."

"We listen when it doesn't actively interfere with what we want to do," Manuela quipped, then smiled when she saw Luz Alana cover her mouth to hide her own smirk. Soon she found herself engulfed in a six-limbed embrace, receiving exactly what she'd asked for.

"Can we go out now?" she asked, her voice muffled. "I've lost sight of the duchess for too long as it is." They let go of each other after a moment, and without words their bond was restored. Their pride as strong as ever.

"Ay, there goes another one of the shippers I must talk to," Luz Alana yelped, already stepping out from behind their curtain. She blew them both kisses as she rushed out into the fray.

"But we were still talking!" Aurora protested, but Luz Alana was already a dozen yards away, pulling one of her business cards from the bodice of her dress. "Why was I cursed with the most stubborn and outrageous friends in the world?" For all her claims of being the most practical one, Aurora could be quite melodramatic.

"Because if not, you would never have any fun and would spend your days elbow-deep in placenta or whatever it is you do at those clinics," Manuela teased. "Come on, enough blustering over potted palms." She tugged a very stiff Aurora back out into the light and was smoothing her skirts with one hand when she heard a surprised squeak.

"What?" Manuela popped her head up and saw the cause of Aurora's distress call. The Duchess of Sundridge and her son were headed in their direction.

The noise of the room melted away as her heart began a concerning staccato against her chest. "Act like I've just said something funny," she urged, smiling madly at Aurora, who looked even more confused than she'd been a moment ago.

"What in the world is the matter with you, Manuela del Carmen? Estas loca?"

"Do it, Aurora," she insisted through gritted teeth as she patted her friend on the arm and threw her head back in silent laughter. "She's on her way here." Manuela snapped her fan open and began to flutter it in front of her face.

"I don't think I've ever seen you like this," Aurora muttered. "You are usually so calm and aloof when men show any interest in you."

"I'm going to pretend I didn't hear that," Manuela told her friend, her attention fixed on the duchess who was headed straight to them.

"Señorita Caceres Galvan, our paths cross yet again," she said in that low, husky voice of hers. There was a mild tone of accusation, which Manuela would've taken more to heart had she not noticed the way the duchess's gaze swept over her generously deep décolletage with undisguised interest.

"Your Grace." She bowed her head slightly, but her eyes locked with those piercing violet ones. "I thought you'd be home drawing up an ironclad agreement for me to sign." She paired the barb with a flutter of her eyelashes. She was still applying herself to the art of ocular flirtation when the duchess pulled something out of her pocket.

"I had to make sure I returned this," the duchess teased, as she handed Manuela the glove she'd left at the restaurant. Manuela reached for it, shivering as their fingers brushed.

"How kind of you," she said as her voice dropped to a rough

whisper. Since she'd left Au Rocher de Cancale, Manuela had been unsure of what footing she'd been on with the woman. She was certain her land was something Cora wanted very much, but she was not quite as sure how the woman felt about her. "I am grateful to you, Your Grace." As she slid the glove into a small pocket of her skirt, the floor under her feet seemed much sturdier. Because the duchess hadn't known Manuela would be here tonight, but she'd kept her glove.

That had to mean something.

A sharp pinch on her side broke her concentration. Right, introductions. How was she expected to observe the rules of etiquette at a moment like this?

"This is my dear friend, Doctor Aurora Montalban Wright. She's a physician in Mexico."

"Duchess," Aurora automatically said, curtsying with such grace and aplomb one would never imagine she'd waxed on about the abomination that was the European aristocracy just that morning.

"Mucho gusto, Doctora," the duchess responded in Spanish, making Aurora's form falter and Manuela gasp loudly. "A practicing woman physician. You must be very tenacious."

"You speak Spanish?" The astonished question was out of Manuela's mouth before she could stop it. "You could've said so during our lunch." She wasn't certain why this seemed like an egregious detail for the duchess to have kept from her. Cora, on her end, appeared quite pleased with herself.

"Are you Spanish?" Aurora asked, as she looked between Manuela and the duchess.

"Chilena, but I haven't lived there since I was seventeen," she explained, smiling placidly at Aurora, then sending a much more incendiary look Manuela's way. "My father was American, but my mother was from Iquique, close to where he had his mines." Her explanation seemed a bit stilted, as if she was unaccustomed to speaking about herself. "I've lived outside of

Chile almost as long as I lived in it. Paris has been our home for almost a decade now. We came here after my husband, the late duke, passed away." A flash of pain passed through her eyes at the mention of her spouse. Even in the short time she'd known the duchess, she suspected that fleeting vulnerability was rare. She was also intrigued about her relationship with the duke. "This is my son, the Duke of Sundridge," she explained, bestowing a look of naked affection to her handsome companion.

"Stepson, and please call me Alfred."

Stepson. The relief Manuela felt at that word was enough to make her knees weak, and she didn't even know why. "If I was her child, she would've birthed me at ten, which unfortunately is not considered nearly as reprehensible as it should be." He leaned in to kiss Manuela's and Aurora's hands, a warm smile tipping up his lips.

"You have made an impression on my stepmother, Miss Caceres Galvan. She was quite stirred by your luncheon this afternoon." By all appearances the duchess remained impassive at the comment, but a moment later the duke cried out in pain, before dissolving into laughter.

"Your stepmother hosts quite an exciting lunch." She snapped open her fan again and waved it very slowly right over the area on her chest where her breasts were pushed up and out by her corset. "My mouth is still tingling." She made sure to bite her bottom lip, right on the same spot where Cora had so tantalizingly suckled it that afternoon. "From the oysters, of course."

"Of course," Cora echoed. Someone—likely Aurora—gasped, but Alfie seemed amused by the conversation happening between Manuela and his stepmother. "Can I speak to you for a moment, Miss Caceres Galvan?" the duchess asked, her face very serious, prompting Alfred into action.

"Would you do me the honor, Doctora Montalban?" Aurora eyed his proffered hand dubiously, but it seemed the persuasive skills of the family didn't solely reside with the duchess.

"We could leave these ladies to talk while you tell me all about your medical practice." That was all it took for Aurora's fortress against the aristocracy to crumble. She let the handsome duke lead her away while Manuela and the duchess exchanged torrid looks. They were standing about a foot apart, but Manuela could feel a wall of heat radiating between them.

After she left the duchess she'd convinced herself her impulsive offer was about getting her last bit of freedom. But right now, standing in front of this woman with her heart in her throat and her body in the grips of burning desire, she had to recognize the overture was as much about the duchess as it was about experiencing Paris. "Have you given my proposal any more thought, Your Grace?"

"I've scarcely thought of anything else." Her voice was so deep and husky. It was a voice made to whisper dark, ruinous deeds in hidden corners. Manuela's clothes felt too tight as she imagined herself leaning against the wall with those full lips brushing her ear and one of those elegant hands up her skirt. "I imagined you'd be on the dance floor with one of these simpering boys who can't seem to tear their eyes off you." Manuela's breath caught at the naked disdain she bestowed upon the men looking in their direction. She was not foolish enough to think it was jealousy, but there was a hint of possessiveness there that intrigued her.

Before she responded she took a step forward, so they were merely inches apart. Her mouth went dry from the proximity, the need to kiss the woman lashing away every ounce of sense. For a moment she could scarcely remember what it was she was supposed to be doing.

Oh yes, staging her attack.

"My apologies if I didn't make myself clearer in our previous meetings. Simpering boys are not of any interest to me, and I didn't come here to dance."

"Given my knowledge of what you entertain yourself with,

I'm afraid to ask what you intended to do this evening, if dance is out of the question, princess." She spoke the words very low, so low that Manuela had to bend down to hear. Their arms brushed for a fleeting second, and the effect of that friction ran up her spine like lightning. But she wasn't so far gone as to miss an opportunity to shock the duchess.

"Well," she started, smiling up at Cora. She liked thinking of her as Cora. "The duchess" didn't seem quite right anymore. Not with the things she wanted from the woman. "I *was* intending to break into the greenhouse at the Brazilian pavilion, but only after I had some refreshments." Cora's eyes twinkled with mirth as two white teeth snagged her bottom lip. God, she was so beautiful,

"What kind of evening would it be if you didn't commit some breaking and entering?" Her tone was very serious, but her mouth tugged into a heart-stopping crooked smile, and again a flush of happiness coursed through Manuela.

"I hope we never have to find out," she taunted, making a laugh escape Cora.

"Dare I ask why the Brazilian pavilion?"

"Flowers—flora," Manuela corrected herself, "are a central theme of my art. The Brazilians have brought hundreds of endemic orchid varietals I've never seen." Cora's eyes widened with interest, just like they had that night at Le Bureau. It was rare for Manuela to receive this kind of reaction when she mentioned her art. The Leonas were encouraging of her, but they didn't light up at the prospect of hearing her go on about her inspiration or aesthetic. The duchess, on the other hand, seemed impatient to hear more. "They even have gigantic lily pads called Victoria Amazonica. I heard they're big enough for an adult to lay on them."

"Crimes de florale," she said, with humor. "You are inventive, princesa." The duchess pressed closer, and for a breathless second their chests touched. The friction sent a jolt of lust right to her core. Maybe it had been a mistake to do this in plain sight.

"My friends would say foolhardy," she refuted in a self-mocking tone that turned the duchess's smile into a frown. "I've tried to see them during the day twice already, but there are just too many people."

Cora considered that for a moment and seemed to be readying a question when a very large man with an unfortunate set of very greasy whiskers approached them.

"Sundridge, I've been looking for you, but finding even one person who speaks French is a damned ordeal in this place." Instantly the interested, warm Cora was replaced by the icy woman from Au Rocher de Cancale.

"Good evening, Blanchet." Nothing about the way Cora greeted the man could be considered anything other than perfectly cordial, and yet somehow it landed like an insult. Blanchet didn't seem to notice: his beady eyes were much too busy roaming lecherously over Manuela. The man's shameless leering made her wish she had a shawl to cover herself with. Cora also noticed, and smoothly placed herself between Manuela and the older man. The simple gallantry of the gesture had quite an impact on Manuela. She couldn't recall another time when someone had so instinctively protected her. "Is there anything you need?" Cora asked, her tone decidedly less friendly.

"Say, did you make any progress with that little chit who owns the land we want?" Manuela thought what she'd seen on Cora's expression after she'd made her scandalous offer was anger, but now she realized she'd been wrong.

"Could you show at least a modicum of manners, Blanchet?" she asked through gritted teeth, the warning clear as day in her voice.

"Such emotion this evening, Your Grace." He didn't spit the words, but he might as well have. "I thought you were congenitally frigid."

Manuela didn't normally care enough about men's opinions to muster up any kind of reaction to their barbs. But hearing Blanchet's brazen insult caused a wave of revulsion to rise in her. And why was Cora not telling him to go to hell?

Without thinking she decided to throw herself firmly between whatever tug-of-war was happening between the duchess and Blanchet. "Monsieur Blanchet, it's a pleasure to make your acquaintance. If you are referring to *my* land in Venezuela, I can assure you the duchess drives a very persuasive bargain. We were just now discussing the terms of the sale."

Blanchet fell prey to a coughing fit once he realized his misstep. The duchess shot her that same look of puzzled admiration from their luncheon and suddenly Manuela was done. She wanted more time with this woman and she was willing to play dirty to get it. "Just now we were settling some final details, weren't we, Your Grace?" Cora would either go along with Manuela and seal the deal, or she would not.

After a long pause the duchess finally spoke. "Of course," she asserted with a nod under the scrutiny of Blanchet's dubious gaze. "In fact, Blanchet," she turned such a deadly smile in the man's direction Manuela almost expected him to cry out in pain. "Would you allow me another minute with Miss Caceres Galvan? We—"

"I don't see why that's necessary," the man interrupted. "Surely I would be privy to anything you are to discuss regarding the acquisition of the land."

Manuela had heard the expression *murderous eyes* before and had always considered it a metaphor, but now she saw that one could indeed see an intent to kill in a person's gaze. Poor Blanchet seemed completely unaware of how close he was to meeting his maker.

"Actually, Monsieur Blanchet," she whispered in her most innocent, angelic voice, "I don't feel at ease conversing about such delicate topics in the presence of a gentleman." She made sure to add a flutter of her eyelashes and an inviting pout. This weaponry had always seemed to mollify the gentlemen of Blanchet's kind.

"Of course, my apologies." He took a step forward and brushed a whiskered kiss on Manuela's gloved hand before stepping back to glance at Cora. "If you would be so kind to find me once you are done, Your Grace." Manuela could almost hear Cora pulverizing her molars at the man's haughty tone, but she mustered up a *yes* before sending him on his way.

Manuela thought she would at least receive a thank you from the duchess, but instead she was grabbed by the arm and pulled into the same hiding place where she'd made her confession to the Leonas only minutes earlier. Lust and apprehension swirled in her belly as she was pierced by very unhappy eyes. Cora stepped up to her until she had her back pressed to the wall, and once again Manuela's mouth was faster than her brain.

"This is a very good place for clandestine kisses." But the duchess was not in a kissing mood.

"You little devil. I had *not* agreed to your offer," she bit out, her tone a mix of helpless amusement and accusation.

"Oh come now, Your Grace," she said in her sweetest voice. "We both know you were going to accept it," she shot back. "I just gave you a nudge." Emboldened by Cora's silence, she lifted a hand and ran a finger up the center of her jacket. "I like this color on you," she said appreciatively. "It reminds me of a black dahlia." She lifted her eyes to the duchess and wondered how she was not being scorched. There was anger there, to be sure, but right beneath, there was the same fire burning through Manuela. One that she intended to see unleashed. "When are you taking me on my first outing?"

Cora's hand clutched Manuela's exploring finger. "There will be no such thing without a signed contract, princess. I will bring one tomorrow with some reasonable terms for this scheme of yours, and once that's signed, we can discuss these so-called out-ings, but there will be no games."

"I wouldn't dream of playing games, at least not ones we both wouldn't enjoy." She let the offer in her words hang in the air a moment, before pressing closer. "Your Grace."

Manuela lifted herself on her tiptoes and brushed her cheek against the duchess's. The contact was so electrifying it took her a moment to get her breathing under control. "I am free tomor-row evening," she informed Cora cheerfully, as if the woman wasn't trying to skewer Manuela with her eyes. "But you must collect me at the Palais des Beaux Arts. They're finally allowing international artists to see their pieces before the exhibit opens to the public. You'll find me with mine in the South American wing." She smiled, then pressed her cleavage to Cora's arm. The duchess reacted with a very satisfying inhalation of breath, and Manuela smiled wider.

"I am not one to boast, but they are two of my best." She pressed her chest just a little further in to Cora and winked. "The paintings, I mean." The other woman stared at her for an agonizingly long time, so long that Manuela began to won-der if she'd pushed too far. It wouldn't be the first time that her impulsiveness backfired, but in the next moment that slender body was pressing Manuela into the wall until all the air es-caped her lungs.

"When I come to you tomorrow," Cora said, lowering her head so that loose strands of hair tickled Manuela's cheek, "it will be with a very long list of rules for this little scheme of yours, Miss Caceres Galvan." Her throat went dry, and she had to clamp her mouth shut to keep from moaning. "The first thing we will have to establish is that there will be no touching and absolutely no more kissing."

"We can work out the details when you are in a more ame-nable mood," Manuela hedged.

Cora was not amused. "It would be in your interest to inquire about my reputation in negotiations before then." She pushed back just as Manuela was contemplating pressing her lips to the curve of her neck. It took everything she had not to cry out in frustration. "Oh, and try not to get caught breaking into any more buildings until then."

Eight

Any hope Cora had harbored regarding her control over her arrangement with Manuela Caceres Galvan had disappeared somewhere between her almost having the girl next to a platter of oysters and the near catastrophic run-in with Blanchet. And now here she was, swallowing up the length of the gravel path leading up to the Palais the Beaux Arts, so she could launch herself headfirst into a farce that would most likely end in disaster. At least she did have a contract for the heiress and intended to get the damn thing signed without falling prey to all those supple curves and bubbling laughter...at least not again.

"Where did you say we could find her, Maggie?" Cora asked of her secretary, whose much shorter legs forced her to follow behind her at a harried clip. With a sigh, Cora slowed down as Maggie gasped for air.

"All the South American paintings are on the top floor of the Rapp Gallery, Your Grace," Maggie informed her as they reached the entrance of the building. She'd been visiting the fairgrounds long enough to recognize the large domed structure behind the west side of Eiffel's shrine to phalluses, but she had not gone inside the palace of fine arts. The building, which she'd heard contained more than seven hundred paintings, was designed by architect Jean Camille Formigé, who was also tasked with crafting the sloping park in front of the La Basilique du Sacré-Coeur in Montmartre.

She mounted the steps to the closed doors of the building, bracing herself for the impact of Manuela Caceres Galvan. It wasn't that Cora could not handle a wildcat, it was that her own reactions as she did the handling were becoming increasingly unpredictable. Cora had never been amused by mercurial, flighty girls who pranced around breaking into gardens at night. She'd always been attracted to sensible women who took themselves and their place in the world seriously. Like that Doctor Montalban, for example. It wasn't that she couldn't be taken with a bit of frilly lace and a nice bosom, but she rarely continued to think about them two blasted days after the fact.

Cora had been prepared for many things when she summoned the heiress to a meeting, and had she met her for the first time at the luncheon, Cora would've have assumed her predictions were right. That the heiress was a product of her world. A little cynical and reckless, if utterly unwilling to give up her comforts. But the woman she'd met at Le Bureau who had climbed furniture barefoot to get a closer look at a fresco, that woman was in love with life. A woman who knew exactly what she was giving up and was granting herself one last taste of it. A woman who evoked her most protective and predatory instincts all at once.

Cora examined the corridors of paintings as she made her way across the first floor of the building. She passed the sections for the United States, Belgium, Sweden and a few other European countries. Some of the artists she knew, like Sarah Dodson, an American who had been a pupil of Jules Joseph Lefebvre, a friend of Cora's. She stopped for a moment to look at one of Sarah's pieces, The Morning Stars. It was intriguing and ethereal, with its pastel colors and prancing nymphs. She wondered what Manuela would make of the blurry maidens in ecstatic dance. Then she reminded herself what she was about today and kept walking.

At any another time, she would've strolled through the gallery and taken her time examining the paintings. But today she was beholden to a certain island princess, who was expecting Cora to take her on an adventure across every ladies' hall in Paris. *That* would not be happening. The only way Cora would get through this month without causing a scandal was to stay well away from temptation. A tall order considering she'd be saddled with the embodiment of it for the duration of this farce. But Cora had a plan.

Manuela had requested that Cora show her the world women like the two of them inhabited in Paris, and she would. It would just be a slightly different set of women than those the heiress probably envisioned.

There was no shortage of septuagenarian lesbian couples in Paris the Duchess of Sundridge could call on for dinner, and she was planning to extract every invitation she could. A satisfied smirk lifted her lips at the thought of beating the little devil at her own game. By the time Cora was done, Manuela Caceres Galvan would be sick of parlor recitals and sapphic poetry readings. So engrossed was she in this minor fantasy involving sumptuous breasts and gnashing of teeth that she almost slammed into a window when she reached the end of the corridor.

"Where exactly did they say her paintings are?" Cora whipped around, realizing she'd crossed the entire gallery and was yet to find Manuela's work. "I thought there were only two floors."

"The gentleman I spoke to earlier said it was in the room at the top of these stairs." Maggie pointed at a very narrow doorway, leading to a narrower staircase. "Perhaps up here?"

"You mean in the attic?" Cora asked, suddenly incensed. Maggie shrugged helplessly, and Cora clenched her jaw. There weren't many people left in the building since it was after the grounds were closed to visitors for the day. But this area of the gallery didn't seem like it got much traffic even when it was open. It was dusty and eerily dim. Clearly whatever they'd stuck up there was not meant to attract much attention. They took the steps carefully as they were not very stable, and by the time Cora reached the top she was indignant. Had they really selected Manuela's work only to hide it in the farthest corner of the place?

"Maggie, why don't you have François take you home in the carriage?" Once again that protective instinct overtook her. The heiress had been so proud when she told Cora about the paintings. She could only imagine how embarrassed she would be to find them relegated to the recesses of the building.

After Maggie left, she carefully climbed the remaining rickety steps, her furious indignation on Manuela's behalf only increasing with each one.

The alcove she found at the top was not very large and she spotted Manuela immediately. Except that the woman she found was a far cry from the flirtatious, colorful creature from the night before or the scandalous vixen from their lunch. Manuela's shoulders, which she'd only seen tilted in seductive poses, were hunched and her head hung low. There was an air of defeat surrounding her. Even in her birds of paradise colors she seemed subdued, like her inner light had been dimmed.

It hurt Cora more than she'd like to admit to see her looking so small and dejected. But still so damn beautiful. The jaunty hat on her head was riddled with ridiculous plumage. The daring red of her walking suit was like a beacon. The skirt began with a very dark red near the hem and the shades lightened as they reached her waist. The jacket was of a darker shade, except for a line running down the middle of her back. She looked like one of the flowers she claimed to include in her work, resplendent in crimson, until one came close enough to notice her crestfallen form.

A need to slay whoever had done this gripped Cora with such

a ferocity her hands shook. "I've heard the Americans have paid off the French to hide any paintings that overshadow theirs," Cora offered loudly as she got closer. The artist jumped at the sound of her voice, but she didn't turn immediately. The thought of this luscious being, with her salacious smiles and lusty laughs, crying in humiliation in this musty, hidden corner made Cora unreasonably angry.

"My art is American too, remember." It was an attempt at levity, but the strain was clear in Manuela's voice. "I'm surprised you could find me here." Cora would've never guessed she'd miss the barrage of shocking comments she'd been subjected to during their last two meetings, but here she was despairing after only seconds of witnessing this diminished version of her princess. "I should've waited for you downstairs, to save you the trouble," Manuela apologized, turning to face her. Her eyes were too bright, and her smile a wan, feeble thing. Once again, Cora found herself ready to beg for a glimmer of the very things that just yesterday had driven her crazy.

"You were so humble in your advertisement of your skills, I had to come and see for myself," she teased, in an attempt pull out a real smile from her. All she got was a small twitch of the mouth. It was absurd to miss the outrageous things that constantly came out of the heiress. And yet, she was dying to be pestered for a kiss or talked into some other wild scheme, anything other than this silence.

Cora turned her attention to the art, hoping questions about the paintings could bring Manuela out from under this shroud of unhappiness. There were two pieces side-by-side, about three feet in height. Even at a glance she could see the enormous talent. She'd always been moved by art, and over the years she'd educated herself on how to appreciate technique, to recognize elements and themes that transformed images on a canvas into a story. There were some tales to be seen here, to be sure.

The heiress had a deft hand with color and shadow. It was

easy to see why she'd been selected: every line was precise, the subjects fleshed out so vividly they could've stepped out of the painting. Her interest in the Brazilian pavilion's greenhouse was also evident—flowers were not merely present in Manuela's work, they were at its essence. That and women. In her art, the feminine didn't just exist it nature, it *was* nature. It was like nothing Cora had ever seen, and it only made her angrier that they'd keep them hidden up here where no one would appreciate them.

"I think I would've recognized these as yours at first glance." She turned to Manuela when she said it and came face to face with a very dubious expression. "It's true," she insisted, but the artist was unmoved.

"You don't have to make me feel better," she said, again in that stoic, dull tone that seemed to cover the sun with a great, black cloud.

"I thought from what you already knew about me, you'd glean that I do very little to make others feel better, princesa," Cora retorted, once again trying to obtain some kind of reaction. She was finally rewarded with a minuscule smile that instantly brought back the sun.

"I'm not upset because I don't think my pieces aren't good enough to be here," Manuela told her, and Cora heard a little of that rebellious spirit returning. "I'm angry because they got my name wrong." She pointed at the little placards under each of the paintings. Cora leaned in to get a look, and Manuela made sound of disgust as she read.

Manolo Caceres Galvan. The bastards.

"Disgraceful." It was one word, but there was such mighty indignation infused into it, such diffidence in her expression, that Cora could not help thinking that she'd seriously misread this woman. Whatever Manuela Caceres Galvan might be, she was not unsure of her worth as an artist.

"Tell me about this one," Cora asked, pointing at the piece

on the left before she said something she'd regret. "I assume this very morose young man with the lyre is Orpheus."

Manuela smiled approvingly, provoking a new and distressing fluttering in Cora's belly. "It's one of my favorites," Manuela explained as she took a step closer to the framed canvas. It was darker than what Cora would've imagined from Manuela, done in black, white and gold, but every image seemed lit from within.

"Eurydice doesn't seem very impressed with Orpheus's musical prowess," Cora commented as she took in the image.

"She was not very happy to be plucked out of the underworld," Manuela added, drolly. "She was having a wonderful time without Orpheus's obsessive pestering and his silly little instrument." Cora grinned, charmed beyond reason by this woman, who for all her frilly lace and apparent frivolity, was quite brazenly feminist.

Manuela's Eurydice was indeed unamused and magnificent standing on a black rock at the center of the scene, with her eyes screwed shut, mouth twisted in discontent. A maiden of the underworld tended to the viper bite on her foot, while vines tangled around her naked form. Then there were the flowers. A black anthurium sprouted from the juncture of her thighs, extending over her hips, while a spray of dark purple orchids covered her breasts. Her hair was very black, the tights coils reaching below her waist. Orpheus, small and surly, stood at the mouth to the underworld playing his lyre, head down in concentration, while his beloved had both hands clapped over her ears.

"The Furies don't seem affected in the same way the myth recounts," Cora commented, tickled by the figures whose faces—instead of wet with tears—were twisted in outrage for the accosted Eurydice.

"Only the men are captivated by Orpheus's efforts. The women all see it for what it is," Manuela answered, bringing to Cora's attention the other figures in the painting. In the background she'd painted a bloated Hades reclining on a throne with a beatific smile on his lips, eyes fixed on the musician. The other men in the composition all shared the same disturbingly besotted expressions. It was so elegantly subversive. A resonant rebuke of men's entitlement, of their unbridled selfishness, but it was so beautifully done one could not help feeling inspired while looking at it.

"This is very powerful. I am not surprised they selected it." Cora shook her head in sincere admiration as she took in the story being told. She also remembered Manuela's words from that night at Le Bureau, her certainty that the fresco could've only been made by a woman, and found herself rethinking, once again, what she thought she knew about the heiress. "I am frankly surprised they had the sensibility to appreciate it."

"They likely gave me a pass because they thought I was Manolo," Manuela muttered, derisively. Cora did not argue—she was probably right—and turned her attention to the other painting.

This one, impossibly, was even more compelling to Cora. It was of a woman at the mouth of a cave which was sealed with one enormous pink iris. Ghostly claws tugged at the hem of her white robes as she desperately reached inside. Shards of light escaped from where her hand pierced the center of the iris. Her face ablaze from the rays emanating from the slit in the flower, her eyes wide and hungry, intent on climbing inside. Eager to escape the darkness pulling her back and into the warmth of that light. It was so lifelike, Cora's heart beat faster as she took in the determination on the woman's face.

"That is not exactly subtle," Cora said with approval. It was truly astounding they'd allowed it in the show. Even if relegated to this small attic.

"Well, men aren't very smart," the artist quipped, a provocatively sly smile on her lips. "And sadly deficient in their knowledge of anatomy."

That was the precise moment it dawned on Cora with un-equivocal certainty that Manuela Caceres Galvan could wreak absolute havoc on her life. Utter madness itched to come out of her mouth. For one, that she was much too good and far too clever for her talents to be wasted posing as some social-climb-er's trophy.

With great effort she managed to remind herself what hap-pened the last time she'd taken on a pretty girl with familial complications. Dammit, she hadn't come here to admire Man-uela's paintings, much less comfort her. Once again she'd been derailed. Her will and her plans undone. She had to get a hold of herself, hold fast to what mattered. Her business, Alfie, re-pairing what she'd broken. She turned her back on the paint-ings and handed the sheaf of papers to Manuela.

"I have the agreement."

Nine

Manuela took the papers from the duchess and went to sit at the lone bench in the room, a bit stunned by Cora's opinion of her work. She'd been close to tears when she'd come in, and the last thing she'd expected was for the duchess to know exactly the right things to say in order to make her feel better.

Despite her bravado the night before, she'd been nervous about inviting the duchess to the exhibition and then had been mortified when she discovered her paintings had not only been relegated to an attic but that they'd gotten her name wrong.

"Thank you for being kind about my work," Manuela said, still staring at the papers in her hands without really seeing the words.

Her expression must have given away her thoughts because the duchess laughed as she took a seat beside her.

"I can't claim that my sensibilities to good art were all my own. My best friend Cassandra has had her share of awful encounters with people who felt the need to let her know her work is absolute filth."

Manuela exhaled in sympathy. "It is one of the drawbacks of creating things that each beholder interprets in their own way."

"I think you are very courageous. All artists are, especially women."

"You are brave too," Manuela said, tipping her head up to look at her. Antonio had managed to gather some information about the duchess, once they realized who it was that Manuela had encountered at Le Bureau. Aside from Cora's seemingly unapologetic romantic proclivities toward women, she was also a well-respected and powerful businesswoman. According to Antonio's sources, she was notorious—and bitterly criticized by some—for her tenaciousness and her indomitable drive.

But however life had hardened Cora, she had been kind in a moment when Manuela needed it. She'd done more than that, she'd noted what there was to appreciate in her work, without bestowing false compliments or empty praise. Everything she learned about this woman made her lose her head a little more. And she was so appealing.

A face made to be painted.

"I am bold in my dealings. I am not afraid of putting myself in a risky situation, but I only let my opponents know what I want them to know. They can't see inside my head or inside my heart. But artists...you put your very souls on display. I could never expose myself like that." It was an olive branch.

Once again, she was arrested with a sense of companionship. It could be her own tendency to romanticize even the smallest kindness. To want to take a sentiment expressed out of politeness and turn it into more than what it was. It was almost certainly that.

"I should read this."

The contract seemed simple enough. Cora would escort her to six events over the six weeks. At the end of that period, Manuela would sell her the land for an exorbitant amount of money. It was more than she'd asked for. Certainly enough for her to live on comfortably for a long time if she had only herself to worry about.

"I'll sign if we set the number of outings at ten," Manuela finally said, attempting to send her most challenging gaze in the duchess's direction.

"I thought artists were bad negotiators," Cora teased, pulling a fountain pen out of her pocket.

The duchess, it seemed, was always a step ahead of her opponents. It pleased Manuela to know that she'd bested her at least a couple of times.

"You must mean the men." Cora's mouth twitched again, something Manuela noticed she did when displaying a shade of her temper.

"How about six?" Manuela balked.

"I might be an artist, but I am also from the Caribbean, and we are born hagglers." This time she got a genuine laugh, for her insolence. "Let's make it eight and I will sign right now," she countered, emboldened by the indulgent grin on Cora's mouth. That pink, lush, bitable mouth. The duchess bit her lip and Manuela licked hers in the exact same spot, and for a moment they were caught in a taut, pulsing moment. Cora was the first to look away, and without a word, she took the papers from her hand, crossed out a line in the contract and replaced it with a note amending their outings to eight.

"There. Happy?"

"I'll be happy when I can finally start my sapphic reverie," she volleyed back, reaching for the contract, but the duchess held on to it, her face grave.

"Why are you really selling the land?" The humor from the previous moment was replaced by a seriousness Manuela suspected was spurned by some niggling in the duchess's conscience.

"Does it matter? You need the land, and I am willing to sell it. I thought that was all that mattered to you." The duchess clearly didn't like it when the questions landed back at her feet, but Manuela was getting quite aggravated with the world's insistence that she be rational all the time.

"It is, but I want to know why it doesn't matter to *you*." The duchess sent her another one of those incisive looks, then leaned back, crossing her legs. This was not the pose a society lady assumed in public, but Manu guessed the woman observed etiquette rules only when it served her.

"I thought the land was lost," Manuela admitted, assuming her own obstinately relaxed pose. "My grandfather purchased the land years ago when my family came to Venezuela in exile from the Dominican Republic. The intention was to open an art school. It was my abuela's dream to have a seaside institute where any woman with talent could come and master her craft, be around other women who shared that passion." At one time Manuela had shared it too. Painting had been such a solace in her life. A lonely only child who had to live in her own head, and the canvas became the place where she could pour herself into. But that dream, like so many others, had died.

"Why did they have to leave?" Cora asked, her eyes curious, but there was no judgment there that Manuela could see. The last century had been one of liberation for the Americas. After the Republic of Haiti was born, the thirst for liberty spread, and freedom never came without strife. Many had been displaced in the path to liberation.

"They had to leave once the War of Restoration broke out and the criollos began targeting the families supporting the efforts to thwart the annexation of the Dominican Republic back to Spain." She still had a hard time comprehending how that scheme had gotten as far as it did. "After that, Abuela didn't have the heart to return home, only to have to leave again. Our family also put a lot of resources into the efforts of fighting the annexation."

"How did they lose the land?"

Manuela looked away at the question, that old pain, fresh again. "The business thrived for many years, but once my father took over… We had some trouble with our finances." It had been more than trouble. Her father gutted the business and eventually depleted the personal savings of the family. "We kept selling off what we had to keep us going, only to be back in the same position a few years later, but by then my abuela was gone." *And it was up to me to save them from ruin*, she didn't add.

"You don't want to build the school anymore?" Cora asked softly.

"I loved hearing my grandmother's plans for it." Manuela smiled at the memory of her abuela sitting in her favorite chair by the window with a view to the sea. She talked for hours sometimes about all the students they'd have. How Manuela would be one of the teachers. "But after the land was sold, she never spoke of it again." And her dying wish had been for Manuela to use the land for something that made her happy.

She lifted her gaze then and found Cora looking at her with unnerving intensity.

"The place where the land is, it has a sentimental value to you." The duchess's mouth pursed a little when she uttered the word *sentimental*, and Manuela almost laughed at how unsavory it seemed to the other woman.

"It *is* sentimental, that's the point," she concurred. "Women in my position can't afford to be sentimental." It was so strange to be speaking about these things that for so long she could barely think about—and to feel strangely unburdened by them. "Wasn't there anything you wanted as a child that didn't quite make sense as an adult?" What she really wanted to ask was which dreams of hers had died with her childhood, but the mood was already somber enough. When she looked up at Cora, she encountered not the forlorn expression she expected but one of defiance.

"No." Manuela laughed at the absolute certainty in her answer. Of course, this woman had been born with a plan of action and had likely begun executing it the moment she came out of the womb.

God, they were so different, and yet this conversation felt like the first time she'd been able to speak freely in years. Because even with her friends, she censored herself. Never wanting to paint things in too grim a light so that she didn't worry them. With Cora she could speak plainly, and she knew there would be no hurt feelings.

"Is it strange that I can perfectly picture you at five years old setting up your dolls and playing at building railways?" Cora's mouth tugged up, and Manuela grinned at the image of tiny Cora in her split skirts bowling over unsuspecting competitors to do her bidding.

"I always wanted to be in business," she told Manuela, but for the first time Manuela saw some cracks in that steel facade. "My father was a self-made man. He came to Chile to work as an engineer in the silver mines and within twenty years had made a fortune. A lot of it was being in the right place at the right time, but he was tenacious, and he was smart." Manuela could hear the admiration in Cora's voice: the man had to have been formidable to be spoken of with such respect from a woman who seemed to think very little of men in such positions.

"Did he approve of your desire to go into business?" she asked and immediately regretted it when Cora's face shuttered.

"He did not," Cora said tautly, after a long pause. The smile on her lips morphed into a fraught thing that made Manuela want to reach over and smooth it with her own fingers. She was certain the duchess would leave her answer there, but to her surprise she spoke again. "When I announced to him my intention to follow in his footsteps, he..." Her face was very blank as she spoke. But something about the way she held herself, her gloved hands gripping her knees, told Manuela the memory was a terrible one. "He went into a rage." Again Cora stopped, this time her eyes directed at the ground. "Within a week, he'd found a man for me to marry."

"The duke?" she asked, horrified. To her surprise Cora burst in laughter.

"No, he was the son of one of my father's associates. I shot him in the leg when he tried to demonstrate how he intended to spend our wedding night." Manuela was certain she'd misheard.

"You *shot* him?" she shouted, staring at Cora in disbelief.

"It was just a graze," Cora said with a wave of her hand. That arrogance returning. "In any case, I paid the price later when I was put on a steamer to London with orders to find a titled husband and stay there for good." She told this ghastly tale so casually, almost too casually. The duchess was very good at hiding her pain, but Manuela was quite experienced in the maneuver herself.

And if she'd been intrigued by her before she was positively ensnared by Cora now.

"That is quite the story," she finally said. Cora scoffed, her eyes bright with amusement. Then turned her attention to the papers in Manuela's hands.

"What about it, princesa?" the duchess asked, pointing to the contract. Manuela lamented the loss of the intimacy they'd forged in the last few minutes, but there would be more time to uncover the mysteries of this perplexing woman. She reached for the fountain pen and signed the line over her name, then stood up.

"That's settled." She grinned at the duchess's serious expression. "What will be the first place you'll take me to? Pigalle, Montmartre?" The excitement in her voice at the mention of those places was not at all feigned. But Cora did not answer, she just looked at Manuela impassively before turning to the narrow door.

"First I think I'd like to see your competition in the gallery," she informed Manuela, dusting off her dark blue skirts. "Then we'll go to dinner."

Ten

———————————————

"Is this my first outing?" Manuela asked as Cora's carriage halted to a stop on the Rue de Montparnasse. They'd both been quiet on the short ride over, and she'd gotten no more information about their dinner.

"Yes. Are you ready?" Cora's husky voice in the darkness of the carriage sent curls of heat through her body, but she was not so far gone she didn't notice the very lacking response.

"I will be once you tell me where we are, Your Grace." Unlike the duchess, Manuela might not have the ability to turn grown men to stone with her eyes, but she certainly knew how to get what she wanted. She made sure to reach for the handle of the carriage door, effectively blocking their exit. Cora raised an eyebrow in challenge, placing her own hand on top of Manuela's. "If you think I won't arm-wrestle you because you're a duchess, you're wrong."

"Are you going to be this difficult about everything, princesa?" Once they'd stepped out of that blasted attic, they'd strolled through the gallery admiring the other paintings. It had been companionable and surprisingly easy, but every time Cora called her *princesa*, Manuela's body reminded her that she wanted this woman, and not as a friend.

"I won't be difficult, if you tell me where I am."

Cora gnawed at her bottom lip, which she'd noticed happened whenever she didn't want to reveal too much. They stayed there for a long moment with their hands tangled together on the door handle before the duchess relented.

"We are at Cassandra and Frede's," she offered with a put-upon sigh, while Manuela made a superhuman effort not to wiggle in her seat or break into applause.

"You're introducing me to your friends, Your Grace," she crowed, wishing there was enough light in the carriage to see if Cora Kemp Bristol blushed. "I'm beginning to suspect you like me."

"You'd better let me out before I change my mind and take you home," Cora shot back, a note of amusement in her voice that made Manuela ridiculously giddy.

"Who else will be at dinner?" Manuela asked, trying very hard to temper her excitement as they took the few steps leading to the door of a small but attractive house.

This Parisian neighborhood was not as fashionable as the Place des Vosges, where Aurora's family had let a town house for them, and she imagined Cora lived in a mansion somewhere. But this little house, while respectable, did not at all communicate opulence. It was certainly not the kind of place Manuela imagined a duchess frequented or where her close friend would reside.

"Some friends, mostly artists, other women like us who are in other trades," Cora told her as she knocked on the door. "A few of them have pieces in the exposition too."

"Oh." Manuela's stomach sank when heard that. They'd walked by some of those pieces. None of them had been banished to corners.

"No, don't look like that, dammit." Cora sounded cross but when she lifted a hand to Manuela's chin her touch was devastatingly gentle. "Your work is brilliant, and no one in that gallery or in this house is better than you." This kindness would be a problem, she thought. It would be impossible to keep herself from wanting more.

"You don't have to say that, you know? I'm not that fragile."

"I say it because it's true." Something fleeting but intense moved over the duchess's face, and Manuela leaned closer. "And given the way you've run circles around me at every opportunity, the last thing I'd call you is fragile, princesa."

The air around them sizzled, as she considered the damage attempting to kiss Cora would cause. Reasonable things floated around her head but none seem to keep her from rising on her tiptoes. It would be quick, just a brush of the lips. Just a taste, a nibble...

"Cora's here!" A door crashed open, sending a dazed Manuela hurtling back right into a pretty, plump woman with skin the color of nutmeg and a very shrewd smile. "You must be Manuela!" she cried out, as she ushered them inside. She was dressed in a tea gown, in a lovely royal blue with delicate teal and purple embroidery on the cuffs, collar and hem. She had a few strands of very dark, tightly coiled curls hanging around her face and a smile that could lift even the most morose of spirits.

"Cassie, this is Miss Manuela Caceres Galvan."

"Miss Aguzzi Durocher." Manuela attempted a bow, but Cassandra instantly pulled her into an embrace.

"Por favor, llámame Cassie," she requested in impressive Spanish, before kissing Manuela warmly on each cheek. "I'm so happy you came. The duchess assured me she would not be here tonight." She sent a reproachful look in her friend's direction but quickly tempered it by leaning in to kiss Cora on the cheek too. For a couple of seconds the two women engaged in a silent conversation with a series of looks, to Manuela's amusement. Cassie shot a raised eyebrow in her friend's direction, which Cora answered with a short shake of the head and very wide eyes. Cassie returned a slightly withering look in response but in the end seemed to relent, because in the next moment she turned her attention back to Manuela. She could not quite tell what had been said, but she'd done this with Luz Alana and Aurora enough times to know important information—probably about her—had been exchanged.

"Now, Cora tells me you're a painter as well," she said as they walked into a small parlor.

"I do paint, but this exposition is the first time I've had my work seen by the public," she admitted, and Cassie made a sound of understanding. Just that small gesture loosened some of the knots she'd had in her stomach all afternoon. She would be among other artists tonight. There were voices coming from deeper inside the house, but their hostess didn't seem in any rush to take them back there yet.

"It can be quite nerve-racking," the Brazilian artist agreed. "I am very eager to see your work." Manuela's enthusiasm waned somewhat at that, but Cora quickly chimed in.

"Manuela's work is exquisite." She was so earnest in her efforts to ease Manuela's embarrassment...and it did help. It more than helped, it made her feel shielded.

"Unfortunately my paintings ended up in an atticlike alcove," she confessed, feeling less humiliated about it now that she had Cora as her defender. "And they misspelled my name. But I *am* there."

Cassie shook her head, chagrined. "It is not easy starting out. But you've made it to a very important exhibition, and now it will be easier to be selected for other ones. And now you will have friends in us to guide you as you find your way." It took a moment for Manuela to understand what she meant, then she shook her head with a laugh.

"Oh, I am not looking to be in more shows," she said, even as she tried to suffuse her bubbling discomfort. "I'm going back to Venezuela to be married, and once I am, I won't continue submitting my work for salons."

Cora cleared her throat behind her, and without looking her way Manuela could sense the disapproval, or maybe it was her own feelings of embarrassment she was ascribing to the duchess's reaction.

"Oh, I see." Cassandra frowned, and for a moment she seemed like she wanted to say more but in the end only smiled and extended a hand to the closed doors in front of them. "Then, I suspect you may be a little bored this evening," she said regretfully, pointing at the doors. "There are a half a dozen painters in there, and I'm afraid you will be subjected to a long discussion on the state of affairs for artists in Paris."

"Oh, I *adore conversing* about art," Manuela rushed to say. "I am certain I'll have a grand time."

Cassandra grinned at Cora's derisive expression. "Our talks are about craft, but also about the business of being a working artist, which may not be as diverting for you."

"On the contrary, I am very curious," Manuela told her honestly. "I'd never really heard it referred to in that way." As far as Manuela knew, there were men who could live handsomely from commission work or with the support of patrons. Even with the advent of photography, portraits were still popular, but she'd never heard anyone talk about painting or any other craft as a profession.

"There are at least half as many physicians and a couple of architects and engineers here to boot. Every profession fueled by deluded self-regard, happily together in one room," Cora added in feigned horror, but her usual undertone of annoyance was replaced by genuine affection. "Be prepared for a room full of people talking to you, at you and for you at once," Cora groused, and Cassie laughed.

"It's not that bad, but we can get a bit boisterous."

Manuela suspected that the duchess was here because she enjoyed the conversation. Cora Kemp Bristol did not seem like the type of woman who spent an evening doing something she didn't like.

Unless she's being blackmailed. Manuela brushed aside that unwelcome message from her conscience and turned her attention to more urgent matters.

"Are they all..." She waved a finger between herself and Cora. The duchess rolled her eyes, then looked to Cassandra, who was watching them with that same curious intensity.

"Cassandra, Miss Caceres Galvan would like to know if you are hosting any sapphists this evening."

The painter's lips tipped up mischievously. "Did you teach her our secret sign?" Cassandra's face was suddenly very serious, and Cora, who was perennially stoic, shook her head in a very weighty fashion.

Secret sign? Manuela looked from one woman to the other, and for the life of her could not determine if they were being serious.

"I am disappointed in you, Corazón!"

Corazón? Who was Corazón? Manuela's mind was already spinning, and she had yet to meet any other lesbians. "Is that your real name?" Manuela blurted out at the same time that Cora shouted, "Not again, Cassandra."

"Your name is truly Corazón?" she asked, fully diving into the deep waters of besottedness. Cora let out an unamused sigh as Manuela's insides churned like lava. She had her head tipped up now, her attention solely on the duchess, whose pink cheeks confirmed to Manuela that she did indeed blush, and it was even more adorable than she could've imagined. Her face was so angular, her cheekbones, jaw and nose so sharp it gave the impression she was chiseled from marble, which made this flush of emotion that much more enticing. The icy duchess was undoubtedly appealing, but this flustered, very human woman was devastating.

"Yes." Cora exhaled with extreme despondence, and Manuela could barely hold back a swoon. "My name is Corazón."

There had to be some deity with a bow and arrow toying with her because this was too perfect. "It's a beautiful name," Manuela said, charmed beyond reason. "Corazón," she said, trying the name out.

Cora grimaced and turned her attention to the door. "It's what one names their pet parakeet," Cora shot back, making Cassandra giggle. Manuela was about to protest when Cora spoke again. "The sign, Cassandra," she reminded her friend, redirecting the conversation away from her name.

"Yes, of course," Cassandra responded and turned to Manuela.

"There's a sign to enter your parlor?"

"Indeed there is," Cassandra affirmed, equally serious. "Not just for my parlor but for any gathering of sapphists. It must be done to be allowed inside."

Cora made a sound of agreement and leaned against a sideboard as Cassandra continued with her explanation.

"What is it?" Manuela asked in a low voice.

"How did Monsieur Coffignon phrase it, Cora, dear?" Cassandra inquired, her countenance the very picture of sober contemplation.

Cora placed a hand under her chin, seemingly considering the question, and a prickle of something began itching at the nape of Manuela's neck.

"I believe the exact words were *quasi-Masonic signs…*" Cora began but paused when the side of her mouth began to quiver.

"Ah, yes," Cassandra continued. "'A quasi-Masonic sign, involving a rapid movement of the tongue and lips, a flutter if you will.'"

"Precisely," Cora choked out as Manuela's jaw dropped.

"A flutter of the tongue and lips?" she repeated, now quite certain she was being had. Cassandra and Cora managed to maintain straight faces, even as the color in their necks became increasingly flushed.

Suddenly the door to the parlor opened and a very blonde woman wearing trousers sauntered out. She wasn't exactly pretty, but she had a kind face, and she looked at Cassandra with enough intensity to electrify the room.

"Darling, are you torturing our guests again?" she asked in a thick accent, then sent a reproachful grin in the direction of the duchess who was hiding behind a supposed fit of coughing. "Cora, I expected better from you."

She extended a hand to Manuela while still sending disapproving—if clearly amused—looks toward Cora and Cassandra. "I am Frederica Holtz-Carvajal, Cassandra's lover. Welcome to our home." With her arm firmly around Cassandra's waist, she smiled warmly at Manuela as if the words she'd just uttered weren't earth-shattering. Two women sharing a home in the middle of Paris. No hiding, no pretending to be friends. An explosion erupted in Manuela at the very notion. The blood in her head rushing so fast she thought she could hear it. Only after a long moment did she realize she hadn't introduced herself.

"I'm sorry," she said, a bit addled. "I am Manuela Caceres Galvan. Thank you for letting me join you." She smiled and shook the hand Frederica offered.

"And I do apologize for these two," Frederica said, contritely while the others grinned. "Since Ali Coffignon published *La Corruption à Paris* last year, they have been entertaining themselves with this ridiculous secret-sign business."

"Ah," Manuela said, understanding dawning on her. "I see," she said, utterly charmed. It would be much easier if the Duchess of Sundridge remained a sphinx, but she insisted on revealing herself to be a woman of a much more complex nature. One that included a sense of humor.

Manuela had one too.

"So, Your Grace," she said, turning so she was facing the taller woman, "are you not going to demonstrate your secret sign? Since I would very much like to attend the gathering, I would be obliged if you'd show me." She batted her eyelashes for effect, bringing on another coughing fit from Cora. Frederica barked out a laugh, and so did Cassandra as she tapped her friend's back.

"Seems like you've met your match, Corazón," their hostess declared. "Let's go introduce you to everyone else." Cassandra took Manuela by the arm as they made their way into the parlor. "There are a few friends I'd like you to meet, and they will be very interested in speaking with you too. We've heard a lot about you." That was delivered with a coy look in Cora's direction.

The parlor was an ample space, painted in a soothing sage and gray, accented with dark woods and leather. There were multiple settees lined along the walls, a few oversize ottomans and four very large wingback chairs in front of the hearth. Art covered almost every inch of the walls. Some she recognized as Cassandra's work, but there was a wide array of styles.

A large sideboard on the farthest side of the room was laden with food. Her mouth watered at the familiar smells from home, which she had not enjoyed since she'd departed from Venezuela. From where she stood she saw a platter of fried fish, what looked like boiled cassava topped with sliced fried onions. There were sweets too. Orange rinds and figs in syrup and even sliced pineapple. It was a tropical feast.

"Ladies, we have a special guest visiting from Venezuela this evening," Cassandra announced. Over a dozen faces turned in their direction at once, before everyone erupted in greetings, and hugs and kisses were offered. The first surprising thing was that in this room, the Duchess of Sundridge was simply Cora. She was not as at ease as she'd been when it had just been Cassandra and Frederica, but the women here evidently knew her well enough to circumvent formalities and greet her by her name.

"To avoid everyone speaking all at once, I will make the introductions," Cassandra offered, projecting her voice with impressive volume. "The first rule of survival in a home with an Italian father and a Brazilian mother is to be louder than everyone else," she joked.

"These two are Louise and Madeline." The two women sitting on a settee in the corner were a little older than Manuela. Louise was smaller with a delicate face and dark hair. Madeline, whose hand she was holding, was younger and strikingly beautiful. "They both teach at Aristide Pasquale's academy. You will have to meet him while you're here." Manuela nodded in astonished silence as she shook hands. Académie Pasquale was where she'd wanted to attend in those brief months she was here in Paris, but her parents wouldn't allow it.

Next she was introduced to Celestine Montrouis, a Haitian sketch artist who also lived in Paris. There were a few physicians, two of them a couple, one from Barranquilla in Colombia, and the woman she referred to as her wife was Austrian and had studied with Frederica. The third couple, Patricia and Diana, were a pair of Brazilian portrait artists, friends of Cassandra, who had arrived for the exposition but were considering remaining in Paris. Although it seemed one of them would likely lose her inheritance if she went through with it.

"Are you here for the exposition too?" Patricia asked. Manuela shook her head, suddenly very aware that all these women had probably in some way walked away from the path she'd chosen in order to live as they were.

"Yes and no," she said. "I have two pieces at the Rapp Gallery, but I have other personal matters here as well." Self-conscious of her cryptic answer, she sent a sidelong glance in Cora's direction. The duchess was staring at her openly, waiting for Manuela to expound on her reply. Thankfully she was saved from having to say more by another introduction. Cora stayed away as Cassandra took Manuela around the room, but whenever she looked up, she found the duchess staring intently at her.

The evening was exactly what she'd dreamed of. Cassandra's friends were warm, talkative, all of them interesting and refreshingly candid about their lives. Celestine recounted how she'd come to Paris from Haiti to be with the woman she loved. Things had not worked in the end, but she'd found work she enjoyed and was able to live well by sketching fashion plates and commercial advertisements.

"I didn't know art could pay enough to earn a livelihood," Manuela told her when she heard about the work Celestine had just finished for a new line of ladies' boots, and Celestine shrugged.

"It was not easy to garner a clientele. Not everyone is receptive to a woman artist, much less a Black woman. But I am good, and there is a lot of demand."

"Yes, and because so much of the work is done through correspondence, one can curtail *some* of those prejudices," Cassandra said from her perch on Frede's lap. Manuela had never considered that, but it was true that often one wouldn't even have to deal with people in person.

"I've also heard there is much demand from the publishing world, for illustrations in magazines and children's books," Louise said, adding herself to the conversation. "I have a few friends doing that."

Manuela's head spun with the information. These women not only lived on their own but they had found ways to use their art as a means of supporting themselves. They might not be living in opulence, but they were *living*. In Venezuela, there were prestigious artists with patrons who supported their work. But Manuela never had the sense there could be enough commercial demand for many to make that their livelihood. In truth, she never considered that her own skills could be transferable to such things as magazines.

"How do you find out about the work?" Louise sent her an approving look, and Manuela warmed to the welcoming way of these women.

"That is one of the problems," Celestine admitted. "One has to be well connected to hear of them. It would be nice if there was a way for them to find *us*."

Manuela hummed as she considered that. She thought of Aurora's plans to organize all the women doctors into a professional association so they could have a place to share ideas and findings.

"I've begun taking some commissions," Cassandra told Manuela before handing her a glass of wine. "I still do studio pieces for galleries, but more and more I am seeking out the commercial work because it's more reliable."

Manuela was surprised to hear that Cassandra needed the work. She'd heard that she came from a family with means. But she supposed that choosing a life with Frede might've come with the sacrifice of that. As she considered that reality, she observed the two of them. The way they touched each other, so lovingly, so familiar. Even when Cassandra was talking to someone else she had her hand on Frede, a bonded pair. Joined even when they were apart. "So how do you know how to set your fees?" She hoped her eagerness was not coming off as rude or intrusive, but again all she saw were smiles and encouraging looks.

"That is one of the more challenging parts," Louise admitted. "Our small group shares how much we are able to secure from different jobs, but very few of the men are even willing to consider us colleagues, much less share how much they earn."

"Maybe you should take a page from Frede's grandmother," Cora said, from the chair by the hearth she'd commandeered, her lavender eyes still trained on Manuela.

Cassandra guffawed at her friend's suggestion, clutching a hand to her chest. "My ears must be deceiving me—our very own sapphic bastion of capitalism suggesting we organize into a union?" Some of the women laughed, while Cora shrugged. Manuela was thoroughly confused.

"Unions?" She probably sounded like a dolt. Aurora and Luz Alana both had their professions, and Manuela knew that more women went into the workforce every day, though it had always seemed to her to be a harrowing way to live. But these women didn't seem downtrodden, they seemed happy, free. Fearlessly speaking about topics that were barely appropriate for men to discuss in polite company with absolute impunity. Manuela felt drunk with all of it.

"I think you've broken our guest, darling," Frede teased in her low voice, before pressing a kiss to Cassandra's neck.

"My apologies, Manuela. See, my beloved's grandmother was Flora Tristan y Moscoso." Manuela nodded. Though she had no idea who that was, she was clearly important.

"The famous radical and feminist," Cora explained, as she sent a friendly look in Frede's direction. "Frede comes from a long line of bellicose women." Manuela noticed that the words were delivered softly, carefully. Cassandra also moved closer to her lover, almost as if offering comfort. Another reminder that these women had suffered losses to be able to sit in this room. "You should tell Manuela about Doña Flora," Cora encouraged her, and by then Manuela was close to begging to hear about this famous ancestor of Frede's.

"My grandmother was raised in Peru, but she came to Paris as an adult after a falling out with her family. Not long before her death she wrote a famous essay calling all French laborers to organize as one union." Everyone in the room stopped what they were doing to listen to Frede's tale. Manuela once again looked to Cora and found the duchess still looking at her with her piercing regard. "She made the argument that if men allowed women, the elderly and the infirm to join with them to fight for workers' rights, we would be undefeatable. It made quite a few waves when it was published in 1843."

Over forty-five years ago, a Peruvian mother had been calling for revolution. "What was the name of the essay?" Manuela asked, buzzing from all she'd learned so far this evening.

"'L'union ouvrière'," Frede told her.

"I will find it and read it," she declared, her head swimming with new ideas. "She sounds like a remarkable woman," Manuela said, and the entire room seemed to hum in agreement.

The conversation seemed to dissipate as people got up to get food and engage in more private talks. Manuela made her way to the sideboard and for a moment just stood in front of the selection of Caribbean delicacies she hadn't seen in months.

"It's quite something, isn't it?" Cassandra asked, before reaching for slice of glistening candied orange rind. Manuela almost swooned from the aroma of cloves and cinnamon mingled with the citrus. It had been her abuela's favorite.

"Where did you find all this? I can't imagine it would be easy to find cassava here," she said, pointing to the buttered boiled cassava.

"We have the duchess to thank," Celestine informed her as she joined them. All three women turned to look at Cora who was conversing animatedly with Frede and another of the guests.

Cassandra laughed, probably at Manuela's look of confusion. "She's invested in a cacao farm in Ecuador. It's owned by a widow she met at some diplomatic event a few years ago. Every time a shipment comes, we are blessed with this bounty." Manuela nodded, dumbfounded, as she watched some of the women fill their plates with the food from home. Food that Cora procured for them, from her business with a widow in Ecuador. Every new thing that Manuela learned about this woman chipped away at a layer of frost from the image of the icy, forbidding aristocrat she showed the world.

"She says it's her way of earning an invitation," Celestine joked. Manuela offered a silent smile, vexed by the contradictions of Cora Kemp Bristol.

After a moment Cassandra excused herself to tend to her hosting duties, and Celestine was pulled into a conversation with Patricia and her partner, leaving Manuela to her thoughts. She slipped out of one of the doors leading to a small balcony. She needed to think about everything she'd heard, what she'd seen in that room. This evening had already been so much more than what she'd imagined. She could hardly make sense of it all. She certainly didn't know how to feel.

For a moment, she leaned on the balcony breathing in the night air, but soon the sound of footfalls crossing the threshold alerted her someone was joining her.

"Has the reality lived up to the fantasy?" Cora asked, as she came to stand beside Manuela, her back ramrod-straight as she looked out into the Parisian night.

"It's wonderful," Manuela said, and even she heard the longing in her voice.

"But..." Cora prompted.

"Nothing," Manuela lied. "Nothing, it's just..." She drifted as she considered what to say. "Patricia said she's walking away from her inheritance to stay here with her lover. It seems like Frede and Cassandra are estranged from their families, too. It's so much to give up."

Cora didn't respond for such a long time, Manuela began to worry she'd offended her.

"Patricia comes from a very wealthy family, and though she will lose her parents' inheritance, she recently came into a bequest left to her by her aunt. She has enough to live comfortably, if not lavishly, for a very long time. Her lover is also the child of a very eccentric shipping heiress who doesn't much care who her daughter takes up with." Cora had taken off her gloves, and her hands were stark in the moonlight resting on the railing of the balcony. "Cassandra did lose her family when she chose her life with Frede, but you've seen them. They belong together." She couldn't deny that. No one who saw Cassandra and Frede could. "Their choices are not yours, Manuela." There was a pregnant pause then, and even through the darkness she could sense Cora's hesitation. "Are you questioning your decision to marry Mr. Kingsley?" Hearing her fiancé's name from Cora stunned her. It felt wrong, like an intrusion, to have any part of her life inserting itself into this moment.

"How did you know his name?" she asked, and Cora sent her a sideways glance that said *You can't be serious.*

"The same way I found out your parents' names and that you would be here in Paris this summer," she informed Manuela, her eyes focused on something in the distance. "Whenever it comes to my business, I always arrive prepared, princesa. That should not be a surprise."

There were many things she could've said then. But she didn't want to talk about any of it. Not her parents, not Felix, not the looming end of this summer in Paris. She didn't want to confess her pathetic money woes to Cora. She didn't want the self-judgment or the bitterness that usually followed any conversation about her future. She'd come to Paris for a reprieve from all that.

"Is your name just Corazón?"

A surprised sound came out of Cora at the change of topic, and again she took her time to answer. "Aymara," Cora replied. "My full name is Corazón Aymara. My mother's people were Aymara." Manuela could hear the hesitation in her voice. No one had told her but, somehow, she knew Cora rarely discussed her mother. "She left the Altiplano to go work as a seamstress in Iquique. She was well-known, dressed all the wealthy ladies on the north coast of Chile. That's how she met my father. He came to have some clothes made for his first wife. Shortly after he took my mother as his mistress, and when his wife died, he married her."

Manuela's eyes widened at that. She'd assumed that Cora's family was one of those old colonial ones that dated back to Reina Isabel.

"My father was born dirt poor. He spent a lot of money trying to erase his origin from people's memory." Like marrying his daughter to British aristocrats.

Cora turned to face Manuela then, her arms crossed over her

chest, a faraway look on her face. Manuela didn't dare speak, scared that if she did, Cora would remember who it was she was telling this story to. "He loved her, but I think he resented her for it too. She was the only thing that revealed to the world who he truly was. That he preferred a working-class woman, someone who came from the same world he did. That's why he became obsessed with marrying his daughters to men with titles. My three sisters are all married to peers."

"Are you close to them? Your sisters?"

"Not really. I am much younger than them. I was the only child of my parents' marriage." She added after a moment, "Do you have siblings?"

"I don't. I'm an only child." In the fragile silence that followed, Manuela asked, "Were you ever close to your parents?"

Cora made a noise that Manuela couldn't quite discern. "My father and I never quite understood each other, and my mother…" Again, one of those long pauses and Manuela braced herself. "She died when I was born."

After that they stood in silence for a long moment, Manuela lost in her thoughts. She wanted to ask Cora about her marriage. She wanted to know how someone who insisted on being so cold and calculating had in a matter of hours shown herself to be considerate and generous—even to Manuela, who had put her in such an awkward position. She had so many questions, but she was certain that bringing any attention to Cora's more gracious side would have a very adverse effect on this fragile intimacy between them.

"I must admit, I didn't think this would be where you'd bring me." She'd expected Cora to uphold her part of the bargain, but she never imagined she'd be granted access to an obviously important part of Cora's life. She didn't know what to make of it.

The duchess watched her for a moment and seemed to be searching for the real question behind Manuela's words, but eventually she only shrugged. "I wasn't planning to," she admitted coolly. "But when I found you at the gallery today, I thought it might be useful for you to meet some of these women."

Manuela didn't know what to say. It had been an altering evening, even if she didn't quite know how exactly. Even now as she looked through the door and watched them all eating and laughing, existing, even thriving in a world that would've preferred to deny their very existence, she felt like a child in front of a window full of sweets she could not have. No, it was more dire than that. She was the child who'd been caught stealing a few sweets and was now denied entrance forever. The truth was that she didn't think she had the courage to give up everything they had, but she did have the remainder of the summer. "I expect you to continue to dazzle me as our outings continue," she added, if only to add some levity to the moment.

Cora laughed quietly. "I've devised a strategy," the duchess replied, her voice so close in the darkness. It made Manuela shiver. "Because I have learned very quickly that you are hell on my plans."

Something tight and hot coiled tight inside Manuela hearing that bewildered want in Cora's voice. It was too dark to see, but Manuela felt her moving closer. Then a hand slid into hers. "Come on, princess. You only get eight of these. You don't want to be wasteful."

Manuela allowed the duchess to lead her back inside and for the rest of the night forced herself to focus on the weeks ahead and nothing more.

This was, after all, a very auspicious start.

Eleven

"Here we are," Cora said placidly as her carriage arrived at Manuela's door just before seven in the evening. "I shall collect you in the morning for a ride in the Bois de Boulogne." It required an immense amount of restraint for Manuela not to scream in frustration. To say that things had gone downhill after that first lovely evening at Cassandra and Frede's was a gross understatement. She'd foolishly assumed Cora had eased her in with that dinner and would take her to increasingly more exciting—risqué—establishments. She'd been sorely mistaken. Manuela had already been on half of her outings with the duchess, and she had yet to be taken to a single scandalous evening's entertainment.

The dinner at Cassandra's was one of the best nights of her life and she'd assumed things would only improve from there. But a full two weeks in, with the exception of those two very early yet promising kisses with Cora, Manuela was still completely untarnished by vice or sin, and quite frankly she'd had enough. And it wasn't as if there weren't opportunities. "I heard there is a gathering in Montmartre tonight," she said suggestively, then watched with frustration as Cora's face immediately shuttered.

Cassandra—who she'd made fast friends with and had seen for tea multiple times since they first met—had personally told her that this very night Cora was invited to a party at a brasserie in Montmartre that catered exclusively to women. So when Cora sent her a message saying they'd be going out that evening, she foolishly assumed she would finally be introduced to Montmartre. Instead Cora had dragged her to yet another lecture, and now expected her to end her evening at dinnertime. It was a damned travesty.

"Montmartre is quite unruly in the evenings. I could take you there in the afternoon next week." At least Cora had the decency to look away when she said it.

The disappointment she was feeling was her own fault. She'd convinced herself that those kind gestures from Cora meant more than they did. That maybe their constant proximity would lead to something more. Then Cora would make a comment about the land and she'd be reminded this was nothing but business for the duchess.

Why couldn't she be happy with what she could have? Why couldn't it be enough to see Paris with Cora? Why did she have to want the woman, too? She turned to look at the duchess, elegant and regal in her burgundy suit. Her eyes downcast, so careful not to touch Manuela, not even a graze of the hands.

Manuela was woman enough to admit she'd made some tactical errors in her negotiations. She should've been more specific about the places she wanted to go. But how was she to know when she'd made the request to be taken into Cora's world that it would be so incredibly dull?

She knew she was being unfair. Some of it—a lot of it—had been gratifying and wonderful, but it was all so tame. Manuela wanted to misbehave…with Cora, preferably in a bed. She was going absolutely mad with want, and she suspected that all these deathly boring excursions to lectures and recitals were the duchess's way of keeping them both from lapsing.

Every time Manuela asked her about an evening in Montmartre or Pigalle or requested to be taken back to Le Bureau, Cora dissembled into some tangent about edifying events and essential sapphic experiences. As far as Manuela was concerned, nothing could be more *essential* than experiencing extremely sapphic intercourse. She had no intention of wasting the weeks she had remaining taking in more harp concerts in drawings rooms full of bores. She intended to be knee-deep in immorality of the lesbian sort that very evening, and if Cora Kempf Bristol refused to take part in it, she'd take matters into her own hands.

"Thank you for another illuminating evening, Your Grace," she said, a little tersely, gathering her skirts to descend from the carriage—what a waste. The small, dark space, with its plush padded walls and the enticing scent of leather, was the ideal place for a tryst. Cora was, as usual, seated as far away from Manuela as possible. The frustrating woman wedged herself into the corner of the conveyance so tightly she wondered if the footman had to pry her out.

Manuela had lost count of the times in the last weeks she'd fantasized of Cora reaching for her and pulling her onto her lap then kissing her hungrily. Of mouths and bodies fused together while they traveled the crowded Parisian roads.

Unfortunately, the ravishing she so desperately yearned for continued to occur exclusively in her mind. Why would a person live in Paris if they were so attached to discipline?

What would happen if she leaned over and kissed her?

Nothing. Absolutely nothing. The moment Manuela made an attempt, the duchess would remind her what they'd agreed on and send her on her way, then punish her by subjecting her to some other dreadfully bland evening.

Cora Kempf Bristol's self-control was proving to be a mighty foe. For Manuela to win this battle, she would have to engage a different set of skills than those she'd utilized thus far. The time for a more forceful tactic had arrived. She might as well begin now.

"Oh dear." Her hand went to her chest.

"What's the matter?" Cora asked, with a promising amount of concern in her voice. This was the most frustrating aspect of their situation: the attentiveness, the protective manner Cora had when it came to Manuela. She was so excruciatingly considerate, yet so maddeningly chaste. Manuela intended to test the walls of that fortress tonight until *something* broke.

"I just recalled I may have plans this evening that will keep me out of bed until a very late hour." She didn't have any such thing, but she knew exactly where to find the kind of diversion she wanted. If the duchess would not take her, she would take herself.

"Plans?" the duchess asked stiffly. That fluttering in her jaw made an appearance as well. Things were progressing nicely already.

"That's correct," Manuela confirmed as she descended the steps of the carriage on the street in front of her house. She looked over her shoulder and was delighted to find a very deep frown and unhappy violet eyes staring at her.

"You're going out with someone else?"

Manuela nodded, demurely, making sure she widened her eyes for the full innocent-damsel effect. "This won't affect our arrangement. But I am afraid that an early horseback ride may be too straining," Manuela advised the duchess, and for a second, Cora seemed almost confused. Like she'd forgotten what it was that they were doing. Like she'd forgotten about the land. And then, as always, the mask fell with its full force. Her mouth flattened, and she leaned back into the carriage, her eyes trained straight ahead.

"I hope you have a pleasant rest of your evening, Manuela."

For a long moment Manuela watched with fascination as Cora's usual impassiveness shifted into something that looked a lot like despondency, even as she fought to appear indifferent. It was there in the strain around her eyes, the pinched set to her mouth. This was a woman holding onto her control by sheer force. But she was too damned stubborn to ask Manuela not to go off on her own.

Yes, she was besotted with the woman, absolutely infatuated with her. And the time had come to force the duchess's hand. So help her, Manuela had gone to her last mind-numbing recital.

"Have a lovely evening, Your Grace." Manuela fluttered her gloved hand in goodbye. Cora turned then and for a second their gazes met. She let the Duchess of Sundridge see what she could have if she would just come and take it. The duchess looked away first.

Satisfied, she stepped onto the sidewalk, and for good measure as the carriage pulled away Manuela happily called out, "Thank you for another invigorating afternoon of art and conversation"—tepid, lifeless, desperately sluggish conversation— before running into the house.

"Aurora," she yelled the moment she walked inside. Luz Alana and her earl had parted to Scotland two days earlier with the plan to elope to his country estate. Their friend had taken her younger sister and Amaranta with her, and Manuela and Aurora were supposed to join her there in ten days' time. Until then they were free in Paris without a chaperone, and Manuela did not intend to spend any more of it bored to tears.

"Why in the world are you shouting, Manuela?" Aurora appeared at the top of the stairs in her usually exasperated state.

"I don't have time for your moods, Aurora," she shot back as she mounted the stairs. "We must ready ourselves for an evening of perdition and immorality in Montmartre."

"Absolutely not. I'm planning to visit a maternity ward this evening." Her friend crossed her arms tightly across her chest, narrowed eyes skewering Manuela. "Weren't you just out with the duchess? Why do I need to be involved in your moral descent?"

"I don't want to talk about the duchess," Manuela said with a stomp of her foot. Aurora's eyes narrowed further. "It is incredibly frustrating to have, for the first time in our lives, two weeks unchaperoned and you choosing to squander it by spending all your time in hospitals, Aurora."

"First of all," Aurora began, fully projecting her medical–lecture voice, "spending time in hospitals is what I am here to do, Manuela." Aurora's hand shot up with two fingers in the air. "Second, the only reason we even need a chaperone is because your mother can't trust you."

"There is no need to split hairs regarding the chaperones," Manuela spluttered, while her friend eyed her with disapproval.

This was not working. She was completely mishandling this situation. Aurora would only dig her heels deeper if she tried to appeal to her nonexistent sense of adventure. But after twelve years she had some tricks up her sleeve, when it came to leading the Leonas astray.

"There will be many women of various trades there you could conduct your interviews with," she suggested enticingly and was happy to see a minor thawing in the set of her friend's shoulders. Since their arrival in Paris, Aurora had been going to working–class areas asking women what kind of medical services they needed. A room full of them was exactly the kind of lure that would have Aurora ready for action.

"I have not even had dinner yet, Manuela," Aurora argued, her resolve weaker this time.

"It *is* a brasserie. They have wonderful food. Cassandra, the friend of the duchess who invited me, said their leek soup and stuffed chicken are the best in Paris." She still had one more weapon in her arsenal but was happy to see that the mere mention of nourishment was putting Aurora in a very receptive mood.

"Stuffed chicken? I've never had those." Manuela made sure

not to react to her friend's greedy tone. Aurora was the most disciplined person Manuela knew. Her perseverance and tenacity were astonishing, but the woman could be led down to the pits of hell with the promise of a juicy roast. It was time for the coup de grâce.

"Oh!" She made a show of slapping her palm to her forehead, as though disgusted with her own absent-mindedness. "Do you know of Frederica Holtz-Carvajal?" Aurora's eyebrows shot up at the mention of the name with obvious interest.

"Of course! She's one the first two women in Peru to practice medicine." Manuela decided her new royal blue dress with the peacock feathers would be perfect for her first outing in Montmartre. The she went in for the kill.

"She'll be there tonight."

"Frederica Holtz-Carvajal will be there?" Aurora shot her a suspicious look, but Manuela kept her expression impassive and patiently waited. She knew that the prospect of meeting a fellow physician—a prominent Peruvian one, at that—would be far too tempting to pass up.

"Her lover is hosting the party. They go everywhere together." She didn't know for a fact Frede would be there, but judging by how devoted they were to each other, she could only assume the woman would make an appearance.

"I know you enough to know that at least half of what you've just told me is a lie," Aurora volleyed after long consideration, but her friend's tone was far less forbidding now. Truly, they made it far too easy.

"But half *is* true. The stuffed chicken at least I am certain exists."

"All right, I'll get dressed," Aurora laughed, completely unfazed by the fact she'd agreed to go to a party full of sapphists. "But you are making a habit of extorting people to get what you want, Manuela del Carmen."

If Aurora only knew just how true that was, Manuela thought as she made her way to her bedchamber.

"Why are you pouting, Corazón?" Tia Osiris demanded while Cora glared at the lit fireplace.

"It's nothing. I am just pondering some things." The things in question all had to do with the heiress who had come into her life to steal her peace and plague her thoughts every waking moment of the day.

"Has that heiress finally grown tired of recitals and reptile lectures?" Tia Osiris sniffed and took another sip of her brandy.

"She has not." Cora was not quite certain it was the truth. Manuela had been less enthusiastic during their last outing, and the way they'd parted this evening...she knew the little vixen was up to something. "Things are going wonderfully. Could not be better." Even she could hear the doubt in her words. "Miss Caceres Galvan only needed a night to herself."

Almost certainly to cause mischief.

As her carriage had driven away earlier that evening, she'd had to sit on her hands to keep from banging on the roof and asking her driver to go back to Place des Vosges. But she needed her own reprieve, if only to restore some of her senses when it came to Manuela.

"I'm surprised the poor girl has put up with it as long as she has." Cora wouldn't take her aunt's bait. All she'd done was try to maintain some sort of decorum in a situation where she felt constantly out of control.

The woman was like an affliction. Cora wasn't content if she was not near her, but it was torture to have her so close and not touch her. Every time they were together she spent every second negotiating what she would allow herself. A brush of a finger to an elbow. How many times she'd permit their knees to graze in the carriage before she forced herself to sit in the furthest corner of the conveyance. It was ridiculous. She was like a schoolgirl—worse than that. Because even as a schoolgirl Cora had never been this...this besotted.

She practically shook whenever she caught a glimpse of the curve of her neck, and the thought of seeing what shade of brown her nipples were robbed Cora of sleep. She was obsessed with the idea of licking up those shapely thighs, of spreading them and... Perhaps it was best to get some distance.

Except that the thought of Manuela out there in Paris getting into trouble on her own was enough to send her running into the streets. And it was not like she could go to Le Bureau and lose herself for an hour or two: that would lead nowhere. She didn't want anyone else.

"She's not a girl, she's a woman, and I've been doing exactly what she asked. She's met half of the lesbians in Paris."

"The stodgy half," her aunt countered, and Cora could not exactly refute that. "For someone considered to be a brilliant negotiator, you are certainly being a bit thick, querida. You are clearly intrigued by this woman. Why not give her what she's asked for and enjoy yourself in the process?"

Cora was gnawing so violently on the inside of her cheek she was certain she'd drawn blood.

"Because I am not involved with Miss Caceres Galvan for enjoyment, aunt." Cora almost cried out in frustration. "The last thing I need is for rumors getting around that I secured the land for the railroad by sleeping with her."

"All the men you associate with do the same or worse," Alfie offered from the other side of the room. It was too much to ask for him to not offer his opinion at some point.

"The men I associate with are amoral, unscrupulous imbeciles."

"And yet, you spend most of your time and energy scheming how to reach the top of that unsavory heap." Her aunt loved her, but she was not fond of her dealings and never lost the chance to let her know. "You should've taken her to Cassandra's party like she asked."

"No, I shouldn't have. She's gotten what she asked me for, and if she doesn't like the entertainments I took her to, she can find her own." Even as she said it, she knew it was a lie. The mere thought of Manuela traipsing around Pigalle rose the hairs on her neck.

She knew she was playing a dangerous game. That the heiress was too smart not to realize what she was doing. To eventually recognize Cora had been appeasing her with tame dinner parties and insipid soirees.

But what was she to do? Admit that she was terrified? Confess Manuela tested each of the barriers Cora had worked so hard to erect around herself every second they were together?

"You know what happened the last time I let my feelings for a woman interfere with my business, Tia," she finally said, without turning to look at Osiris.

"There was no way to know Sally would do that, my dear."

Cora flinched, hearing the name said out loud after so long. The thought of the spectacle she'd made of herself, of the humiliation that had come later, turned her stomach even after all these years.

"If I had not been so busy making a fool of myself all over London chasing after Sally Fraser, it wouldn't have taken so long to realize what she'd been up to."

And she was doing it again, letting Manuela distract her from important business. She'd put off two different meetings this week to gallivant around Paris with the heiress, and now that she finally had a night to herself, all she'd done was ruminate on every word they'd exchanged.

She had a million things to worry about. The first of which was sending word to their agents in Venezuela letting them know to start the process of hiring a labor force to lay down the railway. She had proposals to go over, investments to consider.

There were at least a dozen matters for her to occupy herself with tonight that were more important than speculating where Manuela Caceres Galvan was spending her evening.

A soft knock jolted her back to the present.

"Come in," she called, grateful for the distraction. She hadn't asked for anything to eat, and it was too late for any unannounced visitors. It was a sad state of affairs when she looked forward to dealing with a domestic emergency to get out of her own head. She expected one of the maids, but it was her butler Laurent who stepped into the room with the tray he used for correspondence. Sitting on top of it was a small envelope.

"Your Grace, this arrived just now."

She didn't recognize the handwriting, but the moment she got a whiff of turpentine and lavender she knew exactly who it was from. She put down her glass, heart thudding in her chest, knowing that whatever it was it would make a liar out of her.

She tore into the envelope, certain this was just another stunt. After reading the few lines she had to cover her mouth to keep from laughing out loud. That little diabla.

"She's gone off to Montmartre," she said, standing up. "Laurent, tell the driver to prepare the carriage. I'm going to Claudine's," she informed the servant as impassively as she could manage, then turned toward the two eager faces on the other side of the room.

"I'm merely going up there to mitigate any potential disasters, so don't get any ideas," she warned. Alfie nodded quietly, but the twitch around the corners of his mouth told her he didn't believe a word she said. Tia Osiris had no such restraint.

"If the lying helps you, dear, we won't say a thing."

Cora only rolled her eyes. "This is all Cassandra's fault."

"What exactly did Cassandra do?" Alfie asked, getting to his feet.

"She was the one who told Manuela about the party at Claudine's place, and now she's gone there alone."

"Didn't she make her way here from Venezuela without your assistance, querida?" Tia Osiris asked innocently, while Cora debated whether she should change her clothes and decided it was best not to waste time.

"She has not been to Montmartre. She's not used to the crowd there."

"I thought you said Claudine runs a tight ship."

Claudine Dosantos was a Brasileira who had come to France as the mistress of an aristocrat. When the man passed away, he bequeathed her ten thousand francs that she used to open Le Chat Tordu, a brasserie and gathering place for women. There were other establishments like Claudine's, but at Le Chat Tordu, the clientele mostly consisted of women from the Americas living as expatriates in Paris.

"She does," Cora said grudgingly. It wasn't the issue of security that had her running off to Montmartre. It was more the thought of sultry, delectable Manuela, with her beguiling smiles and those alluring curves, in the midst of all those ravenous ladies of Montmartre.

"Perhaps I should come with you, just to be safe..." Alfie offered.

"That is not a good idea," she told him, making Tia Osiris laugh. "I will be perfectly fine on my own."

"Let her go, Alfred, and we should make ourselves scarce too. I presume my niece is going to want the house to herself when she returns." Her face heated at that, but there was no use denying it. Not when the urgency to go to Manuela felt like it could propel her to Montmartre's summit. This had been unavoidable from the moment they'd met.

Tia Osiris walked up to her, her throat clicking in a sound that was mixture of amusement and affection. "It has been a long time since I've seen that particular hungry glint in your eyes, mi Corazón. It was high time someone made you jump through a few hoops for a change. A woman like you requires a bit of a chase."

What this would require was a lot of cleanup. Things had never gone well for Cora whenever she mixed business with pleasure, and she didn't see any reason why this would differently. This time, at least, Manuela had no interest in her money. "The last thing on my mind is romance, Tia, so please don't look at me like that," Cora told her aunt as she headed for the door.

"Querida, everyone needs a little romance, a little love."

Cora denied that delusion with a severe shake of the head. "I have loads of love. I have you, Alfie, Cassie and Frede. I don't need anything more." She clearly needed something. Why else would she be running after Manuela when she was obviously being baited?

"My hat," she said, practically growling, the frustration of the last ten minutes seeping into her bones. She told herself this was her merely doing her due diligence. She could not finish the railroad without Manuela's land, and she would not get the land if the blasted girl got herself killed in Montmartre.

"Are you sure you don't want me to come with you?" Alfie asked, as a footman opened the carriage door for her.

"Alfie, I love you. You are the light of my life, but I will have Pierre physically remove you from my carriage if you insist on getting in." The strapping footman blanched at her words and her stepson relented with a grin, then threw his hands up in a sign of defeat. "Believe me, son, what is about to happen in that brasserie is not fit for your young eyes."

He laughed, but she was deadly serious. Manuela Caceres Galvan thought she wanted debauchery... Cora would make sure she got exactly what she'd been so diligently looking for.

Twelve

"That message you sent to the duchess will only start trouble, Manuela," Aurora warned a while later as their carriage slowly took them up the hill leading to Montmartre.

"If you recall, Aurora, trouble is exactly what I've been after since we arrived in Paris and so far have not seen even an inkling of." It might be true that the note she sent off by messenger was the equivalent of placing a steak under a caged tiger's nose, but Cora had begun this chess game. Manuela was merely making her move. She was particularly proud of the final line.

Your Grace,
It is with my deepest regret that I write to inform you that I will not be available for our morning ride. I have been called away this evening to attend a divertissement at Le Chat Tordu in Montmartre. I've been advised that their offerings may keep me from my bed until the early hours of the morning. It seems prudent not to make any plans before noon. Please send my regrets to the horse.

Warmest regards,
Manuela Caceres Galvan

Manuela wasn't certain what reaction that taunt would draw from the duchess exactly, but she suspected there would be one. At this point, she didn't much care what it was.

"What games are you playing at, Manuela?"

"I only wish any of this was a game," she exclaimed in frustration. "I bargained for a bacchanalia, and so far all I've done is discuss the benefits of Ceylon tea with Cora's lovely but quite older friends. Then there was the harp recital and the lecture on what seemed to be a species of sapphic beetles." That last one had truly pushed Manuela to the very limits of her patience. If Cora wanted to play dirty, Manuela would see her in the muck, preferably at a location in Montmartre. "If the duchess is unable or unwilling to provide me with the erotic tryst I deserve, then I will find it myself!"

Aurora choked, pointing at the coachman, which only made Manuela more cross. "Oh, for goodness' sake, Aurora, no one cares what we do here. Who is this French coachman going to tell our affairs to?" Manuela reminded herself that Aurora was in this carriage because she was trying to be supportive, and it would do no good to take her frustrations out on her. "I know this all seems silly to you, but it is something I desire greatly. It's a chance I won't have again."

"Manuela, you could just stay in Paris. There are thousands of Caribbean and South American people settled here. You met some yourself at that dinner you went to with the duchess. Paris has always been a place where people come to find their own way of being." Aurora spoke from personal experience. When every door had been closed to her in her own homeland, she'd come here to Paris to study medicine. "It is especially true for women who, for whatever reason, can't pursue what they want in their own countries. Ironically, in some ways, there is more freedom here." Aurora paused for a second, her gaze troubled. Manuela could only assume she was thinking of her own issues with her family, but as always her friend didn't dwell too long on what was beyond her control and focused on what was. "People do it all the time. Look at Antonio," Aurora insisted.

"Antonio is a man and an engineer," Manuela reminded her impatiently. "I don't want to end up in some hovel as a laundress because I decided to pursue my passion." Aurora flinched at that, and Manuela sighed.

Even as she'd said it, she'd considered the women she'd met in Paris. The paths they'd chosen. The lives they'd created for themselves. Perhaps not glamorous ones, but they were lives with dignity and purpose. She thought of her mother, of the whispered recriminations about what she'd cost them all. Her own guilt for what her indiscretions had caused. The reality was that the Parisian life Aurora spoke of could never be hers.

"I just want you to be happy," Aurora finally whispered, her gloved hand reaching for Manuela's. She knew her friend meant well, that she sincerely wished to see her happy, but Aurora didn't quite know the full truth of Manuela's circumstances.

"I never told you or Luz Alana how bad things became with my family." Aurora's hand tightened on hers, but Manuela turned her face away, looking out into the Parisian night. "Father didn't just get into debt with the factory, he lost it. There were a few years after Abuela died when we were living hand to mouth." She heard Aurora's sharp intake of breath.

"Leona, why didn't you tell us?"

"My parents didn't want anyone to know." She shrugged, even as her face heated with that old humiliation. "And you had your own issues to deal with, between your work and your father and brothers. Luz was so preoccupied with the business, and then her father passed." It was more than that, of course. It had been mortifying. She'd never even realized her family was in the situation it was until too late. Until the debtors were coming to the house and demanding their money. Until they couldn't pay the staff who had worked for them for years. Until they almost lost the roof over their heads. "When Felix started courting me, Father had been assaulted by a debt collector only a week earlier. He'd kicked him so hard he'd broken a rib."

"Manuela!" Aurora's shocked voice did nothing to ease her remembered pain. She hated those memories. She'd never spoken to anyone about that day, about those months of constant worry. Of her parents' screaming fights that usually ended with her mother coming into her room to remind her they wouldn't be going through any of it if she hadn't done what she did with Catalina. She'd barely slept for months, tortured by guilt and increasingly desperate as their situation worsened.

The fear of her father being thrown in jail, her mother's frantic sobbing about being ostracized by their friends. That had been the worst of it. To know that their community, the families her mother lived to impress, would all turn their backs on them if they ever knew of their situation. She'd spent long nights fearful of what the future held for them, despairing of what would happen if they were found out. There had been days, weeks, during that dark period when Manuela told herself she'd do anything to never be that afraid again.

"Felix swooped in and offered to make it all go away if I married him." He'd seemed like a godsend then, and for the first time in so long her parents didn't look at her like she was to blame for all their troubles. "He was looking to buy a place for himself in society, a way to gain some influence with the wealthier families in Caracas and the Caribbean Coast as he expanded his business there. Despite my family's troubles, we are still well-established in Caracas. The Caceres and the Galvan names are still respected." Aurora grunted at that, but she didn't argue. She knew the truth of it. "I was the perfect accessory for that process."

Manuela's family, at one time, had been the biggest supplier of candles in the Caribbean and the northern coast of South American. They had also been tied to two of the most respected political figures of the region, the great Juan Pablo Duarte and

Felix del Rosario Sanchez. Consuelo and Prospero Caceres Galvan found their daughter and their self-respect a low price to pay for to regain their financial security.

"I don't want to worry about money ever again. Don't judge me too harshly."

Aurora let out a long helpless breath and put an around Manuela. "I am not judging you. I am *worried* about you." Manuela nodded, and let her friend pull her into a hard embrace.

"I just need a little bit of happiness, and I don't want to feel guilty for it."

"You deserve more," Aurora said with a sigh.

"We all do," Manuela argued, her eyes closed as they ascended the hill to Montmartre. "But right now, I don't want to dwell on what I deserve. I want to take advantage of what I can have. What I want is to be in Cora Kemp Bristol's bed until I get on that boat to Venezuela."

Aurora's laugh was pained as she pressed a kiss to Manuela's cheek. "It figures you'd finally become pragmatic about something like this," she said with a shake of her head. "You heart is too big, and you give it away too easily, and I think this duchess, even if it's not her intention, could hurt you." Manuela was certain of the fact. "I just hope wherever we are going won't involve watching two people copulating...again." Aurora shuddered and Manuela laughed at her friend's horror.

"You are so squeamish, Aurora," she teased, grateful for the change of subject. "You'd think with all the naked bodies you have to look at when you see patients, you'd be less sensitive to them."

"Looking at a patient is very different than seeing a display of fellatio two feet away from my brand-new boots." Aurora could be so delightfully dramatic.

"The chances of fellatio happening in front of you this evening are drastically lower than they were at Le Bureau." She patted Aurora reassuringly on one knee.

"You are vile," her friend said, pushing her playfully on the shoulder, then sighed again. "I will do my best to support you in this extremely ill-advised outing." Manuela didn't miss the trace of humor in her friend's voice and decided to count it as a win.

"Thank you."

"Don't thank me too soon. Are you certain this is safe, Manuela?" Aurora asked again, as their carriage neared the red awning with a sign of a black cat who appeared to be attempting a waltz. The street was teeming with people. She also noticed that there were many more women than men in front of Le Chat Tordu, some defiantly holding hands and canoodling in plain view.

"The Twisted Cat?" Aurora asked, looking up at the sign. "Truly, Manuela?"

"It's probably more like The Inverted Cat," she offered, which didn't amuse her friend. "Only the women will be allowed in." This seemed to ease Aurora's nervousness. Minutes later they were standing on the street poised for Manuela's next adventure.

"How do we get in?" Aurora asked, watching all the people milling around the entrance.

Manuela didn't waste any time and pushed to the front of the queue with the deftness of someone accustomed to inserting herself in places she didn't belong. "S'il vous plaît, madame," she yelled, snagging the attention of a woman of intimidating stature who was guarding the door. Her legs were wide apart, her pinstriped shirt defiantly unbuttoned under her long coat. She raised an unimpressed eyebrow from under the brim of her cap in response to Manuela's greeting.

"I am Manuela Caceres, and I'm here as a guest of Cassandra Aguzzi Durocher." The woman narrowed her eyes, clearly taking stock of both Aurora and Manuela. After a long moment and more than one appreciative glance at Manuela's décolletage, she pulled back a curtain and waved them inside.

"Mademoiselle Aguzzi is upstairs," she grunted, immediately focusing again on the hopefuls who approached her.

AN ISLAND PRINCESS STARTS A SCANDAL

"Is it even really a restaurant?" Aurora asked as the two of them pushed inside.

"From what Cassandra told me, most of the establishments in Montmartre of this sort began as communal tables," she explained as they entered the room. "Many of the proprietresses hosted meals as a way to gather like-minded women. A place where they could safely meet and...commune," Manuela concluded when she couldn't find a more fitting word.

"It would figure that women come up with a way to gather and nourish each other, while men devise dens of vice and violence." Aurora scoffed at the servers walking by holding trays laden with divinely smelling foods.

"Don't be so harsh," Manuela chastised. "I enjoyed my time at Le Bureau."

"Because you landed on a duchess and you enjoy seeing me suffer," her friend countered with humor, as they finally entered the main room.

Le Chat Tordu was not at all like Le Bureau. While the brothel in the Palais-Royal dazzled their clients with luxurious surroundings, this place was...simple. Clean and well-cared for, but a world away from the opulence of Le Bureau. Low lights did a lot to hide the scuffed wooden floors and threadbare furnishings. The art on the walls was not in gilded frames, and the staff was not in fine livery, but the women who seemed to cover every corner of the space made it heaven to Manuela.

So many women of all shapes and sizes. Of different races, but in here they all seemed at ease. High-society ladies in sumptuous gowns sitting in pleasant conversation with bluestockings in stark morning suits. There were card games and singing. The atmosphere as boisterous as it was carefree and safe. Like she could walk up to any of the many tables, sit down and be welcome.

There was something very different about a place that existed solely to cater to women who sought the company of other women. A brasserie not just *à* femmes but *pour* femmes.

"Aurora, esto es un paraiso femenino." For a second she was irritated with Cora all over again for depriving her of this. But this place was so glorious she couldn't even hang on to her irritation for long.

"Oh, look at the band." The band, an all-woman quartet, was playing a lively piece that had the dancers in the room hopping around and laughing. A Black woman dressed in a set of trousers and jacket, much like the one Cora had worn that first night they met, was singing next to the musicians.

"Not a man in sight," Aurora said, sounding pleased. "This is exceptional, Leona." One thing was certain: Manuela might not have had much luck when it came to her parents, but the universe had blessed her with the absolute best of friends. Aurora might have agreed to come against her better judgment, but now that they were here, there wasn't an iota of ambivalence even when faced with a room full of women openly touching, embracing, kissing each other…and more.

"This doesn't bother you?" Manuela asked, giving Aurora a sideways glance. "You were practically running for the hills at Le Bureau." She'd always wondered how she and Luz Alana could be so unwavering in their acceptance of her.

On her better days she told herself it was because they loved her unconditionally. On her darker ones, when she couldn't believe anyone who truly knew her *could* love her at all, she'd tell herself they only accepted it as long as they never had to see it. But here it was, and Aurora was as steadfast as ever.

"Ay, Leona," her friend's teasing tone brought Manuela up short. "When has being friends with you ever been about comfort?" Aurora teased, then eased the barb by putting an arm around her. "Le Bureau was different," she asserted, valiantly unflinching even as two women began kissing with extreme ardor just a few feet from them. "This place is for pleasure, that is true, but mostly it's for women who don't have a place to be themselves to do so. It's their haven, their safe place. Above all things, I want the world to be safe for us. These women can nurture a part of you that Luz Alana and I never could, and I am glad that you've found a community that can. I want that for you, Leona. A place where you can be your wildest, most Manuela self."

Tears clouded Manuela's eyes at the matter-of-fact words from her friend. Aurora didn't much care what Manuela did, as long as it made her happy, as long as she was safe. "Thank you for saying that," she said, voice clogged with tears.

Aurora, not one to tolerate any prolonged sentimentality, patted her on the head distractedly while she looked after more platters of her coveted chicken. "If you're going to cry, do it while you beg one of those servers and kill two birds with one stone, so to speak."

"I will if you admit you secretly love our adventures," Manuela said with a laugh, before kissing her friend on the cheek.

"I most certainly will not," Aurora retorted with equal humor, and Manuela's thoughts drifted once again to the group of women she'd met at Cassandra's. The way they carried themselves in that parlor, fearlessly. Even Cora, who seemed to always be so sure-footed, seemed different with those women, like she'd put her armor down. That was the safety Aurora spoke about, the security of a place where you didn't have to pretend. For the last ten years Manuela had been seeking safety too, for her parents, for herself. And though material stability was necessary, she'd never considered how much she needed to feel protected in other ways.

In the last two weeks Cora had given her a taste of that. From that very first time they met and how she caught her fall. At the gallery she'd sat there with Manuela and talked about her art until she remembered that she didn't need anyone's approval to know what her work was worth. And then she'd given her the greatest gift of all by introducing her to other women like them.

Bewitching lavender eyes and a hard, lush mouth appeared

in her mind, and a pulse of pure, raw longing swept through her like an avalanche. She wasn't even certain what it was that she wanted; her experience with other women amounted to nothing more than a few heated kisses and clumsy gropes with Catalina. But even those fledgling encounters had been enough to make Manuela crave them for years. The memories of being touched like that, of burning with need for a caress, for a brush of lips kept her warm on many nights, long after Catalina. She wanted to experience it all with Cora.

She ached to be the one to melt the icy duchess.

"Leona! Chicken!" Aurora urged, making Manuela jump. "Where did your mind go?" her friend asked in exasperation. "Don't tell me. I can guess from those two red splotches on your cheeks."

"Manuela," a familiar voice cut through the noise of the crowd as Cassandra Aguzzi Durocher made her way to them accompanied by Frede and another woman. In mere seconds, both Manuela and Aurora were enveloped in a flurry of kisses.

"I am so glad you came!" Cassandra tightened her arms around Manuela. "You managed to escape another of Cora's lecture on the sapphic habits of spiders?" she joked.

"It was beetles," Manuela lamented dramatically, which Aurora found absurdly amusing, and even Frede cracked a smile.

"I think we caught a lively one, Claudine!" Cassandra told the taller woman Manuela had not yet been introduced to. As they approached, she noticed that she was being assessed from head to toe. The examination didn't feel intrusive; it was more as if the woman was confirming something she already knew.

"Indeed." From only that word Manuela detected a different accent from the Gallic she'd been hearing since her arrival in France—then she remembered that Cassandra told her Claudine was also Brazilian. "Cassie tells me that you are the cause of the duchess's volatile moods as of late."

Manuela's expression must have given her confusion away,

because the woman laughed and leaned down to buss her on the cheek. "Don't fret, chérie, this is the best thing to happen to us in years. My dear duchess has spent too many years dedicated to her schemes and machinations. She needed desperately to be brought to distraction!" Manuela, who was usually more than happy to accept any and all praise, didn't quite know how to respond to this. "I have not properly introduced myself. I am Claudine Dosantos, the proprietor of Le Chat Tordu."

"It's nice to properly meet you, Madame Claudine." Manuela waved a hand toward Aurora, whose expression had gone from mildly indifferent to utterly rapt since the other women had appeared. "This is my friend, Doctora Aurora Montalban Wright. She's a physician."

"Of course." Cassandra beamed and turned loving eyes toward her quiet lover. "Frede has been dying to meet you." As usual Aurora did not hesitate to start up a conversation with the shier Frede and was soon plying her with questions on all sorts of things Manuela didn't understand.

"I heard the word *speculum* mentioned, so those two will be busy for a while." Cassandra grinned as Aurora spoke animatedly to an attentive Frede.

"Tell us everything," she urged, guiding her to a small table. "Was Cora livid when you told her you were coming here?"

Manuela glanced at the expectant faces, preening internally at the thought of the letter making its way to the duchess at that very moment. "I didn't exactly tell her to her face…"

Claudine raised a curious eyebrow while Cassandra whirled her hand encouragingly at Manuela.

"I sent her a note letting her know I would be up much too late to be able to ride in the morning, and…" She paused dramatically as the other women waited with bated breath. She wondered just how uncommon it was for someone to contradict the duchess. "I did send my apologies to the horse." Cassandra laughed so loud, both Frede and Aurora whipped their heads in their direction.

"Oh, Cassie, how long do you think it will take for our Corazón to burst into this place like an avenging angel?" Claudine asked.

Manuela's heart gave a hopeful thud. "Do you really think she'll come?" It was impossible not to sound impatient.

Cassandra chuckled, still wiping her eyes, and then sent Manuela a knowing look. "I'd say you should take your run of the place now, my dear, because I suspect your lady in shining armor will be here any moment."

Thirteen

The conversation with Alfie and Tia Osiris pitched Cora's thoughts back to the last time a woman had burrowed under her skin like this. She was not prone to digging up old history. She didn't dwell on her past mistakes; she only looked ahead, applying herself to righting wrongs, instead of wallowing in the past. But as her carriage took her up the hill to Montmartre, she did just that.

It started on the second anniversary of Benedict's death. She'd been miserable and missed Benedict's friendship desperately. Even Alfie, who had always been such a sweet boy, had become contrary and withdrawn in his grief. She felt crushed under the pressure of her responsibilities. As though she was constantly giving one hundred percent of herself in every facet of her life, and everyone around her seemed to be receiving barely ten percent.

At Tia Osiris's insistence she'd gotten on a train to Paris for a few days of rest. Instead she'd installed herself in Le Bureau for two days and two nights of fucking and drinking which had only ended when Frede and Cassandra practically carried her out of the brothel and took her to a salon. There she'd met Sally Fraser.

It had all seemed so fortuitous at the time. Sally was also visiting from London and had a brother, Charles, who was eager to be a part of Cora's latest business ventures but had been unable to gain an audience with her or any of her associates. The reason for the denials had been Charles's terrible reputation for absconding on his debts, but Sally had captivated Cora. By the time she returned to London, Miss Fraser was in Cora's bed and her brother in her business dealings.

Cora became consumed and was outrageously careless. Dismissing appointments to discuss matters of the duchy to run off to the country estate with Sally. Kissing in gardens in front of staff. Making love to Sally in parlors. All the while, Sally continued to ask for small favors for her brother. Just a little loan here, to put in a word there. The mere thought of how stupid she'd been made Cora's face burn.

After months of ruinous conduct, of neglecting Alfie, Sally finally informed Cora that she would be marrying. That the Viscount of Demming had been courting her for over a year and that, now that she had a dowry—thanks to the recent boon in Charles's financial situation—she'd accepted the man's hand.

Cora did not receive the news well and made a spectacle of herself. She caused a scene, wept openly in front of the servants, begged Sally not to marry. Offered to give her anything she asked for, if only she didn't leave her. When Sally had turned her away, Cora had lowered herself further and gone to Charles, that spineless pustule, to intercede on her behalf, gone down on her knees, degraded herself—*to a man*—but once his finances were back in working order, he turned her away like garbage.

By the time she realized she'd been quite literally had, Cora had decimated her reputation so thoroughly that she'd had to leave London altogether. Not even her growing notoriety as an avid investor could undo the damage. She'd closed the house in Belgravia and brought Alfie and Tia Osiris to Paris. She swore never to be swayed like that again. She also vowed only to re-

turn to London when she'd accrued so much money and garnered so much power that no peer would dare turn her or her
stepson away or even whisper the name Sally Fraser.

Sally had been so unassuming and would hang on to every
word out of Cora's mouth. She was neither flirtatious and tem-
pestuous like Manuela nor direct and assertive like Cora. She was
comforting, gave herself to Cora so easily, at a moment when
she'd craved that kind of simplicity. Cora had long thought that
was why she'd fallen for her. Sally was so wonderfully uncom-
plicated at a time when everything in Cora's life felt like a series of cyphers.

And now here was Manuela Caceres Galvan, with whom
nothing was simple. Unlike Sally, who allowed Cora to remain
in control at every step, Manuela was as manageable as a tor-
nado. Every time she thought she had a path laid out to deal
with the heiress, she ran off in a completely different direction.
She knew the hellion was taunting her and just this once, because it *was* her damned prerogative, she'd take the bait. She was
not going to Montmartre to make a scene; she was going there
to make a statement. To remind Miss Manuela Caceres Galvan
who it was that she was dealing with.

If the island princess claimed to want her fill of sexual exploits before she returned to her life as a society lady in Venezuela, Cora would impress upon her just how out of her league
the princesa was.

The moment the carriage stopped in front of Claudine's she
hopped out of it without help and ordered her driver to come to
the back entrance of the building in ten minutes. She expected
the whole business to be done in five but, knowing Manuela,
there would likely be interruptions. She strode to the door of
the building, not caring who saw that the Duchess of Sundridge
was at one of the most notorious lesbian establishments in the
city. She never hid her preferences and was a regular at Le Chat

Tordu, which was why the moment she stepped up to the door, Helene, the gatekeeper to the establishment, waved her through.

"Duchesse," the imposing blonde greeted Cora in her Germanic-laced French, "Miss Cassandra told me to expect you." That was added with a knowing grin, which she decided to ignore. But instead of making her way into the brasserie, Cora remained at the threshold, wavering.

"What's all this waffling about, Duchesse?" Helene asked, cannily. "This isn't like you. Whenever you arrive here, you say hello and sod off to hunt down some pretty girls. Not that I don't appreciate a bit of stimulating conversation." Cora rolled her eyes, but Helene was right. For all her bravado on her way here, she was suddenly hesitant to go inside. What if Manuela's note had not been about getting Cora to chase after her? What if she'd found someone she preferred to Cora? Her gut clenched at the thought, and if she had any sense, she'd turn on her heel and go home.

"Oh là là, Duchesse." Helene was smiling wide at her expense now. "I don't think I've seen that expression on your face since those idiots came to start trouble here."

"Don't remind me," Cora grumbled.

Six months earlier, on a busy night, two men had entered Le Chat and assaulted the women there. They'd been visibly intoxicated and rambling about not allowing so-called tribadists to make them irrelevant. They injured three women and struck Claudine in the face before some of the clients overtook them and beat them to a pulp with whatever they could find. By the time the police had arrived the men were worse for wear, but it had made Claudine as well as the women who frequented Le Chat too aware that their little utopia was not as safe as they liked to think.

The reminder of that sent a frisson of unease up her spine at the thought of Manuela anywhere near a situation like that. She needed to find her. "Speaking of trouble, there's something inside that is currently under my purview, and I'd like to get it back."

Helene's lips tipped up like the Cheshire cat. "If the thing you're referring to is that delectable caramel-skinned morsel with the sweet mouth and luscious chest..." The woman cupped her hands in front of her own generous bosom to the delight of the crowd gathered on the street. Cora refused to be amused. "She came through the door about an hour ago with a frowny friend in tow..." Cora had to clench her teeth when she thought of those lush hips swaying as she made her way through the room. She was probably climbing on tables looking at Claudine's art on the walls, falling on some unsuspecting woman, and...

"That would be Manuela," she sighed and Helene's grin reached her eyes.

"Then, I suggest you pick up the pace, Duchesse. The last time I looked in, the girls were circling like sharks."

Cora was already reaching for some coins in her pocket.

The doorkeeper raised an eyebrow in question.

"Empty the back stairs for me."

"The back stairs?"

"Yes," she sweetened the request by sliding a few coins in the woman's hand. "And tell Claudine to send a bottle of champagne to my carriage. My coachman will be at the back door in ten minutes." Helene tucked the money in her pocket and gave Cora a mocking military salute.

"At your service, Your Grace," she called as Cora disappeared through the hallway leading to the main room. "Wishing you luck! That one looked like she's left her fair share of casualties in her wake."

Cora's lips tipped up, despite herself, at the wisecrack. The woman was not wrong. Manuela was dangerous. Dangerous and seductive...and likely the greatest mistake Cora would ever make. All the same, she walked into that room prepared to admit defeat in the war she'd been waging with her self-discipline. The hair on the back of her neck rose, and her muscles tightened in anticipation of what was to come when she finally cut the strings holding her back. In a single second her feet were propelling her across the crowded dance floor in search of the one thing that could get the Duchess of Sundridge out of her house and up on this hill with only a few short sentences.

Fourteen

It wasn't that Manuela was bored, it was that she was frustrated. Frustrated and annoyed at herself, for her absolute lack of interest in the bounty of women who were at that very moment doing their utmost to lure her to join them in the three things she'd said a thousand times she wanted to do in Paris: discuss art, drink champagne and flirt…with other women.

It was a waste. An utter disgrace to sulk for the past hour because every single thing she heard or saw made her think of Cora. It was completely ridiculous, and an absolute ordeal, to finally be exactly where she'd dreamed of being and squander it by staring at the door lamenting her note to Cora hadn't worked.

"Ugh, Aurora, you reek of chicken," Manuela said peevishly while her friend nodded and bit into a chicken leg. "If you eat one more piece, we'll have to start checking you for feathers."

"I know." Aurora was, in an ironic twist of fate, having the most amazing night of her life. "It's delicious, and one of these lovely barmaids said she could put one in a parcel to take with me." To hear Aurora speak, one would think the chickens were made of gold. "Leona, I never knew life could be this way. I just talked about contraceptives for thirty minutes with two doctors and met an architect who had wonderful suggestions for my clinics. There is an Eden on earth, where the women wear trousers, and they serve roasted chicken." Manuela's lips twitched at the utter joy in Aurora's face.

She had noticed that much like at Cassandra's, there were a remarkable number of women walking around in trousers. Very much like the ones Cora wore that first night.

"I would love to get a pair," Aurora mused, then sent a pointed look at Manuela. "I might need you to put in a good word for me with the duchess."

Manuela frowned. "What are you talking about?"

Aurora rolled her eyes. "Do you make any conversation with the woman when you're together, or do you just stare at her with moony eyes?"

"I have never mooned," Manuela flicked her hand, but was too curious to not push for more details. "What is this trousers thing?"

"Apparently the city of Paris has had an ordinance since the Revolution requiring women request a permit to wear trousers in public." Aurora took a generous bite of her chicken. Manuela almost snatched it out of her hands, but that would not get her the information any faster. "Your duchess has been footing the bills for women to acquire these permits." *She had?* Aurora nodded, which meant Manuela must have asked the question out loud. "She has a solicitor on retainer that only manages the permits, she's gotten dozens of them."

That same fluttering she'd had when she heard about Cora procuring the food for Cassandra's dinner party started up in her chest and bad, unwise, impossible delusions cropped up in her mind. It was best to focus on something else, and fast.

"That's very kind of her. Did Frede have anything else to say about medical matters?" Yes, she was desperate enough to submit herself to one of her friend's monologues if it would distract her from thinking about Cora. But Aurora knew her too well, and simply stared blankly at her. "Fine, *I* had a lovely chat with Cassandra."

In truth she'd had quite a few stimulating conversations once she'd forced herself away from keeping guard at the entrance like an obsessed lunatic and joined Cassie's guests. Some had been at the dinner at her house, and Manuela had been eager to reconnect with them. She'd read the essay written by Frede's grandmother as she'd promised—Cora had sent her a copy by messenger the next morning, always so horridly thoughtful—and she'd been eager to discuss it.

Their conversation had been so open, so honest, that Manuela even shared some of the ideas she'd been mulling about an artists' collective. Not for herself, of course, but for Cassandra and her friends. Claudine thought it all wonderful and suggested she share them with Aristide Pasquale, which resulted in Cassandra suggesting that Manuela come with her to the academy the next day.

All in all, it was one of the most encouraging evenings she'd had since she arrived in Paris, and she could not enjoy it because a certain imperious duchess could not do her part in putting Manuela out of her misery. And it was misery: she was practically jumping out of her skin. Every black head and straight back she'd seen all evening had her heart practically galloping up her throat.

"Who exactly are you glaring at?" Aurora asked through a mouthful of something.

"At an imaginary Duchess of Sundridge. I honestly cannot believe she stood me up." She resisted the temptation of dramatically tossing herself on the empty chaise behind them, but only barely.

"But you sent her a note telling her not to bother you."

Manuela shot her friend her most withering glare. "It is called a seduction game, Aurora," she explained, abandoning all semblance of calm. She was absolutely incensed. The insolence to not respond to her note!

"So when you said you were happy to come here on your own..." Aurora began, openly teasing Manuela now, and she was too beside herself not to fall for it.

"I was clearly lying!"

A commotion on the other side of the room distracted Manuela from her impending spiral into despair. She had her back to the entrance, but Aurora's surprised gasp and the pleased smile that followed made Manuela whip around.

"Looks like someone is here for you," Aurora whispered softly, nudging her forward, but Manuela was frozen in place. Her heart skipping erratically in her chest when she finally saw her.

She opened her mouth, but nothing but air escaped as she watched the Duchess of Sundridge, looking to all the world like a surly, raven-haired Amazon, making her way across the room. She cut through the crowd with her decisive stride, without a single person daring to stand in her way.

Not for a second did she take her eyes off Manuela.

Around her, people talked, the music continued, as though Manuela wasn't experiencing the single most dramatic moment of her life. Her blood thrummed, her pulse quickening as she waited like a flimsy boat at sea, about to be capsized by the storm brewing in those violet eyes.

She was ready to be taken under.

She came, she came for me, she told herself again and again as the woman she so desperately wanted was finally in front of her. The duchess was magnificent in her ruby-red topcoat, the collar standing straight up. Her suit, the same one she'd worn this afternoon, in a striking gray-and-blue houndstooth perfectly cut. This was not a woman who walked into a room unsure of her purpose. From head to toe, the Duchess of Sundridge was a study in conviction. Cora Kemp Bristol, imposing and self-assured, was a woman who knew exactly what she was about, and tonight it seemed Manuela was finally—*thankfully*—in her crosshairs.

"Your Grace," she began, breathless and not caring. Why was Cora looking at Aurora?

"Miss Montalban, I have arranged for my driver to come back for you once he's delivered us to our destination," Cora announced in a tone that clearly left no room for argument, as she took Manuela's gloved hand.

"Thank you." Aurora nodded slowly, her usual combative manner replaced by open astonishment. It seemed even her Leona was cowed by the duchess's intensity. In her crimson coat and with those violet eyes flashing, she could've been Agamemnon sailing the Aegean Sea poised to finally conquer the Trojans...which made Manuela a very, *very* eager Troy.

"Where are we going, exactly?"

In response, Cora shot her a look that could only be described as predatory and pulled her closer so that they were flush against each other. "I'm taking you home."

Manuela's first impulse was to jump jubilantly for joy and dash to the door at a run, then she reminded herself what Cora had put them both through. She couldn't just capitulate.

"What if I don't want to go home with you?" she said disingenuously, which admittedly would've had a stronger effect had she not been pressing herself quite insistently against Cora.

"I thought I'd been summoned for that very purpose, princesa." She dared to glance up and was confronted with such wicked promise that all the air seemed to catch in her lungs.

Manuela's limbs, the traitors, immediately loosened at the word *princesa*. It was absurd how much she liked it. It almost never sounded like a compliment. It was probably what Cora called all the besotted girls she seduced...and still every time, the effect was riveting.

Manuela was no stranger to being desired. She'd spent her life being ogled and coveted by men, but it was different when the desire was reciprocated. When the person whose attention you wanted returned it with equal fervor.

"I thought we'd agreed doing this would only complicate things." Manuela tried to follow what Cora was saying, but the duchess was softly caressing her cheek with a knuckle, which made it quite difficult to come up with any thoughts that didn't involve smashing their mouths together. With effort she forced her eyes away from Cora's lips and attempted to come up with something other than begging for kisses.

"I never agreed," she retorted and allowed herself to do some of her own touching. She circled her hands around that regal neck and tried her best not to appear too much the infatuated fool. "If I recall correctly, it was more like you decreed."

"This won't make any of this easier, sweetheart," Cora warned, and she was probably right, but Manuela didn't care. Besides, she was beginning to think there was no such thing as easy. Agreeing to marry Felix had seemed like the path of least resistance, and now that future loomed above her like an albatross. She might come to regret this, but that didn't make her want it any less. In fact, she would walk through fire to get to it.

"There is no stopping this train, Corazón." She dared use the duchess's name, and her reaction was everything Manuela could have wished for. That frosty gaze melted just a touch, that beautiful, hard mouth softened. If it was up to Manuela, neither of them would stop this until there was nothing but ashes left.

She thought of Luz Alana who—much like the duchess—had always been so stoic. And yet they'd all watched as the ember of attraction she'd felt for her Scottish earl transformed into a passion so consuming she was on her way to marry the man merely days after meeting him. Luz insisted that it was all a business agreement, that they would divorce after they each received their inheritance, but one had only to observe the two of them together to see the flames engulfing them.

That was what she felt now. Manuela had ignited the fire, and Cora had arrived to stoke the flames.

"Hello, dear. I am so glad you could join." Cassandra's voice pierced through the tightly drawn silence between them, and Manuela almost cried in frustration. But whatever had been keeping Cora at a distance before had evaporated on her way here. Instead of pushing Manuela away, as she'd done at the dinner party, Cora tugged her closer, so close that her lips brushed her hair.

"I'll talk to you about invitation etiquette tomorrow, Cassandra," Cora admonished her, before pressing a quick kiss to Manuela's head and melting her in the process. "But at the moment I have some urgent business with Miss Caceres Galvan, and I am afraid we must go."

Unlike Manuela, Cassandra did indeed jump for joy. Despite knowing the folly of it, Manuela couldn't help wishing that this could be the start of something lasting. That their well-wishing friends were sending them off to the start of their great love story. "I'll look on you in the morning," she called over her shoulder, as Cora volleyed back a terse *I advise you don't* and pulled Manuela halfway across the room.

"I thought you'd be angry at me." Manuela's mouth would never learn. Cora didn't respond, her sole focus on getting them out of the room. She only stopped when they reached a door at the end of a long hallway and pulled it open, leading Manuela inside. There was a staircase heading up to what she assumed were Claudine's rooms, and there was another door on the opposite side.

Once Cora closed the door, she turned around and pressed Manuela to it. Her face was impassive, unaffected, but those smoldering eyes told a very different story. She looked down at Manuela's mouth and licked her own lips roughly. Her own breath caught, riveted by the sight of that pink tongue.

"You thought you'd get my attention with this stunt?"

She could point out that she'd succeeded, but that would probably backfire. "I've been trying to for weeks. I got impatient." She protested weakly as Cora's fingers traced something on the expanse of skin over her breasts. Her nipples pebbled into hard points in response, and every inch of clothes on her seemed to tighten all at once.

"Here I am, princess. What do you want with me?" Manuela squeezed her thighs together to abate the throbbing between them as she struggled to make words that weren't begging.

"I suppose I'm going to have to learn my lesson for disappointing your horses."

Cora laughed, a husky, enticing thing that slithered right under Manuela's skin. "That's not the lesson you need today, princesa."

Their breaths rose in unison as blood rushed to Manuela's head. Fast and hot, fogging her mind, and all she could think of was being kissed. Those lips, she wanted them on hers so badly she could feel the ghost of them. An impossible ache pulsed at her core. She was desperate for Cora's hands, her mouth.

"No?" Manuela asked, her voice reedy as Cora pushed away from her and turned to the other door.

"No," Cora echoed as she turned the doorknob and cold night air filled the room. "From now on, you *tell* me what you want. Not with little notes or pouts. Or barters."

"Tell you?" The question came out feebly, but Manuela had never felt more alive. There was enough energy buzzing inside her that she imagined she could electrify Eiffel's tower herself.

"You said you wanted to experience for yourself what women like us do in Montmartre… You are about to."

Manuela was hanging on every word out of Cora's mouth, only marginally aware that they were stepping out into the street and Cora's carriage was there waiting for them. "What will you do?"

Cora clicked her tongue, a wicked glint in her eyes. "Not only *me*, darling, *us*. You and me." Cora's voice was a seductive, dangerous whisper as her driver helped them up into the carriage. Once inside, she expected Cora to take her usual place as far away from her as possible. And she did take the banquette opposite Manuela, but this time, she sat right across from her. So close that their knees brushed every time the carriage jostled as it began its way down the hill. Her heart beat so furiously, she wondered if Cora could hear it.

The small lamps on the outside of the carriage windows lent the cavernous space inside enough light that Manuela could see the duchess's face. This was the Cora from that first night, languid and hedonistic. With a glint in her eyes that spoke of long nights of pleasure and the darkest of deeds. Manuela could only hold on to the velvet upholstery of the seats as butterflies swerved madly in her belly.

"I didn't think you wanted me anymore," Manuela confessed, much too aroused to place any kind of restriction on her admissions.

The sound of Cora's laugh cracked through the small space like lightning. She shook her head, an expression of disbelief on her beautiful face. "Want you?" Cora sounded almost outraged. She'd kept her coat unbuttoned, and it was spread over the seat in dark pools of red. Her mouth set in a vicious expression, readying herself to make quick work of what was left of Manuela's virtue. If her teeth could unclench, she would've sneered at just how wrong the Greeks had gotten it.

Hades…could only be a woman.

"Do you know that you've made a liar out of me, princesa?"

"A liar?" Manuela gulped, as she fisted the frothy fabric of her dress to keep from reaching out.

Cora nodded, leaning close enough to slide slender fingers down Manuela's face, her neck, her chest. "I've spent the last ten years ensuring that my work and my desires never cross. I have striven to harden myself to anything that could veer me off the path I set for myself. I was convinced I'd achieved it." She gave a sardonic laugh at that bit and pressed in so close that their faces were merely inches apart. "And you," she breathed out, her fingers curving around Manuela's chin, the side of one rubbing delicious circles on her skin. "You, Manuela, have dropped into my life like a cyclone, and I have not known peace since." She whimpered, she couldn't help it. "These lips." Cora ghosted her mouth over Manuela's as she spoke, making her tremble. "I dream of kissing them, of licking inside. I dream of watching them slide down my body. Of watching you taste me."

"Ah..." The choked gasp escaped her lips, and Manuela had to bite her tongue to keep from moaning.

"Your neck," Cora's hand drifted down, the tip of her nail softly scoring Manuela's sensitive skin, "I want to bite into it, suckle that soft, velvety skin until I leave you marked with my hunger." Manuela pressed her feet onto the floor of the carriage, as she fought for purchase. "I've lain awake at night wondering what it would be like to bury my face between your breasts. Lash my tongue over your nipples and watch them tighten. Suckle them until I hear you cry out for me." Both her hands were there now, grazing softly over Manuela's décolletage, cupping the underside of her breasts until they were lifted high enough Cora had only but to lower her face a fraction of an inch and she could take one in her mouth.

"Please," Manuela begged, a shaky puff of air escaping her lips. Cora made a *tsk* sound, her firm, gloved fingers sliding down Manuela's bodice to her waist. She gripped her for a moment and then continued her journey south until her hands were at the juncture of her thighs. A low, appreciative sound came out of the duchess as her thumbs caressed Manuela.

"This is the prize for all those sleepless nights," she whispered, her mouth against Manuela's ear. "This is where I plan to spend an age, tasting, nibbling, suckling... Has anyone done that to you?"

Manuela's body went molten, her thoughts sluggish from arousal. "No," she confessed, feeling shy and terribly inexperienced at that moment. She knew about this kind of caress, had read about it, even seen art depicting it.

She'd never done it, but she'd dreamed of it. Spent hours touching herself as she fantasized about how it would feel for a tongue to explore such a secret, private place. "But I want it," she rushed to confess, beyond pride.

"Mm, I promise to make it good for you. Perhaps I'll start right here," Cora's index finger was now making circles over that place that throbbed with need. "Do you ever touch yourself there? Slide your fingers inside and relieve that throbbing ache?"

She did. She had, many times in the past two weeks, thinking about Cora. Wishing it were the pads of her fingers rubbing that perfect spot, that it was this woman's making her fall apart.

"I've done it thinking about you."

The groan that escaped Cora's throat was pure sin. Something hot and starved unfurled in Manuela in response to it. The duchess leaned back and shot her another of those sultry looks. "Do you still think I don't want you?" Manuela shook her head, ready to come out of her skin.

"Good," Cora said approvingly, leaning further away, eyes heavily lidded. She seemed remarkably calm, while Manuela shook like a leaf. It was impossible to say anything coherent in that moment, so she decided to watch the other woman. She noticed that though the duchess might appear in control at first glance, when she slid a hand over her lapel it shook, just a little. That there was a tightness in her jaw indicating she might also be struggling with maintaining control. When she spoke, she was looking out the window. "I intend to carry out every single one of the things I just promised to you the moment I get you behind closed doors."

"That's exactly what I hoped for," Manuela whispered, without hesitation into the semidarkness as lust crawled deep in her bones and a frantic sort of greed enveloped her. She wanted to pounce on this woman, sit astride her lap, make her as disheveled and undone on the outside as she made Manuela feel on the inside. She was imagining herself ripping every button on Cora's shirt and kissing every inch of skin she exposed when Cora spoke again.

"There is the matter of our arrangement. Whatever happens tonight won't change what we agreed on."

In the recesses of her brain where rational thinking still occurred, the word *arrangement* seemed to register, and Manuela nodded. "Nothing will change."

She had signed that contract, and she intended to honor it, but she understood what Cora was truly saying. There was no future for them, nothing beyond what they could have in the next few weeks. And Manuela would take it. This was what she'd been looking for after all, something impersonal and fleeting, nothing more. She'd already sold her *more* in exchange for never risking being left with nothing again.

But tonight, in the Duchess of Sundridge's bed, she intended to have absolutely everything.

Fifteen

"Send a tray of refreshments to my sitting room, Laurent." Cora had barely managed to get her coat and hat off before pressing a hand to Manuela's lower back and practically running into the house. "And tell Juliette that I won't need her tonight. I am not to be disturbed until I call for breakfast."

"Of course," the stoic man said, as if this wasn't the first time she'd ever brought a woman home in the decade they'd been in Paris.

"This way." Cora ushered a quiet Manuela to her rooms. She'd been subdued in the last few minutes of the ride, but now she was very alert, looking around the room with open curiosity.

"Is that Celia Castro's work?" she asked, demanding Cora's attention as they made their way down the hallway leading to her rooms.

Cora stopped, smiling at Manuela's weakness for a pretty painting. Even when the urgency to get this woman into her bed was practically propelling her across the house, she was charmed. Manuela didn't just appreciate art, she was fueled by it. There wasn't a painting or a sculpture, she didn't give her full attention once she was in front of it. Even at the Rapp Gallery when she'd been so disappointed by their treatment of her work, she'd patiently perused every piece with Cora. Made observations, answered questions. Manuela was irreverent in almost every way, but she had deep respect for artists and their work. Cora, in turn, respected that quality in her.

"Her shadow work is truly exquisite."

"Sweetheart," Cora whispered, before leaning in to kiss the bare apple of her shoulder, "I cannot overstate how enticing I find your passion for art." She let her tongue flick over the place she'd kissed, eliciting a delicious shiver from Manuela. The reaction made Cora's own body respond intensely. Her hands shook with the need to touch more. "But right now, you cannot expect me to reasonably carry any conversation that doesn't involve the quickest way to get you out of all these clothes." There was a giggle and then a sweet little moan when Cora nibbled softly on that beautiful brown skin.

"Won't someone catch us?" Manuela asked, not quite concealing her eagerness, as she offered more of her neck for Cora to kiss.

"We won't see another human until I call for them," Cora assured her, before lowering her mouth to the pulse point at the base of Manuela's throat and sliding her tongue over the dip there. "In fact, I could undress you right here in this hallway, and no one would know."

"But surely they could hear us," princess persisted, her breaths coming in quick, agitated spurts now.

"You like the idea of my maid hearing you scream for me, princess?" Another one of those delicious moans escaped Manuela, making Cora's head spin. God but she was everything she'd ever dreamed of. "Mm, this is not how I imagined bedding a duchess would be." Cora paused at that and lifted her gaze to Manuela's face. The smile on her princess's lips practically shouted *Debauch me!*

Cora gently pushed her against the wall and leaned in to kiss the valley between her breasts, her tongue dipping into that warmth. "That's because you're about to bed a miner's daughter, querida."

Manuela's mouth tipped up sinfully, leaning lazily between two paintings. "Oh, now I'm intrigued."

Cora licked into her mouth, languidly tangling her tongue with Manuela's, before pulling back so she could unhook her bodice. "I want them in my mouth," she whispered, feeling that sweet tug of desire between her thighs. Once Manuela's breasts were free, she cupped them with her hands, pushing them together. She lashed the tight brown tips of her nipples with her tongue, all the while looking up at the heiress, who had the back of her head pressed to the wall, her bruised lips parted as the most delicious little sounds escaped them.

"Beautiful, the feel of them in my hands." Cora tightened her fingers, as Manuela pressed further against her. "How can a face like an angel's make me want to do such wicked things?" Cora asked, making her laugh. That sound, it was like the first rain after months of drought. She wanted to be the cause of it. Have her kisses, her touch draw them out enough that she memorized it. "I want to do exquisitely depraved things to you." A fluttering of eyelashes, and then those molten brown eyes focused on her.

"Yes, please." Cora would, God, she would spend hours lost in her.

They worked together to undo what felt like hundreds of skirts until the heiress was down to her combination. Finally Cora could reach between the slit of Manuela's garment. Her breath caught as her fingers encountered that slippery warmth. She parted the mound of curls and ran the pad of her fingers down the wet seam.

"Mm, Cora," her princess moaned, her hips pressing into the caress.

"You're so hot and swollen for me," she whispered, searching for that tight little pearl. When she found it and rubbed a tight circle over it, Manuela let out a hoarse scream, already shaking with pleasure. "Mm, yes, you like that," Cora said, mouth pressed to Manuela's neck, her teeth grazing the skin. "Come for me." She gasped, sliding two fingers into that velvety channel, all the while tangling her tongue with Manuela's.

"I'm going to fall apart," Manuela said, voice tight. Cora pressed their mouths together and kissed her hard enough to draw blood, pinching that bundle of nerves at the same time. Manuela's climax rushed through her in the next instant, her body stiffening, her screams of pleasure flowing into Cora's mouth.

Her body was so soft. Cora wanted to drown in her. Touch her until her hands knew Manuela's body as her own. "You needed that sweetheart," she said softly, her hands still roaming over every inch of exposed skin she could find. Feeling the need to touch, to feel this woman's body that she'd craved so fiercely. Even as she realized that having her once had only made her need that much stronger.

Manuela nodded in response, even as she took Cora's head between her hands and kissed her deeply, a fervent, rough kiss that she could do nothing but lose herself in. Her princess was hungrier now. The shyness at their arrival replaced with powerful need.

"Take me to your room," she begged, between biting kisses. "I want to see you. I want to touch you too."

Cora was in the wind, floating in the gusts of this woman. It was always going to be this way. Cora capitulating to this hunger, walking into her own undoing with her eyes wide open. She could already feel it, the craving for more of what Manuela made her feel already at work, eroding her defenses.

"This way," she said in defiance to her own common sense as she took Manuela by the hand. Even a month ago this would've been unthinkable. Cora had never allowed anyone in her bedchamber after Sally. Had never even been tempted, and here she was pulling Manuela into her most private space. "Here it is." She let Manuela go in first and hung behind, the blood rushing to her temples as she waited for the reaction.

"Cora, this…" Manuela's voice drifted as she looked around the room. The wall that looked out onto the garden was almost all glass, giving a lovely view of the illuminated city at night. Eiffel's tower shone in the distance. Cora's heart hammered, suddenly feeling quite vulnerable to be revealing her secrets. "This is so…" The heiress began again, as she turned in circles, adorable in just her linen combination, taking in the room, and Cora came up behind her, wrapping her arms around her. Anxious, but wanting the other woman too much to stay away.

"Eye-wateringly pink?" she finally said in a self-mocking tone, making Manuela laugh with delight. She was unreasonably nervous about this. What did she care what Manuela thought about her rooms? She'd done them this way to please herself. There wasn't a single opinion besides hers that mattered, and yet her heart felt like a fist as she waited.

"It is an explosion of pink," Manuela retorted, eyes wide and bright, but still not saying what she really thought. Cora's bedchamber was large. It took up almost a quarter of the space of her floor in the house. This was her sanctuary, decorated and outfitted to her exact taste, and other than the housekeeper, her lady's maid, Cassie and Tia Osiris, no one had ever entered it, not even Alfie.

"I was expecting a very sober room with dark colors," Manuela admitted, turning to face Cora, beaming. "This is so much better."

"Are you teasing me?" Cora asked, feigning offense.

"Teasing you?" She looked absolutely horrified at the suggestion, and something in Cora's chest pulsed with a feeling that had gotten her in awfully hot water at another time in her life. "I don't think I've ever seen something so absolutely magical.

That chair is made of pink damask!" She pointed excitedly at one of the two armchairs in front of the fireplace. Another one of those very tight coils inside Cora loosened at Manuela's obvious admiration.

How would she get herself back in order…after?

She had always cultivated an image of restraint and moderation. In her dress and in her manner. She made sure she was always dressed finely, not a hair out of place, but in no way giving an inkling of her inner self. She spent her life in hiding, in many ways even from those closest to her. But in this place, she was just Corazón. She'd never known sharing it with someone could make her feel so replete.

"I think," she finally said, her arms still wrapped around Manuela's waist, "I'd like to have a taste of you while you sit in one of my chairs."

She'd brought the large wingbacks from Benedict's household and had had them reupholstered in a dark fuchsia. Manuela was looking at them like they were Queen Victoria's throne. "Only since you seem to like them so much." Manuela made an urgent, needy sound, pressing her delicious rump against Cora.

"I'd like that." Without hesitation the stepped out of her combination and stood there gloriously naked for Cora's view. Manuela was so eager, so unabashedly honest in her desires. It was addictive; it was impairing. She could barely think straight.

"But all your clothes are still on," Manuela protested weakly, as she dropped into the plush pink chair like a hedonistic empress. Her brown skin flushed with a tint of pink, her heavy breasts swaying as her breaths got shorter. Her belly was soft and just below was that thatch of reddish-brown curls concealing that hidden treasure Cora could barely wait to taste.

"I suppose they are." Cora looked down at herself almost in surprise. She was still fully dressed, but the need to possess Manuela was so consuming, she couldn't concern herself with that. Manuela looked like one of the maidens from Cora's fresco. Ripe and luscious and eager to be pleasured. "I can't be bothered with clothes, princesa," she told Manuela, going down to her knees.

In most areas of her life she preferred order. She liked her home, her business, her staff, her domain neat and predictable. But with a lover, in a bed, she reveled in the delicious chaos of it all. If there was one thing she'd learned, it was that pleasure tore off the mask. For those short seconds when the only thing that mattered was reaching for that instant of glory, there was no posturing, no pretending, there was nothing but frantic, raw need, and Cora very much enjoyed being the one whose hands, mouth, tongue could give that gift to another. She took great satisfaction in pulling at all the threads that held them together. Was endlessly gratified to see a lover slump back on the mattress utterly wrung out, a blissful smile on their lips. The difference was that tonight, with Manuela, Cora was unraveling too.

She palmed the satiny back of Manuela's well-formed calves, and slid her hands up them, feeling the taut muscles. "Strong," she whispered admiringly, before licking up a long line from a well-shaped ankle to the underside a knee.

"I like to take long walks on the beach," Manuela explained, with a little shiver.

Cora pulled those firm legs apart and kissed the inside of her thigh.

"You are infuriatingly tempting," she whispered against that warm skin and smiled when she heard a small huff of laughter.

"My apologies, Your Grace." She didn't sound sorry at all, and that irreverent cheekiness was fully back in Manuela's voice. In retribution, Cora took some of that supple skin in between her teeth. Manuela's moan was accompanied by a sweet little hiss as the heiress widened her legs.

"Can I look?" Cora asked, her hands skating upward until she was right at the juncture of Manuela's thighs. The coarse hairs brushed the tops of her fingers. She let the pad of one drift up the slick furrow, feeling that wet heat engulfing her finger.

Manuela gasped and tilted her hips in a silent demand, her teeth snagging her bottom lip. "Oh, but this is lovely," Cora crooned, pressing kisses all along Manuela's thighs until she reached the place that had been haunting her dreams for weeks. She used two fingers to spread open the beautiful, dewy folds of soft pinks, deep purples, and browns, then lifted her eyes. That mouth, red and sweet like the ripest berry. Those bountiful breasts, a feast.

Cora thought of Manuela's painting of her flowers. The women with flowers blooming from their bodies, with petals sprouting from those most private places, and smiled even as the tip of her tongue licked the seam of that perfect place. This woman was a garden, rich, plentiful, nourishing. Food to satiate Cora's yawning hunger, water to quench her deepest thirst.

"I want to consume you," she murmured, her lips parted at the very core of Manuela's body. There was a little cloudy drop of liquid gathered right under her clitoris, and Cora swiped it with her tongue, before popping the finger in her mouth. Manuela moaned, her hands moving to grip the armrests of the chair.

"Do what you promised, Corazón."

Cora froze. No one had ever uttered her name—the name her mother had given her—at a moment like this. No lover had ever known it, never mind been allowed to use it. But this heiress with her smudged fingers and her open smiles that hid so much had managed to penetrate the most guarded corners of Cora's world.

"What exactly did I promise?" she asked, her eyes locked on the pink little bud. She flicked it with her finger, rubbed circles on it, her skin buzzing with need to see Manuela undone again. Cora lifted her gaze, her eyes snagging on her lush curves.

"You promised you'd taste me, make me cry out," Manuela said, flushed, her nipples erect from her arousal. Cora wondered if she'd run out of time before she could have her fill.

"I did, didn't I?" Cora teased, as her thumbs caressed the inner folds, eliciting a delicious shiver from Manuela. "I told you I'd feast on you." She lifted the hood and blew a puff of cool air on the sensitive little peak. Manuela threw her head back and groaned, her wide hips circling into the caress. Cora looked at her in wonder. She could never fully let go, even when she was absorbed in another, she always needed to be in control, but Manuela sank into the pleasure she was being given without reservation. Her body open and her eyes closed as she rode the sensations.

And the sounds she made. Little clicks of the tongue and gasps, as her hands reached for purchase. Every movement saying *Give me more, satisfy me*, and nothing had ever felt more necessary than to give this woman everything she asked for.

"I think honey," Cora whispered, as her fingers glided over the smooth inner labia of Manuela. "That's what you taste like." She pressed her nose to the mound, inhaling the scent that was uniquely hers. This had always been the place of her wildest desires, this earthy, dewy, fragrant, soft and powerful place.

"Have me," her lover asked, her hand cupping the back of Cora's head and bringing her in. She ran the tip of her tongue along the seam, her eyes locked with Manuela's. She used her fingers to pluck her open and invaded. She lapped roughly at the engorged clitoris and her princess's eyes widened before screwing shut. Little gusts of air escaping her lips as her muscles tightened with her oncoming climax. The whimpers that escaped Manuela detonated an explosion of tingles and shivers all over Cora's body. Her own core throbbed, needy and wet, but she was enthralled by this woman. She held her open and ate at her as Manuela's cries echoed in the room.

"I adore your mouth," her princess purred, urging Cora on. "Faster, oh!" her lover gasped, as she slid two fingers inside, massaging those slick inner walls even as she swirled her tongue. Manuela's breaths grew harsher, and her thighs began to shake.

"Corazón, Corazón, Corazón." One strong pull on her sensitive clitoris, with her fingers buried inside her, and Manuela was shouting her orgasm, back arching and her head thrown back. "Oh, yes, yes," she muttered, her head tipped back, a beatific expression on her face.

Cora's breaths were ragged as she pressed kisses to her lover's inner thighs. This woman, this body, all of a sudden felt sacred. Like being the one who got to do this for Manuela, with Manuela, was a higher purpose. Not for the pleasure of it, but for the bond, the connection. For an absurd moment, Cora imagined herself on her knees worshipping right here. A supplicant between these supple limbs, a devoted servant of this princess's pleasure.

A long, satisfied sigh from above brought her out of her sex-addled thoughts, making her lift her head to the smiling goddess on her fuchsia throne. Manuela's arms were over her eyes, her lips tipped up in a very sated expression.

Aphrodite in the flesh.

"Did I fulfill my promises?" Cora asked before swiping her tongue over Manuela's navel. In the next moment, bright brown eyes caught Cora's own.

"Is it possible for one's brain to stop working?" she asked, perfectly serious. "I think you broke mine, Your Grace," she quipped as she slid off the chair. Cora scuttled back to give her space, and soon they were kneeling in front of each other. Manuela's face was devastatingly open and happy as she reached for Cora. Without hesitation she licked into her mouth, hungrily taking, tongue sliding in so sweetly, her hands holding on as she ravished Cora. Teeth nipping, scoring skin, possessing. What a conquering this kiss was, swift and unstoppable.

This was not how she thought things would unfold. She should be in control, she was the more experienced one, after all. But what Manuela lacked in sophistication she made up with enthusiasm. There was no smooth seduction dance, no coy whispers. Manuela was rolling thunder, loud and shattering. Cora could only hold on as this force of nature passed through her.

"Mm," she groaned, as she slid her mouth up to Cora's earlobe and snagged it between her teeth. "Is that me?" she asked in a husky whisper, even as she slid her hands down Cora's back to her bum and squeezed. "That briny taste in your mouth?"

"Yes," Cora sighed, shivering at the delicious things Manuela was doing to her ear.

"I want to do it to you," the heiress said, turning her face again to take Cora's mouth. "I want to put my tongue inside you." She sounded as breathless as Cora felt, and her hands were everywhere. Tugging at clothes, fussing with buttons. "If you don't help me undress you, I am going to rip these off you."

"Good God, are you an octopus?" Cora teased, as what felt like ten different hands worked on buttons and fastenings. In the next moment she was being toppled back and kissed senseless.

"I want to *see* you." Manuela emphasized the request by kissing Cora's ears, her nose, her forehead. Licking her neck, even as those nimble fingers made quick work of her jacket. From one breath to the next, the energy seemed to tip, and Cora was no longer the hunter but the prey.

Her island princess was fully on the prowl now, and Cora for once decided to let go.

Manuela was a madwoman.

What Cora had given her had been life-altering. She'd never thought she could be so fully in her body as she'd been when Cora made love to her. Every kiss, every caress was electric, shocking in the pleasure it brought her. It felt so natural to be like this, so utterly right.

Manuela had not expected that.

Even in the moments when she'd been frantic from wanting Cora, she never expected it to feel so…vital. Like her body was finally being used the way it was meant to be. Like the pulls and levers of her were built for Cora's hand, and she was being unlocked with every touch, and now she wanted to do the same for her duchess. She was crazed with the need to make this woman, who could seem so cold but made love like a lioness, feel as cherished.

"You are like a lamprey!" Cora cried as Manuela straddled her, but her tone was not one of protest. There was a lightness in her eyes, a looseness in her limbs, that made a wellspring of tenderness bubble up inside Manuela. They were on the rug in front of the roaring fireplace, and the flickering flames cast Cora's face in gold. She looked like one of the women in her paintings. So exquisite Manuela's heart skipped.

"You look like you were dipped in gold," she told her and leaned down to kiss the apple of her cheeks where the light flickered in a particularly striking way.

"The way you look at me," Cora said and pressed a hand to her stomach.

"I want you," she said, hoarsely.

"Then, have me, princesa." She could not bear another second of seeing Cora in all those clothes.

"Skin!" she exclaimed in triumph as she managed to rip off Cora's tie and unbuttoned her vest. "Aurora is right, fashion is the first line of defense for women's oppression," she groused, making Cora laugh. "You must sit for me, I need to draw you," she said, quietly, sliding a finger down the side of Cora's face. Tracing those sharp cheekbones and stubborn jaw.

"I am not a very good sitter. I fidget too much." Cora smiled ruefully, pressing her face into Manuela's touch, then playfully taking one of Manuela's fingers between her teeth. She laughed, even as her stomach clenched with something new and scary, something she could not allow to take root. Survival, for her, for her parents, depended on keeping the rules as they'd set them. She distracted herself with undoing more buttons. Cora's own hands gripped Manuela's hips, fingers digging in as more and more skin was revealed.

"My challenge will be to make it so you are nice and relaxed for the sitting, then," she said suggestively, making Cora chuckle again. It was a sound she'd never heard before. Not that harsh, sardonic laugh from their luncheon, or even the warm but aloof one from their dinner parties. This was lusty and slightly addled. This was amorous, languid Cora, and despite herself, Manuela fell even deeper.

After the vest was pulled away and the tie tossed aside, the blouse was next, exposing more of that taut olive skin. Manuela was plump, her bottom and her breasts full and generous. Cora was rangy and slim, her breasts tight and firm. A body that seemed as practical as the woman it belonged to. There was also a restless energy to Cora. Her eyes always calculating. Windows to a mind that was constantly racing. But tonight, there was a serenity in those violet eyes. Knowing she was partly the reason for it broke Manuela open.

I've traded away so much, but this is my prize, she thought, and as she flicked the buttons on the chemise, she leaned down to place a kiss on her lover's lips.

You are my prize, Corazón.

"I don't know what to kiss first," she laughed, tweaking sensitive nipples.

"I have a few suggestions," Cora groaned, as she dipped one of those clever fingers inside Manuela. She rocked into the pleasure climbing up her limbs in seconds. Manuela let Cora explore her, a thumb circling her clitoris, a finger pushing in and out of her heat as she occupied herself with running her hands over every inch of visible skin.

Once every piece of clothing was pulled to the side and every button and hook had been undone, Manuela descended on Cora, ravenously. She pressed biting kisses to that slender neck, licked down the valley between the perky breasts, stopping to give each one a long, hungry kiss. She licked into Cora's navel, all the while feeling those long limbs scissoring under her.

"Are you hot and bothered, Your Grace?" she asked, as she

pushed up the obtrusive skirts. Thankfully Cora was a much more sensible dresser than Manuela, and there were only two layers to reckon with between herself and what she was searching for.

"I am getting impatient," Cora protested, a mix of humor and desire visible on her beautiful face.

"Well, we can't have that. What kind of guest would I be if I made my hostess wait?" Manuela muttered as she pulled up the chemise to Cora's waist. She didn't hesitate and positioned herself right at the apex of Cora's thighs. "May I?"

"If you only would," Cora answered tightly, but there was a breathy sigh at the end and that was all she needed. Her thumbs parted the rosy lips to get a look. She sucked in a breath at the sight. She'd never seen anyone else this close. She knew what *she* looked like. Aurora had lectured her enough times in the importance of being at ease with her intimate parts, and Manuela had heeded her advice to look at herself with a mirror, but she'd never seen another. Cora was beautiful, the textures and scent of her so similar and yet singularly hers.

"This is marvelous," Manuela praised, admiring her lover in the light of the fire.

"I don't think I've ever heard it called that," Cora gasped, as Manuela ran her thumb over the inner labia and felt the supple skin there that was slippery and silky all at once.

"Just like a perfectly juicy mamey," she smiled, emotion suddenly closing her throat. She pressed her lips to that secret place and slid her tongue over the length of it. The smell of Cora, salty, like the earth, like the sea, like everything that held life. She flicked the stiff red peak at the very top and felt Cora stiffen before a tortured little moan escaped her.

She wanted to please this woman, to unravel her. To see this duchess, who had made herself so hard—who the world had toughened—melt. "Quiero darte placer," Manu whispered and licked inside again. She suckled on delicate skin and let her fingers play. Soon Cora's climax rushed through her, her back bowing on the rug, her violet eyes burning Manuela, as a reedy sigh escaped her lips.

After, Manuela kissed her way back up Cora's body, leaving a wet trail along her belly, her breasts and neck until she reached a sweet, smiling mouth. The duchess's face was soft, no tight lines around her mouth, no furrows in her brow.

"You are hell on my plans, Manuela Caceres," she said, reaching for her.

"I am a bit of a disrupter," Manuela admitted, pressing a smiling kiss to Cora's mouth.

"What am I going to do with you?" the duchess groaned, wrapping her arms around Manuela, and her heart kicked up into a frantic staccato. Absurd things flew through her mind at the question, and she pushed them down as far as they could go. She could have this now, if she kept her head. There was no future here, but there was *now*.

Now could be as good as she made it.

Manuela moved up until she was straddling Cora again and ran her hands up that beautiful, bronzed skin.

"I am not sure what your plans for me are, Your Grace," she teased, "But I am not leaving this room until I've gotten to lie on that birthday-cake bed of yours."

"This is why I don't let anyone in my rooms," Cora said ruefully, as she lifted herself up to sitting. She kissed Manuela again, deeply, ravenously, and after a long moment, pulled away. "I guess you'll have to spend the night, then. I can't send you home under the cover of darkness."

Manuela nodded in agreement, turning away to hide her very pleased smile. "You know best, Your Grace."

Sixteen

"Are you certain you don't need my help serving the food, Your Grace?"

"It's quite all right, Marie," Cora insisted as she lifted the lid of one of the platters on the small table in her sitting room. "This smells divine," she praised as the scent of freshly baked bread and fried bacon wafted up. Marie nodded in confusion, clearly at a loss over Cora's sudden enthusiasm regarding food. She was notorious for being indifferent when it came to her nourishment and most mornings missed breakfast entirely, and she *never* took it in her rooms. Today, not only was she famished, but she'd called for it to be served in her sitting room…for two. She bit back a smile thinking of the reason for her mighty appetite this morning.

The luscious, wanton reason who was currently splendidly naked and curled up in the bedchamber. Cora tightened the sash of her robe a bit tighter and grinned at the befuddled maid.

"If I need anything else I will ring," she instructed the girl, then tipped her head in the direction of the door when she remained frozen in place.

"Of course, Your Grace." Only after a none-too-discreet peek at Cora's closed bedchamber doors did Marie finally leave the room.

"Do send the footman with the bag when he returns," Cora called, but Marie was already gone. Mostly likely on her way downstairs to report on everything she'd seen while delivering the food, including Cora's orders to send for a change of clothes for Manuela. The mistress's unusual morning would be enough gossip to keep her house staff buzzing for the rest of the week.

Typically, this was the kind of thing that would send her on a rampage reminding her employees they were paid as generously as they were in order to ensure their restraint when it came to discussing Cora's comings and goings. Today she couldn't be bothered. And to be perfectly fair, this morning had been quite out of the ordinary. For one, it was almost eight and Cora was still in her dressing gown instead of on her way back from her morning ride in the Bois de Boulogne. For another, she had an unannounced guest...in her bedroom. Something which had not occurred since...well, ever.

A frisson of unease snaked up her spine at that thought. Not because she worried about any gaffes from her staff but because she was stepping over lines in the sand that had served her well for a long time now.

But the last time she'd done this, she thought she was falling in love. That last time, Sally pretended to be falling in love back. With Manuela, the cards were all on the table. This was no fairy tale. This was two practical women acquiescing to a mutual desire with the full knowledge that there was no possibility beyond a few weeks of very enjoyable evenings. More than enjoyable. She had to admit, even if only to herself, that Manuela had been right to push her.

She'd needed this.

"Sentimentality is not your strong suit, Cora," she told herself as she poured some coffee into a cup before heading to the bedchamber doors. Anticipation itched under her skin as she turned the handle and was welcomed by a sight that could not be called anything but decadent.

"I was wondering where you'd gone to," her bedmate protested from the middle of the bed. She was still naked but was clutching the white sheets over her breasts in an attempt at modesty. Cora leaned on the doorway, admiring all that toasted-almond skin. Manuela's hair was down now, a mass of cinnamon curls cascading down her back and chest. Her eyes smudged with a hint of kohl. Cora was sorely tempted to drop the cup of coffee on the carpet and crawl under the covers to have another taste of her.

"I brought you coffee," she offered instead, raising the porcelain cup.

"You are an angel," Manuela said, disappointingly extending only one hand for it.

Instead of handing over the coffee, as she'd intended, Cora took a small sip of it and shook her head. "This is very fine coffee, sweetheart. The best in Paris. I'm going to need an incentive to part with it." She made sure to be very clear of what she meant by *incentive* when she directed her gaze to Manuela's chest. It took a moment, but the vixen soon caught up to the bribe.

"That is pure extortion, Your Grace, and I would know," she said with a wink, even as she let the sheet fall and leaned back on her hands, giving Cora a perfect view of her breasts and lower still.

"That's much better," she said approvingly, her mouth suddenly dry as walked over to the bed.

"I have my own requirement too," Manuela informed her as she took the coffee. She had a sip of the drink with her eyes fixed on Cora then made a circle in the air with her finger. "No robes allowed in this bed." That advisement was delivered with a particularly heated glance over the rim of the cup that pulled hard at Cora's core.

"I'm not usually keen on others setting rules in my domain," she said, undoing the sash on her robe, before letting it slide off her body. The heavily embroidered silk fell with a whoosh by her feet as Manuela watched her heatedly. "Happy?" she asked, raising an eyebrow. Her own hair was down too. Unlike Manuela, hers was very straight and dark and hung down her back in a thick ebony curtain. She usually put it in a braid, but this morning there had been no time.

"Very happy," Manuela answered, tipping her head back to drink the last of her coffee before stretching to place the empty cup on the table beside the bed. The movement exposed more of her skin, revealing that triangle of kinky curls that made Cora's mouth water. Manuela's eyes never left Cora's body. Without a word she planted her hands flat on the mattress, lifting that delectable, round bottom in the air.

"They brought breakfast," she said, as Manuela roamed the length of the bed to her. "It's in the sitting room."

"That's not what I'm hungry for," the heiress answered as she reached Cora at the foot of the bed.

She couldn't resist sliding her own hand over the curves of Manuela's back until she reached that plump bottom and took a handful. "What are you hungry for, then?" she asked breathlessly, as her lover kissed her way up, planting gentle kisses on the knee resting on the bed, the inside of her legs. She lifted her gaze as she licked the juncture of Cora's thighs and palmed her crotch.

"I want this," Manuela tightened her hand right there, tugging at the thatch of hair, before lowering her head. "Can I have it?" she asked, and the friction of her mouth right there, was enough to make Cora shake with need.

"It's all yours," she murmured, and the request suddenly felt much larger than the moment. Nothing was simple with Manuela, and even when she wasn't asking, Cora wanted to give her more. Manuela's tongue when it pierced her was hot and slick.

She lapped the length of Cora's furrow, until she reached that engorged point. Her hands were more certain this morning as she pulled Cora's legs apart and with two fingers spread her folds until she was completely exposed.

"I could spend a day right here," she whispered, before diving in. A choked cry escaped Cora's lips at the savage pleasure being wrung out of her. Her insides melted while she strove to press herself into Manuela's hungry mouth.

"Dios mio, Manuela," she groaned, gripping that brown head as teeth, tongue and lips ravished her. The orgasm when it came was abrupt and shattering. Pummeling her, turning her limbs to mush.

"Mm," Manuela moaned as if she could taste Cora's climax. Her tongue rolled around Cora's clitoris again. After a few more chaste kisses to Cora's labia and some ridiculously sweet little cat licks, Manuela finally turned blazing brown eyes on her.

"Heavenly," she declared, before slowly sucking on her fingers one by one while Cora watched, transfixed. "May I please have another?"

Cora pounced. In seconds she had a giggling Manuela on her back as she straddled her hips.

"I thought breakfast was going to get cold," her princess teased as Cora pushed one of her legs back.

"I'm not done with you yet, Señorita Caceres Galvan," Cora warned, burning for her again. "I'd like to try something with you," she said and pushed two fingers into Manuela, who in response let her legs fall further open, her eyes closing in apparent bliss.

"Please," she moaned as Cora fucked in and out a few times, watching her lover's face go slack with pleasure. Cora let her fingers slide out then lifted herself up until their groins were lined up, their folds gliding against each other deliciously. Only when she was at the perfect angle did she rock forward. Manuela's eyes flew open comically.

"What—" she began, but the question quickly became a series of hot, frantic sounds when Cora began moving against her again, the friction making currents of pleasure explode inside her.

"Oh, that's wicked," Manuela moaned as their thrusts fell into perfect rhythm.

"Pinch your breasts, sweetheart," Cora demanded circling her hips into Manuela's.

"Mm, yes," she gasped as she worried brown nipples between her fingers. She pressed the back of her head into the mattress, the cords of her neck tight as she seemed to hit a particularly pleasurable spot. "I'm—" she broke off as her back arched off the mattress. Her top teeth snagging on her bottom lip as she shook with pleasure.

"Come for me, preciosa," Cora said hotly, feeling her own orgasm crawling up her spine. A second later Manuela cried out, and she tumbled down right after her.

Eventually they came out of the room and breakfasted. Manuela enjoyed her food, and Cora could not stop staring as she ate breakfast, naked as a babe.

"Are you certain you don't want one of my robes?" she asked as the heiress walked around the sitting room wearing absolutely nothing.

"No," she said with a very impish smile. "Unless you want me to."

Cora sipped on her coffee and shook her head. "This is the best view I've had in years."

Manuela, who was standing in front of one of Cora's art pieces, turned her head and shot her a dubious look. "I seriously doubt that."

Cora laughed before standing up and going to Manuela, instinctively placing a kiss on a naked shoulder.

"This is quite something," Manuela said, as they both looked at the small painting on Cora's wall.

"It's called *L'Origine du monde*," Cora told her, and Manuela grunted in response. The image was of a torso. Only a single breast, belly and pubic area of the model were visible. It was shocking in its explicitness. Such a rather coarse close-up view of such an intimate part of the body. The patch of dark curls, the pink labia below and the milky skin of the buttocks. Cora had purchased it in jest some years back but had grown strangely attached to it. It was a very pointed reminder of who she was, of the desires—ones that even as she contorted herself for a world that wanted to obscure her—she never denied.

"A man did it, of course," Manuela commented, her head turned at an angle as she examined it.

Cora hid her grin on Manuela's neck and nodded. "It was a man," her voice muffled as she spoke. "Gustave Courbet. He painted it in 1866. It was a great scandal at the time, but I only acquired it a few years ago," Cora explained. She wondered how Manuela would paint the same subject and found herself very eager to see it. Then she berated herself for her foolishness. After a long moment Manuela turned around, her face eager.

"Let me sketch you."

Cora raised an eyebrow, her eyes still on the painting, and Manuela grinned. "Not just those parts of you," she said cheekily, then slid a hand down between them and cupped Cora. "Although, it can't be overstated how much I look forward to getting much more acquainted with them."

Hot arousal shot through Cora as Manuela caressed her possessively. This girl, this woman, taking from her like this. No one in Paris would dare do this, but this princess helped herself to Cora's body in a way that left her breathless. Aching with want.

"I want to draw your eyes and your nose," Manuela said, bringing Cora's attention back to her. "These freckles." A thumb brushed over her cheek, and then a kiss on that spot followed. It was tender and incendiary all at once.

"I haven't had my portrait done in a long time," Cora admitted. "Not since Alfred was about ten years old."

"I saw it," Manuela said after pressing a kiss to Cora's mouth. "It looked like John Singer Sargent." Cora should've known she would guess.

"It is." Cora frowned as she watched Manuela slide on one of her dressing gowns before going in search of something in her reticule.

"I could get some paper for you," she offered.

"No need," Manuela declined happily as she triumphantly pulled something out of the bag. "I've got one of my small sketchbooks." She winked at Cora as she stretched the tight tube of papers, then pulled out two small pencils.

"I have a desk in the other room." Manuela waved her off again. Cora grinned to herself at this new, very self-possessed side of Manuela.

She looked around the room for a second until she settled on a pale pink settee by the window. "There."

Cora allowed herself to be positioned to this side and that, and after a few interruptions which involved a few kisses, the artist was happy with her pose.

"Can I see?" Cora asked, picking up the curled sheaf of sketching paper. Manuela looked up from whatever she was doing to her pencils and nodded.

"That's from the last week at the fairgrounds," she told Cora. The duchess leafed through the images. The paper was so small they were practically miniatures, but the detail and skill of the drawings was astounding. It was mostly faces. There had to be at least a dozen portraits.

"This is only a week's worth?" she asked in surprise and Manuela laughed self-consciously.

"I'm always drawing, the moment my hands are idle, I reach

for my sketchbook," she admitted as she came to stand behind Cora. "You just never notice because whenever I'm with you my hands are distracted."

"It's true," she exclaimed when Cora threw her a dubious glance.

"These are brilliant." She was examining the portrait of a young girl. Her hair was pulled back into a braid, a small smile pulling up her lips. The features were so detailed, the happiness on the girl's face so vivid Cora expected the impish child to wink at her.

"That's Clarita, Luz Alana's little sister, when we took her to Cairo Street," Manuela explained, her eyes softening as she looked at the drawing. "She has a bit of a fascination with the mummies." It was only her face, neck and a bit of her shoulders. She was wearing a black dress, and a small brooch was fastened to her neck, which on closer inspection...

"Is that a spider on her neck?"

Manuela kept her attention on what she was sketching, but her mouth tipped up. Her expression one of indulgent affection. "It's a black widow!" she corrected. "I found it for her at a shop in Le Marais."

"That's an odd accessory for a little girl," Cora mused.

"Luz Alana and Clarita lost both their parents, their father in the last couple of years," Manuela said, raising a shoulder, her face somber as she talked about her friends. "She's been fascinated with death and scary creatures. I know I shouldn't encourage her, but I remember what it was like to be a child among adults and not fully able to grasp all the things happening around me. Feeling misunderstood." She set her pencil down and turned to Cora, her face very serious. This expression of concern and love was so distant from the self-indulgent, spoiled girl she'd believed Manuela to be. "I had my art to focus on, and it helped during the harder times. Clarita likes insects and mummies. What's the harm in that?" She fiddled with the pencil, her focus on the far wall. Cora knew what it was like to feel misunderstood too. Like your pain was invisible, because every adult in your life was too suffocated in their own grief. Her own father could barely stand to look at her most of her childhood.

Cora had lashed out. She had leaned into all the things about herself her father hated and had flaunted them in his face. Her tomboy inclinations, her fixation with business, her disinterest in marriage or any of the things society girls were supposed to want. The more her father insisted on her conforming, the more she rebelled. The more she tested his love, until she went too far and he cast her out. Her Tia Osiris had tried to love her, but even she was bewildered by Cora's rage. Only after they'd set sail for Europe had she let her aunt in, and thankfully with her it had not been too late.

"It's very kind of you to do that for her. Sometimes it's enough for just one person in your life to embrace your strangeness."

"Indulging Clarita helps me in a way," Manuela admitted, before turning attention back to the sketch. Cora wanted to ask what she'd meant, but that was not conducive to observing the rules they'd set for this arrangement.

Grappling for something to distract her, she leafed through more of Manuela's drawings. The next one was done with even more detail than the previous ones, but the style was very different. This one was of an older man. His eyes were screwed together as though he was trying to observe something at a distance. His mouth was pursed. Like he'd swallowed something sour. With his mustache and aged face, he should've looked grandfatherly, but the image made Cora feel as if she was witnessing something perverse. She flipped the page and found another similar drawing, but this time the face was that of a beautiful woman, or at least she would've been beautiful if her eyes weren't wide and bulging out of her face, her mouth half open as if she was gawking at something. The image was just as unsettling as the previous one.

"Where is this from?" she asked, glancing up at Manuela, who seemed to almost recoil at the page Cora was holding up. As if even she'd forgotten just how disturbing her own sketches were.

"It's from the ethnological expositions at the fairgrounds," Manuela said succinctly.

An icy feeling settled in Cora's stomach as realization dawned. "I'd heard they were planning to do that," she said, with distaste. She had not gone to that part of the grounds but had heard from some associates who were part of the planning committees that the French planned to exhibit people indigenous to some of their colonies.

Display them in habitats for crowds to come and see. "It's barbaric," Cora said, looking at yet another monstrous, gaping face. "Do they make them just stand there to be being stared at?"

"They do," Manuela said grimly. Her gaze was as hard as her sketches, which Cora noted were not of the people on display but of the leering crowds coming to ogle them. Now that she knew what it was that the figures in the drawing were doing, the images held a distinctly sinister air.

"I only went once," Manuela admitted, a shiver running through her at whatever she was thinking of. "I couldn't do any drawings of those in the exhibitions. It felt wrong. But the more I looked at the people coming to see them, as though they were in a human zoo, the more upset I became, and suddenly I was drawing them. I didn't want to forget the ugliness of that moment."

"Bearing witness is important. Your drawings are a stark window into what we've grown to accept in our society, how cruel we can be." Cora pulled Manuela by her hand until she was settled between Cora's legs. "That is what a good artist does—reflects the spirit of the moment, for better or worse."

Manuela sighed, her expression rueful. "Last night, Claudine told me you sponsor quite a few of artists."

Cora shrugged and pressed a kiss to the top of Manuela's head, uncomfortable with this line of conversation. Claudine, Cassandra and Tia Osiris had the tendency to paint her in a saintly light whenever they could.

"I believe in the arts. I believe in their power to convey a message, to subvert the status quo. I *fiercely* believe in giving those who don't have the freedom to voice their truths the means to express them in other ways." She gently clamped her teeth on the outer shell of Manuela's ear, eliciting a delicious little shiver. "I am also quite taken with the idea of, one hundred years from now, people realizing that much of the revered and praised art of our time was created by people who society liked to believe didn't exist."

It took Manuela a moment to digest what she said, then her smile turned absolutely radiant. "That is positively Machiavellian, Your Grace."

"Why make sanctimonious blowhards squirm only in this lifetime when I could make sure it happens for generations to come?"

Manuela threw her head back, laughing heartily at Cora's words. A smile that fizzed with naughty approval. "I like you, Cora," she said after a long moment, and Cora found herself wishing for more than that. She felt so good in Cora's arms. All of it was too good. The lies she'd told herself even that morning about where they stood shifted almost by the second.

A loud knock on the door pulled them out of their comfortable embrace. "That must be the footman with your clothes," Cora said, moving to get up. "I'll get it."

"Yes, thank you." Manuela beamed as if Cora had ordered her a stable of ponies. "I am supposed to go to Académie Pasquale today with Cassandra and Claudine, so I'll have to get dressed eventually."

"Don't let Cassandra rope you into one of her passion projects," Cora warned, making Manuela laugh.

"I think I'm the one talking her into things," she said cheerfully as Cora left to get the door. Cora frowned at that. She knew Cassandra and Manuela had gotten together, but her friend hadn't mentioned anything about joint projects. "I've been thinking about that essay by Frede's grandmother is all. I had some ideas for a collective I discussed with Cassandra."

Cora froze, just as she was about to reach for the handle of the door and turned to look at Manuela. Was she thinking of staying? Was she considering calling off her engage—

Cora stopped herself, before she went down a path she could absolutely not go down. If she was going to have a chance at returning to London, she could not leave a trail of scandal in her wake. She could absolutely not afford a single misstep. The French could handle a dalliance, but anything beyond that was more than she could risk when the stakes were this high. Getting herself embroiled with a jilted groom with enough resources to make a fuss was out of the question.

"You can put the bag there," she said distractedly, before realizing it wasn't a footman but her assistant Maggie with the Gladstone in hand. A very harried-looking Maggie at that.

"My apologies, Your Grace." The girl looked petrified, her face pale as a ghost. Cora didn't need to ask if something was wrong. For her assistant to be at her private bedchamber's door when she'd asked not to be bothered, there had to be an emergency. "I know you asked not to be disturbed," she rushed to say before Cora could rebuke her. "But this morning you are scheduled to meet with Monsieur Grinaud about the building. It's in one hour," she whispered.

Grinaud. The building.

"Mierda," Cora spat, immediately furious with herself. She'd been so distracted with Manuela she'd forgotten a meeting she'd been trying to secure for almost six months. A meeting she'd had to bribe half of Paris to secure. "Have the carriage brought around and send my lady's maid. I'll be ready to go in thirty minutes."

Cora closed the door behind Maggie, self-recrimination churning in her gut. Pulling her shoulders back and schooling her face into an impassive mask, she walked back into the room. "I have to go," she told Manuela as she handed her the bag without looking at her.

"Oh." She sounded disappointed. Cora hardened herself to it. "Can I come with you?"

Instantly her mind began producing reasons to say yes. She could drop her off at Cassandra's. If she took Manuela with her, she could ask her about this collective business. But those were only excuses to stay with her longer, to break the rules of what they'd agreed on.

"That won't be possible," Cora said, staring at a spot directly over Manuela's head. "I will ask my other driver to deliver you home. I'll send a maid to help you dress."

Manuela stayed silent, her eyes searching, clearly trying to figure out what had gone wrong in the last two minutes.

"Will I see you tonight, then?" Cora ground her teeth at the guilt slicing through her. God, what had she been thinking? She couldn't do this.

"I have plans tonight," she lied, still not looking at Manuela. "But there are more outings to fulfill." From her peripheral vision she saw the pained flinch on Manuela's face. It took everything she had not to go to her. "I'd like to take you to the opera next."

"I leave for Scotland on Sunday morning."

"Scotland?" She winced at the alarm in her voice. Manuela only stared at her.

"My friend Luz Alana is there. She's just been married. Aurora and I are to join her for a week."

"I see." She tried to tell herself this was for the best. Distance was exactly what they needed. "I will send a seamstress to your house tomorrow, then, for the opera. We will go on Saturday, before you depart."

"I have dresses," Manuela said quietly. "I have a whole new trousseau."

"I would like to give you this one," she said once she could speak, and whatever Manuela saw on her face was enough to make her agree. By the time Cora came down to the foyer to go to her meeting, Manuela was gone.

Seventeen

Manuela was still debating whether she was dejected or furious at Cora's behavior as she walked to the Académie Pasquale.

"You know, for all that you've been informing me of every minute detail of your little adventure with the duchess, I thought I would hear something about last night," Aurora complained as they turned the corner of the Boulevard Montmartre. "You've barely spoken since you returned to the house."

Manuela knew this was as much of an admission of concern from her friend as she would receive. And the truth was she would've said something, if she had any idea of what had happened. It had been perfect until it hadn't. One minute she was having a wonderful morning, and the next Cora couldn't get rid of her fast enough. She suspected it had to do with the meeting Cora seemed to have forgotten about, but Manuela would've understood that if Cora had simply taken a moment to explain. She had an appointment of her own to attend to.

Except she would likely have canceled hers if it meant spending more time with Cora. She'd been considering doing that very thing when they'd been interrupted. She was such a fool.

She'd truly thought something had changed between them last night. Something was certainly different about *her*. Not just because of Cora but everything she'd experienced since they started this adventure.

It was the way they'd made love, it was the Paris she'd seen in Montmartre, it was the women she'd met at Cassandra's and Claudine's.

"Ay, Manuela, habla por favor," Aurora protested, tugging on her arm. "You're starting to worry me."

"Nothing is wrong, not really," she shrugged. "Last night was…" *Revelatory. Transcendental. Devastatingly perfect.* "I just…"

"You want more," Aurora finished for her, but for once her friend's voice didn't have that exasperated undertone. She was also right.

She did want more. She wanted too much.

"You can say it," Manuela sighed, ready for the well-earned *I told you so*s, but Aurora only pressed closer to her side as they weaved their way through the crowded sidewalk. "This was extremely foolish, and now I have developed feelings for a person who I can never have."

Aurora was quiet for a long time, so long that they'd almost reached the entrance to the Passage des Panaromas, where the academy was located, before she spoke.

"Manuela, why would I blame you for playing your last card and hoping for a win?" Aurora turned to look at her, and there was no recrimination there, no judgment. "So what if what you did is not what I would've done? Last night when I was talking to Frederica, she told me that in order to get Cassandra away from her family, they had to essentially pay her parents a ransom. They didn't even need the money, but they wanted to leave the two of them with as little as possible. Make them regret their choices."

Manuela swallowed down the lump in her throat and thought of the stoic Frede and the ebullient Cassandra and their little warm home where everyone was welcome. Of Cassandra, who was even now waiting for Manuela at the academy to introduce her to more artists, more people to make her feel less alone.

"It is true that things have not been easy for me," Aurora continued softly, as if she was contemplating something inside her. "But my choice to sacrifice myself for my dreams of a clinic will only affect myself, and I will never have to worry about my livelihood. Those are not your choices. Women are dealt such a measly hand, we are just trying to make the best of it, and I will not judge you for how you do it, Leona."

"Thank you," Manuela said, as they reached the entrance to the Passage. "I know how hard it is for you to be comforting."

Aurora balked at that and then dissolved into a rueful laugh.

"And thank you for coming with me today," Manuela said as they reached the academy's unassuming storefront.

Aurora shrugged as she peered into the small window on the door. "It is no trouble. I am growing quite fond of these sapphic outings." Manuela rolled her eyes at Aurora and leaned in herself to get a look inside. Behind the glass there was a display which showcased a variety of paintings Manuela assumed were by the students. There was a small sitting room, and beyond that was a large studio where a class was being conducted.

Manuela was debating whether to knock or just walk in when Aurora spoke. "Oh, there's Cassandra." Cora's friend was indeed walking away from the cluster of students and easels and was waving at them through the window. Next to her was an older man, who had to be the famed Aristide Pasquale.

The moment they were inside, they began their introductions, Cassandra speaking to Pasquale about Aurora and Manuela as if they were old friends. "Guess where Aristide and I just returned from?" Cassandra asked.

"I hope it wasn't still at Le Chat Tordu," Manuela teased, making Cassandra giggle.

"We went to the Rapp Gallery and encountered two pieces by

one Manuela Caceres Galvan in a *very* prominent place among the exhibit from the Americas."

Manuela frowned at her words, wondering if Cassandra was mocking her.

"Your work is very good," the master told her, his eyes warm as he took her hand. Manuela thanked him, still confused about where they'd seen her paintings.

"Did they add more paintings to the alcove?" she asked. Cassandra didn't seem to understand the question. "Other than my pieces, there were just two others up there when I visited." Which had been that night she'd signed the blasted contract with Cora.

"No," Cassandra said with a shake of her head. "We found your pieces in one of the larger rooms on the first floor."

"The usher in the room did say they had been recently moved there," Monsieur Pasquale added.

"Right," Cassandra concurred, her brow suddenly low on her forehead as if she had just realized something. "One of the gallery's directors instructed them to do so a week or so ago."

A week or so ago. Could Cora have...? No, it couldn't be. Who would do something kind and romantic like that and then not even mention it?

A stubborn, deeply infuriating woman who insisted on pretending she had no heart. One who quietly made sure her friends had the food from their homeland at their table, who sponsored art students, who paid for women to wear trousers if they chose to, who raised her stepson like her own, who secretly slept in a pink bedchamber, and who was loved and respected by good people. *That* would be the kind of infuriating creature who would pull a stunt like that. Manuela could throttle her, except if she had her in front of her right now all she'd manage was to launch herself into her arms and kiss her until they both couldn't breathe.

Cora Kempf Bristol truly was trying to drive her mad.

"Manuela." Aurora's voice pulled her from the whirlpool of emotions that Cora's confounding behavior had once again pitched her into.

"I'm sorry," she apologized to Aristide, who seemed to be waiting for her to speak.

"I was saying that I was very impressed with your work. I especially loved your flora. They are so vivid. I have never seen anything like it. Your color saturation technique, in particular, is outstanding."

The sincere admiration of her skills brought to Manuela's attention—just as when Cora had done it—how long it had been since appreciation for her work did anything for her. One could only hear so many times that art was for ladies of leisure. That it was a nice-enough hobby for pretty girls while they waited for a husband, before one lost the drive for it. Even her pieces that had been selected for the exposition had been submitted by *the wife* of one of her old instructors in Venezuela.

She'd dreamed of being a great artist once, but she hadn't thought of that for a long time. She'd certainly never thought of it as anything like Aurora's medicine or Luz Alana's rum business. It was merely something she did well. Not something she attached ambition or drive to. But her time with Cassandra and her friends had altered her sense of what a woman could do with her art.

"Cassandra informs me that you will be returning to Venezuela soon, to be married." Pasquale's eyes were brimming with kindness, but his words cut her like a knife. "If you were to stay here in Paris, I'd offer you a position as an instructor. I have been looking for someone who can achieve that kind of detail for our botanicals classes."

"Don't mind him. He is perennially attempting to recruit my friends." Cassandra winked at Manuela. She assumed Pasquale was referring to classes for his children, since she'd never heard of women instructors at a formal institute. Académie Pasquale was the most successful art school for those preparing for the entry exam at the Académie des Beaux-Arts. She couldn't imagine them allowing women to instruct the students looking to enter the rigorous program.

"Manuela is much too talented to be instructing children how to doodle daisies," Aurora, who had clearly made the same assumption, chided Pasquale.

"Aurora," Manuela rebuked her friend, but the master only laughed, that same kindly expression on his face.

"Oh, she would be teaching adults," he assured her. "In addition to the instruction to those preparing for the entry exam, we also impart classes for illustrators, sketch artists, even cartoonists." He turned to Aurora with an apologetic smile and directed her attention to a large, framed illustration of the different parts of the human brain. "We even instruct artists on scientific illustrations. We've had an increase in demand for commercial art, you see," Pasquale whispered as they passed a class of about ten students gathered in a circle drawing a model sitting on a banquette at the center of the room. Three of them were women, and no one seemed very concerned about that.

"You have mixed classes," she commented, and Aristide sent her an amused look.

"We do. Not all of our male students are willing to participate, but many are. Paris is not London or New York. We've always taken pride in bucking convention."

"Mostly because we're too busy engaging in all matter of sin to care," Cassandra joked, and they all laughed, but Manuela's attention remained on the group of students.

"I have noticed that many businesses, especially those selling food and beverages, are using posters as advertisements." Pasquale nodded approvingly at her observation. "It is becoming more and more popular, and many studio artists are taking them on to secure a more stable income."

"It seems like the working artist could be a viable profession,"

Aurora announced pointedly. Manuela didn't dignify that with an answer. Thankfully Aristide had a sketch of some craniums to distract her friend and she was able to slip out of that potentially distressing conversation.

"How did things go last night?" Cassandra asked, catching up with her in front of a row of illustrations for children's books.

It was definitely uncouth to discuss any details of the previous evening and that morning, but she was desperate to obtain some perspective from someone who knew Cora. The trouble was that the things that bothered her were well beyond the boundaries of their agreement.

"Did they truly move my paintings?" she asked, heading off any talk of her feelings about Cora, while at the same time indirectly probing Cora's feeling toward her. She barely made sense to herself these days.

"Yes." Cassandra sent her a curious look but respected Manuela's change of topic.

"And fix my name on the plaque? Because before it said *Manolo*."

"They did, and it was correct."

"Was it her?" Manuela asked, unable to contain herself.

Cassandra sighed deeply, then lifted a shoulder. "I wondered, since you'd mentioned it that night at dinner. But Cora has the very unfortunate habit of hiding anything and everything she does for others. She'd kill me if I told you even a tenth of it."

This was exactly the opposite of what she needed to hear. She wanted to be apprised about the many instances in which Cora had behaved like a complete comemierda, so her heart could stop clenching every time she heard the blasted woman's name.

"Your friend is confusing." The outburst earned her a sympathetic look from Cassandra who seemed to take in stride that her best friend was out there driving unsuspecting women mad.

"I assume she was not a gracious host this morning?" The

cringe on Cassandra's face almost made Manuela laugh, then she remembered how quickly Cora had gone cold.

"That's the confounding bit," she admitted, leaning to look at the portrait in front of her. "Things were going so well, and then she realized she'd forgotten a meeting and flew out of the room like the house was on fire." And what was the point of even discussing this? Just because she had put her marriage out of her mind, it didn't mean it wasn't happening when she returned to Venezuela. "It doesn't matter," she finally said, averting her eyes from Cassandra's. "Cora is just keeping to our agreement."

The disgruntled exhale from behind told Manuela that Cassandra didn't like that explanation, but in the end Cora's best friend's opinion didn't matter either.

"The sad thing is that she is not keeping to it at all," Cassandra said to Manuela's back. "That day that you two met for lunch, she swore to us she would never bring you to any function or events where we could meet you."

Manuela turned to look at Cassandra who was brandishing a raised eyebrow in her direction. "She probably forced herself to break that promise because she felt bad for me due to my paintings." Which she had then gotten sorted for Manuela.

"I've known Cora for a long time," Cora's best friend told her. "She doesn't allow just anyone into her private life, no matter how badly she might feel for them." Cassandra bit her lip, clearly debating how far to delve into her friend's past. "She'd just lost Benedict when we met," she began, at length. "And she was..." Cassandra's voice faltered then, as though even recalling the state Cora had been in then still affected her.

"Were they in love?" she asked so quietly that she wondered if Cassandra heard her. She assumed, given Cora's proclivities, that their marriage had been in word only, but maybe she was wrong.

"No, not in love." Manuela noted Cassandra's emphasis on *no*, expecting there to be more. "She couldn't love him, not like a wife loves a husband, but Benedict knew that. He was ill when they met, and all he wanted was for someone to look after Alfie when he died." Cassandra's eyes were far away as she looked inward. "He didn't want his son to be left in the hands of relations who would only want him for his money." That explained, at least in part, her connection to her stepson. "They married when she was eighteen, and his illness took him five years later." Cassandra lifted a hand to the glass enclosing the illustration and traced it with her nail. "For more than a year she was like a ghost. Her Tia Osiris helped as much as she could, but we grew worried. All she did was work. Benedict was not very good with business, but he encouraged her in it. By the time she was widowed, she was managing all of the duchy's holdings and growing a fortune in her own right. She was grateful for the freedom he gave her, for the faith he had in her."

Manuela thought of the story Cora had told her about her father. Finding a man who reacted with encouragement instead of scorn to her ambitions must have been wonderful. Just as losing him would've been devastating. "She cared about nothing other than Alfie and fulfilling her promise to Benedict to raise his son. Then she met someone." Manuela noticed that the usual warmth in Cassandra's voice disappeared at the mention of this someone.

"She fell in love then?" Maybe that was why Cora was this way. Maybe her heart belonged to someone she couldn't have. It wasn't exactly uncommon for women like them.

Cassandra's smile was as sharp as a blade. "I don't know if it was love, but she lost her head for someone who wanted to use her." There was a short, taut silence. "Someone who was already engaged to be married."

"I thought it wasn't unusual for married women..." Manuela started, then quieted when she took in Cassandra's bleak expression. "Ah, she never told Cora about the engagement."

"She didn't, and she took advantage of Cora's connections to repair her brother's finances and increase her dowry to boot."

No wonder she had been so resistant to get involved with Manuela. "When she found out—" Cassandra grimaced as if the mere memory of the incident caused her physical pain. "Let's just say Cora was not discreet about her heartbreak, and since then she's seemed determined to never expose herself to that pain again."

"That's awful." Manuela couldn't come up with anything else to say. But God, poor Cora! Losing her husband and then the first time she risked her heart…to be betrayed so terribly.

"I know your situation is not the same," Cassandra started, but Manuela shook her head to stop whatever she intended to say. She could not bear to hear it.

"Our situation is temporary. For Cora this is a business transaction, and for me…" Now she was the one grimacing at the thought of what awaited after this. "It's a mutually beneficial arrangement, where everyone knows where they stand. When it's over, she will have her land, and I will get married." She pressed a hand to her throat and forced herself to smile. She would have to work on her reaction to the prospect of a life with Felix.

"In the years I've known Cora, she has never brought anyone to my home, or hers," Cassandra told her, and Manuela wished she could cover her ears.

Again she shook her head, denying Cassandra's words. What was the use in any of this? She couldn't change course now, not without disgracing herself. Not without once again costing her family everything.

"Cassandra, I am happy that you could make a life here with Frede, but I don't have that freedom. My parents depend on me." Felix had paid a fortune in debts, in trips, in dresses. He'd paid for Manuela. "If it was only me, perhaps…" No. This was futile and would only make things worse later.

She wished she hadn't learned of the concessions Cora had made for her. She wished she was strong enough to end this now, but after last night there was no staying away. If Cora wanted her in her bed, Manuela would go. She could nurse her pride all the way across the Atlantic.

Cassandra's eyes were haunted as she reached for Manuela's hand, her grip so tight it was almost painful. "You deserve more than what you've been told you can have."

"I am leaving to return to Venezuela in a few weeks," Manuela insisted, as much for her sake as for Cassandra's.

"But you could come back here. That idea you had of organizing Aurora's friends has been circling in my head for days now too. We must speak with Aristide about it today."

She'd wondered if this collective could fulfill grandmother's dream in some ways. But it was impossible. Felix would never allow her to be going back and forth between Venezuela and Paris. It would only hurt more if she fooled herself into believing any of this was plausible.

"I don't think so, Cassandra," she said apologetically. "I'm so sorry to have wasted your time, and Aristide's." But at least she wasn't lying to herself or anyone else.

Eighteen

This was pure indulgence, Cora thought as she walked into the room where Manuela was being fitted for her new gown.

"Am I interrupting?" she asked, striding in, her gaze fixed on the woman standing on the dais.

She'd almost called off the whole thing a dozen times. It had been impulsive to summon one of the most popular modistes in the city, demanding she clear her schedule to make a dress for Manuela in a matter of days. But the way the bright magenta sat against her lover's skin made it look like burnished gold. Cora's vision filled with her as her heart whirled around hopelessly in her chest. The design was fairly simple, but Bernadette, the dressmaker, had cut it in a heart-shaped neckline that displayed Manuela's attributes to perfection. The dress hid nothing of her form: on the contrary, it accentuated every one of her beautiful curves.

"Where's Bernadette?" Manuela asked, surprised, her arms clutching the front of the dress which was only held up by pins.

"I told her I'd help you change," Cora informed the heiress, who didn't seem very thrilled to see her.

"I can change on my own." She couldn't: the bodice was still not sewn to the skirt, and once she let her arms fall to the side the whole thing would crash to the floor.

But for once, Manuela wasn't the sunny, easygoing, princess. She was cross with Cora and wasn't attempting to hide it.

Had it really only been two days since she'd seen her? It felt like years.

"Let me help you, cariño," Cora cajoled her and received a very bellicose stare in the mirror.

"No," Manuela volleyed back, her hands clutched in front of her, the sway in her hips hypnotizing as she walked around the dais and came to stand in front of Cora. "What are you doing here?" Her usually inviting gaze was dark and furious.

Cora found the soft, luminous Manuela intriguing. She loved the coy smiles and come-hither looks. But explosive, furious Manuela was irresistible to her. "I expected you to keep hiding from me," she tossed over her shoulder, as she pretended to look at herself in the mirror.

"I was not hiding from you, Manuela," she said in her most reasonable voice. She was right, of course. She had been hiding. For two days she'd been reckoning with the way she'd forgotten herself that night after Claudine's. She'd run off to that meeting with Grinaud, only to realize she didn't much care if she got the building or not.

She sat there for an hour hearing the man drone about some obscure grape he'd found for his private vineyards and wondered why she was there. Why she'd left a woman who had given her the best night of her life to chase after something she knew couldn't make her happy. She'd gone from that damn meeting with Grinaud straight to the Palais des Beaux Arts to make sure Manuela's paintings had been moved, like she'd asked them to the day after they signed the damned contract.

"What does one call leaving a half-naked woman in your

bedroom and flying off to a meeting, then?" The clear hurt in Manuela's voice shamed her enough to make her look away.

"I had obligations, Manuela," she said, instead of begging for forgiveness. "I can't disregard my business."

"Then why are you ordering dresses for me, Cora?" her princess demanded, face thunderous as she whipped around. "Why did you send boxes of undergarments to my town house yesterday?"

Because I couldn't stand the idea of taking you to the opera wearing a dress he paid for. Because the mere thought of anything from him touching your bare skin makes me want to break things.

"I wish I knew!" she burst out, genuinely at a loss over what was happening to her. Her life was in utter chaos since Manuela Caceres Galvan had dropped into it. "I don't know," she repeated, helplessly. "There is no script when it comes to you."

"Stop saying things like that, Cora. It's just going to make things harder."

It's already going to be hell, Cora thought.

Manuela sighed and turned away from her to face the mirror. It was indecent the way she filled that dress. All Cora could think about was tearing it off her. "How did you get a modiste this fast anyhow?"

"By paying a fortune," she admitted, looking around the small dressing room.

"She is very good," Manuela conceded, as she admired her reflection. As mad as her princess was, she did love a pretty dress. Cora had never fancied women who seemed partial to vanity. She'd always prided herself in not attracting that kind of attention. When men spoke about her it was because of her gift for numbers, for her business acumen. Manuela, on the other hand, loved being looked at, even now when she was clearly cross with Cora, she wanted the praise, and for the first time in her life, Cora felt the impulse to shower someone other than her stepson with it.

"That color makes your skin look lit from within," she whispered and received a sultry, sideways glance and a little *hmph*.

"Bernadette said she worked for Empress Marie-Claire of Haiti," Manuela offered in answer.

No truce yet, it seemed.

"Her grandmother was the modiste to the empress until her death," Cora confirmed, then had to bite her tongue not too laugh at Manuela's visible struggle with her curiosity.

"I knew she lived in exile here in Europe," she said, her tone a mite friendlier and those brown eyes alive with questions.

"After she left Haiti, Empress Marie-Claire lived near Pisa with her daughters for many years." Manuela kept running a finger along the edge of her bodice as she listened, which Cora found utterly entrancing. She had to force herself to continue talking. "Bernadette's grandmother came with her as a young woman and married an Italian. They remained there after the empress passed."

"Fascinating." Cora smiled at Manuela's thoughtful expression. She could not remain angry for very long. One more thing for Cora to be absurdly smitten with. "Exile is so much more vast than those grand figures," she said reflectively, and Cora could see this musing was about much more than Bernadette. "So many displaced by war." It was Manuela's own story, in a way, having left her home country so young, due to her own island's struggles for autonomy. "I'm glad that Bernadette has continued her family's legacy."

Cora nodded in agreement as she came to stand behind Manuela. This woman looked at the world with a sort of magic. She could find a glimmer of light, a trace of beauty in almost everything. Maybe that was how she managed to keep that light that seemed to emanate from her. The large mirror in front of them gave her a very lovely view of the front of the dress. Cora wanted to peel it all off. She'd hardly thought of anything other than making love to her again since they'd last seen each other.

"She was one of Worth's best modistes, but he wasn't paying her what she deserved," Cora explained, getting closer. "Bernadette is a friend of Claudine's. When I heard she was looking to start her own shop, I invested. She makes dresses for all the diplomats' wives and society ladies from the Caribbean. She understands their lines better," Cora murmured, unable to resist running a hand down the curve of Manuela's waist.

"I am still very cross with you," the heiress informed her, even as her lids turned heavy and her body softened to Cora's touch.

"So I heard," Cora whispered, sweeping away curls at the nape of Manuela's neck and leaving a trail of kisses in their place. "Cassandra said you were not very happy with me."

"I hope your meeting was successful, since it seemed so important." Cora lifted her gaze from Manuela's neck and found hurt brown eyes staring at her in the mirror.

"I shouldn't haven't rushed out like that." She ran a finger down Manuela's arm as she spoke and felt a shiver go through the body in her arms. "I was mad at myself, and I punished you for it." She laughed at the challenging gaze in the mirror that practically screamed *You are going to have to do better than that.*

"I've been trying to buy a building in Boulevard Saint-Germain for over two years now, and the owner had finally agreed to see me that morning. I was angry at myself for forgetting." Noticing the minor thawing in her princess's eyes she risked wrapping her arms around her waist and squeezed, almost sighing in relief at the contact.

"You could've just told me, you know," Manuela said, turning that wounded chocolate gaze toward Cora. "You didn't have to make me feel like you didn't want me there."

Cora had become unaccustomed to admitting her shortcomings. For so long she'd been dealing in a world of people she reviled on principle that she'd barely listened to anyone outside of the few she truly trusted. But Manuela was not the men she did business with. She was a woman who like her was trying to do her best by herself and by those who depended on her. A woman who had given Cora the only moments of true happiness she'd had in a very long time. She deserved better.

"I acted terribly, and you are right to be angry with me. I'm sorry." She was awarded a small nod, even though Manuela kept her eyes cast down.

"I went and saw my paintings again." There was a hint of recrimination in her voice. "You were the one who had them changed, weren't you?"

"It was a travesty to hide them like that."

"You make my head spin," Manuela lamented as Cora inched closer, an eyebrow raised. "One moment you insist we are to maintain the terms of our agreement and the next you do something utterly romantic and kind. It is absolutely exhausting."

"I'm sorry." She pressed a gentle kiss to the spot right behind Manuela's ear that fascinated her, and she exhaled in that soft, warm way she did when Cora touched her in the exact way she liked. "It was awful of me to be thoughtful," she teased. "And just when we had finally agreed I was terribly rude."

"Yes," Manuela exclaimed, those dark eyes flashing with humor. "I finally had myself under control, and you had to ruin everything by doing something wonderful, and now you have my body in chaos again." Cora laughed at the very hostile way in which she uttered the last word.

"Perdon, princesa," she apologized again, this time placing her hands over Manuela's which were still clutching the top of her dress. "Might I ask where the chaos is occurring?" she taunted, eliciting a grudging smile from Manuela. "Could it possibly be here?" She ran the tip of a nail over the mound of one breast. "Or perhaps down there?" She slid a hand into the pocket she'd ordered Bernadette to sew into the skirt. Manuela gave a delicious little gasp as Cora's fingers caressed over her sex.

"That is depraved!" she cried, eyes as round as saucers, while Cora added her other hand to the second pocket and cupped her with both hands. "This is absolutely not duchess-like be-havior. Did you do—" She gasped when Cora's thumb pressed right over her clitoris. "Mm," she moaned in a mixture of sur-prise and raw lust. Cora watched in the mirror as Manuela's eyes fluttered closed, lost already. Fully trusting of the pleasure she was about to receive—and Cora wanted to give her everything. To spend days and days making this woman cry out in ecstasy, turn her bones to water with her mouth and hands.

"Let go of your bodice, sweetheart. I won't let it get ruined," she instructed very gently, as her hands worked Manuela under the skirt. She'd slid two fingers into the slit of her combination and into that delicious heat. Once the bodice was gone, Manuela unbuttoned the undergarment so Cora could see those beauti-ful breasts spilling over the corset.

"I've missed them," she groaned, her voice greedy as Manuela touched herself in Cora's view. Her small hands tugging at the tips of her breasts, eyes screwed shut, short puffs of air escaping her lips. "You're so hot inside," Cora praised and felt Manuela clench on her fingers. "Mm, wonderfully wet," she said approv-ingly as she moved her fingers in and out of her lover. "Rock into my hand, darling." Manuela did, her hips canting back and forth into Cora's touch until they were both panting. When she felt as though she would combust, Manuela shifted, ripping one of her hands from her breast and pulling Cora down for a hun-gry, frantic kiss. Their teeth clashed as their tongues stroked and tangled, while Cora rubbed circles over that tight nub, pinch-ing when she felt her princess start to tremble.

"Yes, come for me, sweetheart." Almost instantly Manuela's body stiffened, and soon those little moans of pleasure were fill-ing the room.

A series of light knocks on the door could've been thunder clapping inside the room. Cora's first instinct was to hide Man-uela's nakedness, and she moved to shield her from the view of the door, but no one came inside.

"Your Grace," the quiet voice drifted inside. "Do you need my assistance with anything?"

Manuela, who had shifted and was now plastered to Cora's front with her face hidden against her chest, began to shake at the question.

"That won't be necessary, Bernadette. We shall be out in a few minutes."

After a short pause the other woman spoke again, while Cora pressed kisses to the top of Manuela's head. "Yes, of course. I shall let your carriage driver know." The modiste took great pains to walk away with heavy feet. Manuela's frame still shook. Worried, Cora looked down at the heiress and found that the shaking was not from nerves but from laughter, and soon she was laughing too.

"That was quite debauched." Manuela beamed as she pushed up for a kiss.

"I am happy to know I'm finally living up to my end of the deal." For a second a shadow passed over her face, and Cora wanted to kick herself for mentioning the damn arrangement. But Manuela recovered quickly and bravely offered Cora one of those luminous smiles that made her heart skip a beat. "That is all good and well, Your Grace, but now that you've sent Bernadette away, I will need some help with this." She waved a hand in front of her undone combination. Cora snatched one of those hands which, as always, carried a few smudges from charcoal and paint and kissed the tips.

"I will be happy to assist. Besides, we should hurry up," she said, pointing at the clock in the mirror. "We're going to be late for the surprise I have for you."

Manuela frowned as she undid the fastening at her waist, then looked up at Cora with a shy smile on her lips. "I do like surprises." Cora pushed a fist into her chest to keep her heart inside it. "But will this count as the eighth outing?" she inquired, all business now. "Because after the inverted-beetle lecture, I am going to have to demand some information before agreeing to go." It was hopeless to even try to smother a grin.

"No," Cora said, equally serious now. "That will be the opera." She could see her own misery reflected in Manuela's eyes. "Let's call it a bonus. I think you will like this one very much, but we must make haste." She managed to sound cheerful enough and tried to get them on better footing by veering to more familiar ground. "I didn't intend to get distracted, but you are impossible to resist." She was gifted with a scorching sideways glance for that, as the two of them made quick work of divesting her of the bright pink dress and getting her back into her day suit. After a few very heated kisses and more than a few gropes of that delectable rump, Manuela was dressed and ready for her adventure, and Cora could barely remember what had been so important that she'd kept herself away from this ray of sunshine for two entire days.

"Are we going back to the Rapp Gallery?" Manuela asked, her head turned up to Cora, who had so far been aggravatingly vague about the surprise.

"You will have to see," the duchess declared with a sly grin as they made their way across the Pont d'Iéna to one of the entrances of the fairgrounds. This gate lead straight to the area under the tower and the Sun Alley that hosted the exhibits from the Americas. It was late afternoon now, and most of the exhibits were closing down, but there were still hundreds of people enjoying the offerings.

By some miracle they'd managed to leave Madame Bernadette's shop without being caught—or, at least, caught in flagrante delicto.

She hadn't been joking when she said Cora made her head spin. She could be so forbidding, so indifferent. Like nothing could get past her defenses. And suddenly she was ordering Manuela expensive dresses, organizing surprises, or ravishing her in a dressing room with half a dozen people merely feet away. It was tantamount to psychological warfare, and the rub of it was that as long as there was even the slimmest likelihood of ravishment, Manuela would not be able to stay away.

"What is the building for?" she asked, knowing full well the more she learned about this woman the harder it would be down the road. "The one you finally got your meeting about?" She didn't expect an answer.

"I intend to build a club," Cora said, surprising Manuela, once they reached the St. Vidal fountain under Eiffel's tower. Manuela took in Cora's demeanor. She seemed to puff up as she shared her intention. That light frost that enveloped her whenever her business prowess came up altered even the sound of her voice.

"A ladies' club?" Manuela asked, even though she was quite certain that Cora Kempf Bristol would likely set herself on fire before purposing an entire building for ladies of leisure to knit and drink tea.

"A very exclusive business club, for gentlemen," she corrected, then waved a hand in the direction of the pavilions. "Shall we?"

Manuela wanted to ask more, but she knew she'd probably sour the mood if she did, and besides, what did she care what Cora was doing? She would not be here for any of it. "Is that where we're going, to one of the pavilions?" Manuela asked, dying of curiosity, but Cora only laughed and slid her arm into hers.

"It is a surprise," Cora reminded her in a low, husky voice that made Manuela quiver. It was, of course, a perfectly normal thing for ladies to do with each other, walk arm in arm. No one who saw them strolling there, taking in the wonders of the exposition, would imagine what they'd done with each other just an hour ago. Or the many other things Manuela wanted to do.

"Oh, all right," she huffed in feigned annoyance. "Then, tell me about your club. I need a distraction."

Cora sent her a look but then began to talk. "It's something

I've wanted to do for years now," she said, her gaze intent on where they were headed. "It will be a club only for those who have reached a certain threshold in their connections and business success," she explained, and Manuela nodded, even though she could hardly think of a more horrible way to spend her time. "There are many exclusive clubs in Europe, but in mine, you will have to prove that you have the gravitas to manage yourself in the company of the brightest, most innovative minds in the world."

It sounded like a place that Felix would kill to belong to and Manuela wouldn't be caught dead in. With effort, she smoothed the lines on her forehead. "But why not make your own women's club? Wouldn't it be better to have a place where women who do business felt welcome?"

"Because I want to build something they can't ignore."

"Would *they* be willing to join if it's owned by a woman?"

Cora's expression turned wry. The Duchess of Sundridge was always a step ahead. "I will be setting very high standards for membership, and some will do it just as a point of pride," she explained. "If that fails, I have a few associates who owe me favors that I could..." she stopped, as if considering what word to use "...convince to join in order to lure others." From the set of Cora's shoulders, Manuela figured the persuasion would be rather aggressive. "But I think they'll come. Men like that can't tolerate the idea of a door being closed to them, you see."

Manuela thought of the women she'd met at Cassandra's. It would be virtually impossible for any of them to be allowed in a club like the one Cora was planning to open, and yet they could benefit greatly from something like it existing. A physical place where they could meet to discuss job offers, compare rates or even have studio space to work on commissions. From what she knew of Cora, she'd probably be open to building that too, she just wouldn't participate in it.

She did that: gave money to help her friends do what made

them happy, but she stayed in this world *she* didn't seem happy in. Like Claudine had said, always scheming, always devising a way to outsmart the men she dealt with.

Manuela thought of her own choices, of the marriage she'd agreed to enter, to save her family's status, to protect their standing among people who didn't deserve their regard. And decided she and Cora were not so different after all.

They remained quiet as they made their way through the crowds. Manuela was deep in thought when Cora spoke again. "There's a club here in Paris, the Cercle Agricole, and it's very exclusive. Like White's in London." There was a strain in Cora's voice, like she wanted Manuela to understand why she was doing it. "Women are not allowed to be members, but they can come for a lunch." Something told her something unpleasant had happened at this club. "About five years ago, a few of my associates invited me to a meeting there. I'd brought them an investment for a shipping line out of the South Pacific and was there to report the news that our profits had been more than twice what we'd expected in the first year." Her lips were turned up, but it was not smile. "When we arrived at the door, they informed me I had to enter the building through the ladies' entrance and meet them inside. *I* had to walk around the building and enter through the same door where the delivery men dropped off the produce in order to have the honor of informing men who couldn't do basic arithmetic without my help that I'd made them a fortune."

Manuela could see the fresh humiliation on Cora's face, the unhappy notches around her mouth as if it had only just happened. Manuela, who had been the subject of so many slights by men who saw her as nothing more than a bit of flesh for them to grope and look at, understood that rage. But what she couldn't comprehend was why Cora hadn't walked away. Manuela certainly would if she could.

"Then, why do business with them?" she asked, vexed. Manuela was not naïve—she was marrying a man she could never love, but that was because she had to. Cora didn't need these men. She was wealthy; she had power. She was a duchess.

"I do business with them because after my husband's death, I learned the hard way that the only way I could protect myself and Alfie was to harness power." Manuela thought of what Cassandra had said about the affair she'd had. Cora didn't appear very concerned about people knowing she preferred women, but maybe that was the price she paid to secure that liberty. "If they need me, they can't turn their backs on me. If I save them from ruin, if I use their own greed against them, I never have to worry about Alfie being punished for my choices."

What an exhausting way to live. Always braced for battle. "When will you know you're safe? When will you have enough power?" Manuela asked, causing Cora to send her a surprised look, which was almost immediately replaced by a defiant one.

"Getting my hands on your land will be a coup," she said, and a hole opened in the pit of Manuela's stomach. "That will help with my plans for Alfie's return to London, at least. But the truth is that it's never enough." From looking at Cora, the way she lived, one would think she'd managed to overcome the fears most women had to live with. But she seemed just as trapped as the rest of them.

"We are here," Cora announced, and only then did Manuela realize they'd reached the rear entrance to the Brazilian pavilion. The one that led to the greenhouse.

"Is this—" she began to ask when Cora nodded, waving a hand in the direction of the closed door. It was empty now, and though there were a few people milling around the gardens, there was no one inside.

"Have you been in it yet?"

Manuela shook her head, her heart beating fast. "I never got around to it." For some reason, her eyes stung. "But it's closed."

Cora laughed, then put a hand on Manuela's lower back to

guide her to the glass structure. "You seemed so unconcerned with potential breaking-and-entering charges the last time you intended to come here that I thought you'd be more than willing to engage in a little crime for the sake of your art."

Manuela's eyes narrowed at that. "You're telling me that your surprise is helping me break into the greenhouse?"

Cora's mouth twitched, which only made Manuela's own smile wider. "I called in a few favors and asked to be allowed in after hours."

"Breaking the law for me would've been far more romantic," Manuela countered, unable to hide her happiness at the gesture as they walked inside. No one had ever done something like this for her. Indulged her in this way. "This is wonderful," she said, as she took in the space. There were plants everywhere, sprays of birds-of-paradise and a dizzying array of orchids covering every inch of the many tables lined up and down the structure. They were at the center of the room where they'd set up a cluster of palms, which were conveniently hiding them from view. Unable to resist, Manuela reached for Cora and pulled her in for a kiss. First her jaw, then her cheek, then that mouth which was slowly becoming her favorite place. "Thank you," she whispered and stopped herself.

"You're welcome." They kissed slowly, tenderly, already practiced in the give-and-take of that intimate caress. Their tongues gliding together as they stood in the balmy heat of the greenhouse. Tropical birds chirped somewhere, and the water from the fountains scattered around the place gurgled as Manuela let herself imagine that this woman was hers and that this was but the beginning of a future full of big and small loving gestures. Of easy affection and scorching nights of lovemaking.

What a world to imagine: one in which this body pressed to hers, this mouth tasting hers could belong to her forever.

This woman of contradictions. Who arranged for her to see a greenhouse because Manuela said it mattered for her work. Who made sure her art was given not only its place but respected. Who, even when she was unkind, managed to be thoughtful.

With one last ardent kiss she pulled back, pushing aside any melancholy thoughts that would rob her of the happiness of this moment.

"Shall we go look for the lily pads?" she asked a little too brightly.

"They're this way." Cora waved a hand toward the depths of the greenhouse, then patted Manuela playfully on the bottom the moment she started to walk.

"Very unladylike, Your Grace." It was impossible not to smile.

"I thought you liked it when I didn't behave like a lady." That low, velvety voice, it made her melt.

"I more than like it," Manuela said, coming closer again, practically swooning when Cora's hands slid down to her rump and squeezed possessively. "Mm," she moaned as she was peppered with kisses on her neck and jaw.

"Didn't you say," Cora whispered, her mouth flush against Manuela's skin, "that you had some very important flowers to see here?"

"I did," Manuela admitted. "But your mouth is so enticing." Cora slid her tongue along Manuela's languidly, while her hand reached up to circle over her nipple. "Mm, that's going to delay things." A grin spread against her mouth.

"I would love nothing more than to have my way with you against one of these enormous potted palms." The duchess emphasized that point by sucking on an earlobe that pulled out an inhuman sound from Manuela. "But we only have about an hour." Manuela groaned, pressing her forehead to Cora.

"All right, but after this you are taking me back to your pink cavern and absolutely demolishing the last dregs of my virtue." That fizzy laugh—she was beginning to think of it as the sound of bliss. She wished she could bottle a bit of it and keep it with her for the unhappy times ahead.

"I will not rest until there is no trace of it left," Cora vowed, then pulled her in for one last kiss. "I'd keep you in bed until the moment you leave for Scotland, but I want to see you in that dress at the opera." Cora froze when she realized what she'd said. The wind went out of Manuela's sails, but she would not let sorrow have this moment.

"I am more excited about the parts when you take *off* my dress," she said, refusing to dwell on what could not be changed. She tightened her arms around Cora, then tipped her head up. How wretched it was to know you've found exactly what you've been looking for but it can't ever be yours.

"The opera will be our last outing." She didn't need to say what would happen at the end of their time together.

"I know." Cora pressed a kiss to the top of her head. She sounded hoarse, like she was fighting tears, but when Manuela lifted her gaze to her, those violet eyes were dry.

Stoic, strong, unwavering Corazón.

The woman she loved. She couldn't say it. It would be the end of this if she did. *But she could know it.* She could keep that truth in her heart, and it would be the flame she carried.

Nineteen

"Is it too bright?" Manuela asked as Cora's carriage conveyed them to the Théâtre Lyrique. She couldn't help smiling at the shameless fluttering of eyelashes that accompanied the question or the saucy pout trained in her direction.

"I thought you knew from having been in my rooms for most of the past two days that there is no shade of pink I find too extreme," Cora said, knowing her failure to provide the praise Manuela was after, combined with the reference to what they'd been doing in her rooms as of late, would likely lead to a more overt—and sensual—cry for attention. Her lover did not disappoint.

"But you haven't commented on the brooch."

The jewelry in question was made up of gray teardrop pearls and diamonds done in the shape of flower, and it was clasped to Manuela's dress right where her breasts met. Cora had seen it at Cartier, bought it on a whim and given it to her that morning. She could still feel the lingering ache between her legs from the heiress's very effusive gratitude.

"I've seen it. I bought it," Cora countered and received a very cheeky clicking of the tongue in response. "And *you* are fishing for compliments." She had to bite back a laugh at Manuela's huff of frustration, which preceded a subtle, but firm, shift in position that placed her bountiful bosom decidedly in Cora's range of vision. "I most certainly am fishing for them, and so far, mi duquesa, you are not showering me with the appreciation this décolletage commands," she shot back, that mischievous glint blazing in her brown eyes.

Cora obliged by running the tip of her nail very gently along in the space between the dress's neckline and that luscious cleavage. "Given the lengths I went to this morning to impress upon you how fond I am of this part of your body, I thought it would be superfluous to say it." A sharp intake of breath told her she was finally delivering the kind of adoration that was expected of her.

She'd made love to Manuela's breasts for hours, worrying them between her thumbs, swirling her tongue around the nipples, sucking the underside, burying her face between them until Manuela had climaxed just from the stimulation.

"You did make a fine argument," Manuela admitted a little breathlessly, as Cora circled a nipple with the pad of her thumb.

"But," Cora began, before bending to suck a bit of skin right on one of those delectable mounds, "I admit I could've been more effusive in my accolades," she said very seriously, before pulling out a breast from the bodice and sliding her tongue over it as she looked at Manuela. Manuela's answer was a tantalizing little moan, which she followed by turning herself until she was straddling Cora on the seat of the carriage.

"Just doing my part to facilitate any more praise you had in mind."

That sweet ache that was a constant since Manuela had come into her life sent a wave of heat coursing through Cora. Her shameless, greedy heiress, who was never content with just one kiss. Who always demanded absolutely everything from Cora.

Despite herself, she once again wished they had more time. That there was a way to keep this joy in her arms a little longer. That both their lives weren't already on courses that would require much destruction to alter. It was best not to think of that now. That reckoning would come later, but they still had tonight.

"Will your stepson be at the opera?" Manuela asked, too casually for there not to be some hidden question underneath.

"He wasn't invited," Cora told her, leaning down to press her lips to warm, buttery skin. "If he was allowed to come, then Tia Osiris would ask to come. And that would've led to Cassandra also inviting herself." Cora shook her head, turning her eyes up to Manuela, who was looking at her expectantly. "I wanted you to myself tonight."

They had avoided discussing what would happen after this last outing. Manuela was set to depart for Edinburgh in the morning, and after that their arrangement would be done. The deed would come to Cora soon after and she'd finally have what she needed to step into her rightful role as chairwoman of the South American Railway. Blanchet knew it was coming and had been pressuring her to produce the contract she'd signed with Manuela, but that would not do. Not when they'd see what she'd agreed to. She'd stalled, reminded him in front of the rest of the consortium he'd met the heiress himself. She'd shamelessly lied and bought herself more time. Now she was merely days away from what she'd been working toward for years. Instead of the satisfaction she'd imagined, all she wanted was to push it off.

She'd told herself tonight would be the end, that she'd bring Manuela to the opera and let her go. The mere thought suffocated her, and yet she would do it. She had to. Manuela was already a liability. She had to be strong: for herself, for Alfie, and even for Manuela, because ending her engagement would destroy her. That, paired with her family's past financial troubles, would be more than the respectable families in Venezuela could overlook. She'd become an outcast, and the heft of Manuela's demise was more than Cora's conscience could carry. Her arms, instead of loosening, tightened around her lover. As if her soul were protesting the demands her common sense was making of her.

Thankfully a jolt of the carriage coming to a stop relieved Cora from her spiraling thoughts.

"We're here," she said, pressing a kiss on Manuela's neck before she dismounted Cora's lap, right as the footman opened the door. For a breathless moment Cora wished he'd opened it a second sooner and everyone arriving at the opera house would see them. That the decision would be taken out of her hands.

"Georges Clairin made this," Manuela said as they mounted the steps, pointing to the placard displayed behind glass along the front of the theater. They would be seeing *Esclarmonde* tonight, which Jules Massenet had written exclusively to be debuted at the Exposition. "I heard he's been experimenting with Japanism," her artist explained. Her face very serious as she traced edges of the illustration with her gloved hand. "See the clouds? That's part of the aesthetic." The piece was done in a palette of blues and yellows. The woman standing under a beautifully rendered arch was dressed in long robes, a Byzantine crown on her head. Her eyes were stark and haunted as she held her veil away from her face. "There are so many elements, yet the effect is so clean and precise," Manuela marveled. Cora wanted to kiss her, would've given not a small amount of money to be able to take her by the hand and lead her into that theater, letting the world know this glorious creature was hers.

"Manuela, is that you?" They'd both been so engrossed in looking at the poster the newcomer caught them by surprise. Manuela paled when she saw the woman, prompting Cora to step back.

"Doña Amadita." Manuela beamed. She looked and sounded delighted, but Cora had learned to recognize when her lover was merely pretending to be so. "So wonderful to run into you here. This is the Duchess of Sundridge."

Doña Amadita's eyes widened. "Your Grace."

Cora was accustomed to a barrage of effusive greetings once her title was offered up, but none were forthcoming from Doña Amadita, who though polite, kept sending suspicious looks between Cora and Manuela. The older woman had clearly heard about Cora's reputation.

"Duchess, Doña Amadita's husband is a diplomat. He was the Venezuelan Ambassador to Britain for a number of years." This explained some of the lady's chilliness. At one time Cora had been a very hot topic of discussion, and for all the wrong reasons. Her rumored love life was bad enough, but her insistence in engaging in such lowly, disgraceful things as business and commerce incensed a large swath of the women of her class. Many of them were more disapproving than the men.

"Are Prospero and Consuelo inside?"

"No, my parents are still in London." Manuela's effusiveness was beginning to crack under the older woman's censure.

"I hope your fiancé is all right with your parents granting you so much liberty." The mention of Manuela's fiancé was a slap in the face. Manuela never mentioned the man and Cora more and more avoided the very notion of his existence.

"He is, of course." Manuela's non-answer seemed to further aggravate Doña Amadita, who continued to send unhappy looks in Cora's direction until she was finally pulled away by an equally sour-looking matron. The two of them walked off, Doña Amadita still loudly espousing her general discontent with "the many liberties unmarried girls took these days" as she entered the theater.

"She's an old friend of my mother's and a desperate chismosa," Manuela explained needlessly, sending a concerned look in the retreating woman's direction. After a moment she seemed to snap out of it and turned to the poster again. She examined it quite closely, her eyes darting back and forth over the illustration. Cora, who had never been able to stand still for very long, thought she could remain there for hours, if it meant watching Manuela take in a piece of art that interested her.

"I wonder if he is under contract with the theater," she mused, with a shrewd expression on her face Cora had not seen before. "Or if other theaters need that kind of work done."

"You are thinking of your artists' collective?" Cora asked, as they headed inside.

"Well, not mine," Manuela prevaricated as she'd done every time Cora implied she might have a permanent connection to the endeavor. "Or anyone's, really. So far it's been more my brain firing off silly ideas and me pestering Cassandra about them." Manuela had talked to Cora for almost an hour about her thoughts on the collective as they'd walked around the greenhouse. And her ideas were far from silly. She had a solid concept for how to organize artists in order to leverage better fees and steadier commissions. She even had the idea of compiling a catalogue with their work they could send to companies and publishing houses. There was something there, and it was clear it excited Manuela greatly, but so far, she'd staunchly insisted she would be returning to Venezuela to get married.

"From what I heard from Cassandra, she thinks all your suggestions are brilliant."

"They're not all mine, not really." Despite the folly in it, Cora wanted to push, to ask her if she was interested in working in the collective more formally. But that would lead to other questions, like how she'd be able to be involved in something that was happening across the ocean from where she lived.

Cora was not yet so reckless to enter into those marshlands.

"And I don't know about brilliant." Manuela blushed, her brown eyes glowing with a mix of longing and hope. "She did seem intrigued and said she'd discuss it with Monsieur Pasquale and the ladies from the dinner club. I even thought of offering the money of the sale of Baluarte to help with getting it off the ground. But I was very clear I would not be of much help once I leave Paris."

Cora would've never imagined that the same woman who had offered her land in exchange for a bit of fun would be standing before her, glowing at the prospect of using the funds to help artists unionize. Then again, she, like probably everyone in Manuela's life, had completely missed the heart of a lioness hidden in this woman. "My mother would have my hide if she ever heard I was involved in something like this, but I can just add that to the many ways in which I've disappointed her." She said this breezily but the same stark devastation Cora had seen when Doña Amadita walked away settled in her gaze.

"Is she hard on you?" she asked, unable to contain herself.

Manuela gave her another one of those shrugs that seemed to encompass a world of disillusions. "She's under the impression I am to blame for all of her worldly troubles. Which is why I must make up for it with this marriage."

A scandal at the moment would cast a shadow over Alfie's return to London, Cora told herself, in place of speaking. She had duties that superseded whatever personal losses she might experience.

A suffocating silence rose between them as they stood in the threshold of the theater. She wanted to make this evening memorable for Manuela, but Cora was struggling to keep her emotions from clouding her judgment.

"This is beautiful," Manuela said, valiantly mustering up a smile as she looked up at the gilded walls and the marble staircase.

"It's one of the newer theaters in the city," Cora told her, thankful for any excuse to get out of her own head. "It was seized at the end of the Paris Commune and mostly destroyed."

Manuela continued to observe, her eyes turning this way and that as Cora guided her up the marble staircase. Her pink dress contrasted beautifully against the gild and white marble. She was luminous, made for Parisian nights. Manuela Caceres Galvan, always in full bloom. Cora swallowed down the bitter taste in her mouth at the thought that this living, breathing garden would soon belong to someone else.

By the time they got to Cora's box Manuela's mood seemed lighter, while Cora's darkened with each passing second.

"I've been in opera boxes before, but this is the most lavish I've ever seen." Cora had seized the box in lieu of payment from a French duke who could not repay a debt in time. Usually she was eager to share the anecdote of how she'd bested the monetarily delinquent peer, but she had no appetite for it tonight.

"It was quite shabby when it was passed to me."

In fact, it had been in tatters and she'd made a point of turning it into the best one in the house. A loud reminder to all the men who liked to look down on her that she could not only have a box, but that she could have one far better than theirs. God, how had she managed to delude herself with the lie that these hollow little victories over mediocre men brought her any kind of glory?

This line of thinking would lead nowhere. She clenched her jaw at her errant, unhelpful musings and turned to Manuela's expectant gaze.

"There is not much one can do about the space constraints, but the designer I had made the most of it."

"I love this little room," Manuela said, turning around in a circle to take it all in. "This is so luxurious." Manuela leaned into the dark green velvet-covered wall and ran a reverent hand over it.

"That was made by a group of women in Lyon." She wanted to tell Manuela that the owner was a friend who'd fought to keep the house open after her husband died. That Cora had seen the quality of work she did and given her a loan when the banks refused to. She could almost see the delight on her face when Manuela found out that Madame Colbert, in only three years, had grown her textile firm to double the size of what her husband had managed in twenty. She didn't say it because that would make Manuela light up—she'd smile and ask questions. Her eyes would glow with curiosity and Cora would be caught in the web again. So, she remained silent as the heiress walked around the room, exploring with that unquenchable inquisitiveness of hers.

They moved into the even smaller alcove, Manuela at the fore and Cora behind her, close enough that the back of that bright pink skirt brushed against her own dark blue one.

"This is cozy," Manuela whispered suggestively, and immediately that flash of heat crackled inside Cora. They were in tight quarters, here in this intimate space curtained off from the balcony.

It was serviceable enough to sit with a handful of guests and enjoy some privacy during the intermission, but it was small. The entirety of the accommodations consisted of a table, two chairs, a settee, and a chaise, which Cora had once imagined as the place where she'd ravish society ladies under their husbands' very noses.

Of course, she barely ever used it. She was always too busy. But that was all part of the specter of The Duchess: she made a point of distinguishing herself from the other women of her class. The Duchess of Sundridge did not indulge in leisure, she outworked the tradesmen and outsmarted the peers. Although in the past few days she'd wondered what it would be like to slow down. To stop working long enough to enjoy the fruits of her labor.

With a woman like this you would have to, she thought as Manuela strolled along the narrow passage to the seats, her hands brushing the polished wood. She wouldn't just have to slow down. She'd want to. She'd even thought of taking Manuela on a picnic, for God's sake.

How had the time gone by so fast? When they'd made the deal, the prospect of having to amuse a frivolous heiress had been daunting, but Manuela had turned every expectation Cora had on its head. *She will only be in Scotland for ten days* a voice that sounded very much like Cassandra nudged her. Manuela still had a few weeks left in Paris once she returned. They could...

The words were like acid in her mouth, burning holes on her tongue. The absurd, impulsive words aching to come out.

"If your mother would disapprove of you using your funds for the collective, I could help," she offered instead, somehow delving into even more treacherous territory.

This was not the path to ending this evening, this arrangement, on a good note. Wading into Manuela's trials with her parents, the reasons she continued to pursue this ridiculous engagement when she clearly didn't love the ridiculous man she was to marry, wouldn't make their parting any easier. And yet, once again she opened her mouth. This time it seemed determined to self-sabotage. "I could pay for some—"

Manuela's fingers came over her lips and she tsked with her tongue. "Your Grace, the last thing you want to do is hear about my baggage when you are merely hours away from being free and clear of me and my demands." In the darkness of the hallway Cora could only listen for what was not being said. She wished she could see her face. She should be glad, grateful that this woman who had at every turn upended her plans was for once holding fast to the rules. Manuela was, finally, doing exactly what Cora had asked of her, and she hated it.

"What would you have me do then, princess?" There was a suffocating tightness inside her, like there were two people ruthlessly tugging on either end of a rope coiled around her chest. Her good sense was stretched to the brink of snapping, and still this hunger ravaged her. All this shame, this want, this unbridled need spilling over.

"What you always do, Your Grace," her heiress said, as she

slid a hand over the bodice of Cora's dress, up to the triangle of bare skin on her chest, until Manuela had her palm clasped around her neck. "Make me forget what happens after this. Remind me that today is for pleasure."

"Are you wet for me?" she growled in Manuela's ear, as her princess dug her teeth into Cora.

"I always am for you," she purred, pressing herself closer, rocking into that touch. It was madness to do this, to fuck her when someone could knock on the box door at any time. Just feet away from a curtain that would reveal them to the very people who could destroy her. But her notorious self-preservation instincts escaped her tonight. She'd take her right against this velvet and use this room for what she'd built it for, finally.

"Anyone could see us through the opening in the curtain," she said, before biting on an earlobe as she dug her fingers deeper. Manuela moaned, her legs opening wider, eager for Cora's touch. "Mm, you like that, you dirty girl. Does that make you hot? Thinking of an usher walking in on us while I have my head between your legs? While I make you scream for me?" Manuela bucked into her then, her inner walls squeezing Cora's three fingers.

"They'll know I'll let you have me anywhere. That I live for your touch, for your tongue." Cora froze at the words, her heart hammering in her chest at the savagery of her need. But her princess was chasing her climax, lost in her need. "More Cora, please. Make me fall apart." In the next second, she felt that delicious squeeze against her fingers, and her princess's tongue sliding between her lips. They kissed hungrily, that hot velvety caress mirroring what Cora's hand did between Manuela's legs.

"Mm, yes, make me come like this," her lover pleaded as her fingernails scored Cora's skin. She pressed a fist to her mouth when Cora pulled down the edge of the pink bodice to expose one of those gorgeous breasts.

"Tell me no one else has ever made you feel like this," she

demanded, as she circled Manuela's clitoris with the pad of her thumb.

"Taste me," her lover growled instead, denying her, and Cora smiled at her demanding princess.

"You want me on my knees for you with half of Paris outside the door?" She heard eager sounds as Manuela's hands tightened on her shoulders.

"Yes," Manuela whispered against her mouth before taking Cora's lip between her teeth and sucking it hard enough to sting. "Every time you come in here, I want you to remember me. I want you to crave my taste on your tongue. I want you to miss me." She was angry, she sounded furious—and jealous—and God help her, Cora loved it.

"Lift your skirt." Cora was rewarded with a wicked, lusty laugh that made her blood sing.

"Only if you get on your knees." The defiance in her voice annihilated Cora.

For once, she took her orders without protest and soon she was dipping back into the opening of Manuela's combination. She could hear people outside, arriving at their boxes, gossiping about dresses and whose mistress was present that night.

For one second of madness she allowed herself to imagine what it would be like to turn her back on the life she'd built. To lay waste to her reputation, her position, and live openly with a lover. She knew she couldn't do it. Which was why she'd never ask her to throw away her life only to be Cora's paramour for a few months.

"At what time do you leave in the morning?" she asked from her place at Manuela's feet.

The light in Manuela's eyes dimmed at the question, but when she finally answered her voice was strong and clear. "The train leaves at ten," she said, and leaned down to cup the back of Cora's head. A gentle but urgent touch.

Cora closed her eyes, hiding from seeing in Manuela's the

same despair she was feeling. Instead she blindly wrapped her arms around her thighs, squeezing with all her might. She pressed her nose to her lover's heat. Inhaled her, touched that sacred place and drank from it. Let herself be consecrated by this woman's flesh and poured everything she had into making love to Manuela Caceres Galvan.

A cry and whispered yes tumbled down to Cora's ears as she licked and touched. She dipped her fingers into that fire, she'd always crave. She made love to Manuela like the fires of hell awaited in the wings. She heard a breathy gasp as fingers dug into the back of her head. She kissed the wet folds, the juncture of her thighs, every bit of skin that was bare to her before lifting to her feet, willing herself not to think of the morning.

"Was that to your satisfaction, princesa?" She leaned in for a kiss, Manuela's taste still on her tongue. Cora palmed that lush derriere and even over the layers of fabric she felt her warmth. One that Cora would never stop wanting. This woman, her smell, the unguarded way she gave herself to Cora were indelibly printed in her very essence now, and that would have to be enough.

When they sat down in the plush velvet chairs and leaned in to watch Esclarmonde and Roland's treacherous road to love, Cora could almost convince herself her heart wasn't being torn into a million pieces.

Twenty

She was going back to Paris, Manuela decided, as she sat in Luz Alana and Evan's drawing room after a day that could only be described as harrowing. She and Aurora had arrived several days earlier, and in that time, Evan and his half-brother—who had turned out to be none other than Aurora's detested dance partner from the Mexican soiree—had exposed the Duke of Annan as a thief and a liar. Then they'd woken up to the news that the warehouses where Evan kept his whisky were on fire. While he was tending to that, Luz Alana got herself held up at gunpoint, all before dinnertime.

In short, Manuela would've been quite done with Scotland even if she wasn't missing Cora every second of the day. That last night together had been as agonizing as it was glorious. They'd made love until they'd fallen asleep exhausted in each other's arms, and when the morning came they'd parted with bruising kisses and choked goodbyes. Cora had been stoic, attempting to reassure her. She'd gone on about the funds for the sale, and it was all Manuela had been able to do not to fall to her knees and confess that she'd fallen in love. That she couldn't bear the idea of returning to Venezuela now. That she was certain Cora cared for her too.

But she hadn't: the fear of Cora's rejection had kept her silent. At the opera there had been moments when she'd almost thought her lover was holding something back. But if there were any confessions of true love hidden somewhere inside the duchess, she'd kept those to herself.

Manuela had arrived at the house at Place des Vosges almost at daybreak with Cora's scent on her hands, her mouth, her tongue, and boarded the train in a fog. She'd been so morose even Aurora—for once—bit her tongue.

"I thought you were the boisterous friend," Apollo Cesar Sinclair Robles, the new Earl of Darnick, commented, pulling Manuela out of her sulking.

"Don't *you* have your own house?" Aurora had always been direct, but with Evan's brother she was shockingly rude. The most confusing part was that he seemed delighted by her vitriol.

"You've got cream on your lips, Doctora." He leaned back and brushed his thumb over his own mouth, looking at Aurora's. He was clearly trying to provoke another tongue-lashing from her. He was bafflingly fond of seeing her friend lose her temper. "You do enjoy your sweets. What is that one called again?"

"You know very well it's a cranachan."

The two of them launched into another row. Manuela sighed and turned to Luz Alana and Evan in the hopes of distracting herself from the incessant barrage of thoughts plaguing her mind. But the newlyweds only had eyes for each other and were engaged in an exchange of such heated glances it was a miracle their clothes were not incinerating, which frankly did not help her own mood in the least.

She knew returning to Paris so soon was impulsive. That her friends would worry she was acting rashly again. And maybe she was, but she missed Cora and wanted to see her. After what they'd all lived through over the past few days, seeing how close

Luz Alana and Evan had come to losing each other out of sheer stubbornness, she couldn't stop thinking about Cora. About the way they'd left things. It couldn't be the end, or at least she could not allow it to end without telling her how she truly felt. Telling her their time together had changed her irrevocably, that she'd reclaimed parts of herself she'd thought were lost forever. It was more than just what she felt for Cora: for the first time, Manuela had found people living a life that seemed worthy of risking her safety.

The Manuela who arrived in Paris was too scared of the unknown to ever take a leap like that, but now, she'd seen there were possibilities for someone like her. A woman, a lesbian, an artist. She only had to be brave.

There would be complications. She knew that. There were her parents, and there was Felix, but she had her art. Her skills which she now trusted could be a means to support herself. She had a group of friends who would help her make her way. She even had that tiny ember of ambition to create something lasting through the collective. Something that would help women like her find their own independence.

The Manuela who had accepted Felix's offer of marriage believed that was her only path, but this past month had shown her that women could forge their own.

"What is the latest train to London?" she heard herself ask. The other three turned to her at once.

"There is a midnight train to Charing Cross," Evan told her, with a confused look on his face.

She looked at the clock and saw that it was nine o'clock, stood and for once refused to question her impulses.

"Is there something wrong, Leona?" Luz Alana asked, her face concerned. Manuela knew they would likely disapprove of this, once again accuse her of being rash, but the truth was she didn't care. Manuela looked between Aurora and Luz Alana. Her best friends, the two people in the world who knew her best.

The two people in the world who wanted to see her happy and hoped they could once again be there for her, unconditionally.

"I'm going back to Paris," she announced, surprised by the steel in her voice. She was certain now that it was the right decision. Even if Cora was truly done with her, she had to at least tell her the truth. That she'd been the water Manuela's courage needed to flourish.

"To Paris?" Aurora asked, surprisingly calm.

"Yes." She sent an apologetic look to Luz Alana, who was now sitting straight up, eyes alert. "I know we promised we'd stay a week, Luz, but I have to return." She wrung her hands in front of herself, not from embarrassment but because it was taking an extraordinary effort to not bolt out of the room to start tossing her things into a trunk. "I feel as though there is unfinished business with me and Cora, and if there is a chance to spend the rest of the time I have before going back to Venezuela with her, I don't want to waste it."

"But I thought your deal was done?" To her amazement there wasn't a trace of exasperation in Aurora's question, only sympathy.

"It is," Manuela said awkwardly. "I just need to tell her how I feel, even it's too late... I'm sorry, Luz."

Her friend waved her away, standing up from her place on Evan's lap. "I can't advise you not to take a chance when you were the one to remind me again and again I had a right to find my own happiness when I refused to accept my true feelings for Evan." At the mention of his name, Luz Alana's husband reached for her hand. They looked at each other with such tenderness that something inside Manuela screamed. It wasn't jealousy so much as longing, of yearning to have that, and she knew exactly the person she wanted it with.

Apollo cleared his throat. "I can escort her," he told his brother. "I have business in Paris I need to take care of. I was leaving in the morning, but I'm sure my man could get us two tickets on the midnight train."

"Three," Aurora announced, placing her empty dish on a small table. She shot Apollo a dirty look, then sent a surly one to Manuela. "I am *not* letting you travel alone with this cretino."

"All these endearments are going to go to my head, Doctora."

Manuela truly feared for Apollo's life when he insisted on taunting Aurora like this.

"Perhaps I can come back in a few days' time—" Manuela began, but Luz Alana didn't let her finish.

"What do you need, Leona?" her friend asked, no hesitation in her voice, the final straw after days of holding in a heartbreak so wrenching she'd felt like air was scarcely entering her lungs. She threw herself in Luz Alana's arms, sobbing with relief to finally be able to allow her friends into her secret misery.

"I need Cora, to see her," she confessed, as the tears she'd not allowed herself to shed in years finally came, and she felt another set of arms and noted Aurora's familiar scent at her back. There was movement in the room, and Evan's and Apollo's hushed voices as Manuela let herself be anchored by her friends.

"Are you still going to marry him?"

Even though Luz Alana delivered the question with utmost gentleness, she felt the sting of it. But this was the question, was it not? With her cheek still pressed to Luz Alana's shoulder, ensconced in the cocoon her friends had built for her, Manuela could finally admit what she truly wanted.

For so long she'd fed herself such lies about what would make her happy, what she could have, what she was willing to accept. None of it was what she truly desired. In a way her preferences, knowing she could only truly love another woman, had made it easier. She could tell herself there was no possibility of a life in which she could live from her art or coupled to another woman. Knowing the life she would've wished for herself was impossible made it easier to tolerate one she detested. But now she'd seen it *was* possible, and she couldn't look away.

It was choking her, the need to say it, if only to give it air.

"I don't want to," she admitted, comforted by her friends' embrace. "I don't want to, but I fear it's too late. Felix won't take this well, and my parents will never forgive me for the humiliation." Aurora made a disgusted noise, but instead of her usual barbs, she only held Manuela tighter. "I thought it would be enough to have this time of freedom. To have this one experience to look back on. That the comforts of the life I'd have with Felix would somehow be enough, but I can't do it." She was crying again, but with every word she said she felt lighter, clearer.

Luz Alana looked wretched, her eyes brimming with tears. "We should've known you were struggling, that you were just putting on a brave face. I am sorry, Leona."

"Don't," Manuela said, even has her friend's words soothed a deep ache in her. "I hid everything from you. I won't ever again."

"You don't have to keep things inside," Luz Alana told her, eyes fierce as she took Manuela's face between her hands.

"You deserve to have exactly what you want, Leona, not the dregs left over once your parents have their fill," Aurora said in an unusually raspy voice.

"There is no future with Cora," she insisted, if only to prepare herself for what would happen when she returned to Paris. Regardless of what she felt, of what they'd shared, the duchess had not spoken a word of wanting more with her. "She'd never risk being tied to a scandal like the one Felix will almost surely cause if I end the engagement."

"You don't know that for sure," Luz Alana told her. "Maybe she's in Paris feeling exactly as you do." Her friend sent her husband a look of such unguarded love, Manuela ached. "Go to her, tell her how you feel. If she can't give you what you want, at least you'll know for sure."

Her friend's words helped, but she couldn't lose the niggling of doubt. "She's very invested in making sure her stepson can return to London without any rumors trailing him from Paris."

Apollo made an unhappy huffing sound from his perch at the table. "Isn't this duchess Chilean?" He made a sound of disgust when Manuela nodded. "Why do any of you care about what people with the moral high ground of an anthill think about what you do?" The Earl of Darnick was unable to maintain his mask of indifference for once. "They came to our countries and did what they damn well pleased. Why can't we do the same? Who cares about the opinion of some soulless ghoul sitting in one of those marble mausoleums on Curzon Street? Que se jodan todos."

Although she couldn't disagree with the sentiment that moralistic zealots could all go to hell, it wasn't quite that simple. They might all be South American, but that didn't mean society rules didn't apply to them. Then again, the fact that she was contemplating running back to see her female lover to confess her undying love already placed her well outside the confines of polite society.

Manuela didn't want to spend one more minute of the time she had left in Europe thinking about anyone's *opinions*. All she wanted was to spend it with Cora.

"Que se jodan," she echoed Apollo, as she pulled away from her friends. Her Leonas, her pride. "I cannot miss that train."

"Then, we better get moving," Luz Alana declared, at the same moment that Aurora clapped her hands and ran off to pack them "refreshments." The rest of the evening was a blur. In one hour they had their trunks packed and ready to be loaded on the carriage, and in two they were arriving at the station.

At exactly one minute past midnight Manuela, Aurora and Apollo pulled out of Waverley station, headed for Paris.

"Querida, you made Laurent cry," Tia Osiris chided as they walked around their private garden. An activity her aunt had insisted on since she was apparently tired of watching Cora sulk in her study.

"I did no such thing," she protested, as they rounded a cluster of perfectly manicured topiaries. She couldn't even muster up any remorse for her horrid behavior. She had been an absolute misery to be around for the past week. She'd lost her temper twice in a meeting, which she was certain resulted in rumblings about her becoming hysterical. Not even finalizing the purchase of the building from Grinaud could lift her mood.

"You *almost* did," her aunt argued as she leaned down to pick up a sprig of rosemary and pressed it to her nose. "Querida, why don't you write her a letter? Tell her you miss her." Cora pressed her lips together and looked up at the beautiful sky, striving to gather patience so she didn't yell at her elderly aunt.

"Tia, please, you must stop this," she pleaded. "There is nothing to be gained from having this conversation. I don't miss her. Our agreement is *done*." There was no helping the exasperation in her voice, not that Tia Osiris was even remotely intimidated by Cora's outburst.

Yes, she was…mildly irked this week. It was true that she had felt Manuela's absence in a way she had not expected. But that didn't alter the circumstances around their arrangement, nor did it have any bearing on what Cora intended to do. "In a week's time, the deed will be reverted to me, and it will be done. My personal feelings were never a part of this."

"Why do you lie to yourself?" Tia Osiris asked, and Cora sighed, wishing she was somewhere with a closing door.

"I'm not lying, I'm being sensible," she insisted for her own sake as much as Tia Osiris's.

"You are being a total arsewit."

This offering came from Cassandra, who had arrived an hour earlier to regale Cora, once again, with a lecture in all the ways she was a dimwitted imbecile for letting Manuela go to Scotland without confessing her true feelings.

"I can't be involved in another scandal," she said looking at the women on either side of her. They looked back at her, stone-faced, from under their bonnets. "I am serious. Alfie is mere weeks from returning to London. Not to mention I finally have the building for the club. Or that I'm poised to lead the biggest railway project of the last twenty years." She stood there, shoulders hunched up to her ears, pressing two fingers into the stinging in her eyes and swallowing down the despair crawling up her throat. "Manuela." Cora had not uttered her name for days, and hearing it now made something painful and wretched twist in her chest. "Manuela and I had a deal, she has her obligations, *her duties*, and I have mine. How we feel doesn't matter. I don't miss her, I'm just tired," she lied as her aunt and friend sent her matching disbelieving glares.

"So you are telling me that this reign of terror we have all endured has nothing to do with the fact that the woman you have been utterly infatuated with is gone," Tia Osiris scoffed.

"I have never in my life been infatuated," Cora retorted, ignoring her aunt. "And yes, that is what I am saying. I am stressed and tired of being pestered in my own home. My mood has nothing to do with Manuela," Cora insisted stubbornly, through a painfully clenched jaw. "I—"

A footman running toward them interrupted her from listing another reason why they were all dead wrong about what she wanted.

"Your Grace," he croaked the second he reached them. He looked completely terrified. It seemed Laurent had taken himself out of the line of fire. The coward.

"I thought I said no interruptions!" she wailed, wishing she'd gone to her cottage in Nice like she'd intended.

"Mademoiselle Caceres Galvan is here to see you."

Cora whipped around in the direction of the house so fast, she became lightheaded. Her ears were ringing. "What?" Somewhere in the recesses of her mind, the footman's words rang like cannon fire.

Mademoiselle Caceres Galvan. Bang.

Here. Bang.

To see you. Bang. Bang. Bang.

"Miss Caceres Galvan is here." he repeated, his voice shaking. In her periphery she could see her aunt's and Cassandra's discreet smiles. But she was frozen in place. Her hands worryingly cold as her heart pounded erratically. Hope and elation whirling inside her. "It seems she has just arrived from Calais and would like an audience."

"Yes," Cora said, before finally moving toward the house. "Yes, I will see her. Tia, Cassandra, I must go."

"I thought you said you were done with her?" Cassandra teased.

"I was obviously lying through my teeth," Cora groused as she set off at a run.

"Can we meet her in the morning?" Tia Osiris called after her, but Cora was already halfway up the steps to the house and then there she was. Travel-worn and weary. A riot of chocolate curls all over her face, and she looked like she was dead on her feet. Cora had never in her life seen anything—not the Sistine chapel, not *The Birth of Venus*—that could compare to what she had before her.

"You're here." Even she could hear the awe in her voice.

"I am," Manuela said with a small, nervous laugh. She looked wary, like she didn't know how she'd be received. Like she expected to be turned away. Cora almost dissolved into laughter at the thought of all the lies she'd just told her aunt and best friend. "I know our agreement is done, but—"

"I've missed you," Cora said, reaching for her, unable to keep the truth from Manuela. Not when she'd been braver than Cora. She placed a hand on Manuela's cheek, and her princess immediately pressed into the touch. Always so open, so devastatingly honest.

"I've dreamed of your hands," she whispered and turned her face to press a kiss to Cora's palm. She groaned as need cut through her and moved to kiss her brave princess. They had an audience and she didn't care.

In front of Laurent, the footmen and whoever wanted to look, she tightened her arms around her lover's waist and gently nipped at that plump, delectable bottom lip.

"I missed every inch of you." One of those little lusty sounds escaped Manuela, and Cora slid her tongue in for a taste. Manuela returned the caress in earnest, sliding her own tongue along hers, and soon they were kissing hungrily. Hands gripping hard enough to tear at their clothes, ragged breaths echoing around them. Cora let herself go and poured everything she'd been holding in for days into Manuela, weak with gratitude, blazing with joy.

"My love," Manuela whispered, and Cora's heart broke open. Desire, yearning, love, rushed out of it like an avalanche. "I don't know what I will do next," she said, those brown eyes open and honest. That was Manuela, wearing every one of her feelings on her sleeve. Her love, her fear, her sadness, there for the world to see. "But I knew I needed more time with you."

Cora didn't know what there was to be done. She had spoken the truth earlier when she'd said she could not risk a scandal, but now standing here with Manuela in her arms, she knew for sure she couldn't just walk away. There were no clear answers, and there would not be any easy solutions.

"I am so glad you're here," Cora said as she ran her hands over that lush body she'd so desperately missed.

"Really?" Manuela asked, her eyes shadowed with uncertainty. "This is one of the many downsides of being impulsive," she said, her shoulders drooping. "The realization of how monumentally reckless you've been usually crashes on you all at once, which usually leads to utter mortification."

Something inside Cora shattered at Manuela's confession. She could never be this strong. Not even with Sally—yes, she'd begged and pleaded, but she'd come to realize it had been out of bruised pride, not love. Sally had made everything easy for Cora. Had agreed with every opinion, concurred with every decision. She'd inflated Cora's vanity, and when she'd cast her aside, she'd lashed out. Nothing with Manuela had been simple or comfortable. At every turn this woman had challenged her notions of herself, of what it meant to be strong.

"Come with me," she said, too much emotion clogging her throat to say more. Thankfully Manuela allowed herself to be led into Cora's bedchambers.

Once she'd closed the door, Cora couldn't wait and pressed Manuela against the wall to kiss her again.

"The only one who should be mortified is me. I should've been on a train for Edinburgh the morning after you left. Did you truly come back for me?"

"Cora," Manuela's tone was reproachful, like she couldn't believe she dared ask. Then her expression became a bit more determined, stronger. "In truth, I also wanted to make some arrangements regarding the collective," she added. Something about the way she said it made Cora frown.

"What kind of arrangements?"

"I was considering having the funds from the sale of Baluarte put in a trust, to fund the first few years." Cora did not like the sound of that. If Manuela gave away those funds, she'd be left with no means of escaping that blasted marriage in the future.

"I have already talked to Cassandra about helping them," she lied. She hadn't done any such thing, but she would if it meant that Manuela didn't throw away her only protection.

"You did?" Manuela cried, happily, circling her arms around Cora's neck.

"Yes, and I will help them, but I don't like the idea of you parting with the funds from Baluarte."

Manuela gave her a wry look, clearly confused by Cora's insistence. But after a moment she smiled, pressing herself closer. "Tell me you missed me," she said.

She had no idea how any of this would work. She was set to announce the railway at a reception at the British embassy in a week. The consortium was waiting for the deed to vote for the chairperson. All the things she'd been working for years to achieve, and yet nothing in that moment felt more important than showing this woman the ferocity with which she needed her.

"More than air, princesa. I promise there will be no doubt in your mind how much, by the time I've had my way with you," Cora stated with absolute honesty, as her hands worked to undo the fastenings of Manuela's skirts. When she tried to help, Cora shook her head and took a playful bite out of one breast. "I'll work on the bottom, you work the top, sweetheart. I want you naked and with my head between your legs in the next five minutes, and that will require a concerted effort."

Manuela, bless her nimble fingers and horny heart, had herself in nothing but her chemise in seconds while Cora pulled off her own skirts, petticoats and boots.

"Unbutton it," she demanded, her voice hoarse.

"You too," Manuela commanded, and Cora, who had only been in a tea gown, quickly began undressing herself while she watched. Manuela took off her chemise with impressive patience. Slowly, so slowly, undoing one button after another until Cora could see a strip of golden brown skin down to her navel. She tugged on the edges, exposing those beautiful, heavy breasts.

"They're hard for me," Cora whispered, forcing restraint. She didn't think she'd have this woman again, and she'd be damned if she rushed it. "Pluck on the tips, love," she asked in the quiet of the room. She watched her lover tweak and pinch, feeling her own arousal pooling between her legs, but unwilling to relieve the ache yet.

Manuela Caceres Galvan was a feast to be savored. A woman to love languidly, with deliberate focus. Plundering and conquering was for men: women plowed, cultivated. Manuela's body was sacred ground, and Cora would give it the devotion and nurturing it deserved until she harvested a bounty of moans and cries of pleasure.

"Let me see your concha, amor."

The Spanish surprised Manuela, a naughty little smile tugging up her lips as she said, "Sí, mi duquesa." She slid the straps of the chemise off her shoulders and soon the lace-and-linen garment was pooled at her feet, revealing all that lushness for Cora's enjoyment. She had to breathe through the need clawing at her.

"Bed," she managed to say.

She looked at Manuela lying on the bed with her curls fanned out on the satin sheets. A goddess, the reward Cora didn't deserve but would humbly receive.

"Make love to me," Manuela whispered as she planted her feet on the bed, her knees wide apart. Cora's mouth watered at the sight and climbed between her lover's thighs. She traced a trail of kisses up one leg then the other, encouraged by Manuela's sighs and moans.

"I have been dying for this," she said, her mouth pressed to that hot, wet heat, and spread her with two fingers. She licked inside, quickly turning sweet sighs into urgent cries.

"Harder, darling," Manuela asked, rolling her hips in Cora's mouth and fingers. She pinched the clitoris, then rubbed up and down the slippery folds while her princess writhed under her, clutching the sheets as she cried Cora's name.

"Mi amor, to boca," she begged, and who was she to deny this woman anything. She sucked on those dewy lips, grazed them with her teeth as her fingers scissored in out of her slippery channel.

"You are so sweet." As she talked, she kept rubbing that spot inside while Manuela's leg shook with her cresting climax. "I love hearing your scream for me," she said, before dipping back in and sucking hard on her lover's engorged clitoris. She tasted the climax as strongly as she felt the waves of it crashing through

Manuela, until she slumped boneless on the bed. "That's it, sweetheart," she cooed, still tasting and licking until she felt Manuela's hands tighten on her. She raised her head and found her lover staring back at her with hooded eyes and a sated look that rearranged everything inside Cora.

"I want to taste *you* now," Manuela said, eliciting an almost painful tug between her legs. "Will you let me?" she asked, eyes hungry. Her lusty princess. Always wanting more.

"What exactly did you have in mind?" Cora asked innocently, even as she sat up and straddled Manuela's hips.

"I'd like for you to come up here." She circled a finger over her face, her eyes still on Cora. The walls inside her clenched with need in response. She was aching for Manuela's mouth.

"What would you do with me?"

That devilish smile sent a shiver through Cora's spine. Her body readying itself for the pleasure it knew would come. Manuela didn't waste time in describing her plans for her.

"I'd use my hands to get you in just the right position, cant your hips so you're at the perfect angle to be devoured," she explained, her fingers simulating how she'd presumably spread Cora's folds. "Then I'd use my tongue on you. Just little flicks at first." She gestured, that pink tongue flickering enticingly and again, that sweet tug made Cora squirm on her lover's lap. "Then I'd give you deep, long strokes. Mm." She made a sinful sound, her eyes closed as she licked her lips, while Cora shook. "I'd bury my tongue so far inside you, I'd feel you tighten against me. My fingers would be next and they'd slide inside, on all that dewy passion you always have for me."

She winked, and Cora felt liquid rush out of her. "Then…" she said as she tapped her chin and raised her gaze to the ceiling, apparently considering what to do next. "Then I'd eat at you until you flooded my mouth and screamed my name…more or less. The order could vary."

Cora was panting by the time Manuela was finished talking,

trembling with need and ready to crawl up and demand that she do every one of the filthy things she'd promised. But she didn't have to. Her lover, without the need to be asked, diligently delivered on every one of them, down to Cora very loudly shouting Manuela's name during a mind-shattering orgasm.

"How can anyone be so beautiful?" Cora asked a while later, looking at Manuela as she lay on her stomach, her curls cascading down her back.

"You tell me, Your Grace." She bit her bottom lip and looked wantonly over her shoulder, that cheeky grin undoing Cora's control. She knelt on the bed and ran her hands over that round backside, then unable to resist, leaning in to take a bite.

"Mm, I like that," Manuela purred, tipping her rump in the air. Cora laughed, then licked the spot where she'd bitten, before sucking a love bite on the other cheek.

Manuela sighed, resting her head on her arms as Cora fondled and touched her back and rump. "You certainly know how to make a weary traveler feel welcome." Her voice was a little slurred, probably the days of travel and their frantic lovemaking catching up to her.

"I'm going to order up some food, so I can keep you in bed as long as possible," Cora told her.

"That is not the threat you think it is, Duchess." Manuela lifted her head for a kiss, an achingly sweet smile on her lips.

Cora continued to touch her, rubbing circles on her back, leaning down to place openmouthed kisses on her warm, sweaty skin and tried very hard not to offer things she would later regret. She had planned her life so meticulously, been so careful, only to be undone by the woman who was supposed to help her claim her biggest feat yet.

"I can't believe you came back to me."

"I missed you," Manuela told her again, clear and strong. Unafraid. Cora would be brave too.

"I missed you too, so much," she whispered into the silence

of a bedroom that no longer felt hers. That had been unbearably empty and cold without Manuela's smiles and cries of pleasure. Manuela sat up to face Cora, her expression a mixture of affection and dread.

"I don't think I can betray my parents," Manuela admitted, her eyes filling with tears. And Cora could not risk any disruptions with the railway, which would almost certainly happen if she decided to help Manuela get out of her engagement. Not that she'd said she wanted that. "I want you so much," she said and gulped visibly, "but I don't know if I can do it. I'm afraid."

"I'm afraid too." Cora had never uttered those words before, had barely ever admitted them to herself. And here she was, thirty-five years old, electrified by the prospect of a future she'd buried long ago.

A future that would cost a hell of a lot to secure but might just be worth it.

Twenty-One

"Cora, you didn't say this was an actual palace!" Manuela exclaimed as their carriage slowed down at the end of a long row of conveyances waiting to deliver their passengers to the residence of the British ambassador for a reception to honor the various businessmen—and businesswoman—from the United Kingdom living in France.

"I told you it was called the Charost Palais," she laughed, leaning in to kiss Manuela on the cheek. She was resplendent today in a yellow dress. She looked well pleased, well fed and well…bedded, and Cora was exceedingly proud to know she was partly responsible for it.

It was the evening they'd planned to announce the completion of the railway.

Mere weeks ago, if someone had told Cora that she would be setting out to announce her greatest victory accompanied not only by her new lover but by her new lover's rather prickly best friend, she would have insisted they were mad. And yet…

The last week had been a watershed for Cora. Manuela's return to her had done away with any notion she harbored about continuing on as she had been, though there were too many unknowns to rush into anything.

Manuela had her parents to think about, and Cora had Alfie and her railway, not to mention Manuela's imminent marriage in Venezuela. They'd been through at least a dozen iterations of how to do it and inevitably arrived at the conclusion that whatever it was would involve at least *some* scandal. Neither of them had made any promises. Cora's life and her dealings didn't exactly allow for domesticity. But perhaps if she could help Manuela get settled here in Paris... If she could help her with her idea to organize a guild for commercial artists... If Manuela had the means to stay...

Faced with the daunting string of *if*s, Manuela proposed that Cora focus on getting the sale of Baluarte settled, and once that was out of the way and their deal done, they could make future plans. Cora swore to never again put herself in a situation where her feelings for a lover could risk her reputation. But how could she not? Who could resist closing their hand over a star if it landed in the palm of their hand?

"Was it really a palace before, or is this just the Brits being pretentious?" Manuela asked, clearly trying to get a rise out of Alfie, who laughed heartily at the jab. Her stepson, like every other living thing whose opinion Cora valued, had fallen as madly for Manuela as she had in the last week.

"It truly was a palace. It was built for Napoleon's sister," Cora explained as their carriage made infinitesimal advances to the front of the line. "The rumor is that she hosted orgies where she came out to welcome her guests in the nude atop an uncovered palanquin carried by four men dressed only in loincloths."

"No one can blame the Bonapartes for their subtlety," Manuela said with a giggle, and Cora leaned over and kissed her, right under Alfie's nose. And wouldn't it all be so easy if it was a matter of her loved ones falling for Manuela? Of them loving each other, of her small circle of friends welcoming them home?

Two days earlier in a moment of madness, she'd actually considered doing away with the purchase of Baluarte, of trying to find some other piece of land. But that would absolutely destroy her name. Everyone would know why she'd done it, and the rumors would start—and immediately. Then the regrets would closely follow.

"You're so quiet, querida," Manuela whispered, with those plump lips brushing Cora's ear enticingly. Heat radiated under her skin instantly as she turned her face down to catch the jutting bottom lip between her teeth. "Mm, that's better." Her lover crooned, pressing closer.

"Are you thinking the same thing I'm thinking?" Manuela asked against her ear, pulling Cora out of her grim thoughts.

"Unless you were also just contemplating how long it would take to get you out of that bodice and corset on the carriage home, princesa, then no, we were not thinking the same thing." That pink flush and softening eyes would be seared into Cora's mind forever.

"Manuela, do you mind?" Aurora sighed, but her princess was undeterred and continued to press kisses to Cora's mouth. "It's not enough that dolt Apollo will be there, I have to deal with this." Aurora waved a hand to Cora's lap where Manuela had been sitting for half the ride.

"Would you have preferred to be having tea with Doña Amadita?" Manuela demanded, which seemed to allay the fire in Aurora's annoyance. The diplomat's wife they'd encountered at the opera had been keeping tabs on Manuela since she'd returned from Scotland, even going so far as to show up at the Place des Vosges and inviting herself in for tea with Aurora.

"No, I would not prefer to be at Doña Amadita's, hearing all her horrid gossip," Aurora griped, roughly tugging at the bodice of her gown. "This blasted thing just puts me in a temper."

"Ay, Aurora, you're going to tear the lace," Manuela cried, pulling back from the kiss. "You are so brusque. Stop that." She pushed her friend's hand from the hem as Cora and Alfie exchanged amused glances.

"I just don't understand how we are expected to have a conversation when our lungs are pressed to our spines like this." Aurora continued her litany but got no sympathy from her best friend.

"Your lungs are perfectly fine," Manuela said, patting Aurora on the head like a wayward child. The usually imperturbable doctor responded by snapping her teeth.

"Now, children, behave or we'll have to withhold your champagne," Alfie drawled, winking at Cora.

"Oh, thank God," Aurora exclaimed when the carriage door opened, practically launching herself out of the vehicle.

Manuela waved a hand in her friend's direction as she slid off Cora's lap. "Ignore her. She's antsy about seeing Apollo again. Where were we?" she asked as they made their way into the ballroom. "Oh yes, the imminent divestment of my clothes. I am willing to wager you would not tear a single button." They were walking side by side, with Manuela using her fan to conceal their conversation. If the titans of business could see Cora now, wrapped around the finger of the same young heiress she had assured them she would vanquish during the course of one luncheon.

Cora ignored the wife of a viscount who she'd spent a couple of very pleasant weeks in Capri with a few years earlier, who was attempting to wave her over. Instead she snatched two coupes of champagne from a tray, handing one to Manuela. The imp finished it in two gulps and proceeded to lick her bottom lip in such a sensually explosive manner, Cora's mouth went dry.

"I thought that aristocrats were better about coy flirtation," Aurora groused from somewhere behind them, making Alfie laugh. "I feel like I am going to burst into flames solely based on proximity." Cora couldn't even feign embarrassment. She was much too happy to care.

"Would either of you care to dance?" Alfie asked, looking between Aurora and Manuela. Her stepson knew better than to ask Cora.

Aurora scrunched her nose at the question, clearly uninterested. "Not at the moment," she answered, her eyes on the tables at the end of the room laden with food. "I might venture over to the refreshment tables."

"Are you sure? The band is quite good." Manuela's tone was happy enough when she asked the question, but Cora noticed a shadow behind her eyes when she turned her gaze toward the dancing couples. One thing Cora had learned about Manuela was that when she was subdued, she was at her unhappiest. "It would be lovely to step out on the floor with my preferred partner, but this ballroom doesn't allow for that," she finally said.

"Perhaps after things are done here we could make our way to Montmartre," Alfie suggested sympathetically. "I'm sure we could convince Claudine's band to play a waltz for us."

"That is a wonderful idea. Could we?" Manuela beamed at the proposal, and Cora wished more than anything she could take her in her arms and promise to throw her the biggest ball Paris had ever seen. She had to conform with a slight nod and an *of course*. She wished they could go now.

It was one of those things that had never occurred to her as a deprivation, until these last few weeks with Manuela. Before, not being able to dance with a lover in a place like this would not have ever bothered Cora. After all, she could dance at Le Bureau, she could dance at Claudine's, she could dance at home. But with Manuela she wanted the light. Couldn't imagine being able to hide her feelings. Anger rose inside her at the mere thought of having to. She recalled something Cassandra told her when she asked her why she hadn't accepted her parents' offer to remain in the family if she kept her relationship with Frede a secret. Her friend said it would've been pointless to accept it because she couldn't hide what she felt for Frede any better than she could stop her own heartbeat.

Cora had never really understood what she meant. Now… well, there was Manuela.

Her errant thoughts were interrupted by Manuela's yelp when Aurora gripped her arm. "Oh no, it's him," she whispered, her attention on a very tall and handsome man walking in their direction. Manuela's friend was a remarkably strange girl. "You need to dance with me!" she informed Alfie, who had cut his teeth on managing the demands of strongheaded women and gracefully refrained from reminding the doctor she'd turned him down only a minute earlier. When Cora turned to Manuela for an explanation, her lover threw her hands up in exasperation.

"Aurora, you should just admit you're attracted to the man, bed him and get your nerves back in working order." Manuela turned to Cora. "That's Apollo Cesar Sinclair Robles, the new Earl of Darnick. If you hadn't guessed already."

"Do not tease me, Manuela," Aurora protested through gritted teeth while she tugged on Alfie's arm. "Dance floor, please!" By the time the earl came to stand at their side, Aurora was painstakingly swaying to a waltz on the dance floor while Alfie did his best to keep a straight face.

"Señorita Caceres Galvan, I see you've settled back into Parisian life without trouble."

Cora didn't think she imagined the heavy dose of innuendo in the man's comment. Manuela didn't seem too concerned. "I'm very well. Thank you for asking, Lord Darnick. Have you met the Duchess of Sundridge?"

"Your Grace." The man's greeting was very elegant, but his attention was clearly on Aurora. "You friend has escaped me again. I wonder if running from rooms is one of the courses at the medical school at the Sorbonne."

"She is very spry," Manuela concurred, amused. Apollo's furrowed brow and vexed expression were ones Cora had grown very familiar with in the last month. She could not help but sympathize with the Earl of Darnick, who seemed to be the latest victim to be swept under the tide of the Leonas.

"How are you finding your continental adventures, my lord?" Cora probed. He was a strapping man. Not like Alfie or Benedict, who were fine-boned and almost pretty. This man was a gladiator. Tall and imposing. Shoulders that could hold up a building, with keen eyes that appeared to take the temperature of the room in one glance.

"I am finding my footing," he said, his gaze still decidedly on the dance floor. "But I have the advantage of not having much of a conscience and even fewer scruples, which makes things much simpler." An amused laugh escaped Cora's lips, and Manuela's tipped up at the man's brazenness.

"I wish you luck, then. Miss Caceres Galvan and I are going to take a walk around the palace grounds," Cora said, taking Manuela by the hand. If the earl noticed anything about the gesture he did not say.

"He is an interesting one," Manuela said as Cora led her away from the center of the room, "and he is very intrigued by Aurora, which of course drives her absolutely mad."

"Does she not like the man? Is he bothering her?" She didn't care what title he held: if he was making himself a nuisance, Cora would make short work of him.

"I think what's bothering Aurora is that she likes Apollo too much," Manuela answered coyly, still looking wistfully at the dancers.

Cora was out of practice in this, in being unable to solve a problem for someone she cared for. She didn't like to see her loved ones unhappy, and to bring a lover into her world would mean being the cause of their constant disappointment.

"Come with me," she said, putting future troubles out of her head for the moment, and pulling Manuela out of the door and toward the terrace. This would be a liability later, but she could not bear watching Manuela long for something as simple as dance and not give in to her.

"Are we about to engage in scandalous tribadist behavior?" She sounded absolutely thrilled at the prospect.

There was an endless list, it seemed, of things about Manuela Cora found beguiling, but the easy way in which she embraced any new adventure was by far her favorite.

"Just emulating the fine example Miss Bonaparte set out for us."

"And here I thought *I* was the bad influence on young society ladies." Manuela laughed, a sultry, velvety thing that crawled through Cora's marrow and swirled hot in her groin. She couldn't help stopping to take a look at her, this chimera who made everything so confusing and good, so good.

"You are the most alluring thing in Paris," she said, unable to contain herself, even as other guests milled around them.

"I beg to differ, Your Grace," Manuela argued, hands clasped at her front, shoulders relaxed as she directed that glowing smile up to Cora. "It is me who is looking at the most striking woman in all of Paris, all of France." A gloved finger softly grazed her own, and just that whisper of a touch sent off blaring trumpets inside her. Cora had never been looked at like this, with such adoration. "My woman, my lover. The one who makes me weak, whose eyes melt me in seconds. The one whose taste I carry on my tongue, on my hands. Corazón." Manuela always said her name like a benediction. "Your name, and the part of me you own." Anyone who passed them now, two feet apart, hands folded in front of them, would see two high-society ladies discussing the virtues of a bit of fresh air between waltzes. They'd never know that in that moment, with a few simple words, Cora's soul had been claimed by the woman in front of her.

"If you are going to say things like that, we might have to go into the maze," Cora said with a shake of her head. "Just to avoid my mauling you in front of half of the diplomatic corps."

"Aren't there people inside it?" Manuela asked, even as she followed Cora.

"Anyone currently in that maze is not in a position to divulge others' secrets."

Once they were far enough in not to be seen, Cora took Manuela into her arms. She'd never been one for ballroom dancing, finding it tiresome to let herself be led around by a man. But Manuela in her arms was entirely another matter. They swayed together, Manuela's arms circled around Cora's neck, while her own hands clasped at the small of her lover's back.

"I never want this to end," Manuela finally said, her eyes hidden from view. A pained sound escaped Cora. "You have given me memories to cherish for the rest of my life." Manuela sounded resigned. Like a woman preparing herself for the gallows. Again Cora wished she could promise her forever right then, instead of empty *maybe*s.

"Why don't I take you home, so I can ravish you properly." Cora attempted and failed to sound anything but wrecked. Manuela looked up at her then, and her eyes were burning with that ever-present want. She could be burned in those honeyed depths. Even now when there was a brittleness to them, Cora could still feel the flames of desire moving through her.

"After the announcement," Manuela asserted, and for a moment Cora couldn't understand what she was saying, then laughed awkwardly, realizing she'd forgotten why she'd come to the embassy tonight.

"I was so entranced by you, princesa, the announcement flew out of my mind."

Manuela smiled, but it was a wan thing. She wanted to tell her she loved her then. Voice the thing that had been growing wildly inside her.

"Let's get it over with, then. I'll have us in the carriage and home before you know it." With that she tightened her hand on Manuela's one last time before stepping out of the shadows.

★ ★ ★

The moment they stepped back in the room Cora spotted Aurora and Alfie, who were practically running in their direction, matching expressions of dismayed relief on their faces.

"Oh no," Manuela moaned, alarm clean in her voice. When Cora turned to her, she noticed she wasn't looking in Alfie and Aurora's direction. Her attention was focused on something on the other side of the room. Whatever it was made her eyes widen in terror.

She knew who he was the moment she laid eyes on him.

"It's my fiancé."

Manuela sounds so odd, Cora thought as the reality of what was happening pelted her like hail. Her lover's voice, which only minutes ago had been charged with emotion, had been burrowing straight into Cora's soul, now sounded dead. Like there was nothing left inside her. Like every drop of life had been drained from her body.

"Manu, I've been looking all over for you." Aurora gasped, winded, eyes darting back and forth between them and the man headed in their direction.

Manuela turned those pleading amber eyes on Cora as Felix Kingsley—who was comely enough if not particularly refined in his manner—approached them with an easy gait. Desperation took a hold of Cora like a fever.

Her breathing coming short, her body shaking as she forced herself to remain calm. She told herself again and again that she was in a room full of people who would love to see her make a spectacle of herself. But the urge to shield Manuela from Kingsley's hands—by force if necessary—was overpowering. Recalling the way she'd humiliated herself with Sally made little difference.

"Querida, I thought you'd been nabbed by a satyr in that maze!" the man joked, as he pulled Manuela to him with the air of someone who had paid handsomely for the privilege. A noise of distress escaped her, as she fought the urge to rip Manuela away from him. "You look lovely, my dear." His hands were on Manuela's cheek, his finger touching the exact place Cora had kissed minutes before.

He was so close, too close.

Every time he laid a finger on Manuela, Cora felt as though her mind would unravel.

"Seems the checks I've been sending to half the dressmakers in Paris have been well worth it. You are a vision." Cora bit her tongue not to scream.

"What are you doing here, Felix?" Manuela finally choked out. Her eyes were bright with unshed tears.

"Did you not miss me, darling? Or was spending my money occupying all your time?" Cora's spine went up at the disrespectful comment. This man was a buffoon. Was she really going to let this happen? Was she going to allow Manuela to throw her life away on this weasel?

"Of course I missed you," Manuela managed, even as she visibly recoiled from his touch. "I just didn't expect to see you until I got to London."

She was like a rag doll in the cage of his arms. Her limbs hung limply, defenseless. Fury, possessiveness, and raw, toxic jealousy ran through Cora's veins. With half of the railway consortium in the room, she was as trapped by circumstances as Manuela was in that bastard's arms.

Despite that, it took everything in her power not to scratch his eyes out when he dared to kiss Manuela's nose.

"Your parents are here too, darling," he said, amiably, either unaware or intentionally ignoring Manuela's distress. "They are very eager to see you." The man seemed completely unaware of her state. Did he not notice that she was in distress? That Manuela didn't like to have her hair touched?

"My parents? They never said they were coming to Paris. Neither did you." Manuela finally tugged her hands out of his grasp. The movement was so sharp that she stumbled forward.

For once Manuela's easy, casual manner was gone. That ever-present shield of a smile and flirtatious humor evaporated.

Finally, it appeared to dawn on him that his fiancée was not as pleased to see him as she claimed and his benign expression suddenly turned hard. His grip on her arm tightened, his eyes narrowing maliciously.

"It seems you're under the impression that I need to explain myself to you, querida." His tone was once again amiable, but there was a menacing undertone that spurred Cora into action.

"Manuela, you haven't introduced us." She moved forward, reaching for her beloved—she couldn't bear to see Felix touching her for another second.

"Yes, of course." Manuela nodded woodenly, without meeting Cora's gaze. "Felix, this is the Duchess of Sundridge, she's been my—" Manuela pressed her lips firmly together as she swallowed again and again. Cora watched helplessly as the woman she loved stood there, eyes downcast, engulfed in misery. How could she ever think this would end well? That they were headed to anything other than this agony? "She's been my guide through some of the art world here in Paris," she finally got out. Her voice was surprisingly strong, but when she lifted her dry eyes to Cora they screamed, I thought we'd have more time. Felix, still blessedly unaware of the drama unfolding under his nose, bowed and kissed Cora's hand with all the finesse of a bull running through the streets of Pamplona.

There had been a time in Cora's life when daring to be who she was felt like an endless web of traps and pitfalls. And so, she'd worked very hard protect herself from most of the dangers that could befall her. She had more money than she could spend in four lifetimes. She had earned a place in the innermost circle of the people who ruled most of Europe. For ten years she'd prepared for almost any potential disaster, and here she still was, undone. Ready to give almost anything for a sword she could run through every rope that kept Manuela tied to this man. To her parents.

But she wouldn't, because doing so would ruin them both.

"Your Grace, how kind of you to entertain my beloved." Kingsley was much too unrefined to conceal his curiosity, but if there were things he knew about Cora, he did not speak of them then.

She had to leave. She was so close to destroying everything. "It's a pleasure, Mr. Kingsley. We've tried to take very good care of your lady."

Aurora and Alfie both winced at her words, while Manuela stood there like a salt statue.

"I had no idea you'd made such fashionable friendships in Paris," Kingsley told Manuela, sounding impressed. Cora wanted nothing more than to slap him across the face. "If I had known, I'd have secured a larger church for the ceremony."

"Ceremony?" Manuela asked at the same time that Aurora clasped a hand over her mouth. Cora could only guess it was to stave off a scream.

"Well, that was part of the surprise." Kingsley's face shone with excitement as if he could not see Manuela's ashen expression.

"Your parents and I talked it over and decided it would be silly not to take advantage and have our wedding in the most romantic city in the world." His tone was jovial enough, but his eyes were flinty as he looked at Manuela. That's when Cora realized the man enjoyed toying with his fiancée. Enjoyed reminding her how little agency she had in even the most minor details of her future. "I arrived a few days ago and managed to get a special license to marry here in Paris through the Venezuelan embassy."

No. No. No.

Felix continued to talk, unaware of how dangerously close he was to being assaulted by a duchess. "The French are refreshingly accommodating if one is willing to part with enough francs." Manuela's legs seem to give out on her and Felix held her tighter, his lips tipping up. "I knew you'd be delighted, but not that you'd swoon from excitement, my love." Cora's vision blurred for a second as reality descended on her like a pile of bricks.

Manuela's throat moved as though she was holding back a roar and Aurora seemed ready to commit murder. Cora couldn't breathe. Something stung behind her sternum with such intensity she was overtaken by a coughing fit. Her eyes burned, she couldn't see. There had to be a way out of this. What was all this money for? What was all this influence for, if she couldn't stop this?

"Cora?" Manuela's panicked voice brought her mind out of the depths it was drowning in, but looking at her love with that man at her back only made things worse. She was going to fall apart. She was going to go down on her knees and beg, just like she'd done the last time. Ten years of atoning only to once again break her promise to Benedict.

"I have to go," she heard herself say, smiling until she thought the muscles would snap. "It was very nice to meet you, Mr. Kingsley."

This was not the first time in the past decade Cora had looked the other way in order to protect herself. Until today she'd never despised herself for it. "I trust that you can see Miss Caceres Galvan home." The words tasted like poison. A searing, hot pain shot through her chest when she saw Manuela brush a tear from her cheek.

"Wait," Manuela said, her mask fully gone now. Every emotion naked and visible on her face. "Will I see you soon?"

Cora wanted to tell her she'd fix everything. That she'd get rid of this villain and make sure they never had to be apart. But instead, like a spineless, feckless coward, she ran.

"Congratulations to you both," she said in answer, before walking away.

"What do you need?" Alfie asked, slipping into step beside her, his strong hand sliding into hers as she fought for control.

"To not be here," she said as she rushed out of the ballroom.

"Your Grace." The commanding masculine voice made Cora slow her steps, long enough to search for its owner.

"Bloody hell," Alfie whispered when he turned his head to the man walking toward them. "Blanchet truly had a gift for being in the wrong place at the wrong time."

"What do you want, Edouard?" Cora demanded, utterly unable to maintain any façade of civility.

"To announce the railway, Your Grace. That is what we are here to do." The reproach in the man's voice told her he'd probably been watching her near breakdown.

"Mama, if you want to go—" Alfie whispered in her ear, but she shook her head, willing herself to do what she'd come to do. Once she announced the railway there would be no going back.

"We can announce."

Blanchet shot her a dubious look.

"I can't go, dear," she said shakily to Alfie. "Edouard is right. We must do what we've come here to accomplish." The other man was still looking at her suspiciously, but when she began walking, he followed. Cora launched herself into the task at hand as if her next breath depended on it. She boasted about the new railway. She toasted with her associates as she made herself push away the thought of Manuela in a carriage with that man.

She smiled and accepted congratulations on securing the last parcel of land needed to complete their unprecedented venture, and not once did she break down at the thought of at what cost she'd done so. She volleyed a few barbs at those in the group who had doubted her and by some miracle didn't fall to the ground and sob for what she'd given up.

When it was over, and she finally left the palace with Alfie at her side, she looked straight into his eyes and confronted the judgment and pity in his gaze. They rode away in suffocating silence. Cora looking ahead, her spine straight and hollow inside and it was no one's doing but her own.

Twenty-Two

"I can fake an illness if you need some time," Aurora whispered in Manuela's ear as they made their way into the parlor where her parents waited for her.

She shook her head, grateful to her friend, but there was no use in delaying this confrontation with her parents.

"Hija, that is the dress you wore to meet the British ambassador?" Manuela's mother said in greeting as she entered the foyer of the town house on Place des Vosges she had not set foot in since before her departure for Edinburgh.

"Mamá," she said, woodenly leaning in to be bussed on the cheek. Then looked down at the gown that Cora had threatened to tear off her body just an hour earlier. Manuela had felt beautiful and adored, then. In mere seconds her mother had managed to obscure even that small ray of light for her.

"I think I was too successful with our surprise, Doña Consuelo." She stiffened at the sound of Felix's too-placid voice, which was beginning to seriously grate on her nerves. "Our girl seems to have been stunned into silence." She wasn't *his* anything and just hearing the words revolted her. It had taken everything in her to get through that carriage ride without flinging herself from it.

It was all so disgusting. The lying, the pretending. Felix didn't care about her, and he cared even less about trapping her in a marriage for his own benefit.

Manuela was done with all of it.

For once she wouldn't dwell on her mother's comments about her clothes or her appearance. The only thing that mattered was fixing things with Cora. But first she had to stand up to her parents. She had to tear away the guilt and duty they had unfairly bound around her for so long. She hadn't ruined them, they'd ruined themselves, and again and again other people had had to fix it. Manuela was done being the collateral damage for their wastefulness.

"I need to speak with you," she whispered to her mother, who was eyeing her with almost hostile intensity.

"We do need to talk, hija." She squeezed Manuela's shoulder too tightly and lifted a beaming face to Felix, who was standing with her father, and was yet to speak or even look at her.

Doña Consuelo sent a withering look to Aurora, but her friend thrived under the disapproval of her elders and remained unmoved, shoulder to shoulder with Manuela. Her mother considered Aurora's insistence on becoming a physician unseemly and had almost forbade her from staying at the house the Montalbans had leased for their stay in Paris. That was until she heard the fashionable address and decided that she could overlook her distaste.

"Felix, it is so good of you to bring her to us, but we'd love to sit with our Manuela for a visit, just the three of us. It's been so long since New York." Her stomach dropped at her mother's tone, the way her lip curled when she spoke.

They knew. Somehow, they knew.

"Of course, Doña Consuelo," Felix assented. He looked at Manuela in that appreciative yet detached way he always did.

Like she was a collectible piece that he didn't want lost or broken. "I will go back to my hotel but will be here in the morning to finalize the invitations for the wedding. There are so many prominent South American families here." He seemed to savor the words. "It truly was an oversight to not consider a Paris wedding earlier." He grinned again and took Manuela's hand so firmly she had to resist snatching it away. "Or maybe that was your plan all along, querida mía." It took everything she had not to strike him. He seemed oblivious, so indifferent to her discomfort, even when she did nothing to hide it. He simply didn't care about how she fared in this arrangement.

Her well-being, her own happiness, had never truly mattered, had it? Not to him, not to her parents. Her purpose consisted of gaining him access to the higher echelons of Venezuelan society. To be received in the grand homes of the old families of the northern coast of South America. It was what he was paying for. What *she* would be paying for, forever. Her mother, unaware—or simply ignoring—her obvious distress sent Felix another one of those indulgent looks she'd grown to hate. It was so clear to her now that they'd never really cared who they cleaved her to, as long as they got what they wanted.

"We have so much to do!" Consuelo chortled as Felix said his goodbyes and Aurora reluctantly went upstairs. "We will be ready at first light, Mr. Kingsley."

The moment the door closed behind the man, her mother spun on Manuela.

Could it possibly only have been months since she'd last seen her mother? She felt as though she'd lived an entire lifetime and was ready for the next. But first she had to free herself from the trap set for her by the people in this room. She tried to think of Luz Alana's and Aurora's words in Edinburgh. That she didn't have to keep everything inside. The way they'd asked for her forgiveness because, like everyone else, they'd made assumptions without looking closely enough to see all that Manuela was carrying. But Cora had seen it. She'd seen everything. What Manuela still didn't know was whether the duchess wanted it.

"It was nice of the embassy to invite you. I had no idea the British were so interested in women artists from South America." She hated this most of all. Her mother's insistence on maintaining civility. Even when she was visibly furious, she put on this charade. This pretense. As a child she'd abhorred her mother's games. How she'd circle around her, asking superfluous questions while Manuela squirmed, wondering when she'd tear into her. It went on for hours some days, until Manuela couldn't bear it anymore and begged for the punishment, just so she didn't have to watch her mother look at her with such naked loathing.

Consuelo Galvan de Caceres had many reasons to be angry at her daughter. Manuela had lied to her about what she was doing in Paris. Neglected to inform her parents that Amaranta had gone to Scotland with Luz and she'd remained behind. She'd put in jeopardy her engagement, and much more. They had plenty of reason to yell at her. That was not her mother's way. It was much more effective to silently condemn. To remind Manuela of all the ways the family had sacrificed for her. What she'd cost them.

For the first time since that night she'd been discovered with Catalina, she didn't let her mother's judgment shame her. "I wasn't invited by the embassy," she said, taking a seat by the fireplace. "I was a guest of the Duchess of Sundridge."

"Yes, we've heard about the company you've been keeping," her mother seethed, while her father did his best to appear invisible.

"I thought you would be delighted to hear that I was dutifully climbing that social ladder you value so much, Mother." Consuelo Galvan de Caceres reeled back from Manuela's caustic tone, but she promptly recovered.

"Don't play games with me, Manuela del Carmen. You know very well what I'm talking about. I don't care if that woman is the Queen of England. I know what she is." Her mother's voice did rise on that, but Manuela remained undaunted. "You promised us you'd never do anything like that again. Haven't you disgraced us enough?"

That was how they'd kept her in this trap. Reminding her again and again that what happened with Catalina—the daughter of an investor in his father's candle business who had rescinded his offer after they'd been caught kissing—was the root of every disaster that had befallen their family. But the truth was that even if she'd cost them that investor, her father was who ruined their family, not her. She was done being their scapegoat.

"You mean what *I* am, Mother?"

Both her parents twisted their mouths in disgust, and for the first time Manuela felt nothing. "Let's speak frankly of these things—"

"No," her mother shouted, and her father paled. "I will not abide this. You were seen at the opera with that—" Her mother fluttered her hands in front of herself, which Manuela assumed meant *lesbian*. She remembered Cora's joke about the secret signal and wondered what her mother would do if she began fluttering her tongue.

"Niña, are you even listening? I could not believe my eyes when Amadita Carrillo's letter arrived at our hotel in London."

It had been Amadita Carrillo. She should've known.

"Are you intentionally trying to ruin yourself and this engagement, Manuela? Are you truly this imprudent?" Manuela probably should be furious at her mother's hypocrisy. At the blatant attempt to make this about her indiscretions and not the fact that Manuela was giving up her freedom to keep them all in luxury. But she found that even in her misery, there was some relief in not needing to wear the mask anymore.

"How exactly am I the imprudent one, Mamá?" Manuela demanded, her control fraying at the seams. "Why not tell the truth, for once? Whatever I have been doing here is no worse than Felix carousing around Italy with his mistress. Did that not embarrass you, or was the suite at the Langham he paid for enough to your mortification?" Manuela had never allowed herself to indulge in rage. She'd always known that her very sanity depended on not dwelling very long in anger. But there was no shoving back in the poison that was seeping out of her.

Her mother blustered almost comically at the recrimination. "He is a man, and he can do whatever he pleases."

"Manuela, do not disrespect your mother!" Her father would never take her side.

"I will not," she shouted loud enough to make Prospero Caceres take a step back. "I had three months. That was what I was promised," Manuela protested, fighting back tears. "As long as I was securing my trousseau, I could stay here with Luz Alana and Aurora and when I was done I'd meet the three of you in London."

Her mother's eyes narrowed, her gaze unwavering. "Do not take that tone with me. You know very well that engaging in that filth and getting caught socializing with people like that would never be all right with us."

"With people like me, you mean? Women who want to be with other women. Who take women as lovers." Her mother flinched at her words, and her father roared.

"That is enough! I will not have that kind of language here."

"Yes, we will. We will speak the truth. If I have to live with it, then so do you, Papá," Manuela cried, accusingly. "Your gambling and your careless managing of our finances put us in this position, and I am sacrificing *myself* to fix it." She slapped a hand to her chest, the tears that had been blurring her eyes finally spilling over. "I won't let you sweep that aside."

"What has gotten into you, Manuela?"

She almost laughed at her mother's horrified expression. "What's gotten into me is that I'm no longer willing to pretend this isn't anything other than a sale. That you are not trading me, my life, for your comfort."

"Don't pretend that you don't want the comforts too, Manuela. You enjoy all this as much as we do," her mother rebuked. "Felix has shown me the accounts of your expenses. Don't make this about me." It was true. Amassing pretty dresses and luxuries had been just another one of the ways in which she'd lied to herself about the path she'd chosen. But there was another path for her, if she was strong enough to take it.

A knock on the door made them all turn around. The porter stepped quietly inside, though his face was flushed with red.

"What is it, Damian?" Manuela asked, hoping Felix had not returned.

"Mademoiselle, the Duchess of Sundridge is requesting an audience with you and your parents."

Manuela turned toward the door in an instant, her heart thumping in her chest.

"The duchess?" Manuela's mother asked, flustered. It was one thing to disapprove of her daughter's association with an aristocrat, it was something quite different to have said aristocrat in your home.

Cora had come for her. She'd come.

"I'll go fetch her," she mumbled, already heading to the foyer, her heart pounding in her throat. She'd come here to help Manuela, to help her break free from this at last, so that they could be together.

"Cora," she gasped, her throat convulsing at the sight of her beloved. Manuela flung herself at her. She should probably be more discreet, but she needed the reassurance of this embrace after enduring Felix's. "I didn't think—" She cut herself off, not wanting to voice the terrible fear of the last hour. Cora wrapped her in an embrace for a moment, her arms so tight around Manuela it was almost painful.

And then let her go.

"Where are you parents?"

Manuela stiffened at the chill in Cora's voice. When she looked up, she didn't find a trace of the warmth she'd seen there in the past week. This was not the woman she'd danced with in the maze. This was the forbidding, haughty Duchess of Sundridge.

"I have been talking to them," she said cautiously, wanting to reassure her that she hadn't just accepted her fiancé's return. That she was ready to fight this battle with her family. "I was about to tell them that I won't marry him."

"Take me to them."

Manuela's initial elation at Cora's arrival began to flag when she refused to look at her. But she told herself that it was probably how she was preparing for what awaited them. That this was Cora putting on her armor of the duchess before facing a very ugly scene. Without a word, Manuela showed her to the room.

Manuela's parents scrambled to bow to Cora, their words and their movements awkward. But if Cora noticed the clumsy greeting, she did not give them any indication. She got straight to the point.

"Podemos hablar en español." Every word out of her mouth sounded like an edict. Even the way she stood was different now. Her back straight, her head tilted in a manner that placed a distance between herself and everyone else. It was like the Cora who had woken her up this morning with dozens of kisses had been swallowed up by this icy, unfeeling woman.

"Would you like to sit, Your Grace?" her mother offered meekly, the bravado from minutes ago dissolved in the face of such a commanding presence.

"I prefer to stand," Cora declined, her gaze locked in the empty space between Manuela's parents. "Your daughter signed a contract agreeing to sell me a parcel of land in Puerto Cabello, six hundred hectares of coastland. I believe you call it Baluarte," she began.

Was this why Cora was here? To make sure Manuela didn't go back on her promise to sell her the land?

"Manuela, what have you done?" her mother cried.

"Abuela always said I should use the land for something that was mine and mine alone," she told her mother defiantly. Even now, as she realized that Cora was apparently only looking out for her own interests, she didn't regret what she'd done.

Cora continued as if Manuela hadn't spoken. "I am willing to offer you whatever price you ask for the land. In exchange, you will let Manuela out of her engagement. You will forbid him to make claim on any more of her time, and you will leave her be."

Manuela's legs refused to hold her up after that, her head spinning. Happiness and disbelief thrumming through her veins like fire.

"That is preposterous!" her father cried. "You have no right to tell our family what to do."

"I am not telling you what to do. I am buying the right to do so," Cora countered in the same impassive tone. Manuela's mother's nerves seem to give out, and she tumbled onto the chair she'd been leaning on.

"What is your price? Fifty thousand pounds?" Cora asked, unconcerned with the chaos around her. Manuela's father was purple with fury, his countenance a mask of disbelief. "A hundred thousand," Cora threw out when no one spoke. She crossed her arms over her chest as she continued to pile more money on the offer.

In her twenty-eight years of life, Manuela had never seen her mother at a loss for words, but now she was standing there, mouth in a silent O, as if speech had completely deserted her.

"I don't understand," Consuelo Galvan de Caceres finally said, her voice almost a whisper.

"I don't want that man to marry Manuela, and I will pay you to release her from the engagement," Cora repeated impatiently. "Tell me how much you want."

Her mother blinked, and when she opened her eyes, Manuela could see that familiar greedy glint in them, but her father, for the first time ever, spoke first.

"I will not allow this family's name to be tainted. We will not break our word to Mr. Kingsley so Manuela can run off and disgrace herself." Of course that would be what he cared about: the family's reputation. Even after his own behavior had marred it for years.

"Father, you can't stop me from going with her," Manuela declared, ready to face this down, no matter what it cost her. "I don't want to marry Felix. I have a right to be happy. I lo—"

"No, Manuela," Cora interrupted, and when their gazes locked she found a set of hollow bleak violet eyes staring back at her.

"You misunderstand my intentions." Cora's voice was hoarse, as if she was using the last vestiges of it to say the words. "This is only so you can be free of that man. It will give me great comfort to know that you were spared from an unhappy marriage when I return to London, alone."

Twenty-Three

"Please stop acting like someone died," Cora demanded of her aunt as she sat down to breakfast. Her hands shook from lack of sleep, her eyes were bleary and swollen, the skin around them tight from...no. Thinking about it would make it happen again. She needed something to do. "Where's the newspaper?" she asked, bolting up from the chair.

"In your office, where they leave it every day, querida. And I would stop acting like someone died if you weren't behaving like you're in mourning." She knew Tia Osiris was only concerned, but she was at the very end of her rope. She closed her eyes as that constriction in her breathing began again. It had been happening constantly over the last two days.

She'd be fine and suddenly a fist would tighten around her lungs, another would jam up her throat and all the air would leave her body. She couldn't make a sound when it happened. She couldn't swallow, either. She just sat there, unblinking, gasping for air, a searing pain like nothing she'd experienced radiating in her chest. As if everything inside her was turning to dust.

"Mija, please eat something." She couldn't stand this either, the pitying tone in her aunt's voice. The petrified stares from the servants, as though she'd lost her mind.

"I'm not hungry," she declared, even as she dropped into the chair across from her aunt again. She clumsily reached for a plate of coddled eggs and spooned some onto her plate. The thought of taking a bite made bile rise in her throat. "I have things to do this morning to prepare for the meeting with the railroad consortium tomorrow."

Her aunt stared at her, a determined look on her face, and Cora held a hand up. "Don't. Please, Tia. Don't say her name," she begged, choking through the tears that wouldn't come. "Please."

Her aunt shook her head, her face bleak. "I can't stand seeing you like this, Corazón, please—" Osiris cut herself off at whatever she saw in Cora's face. "Is Juliette off today?" her aunt asked instead, offering her a reprieve. Cora looked up from staring at her plate, the question forgotten already.

"Sorry, what did you ask?" Tia Osiris reached for one of her hands, but Cora slid them both onto her lap. She couldn't bear the thought of anyone touching her. She didn't want comfort and she didn't deserve it. Not after what she'd done. Until she took her last breath, she'd be haunted by the memory of Manuela's eyes when she realized what Cora had been there to do.

A strange sound came out of her, something like a groan. That painful tightness in her neck and chest robbing her of air again. She wanted to pace, to run out of this room, go out into the street and exhaust herself. She wanted to throw herself on the floor and weep. But she couldn't. She couldn't sleep, she couldn't cry.

"I asked if your maid is off today?" Her aunt was looking at her shirt. Cora lowered her gaze and noticed she'd missed two buttons and that there was a stain on her tie.

"Yes, I gave her a few days off," she said without looking up, dabbing her napkin in water and rubbing it over the crusty spot on her clothes. Since she'd come back from the Place des Vosges she had barely left her room. She'd slept in the gown she'd worn to the Charost Palais because it was the last thing Manuela had touched. When Juliette had come to clean her room in the morning, she'd sent her away, clutching an empty cup of tea Manuela had left by her side of the bed like a madwoman. "I don't want people in my rooms."

She couldn't tolerate anyone touching any part of her body that Manuela had touched. She hadn't bathed, avoiding washing her off. She hadn't brushed her hair in days. Her clothes were wrinkled and she smelled terrible.

She'd gone into hysterics when they'd attempted to change the sheets on her bed, wrapped herself in them like a mummy and leafed through the lewd doodles Manuela left for her on napkins and scraps of paper. Stuffed her pockets full of them. She couldn't let go of even the smallest shred of her. She was behaving irrationally. Madly, and she couldn't stop herself.

Cora Kemp-Bristol, the unflappable Duchess of Sundridge, the woman who had challenged every convention and won, was coming apart at the seams. She thought she'd made herself harder. She thought in the last ten years she'd built defenses to see her through any test, any catastrophe. She thought losing Benedict, then what had happened with Sally, had prepared her for any loss. But how could anyone prepare to lose Manuela?

What she felt was beyond emptiness. Beyond heartbreak.

Strong, thin arms wrapped around her shoulders. "You're shaking, querida." Her aunt's voice was low, steady as she sat there, her unseeing eyes dry.

"I'm fine," Cora said, not quite managing to sound it.

"No me mientas, Corazón," her aunt chided, embracing Cora tighter. "We've fought too many battles together for me not to see when you're wounded."

No one had done this to her. Cora only shook her head, biting her tongue enough to taste blood, keeping in the screams, the wretchedness she couldn't allow to come out.

When she left Manuela's house that night she'd told herself she'd walk away unscathed like she'd done with Sally. That she'd lament her moment of weakness, then dust herself off and carry on. But it had been days now and she was still in agony. Barely able to stand.

"I don't know what to do," she confessed, eliciting a sound of sympathy from her aunt.

They stayed like that for a long time, until a knock on the door shook Cora out of her stupor. Laurent entered, wearing the same petrified look everyone in the house seemed to have anytime they had to interact with her.

"What is it, Laurent?"

"There is some correspondence for you." He spoke very carefully, clearly fearful of causing another fit.

"Leave it there." She felt nothing but exhaustion at the thought of dealing with one more note from Blanchet arguing over every one of her recommendations on the bonds issue. The mere thought of discussing the railroad that now represented the mess she'd made of her life turned her stomach.

"Your Grace," Laurent insisted. Cora whipped her head around with every intention to send him away, but before she could say a word, he thrust the envelope forward. "It is from Mademoiselle Caceres Galvan." The words cut through her like a blade of fire, burning through her stupor, as she stared at the elegant penmanship of the woman she loved.

She did love Manuela. She at least would not turn away from that truth, even if it was a wound she carried for the rest of her life.

"Thank you, Laurent," she told the man as she quickly snatched the envelope to hide the trembling in her hands. She didn't even have the strength to be ashamed of this display of emotion. What did it matter? Like her entire staff, he knew

Mademoiselle Caceres Galvan's absence was the cause of Cora's week-long despondency. She'd been slowly undoing every thread that held up the life she'd built for herself since she met Manuela. An inglorious string of rash decisions and impulsive faux pas.

It had been the happiest time of her life.

Once Laurent quietly closed the door behind himself, Cora stared at the envelope in her hand scared to open it and read the words that would cement the truth of what she'd done. She could feel the weight of her aunt's stare over her shoulder, but Tia Osiris didn't rush her.

Cora brushed the back of her hand over her dried lips, revolted by her own cowardice.

She'd acted abominably. She knew it, but she could not bear the thought of Manuela married to that buffoon. If she was to be a villain, she'd be one for giving Manuela the freedom to leave. But Manuela hadn't seen it as help. When Cora told her she'd be going back to London alone, her eyes filled with tears that spilled as she'd stared at her in disbelief. Without another word she'd turned on her heel and walked away from Cora. That was the last time she'd seen or heard from her until now.

She needed a drink. With shaky legs she went to the cart and with one hand poured herself a dram of whisky. The intense scent of peat made her stomach roil—it was barely half past nine in the morning after all, but before the glass reached her mouth Tia Osiris snatched it from her hand.

"Enough, Corazón," her aunt rebuked, tossing the spirits into the fire, making the weakening flames roar back to life. "Ya basta," she repeated, and though there was censure in her voice, her brown eyes were kind. "Pull yourself together, mija. This is not the time to fall apart." Tia Osiris tugged the envelope from Cora's hands and pulled out the small sheaf of papers. "You are strong enough to face this." Her aunt spoke with the same steel that made Cora get off that ship in London after they were banished from Chile. The same steel that drove her to pick herself up after Benedict had died.

"All right," Cora said, sitting down to read. She wasn't surprised to see the deed on top. Now that Manuela's parents knew of the offer, they'd likely force her to sell. Just one more way in which Cora had made a mess of things. She closed her eyes before unfolding the accompanying note, a feeling of dread crawling up her body as she did. Then she read it and the dread quickly transformed into horror.

If I am to be bought and sold, only I will dictate the terms.
M

"What is this?" She frowned at the message, frantically scanning the page, hoping to understand what Manuela meant. The terms were all the same, the amount they'd originally agreed to unchanged. Then she reached the signature page, where Manuela had left instructions to deliver the full payment to Cassandra and Pasquale, to be used for the collective. "This can't be right," she muttered. Cora had hoped that her parents' greed would win and they'd let Manuela out of the engagement, but instead she was giving up the only thing that could buy her freedom. Instead of helping herself, she would help a group of women she barely knew.

She stood, her legs unable to stay still with her mind racing as it was. That was when she noticed a creamy white envelope by her feet. Something told her not to pick it up, not to touch it, but she would not be a coward again. Slowly, she placed the deed on the chair and bent down. She shook off the tremors in her hands and extracted the card inside—except it wasn't a card. It was an invitation. She read it with her heart pounding loudly and sweat running down her back as a hole that could swallow her whole bloomed inside her.

Manuela was getting married in only a few hours.

Cora's hand slipped, and the tray of decanters crashed to the carpet like fireworks. Not a second later, Tia Osiris was at her side and Alfie was bursting into the room.

"What's wrong?" her son asked, but Cora was suffocating. She walked away from the cloying smell of spilled brandy and whisky, her mouth open, gasping, but air would not come. Alfie came to her, gripping her arms as he looked down at her, terrified. "Mother, what's happened?"

"She sent me the deed," she finally told him, her voice barely a whisper. "She's giving the money away." Her voice broke then and she crumbled to the ground. She brought her knees up, her head in her hands. She looked up at Alfie who was kneeling beside her, his face marred with worry.

"She's going to marry him." Cora felt far away, like she was speaking from the bottom of a well.

"Oh, Mama." She flinched at the love in his voice. At the sympathy she didn't deserve.

"Maybe, it's better this way," she lied, even as her heart was torn from her chest.

"She's better off marrying a man she loathes?" Tia Osiris asked from somewhere in the room, but Cora could barely see. What was wrong with her eyes? "You're better off knowing you let her go, to one-up those heels in the consortium?" her aunt asked, her tone a mixture of disbelief and exasperation. "To prove yourself to a group of men who can barely stand the sight of you? Corazón, what has all this been for if you are miserable in the end?" Cora knew her aunt was attempting to make her see the error of her ways, but Tia Osiris had never failed like Cora had. She'd never had to live with the knowledge that her actions had hurt someone she'd vowed to protect.

"I did what I did to make up for the damage I caused. I made a promise to Benedict," she reminded her aunt, then turned to Alfie. "Your father trusted that I would shepherd you to your rightful place in London society and instead I disgraced your family's name with my stupidity. My selfishness. I can't destroy everything when we are so close," she pleaded, needing him to see why she'd had to do it. Why she couldn't be associated with Manuela's broken engagement, with any of this. "I have finally been able to erase the stain I've left on your name."

"Who cares about Blanchet? Who cares what the London peerage thinks? You got the land for them, isn't that enough?" Alfred said, his voice so strong. "I know you don't think so, but you kept your promise."

"My promise was to make sure you assumed your place as the Duke of Sundridge." She looked at him his face so much like his father's. But where Benedict had been mercurial and fragile at times, Alfred was a man who could weather any storm. Knowing he would be a force of good, a man who could look to the future and face it with humanity and fairness, had been worth all the sacrifices. She would not allow for that path to be tarnished again. "You've had to live in forced exile because of me."

"No, what you did was not leave me to the fate of tutors and a boarding school where I'd be bullied and neglected." Alfie pulled her back on her feet. "Any of my other relatives would've been happy to take up in that house in Belgravia and ship me off to boarding school without a second thought." She shook her head at that, as if she'd ever abandon him, or forsake him like her own father had done to her. She would've died before doing that to Alfie.

By some miracle Benedict had been at the very first dinner she'd been invited to in London. Bedeviled by the financial mire his father had made of the duchy and looking for a new mother for his five-year-old son. He'd told her his wife had been the love of his life and he had no interest in replacing her, but that if she helped him raise Alfred, he would give her protection—and he would be a friend. For five years he never, not once, faltered on that promise. All she was doing was trying to keep the one she'd made to him in return. Why couldn't they see that?

"If I don't follow through on this deal, I will lose my footing. My word is all I have with these men."

Tia Osiris let out a cry of outrage, but Cora didn't look in her direction, needing to make Alfie understand. That this was necessary. That she would sacrifice herself for him. That she would not let him down.

"Your word is not all you have, Cora." Her given name coming from Alfie's lips was a slap in the face. He hadn't called her that since he was a boy. "You have family who loves you, friends who respect you. A fortune to spend living a life that makes you happy, doing good in the word, living the life you deserve."

"No more, Corazón Aymara." Tia Osiris tugged on her hand, her face stern when Cora looked up. "Everything isn't your fault or your responsibility. It's not your fault my sister died, mija." Cora shut her eyes, shaking her head in denial, not wanting to hear those words. "It's not your fault your father was too weak to love you when you needed him."

"No, Tia," she croaked, feeling the tears streaming down her face and the misery spewing out of her in sobs.

"Stop torturing yourself, mi amor," her aunt pleaded.

"But if I stop now, if I let them have the railway, then what was all this for?"

"The only thing that matters is what you do from now on. Are you going to let men like that take even more from you?" Tia Osiris held an iciness in her voice that Cora had never heard before. "Are you going to let someone who doesn't deserve her take the woman you love?" Her aunt's words sent a lightning storm through her veins. What was she doing? Crying helplessly as if she didn't have choices, when the woman she loved could be lost to her forever.

"This could all go sideways," she said, feeling her strength come back now that she had a clear goal in her sights. If she lost Manuela it wouldn't be because she didn't let her know exactly what she felt for her.

"Go fight for her," Alfie begged. "I can make my own way in London. You've given me everything I need to do it."

The clock chimed then. In mere hours Manuela would be walking down the aisle to seal her fate.

A stab of pain cut through her as Cora recalled the way Manuela had looked at her when she'd come to see her parents. The hope, the love in her eyes.

"It might already be too late," she said to no one in particular as she stared at the invitation.

"You are strong enough to face whatever it is you find there, querida," Tia Osiris said, as she walked up to her again. This time her eyes only held unflagging love.

"If I stop this wedding, we will never recover from the scandal." It had to be said. She looked at Alfie who seemed utterly unfazed by the prospect. "We will be outcasts."

The Duke of Sundridge stood up to his full height and pulled her to him. "They need us too much to cast us out, you made sure of that. And they're all too scared of you," he told her, making her smile despite her nerves. "If there is scandal, we can weather it, but I cannot watch you do this to yourself anymore. You have fulfilled my promise to Father, to me, a hundred times over. Besides, what I plan to do at the House of Lords will make me unpopular enough without your help." She rarely gave herself credit for what she did, always looking toward the next hill to climb, the next feat to conquer, but this morning, feeling the strength of the man she'd raised, Cora felt proud.

"Your carriage is waiting to take you where you need to be, Corazón," her aunt told her as she was pushed out of the room.

She let out a trembling breath, shaking her head helplessly. They were right. About all of it, they were right. Like the last time, there would be scandal, but the difference was that this time it would all be worth it. Manuela was worth it.

"I hope I get there in time."

Twenty-Four

"Stop looking at me like that, Aurora," Manuela grumbled for the hundredth time that morning. It was surprising how easy it was to maintain one's composure once your heart stopped working. One thing she'd discovered in the last two days was that it was so much easier to live when one could not feel at all. No agonizing over or guessing at another's emotions, or your own. None of it mattered when you were dead inside.

"I'm worried for you," Aurora confessed miserably. Manuela could not even muster up sympathy for her friend's rare admission of distress. Aurora had spent the last day and a half begging Manuela not to marry. Felix being present had not interrupted her pleading in the least, which had been somewhat morbidly amusing to witness. But now, when Manuela only wanted it all over with, it was beginning to grate.

"Can you help with the train of the dress?" she asked, looking at herself in the mirror. The gown, which had been delivered from the House of Worth while she was in Edinburgh and had not been unboxed until the evening before, fit her perfectly. She'd chosen a pale pink satin with a spray of ecru silk roses that ran from the waist down to the hem. The collar was modest, made of a panel of delicate ivory lace that reached the base of her neck. She'd even agreed to a bustle which cascaded into a long train. It was the ideal bridal gown, elegant and whimsical. The sight of it made Manuela want to cry.

There was a knock on the door. Manuela froze, thinking it was her mother. They'd barely spoken to each other after Cora's visit, and Manuela had forbidden her to come anywhere near her today. That didn't mean Consuelo Galvan de Caceres hadn't tried to bully her way into the room where Manuela was getting dressed. But if she was going to go through with this, she refused to pretend anymore. She would not make anything easy for her parents. The only thing that gave her any solace was the prospect of reminding them, at every opportunity, how callous and horrid they were.

"And what is he doing here?" Manuela pointed at Apollo, who had self-designated as one of the bridal assistants.

"Don't ask me," Aurora cried, throwing her hands up. "I can't stand the sight of him." Apollo seemed to think Aurora's insult was hilarious, and after a hearty laugh and more than a few heated stares, he turned his attention back to Manuela.

"My brother thought you might need reinforcements." He sent a pointed look to a miserable-looking Aurora. "I can't say I disagree."

Manuela narrowed her eyes at him and peeked from behind the curtain into the small chapel. To her relief she saw there were barely any people sitting in the pews. Felix's parents were deceased. His only relative was a sister in Boston who was to be present at their wedding in Venezuela but given the change in plans was not here today. The handful of guests in attendance consisted of Doña Amadita and her husband and a couple other of her cronies, who were probably there just to collect gossip to disseminate among every Spanish speaker in Paris the moment this fiasco was done.

Felix stood there waiting, benign and impassive in his morning tails. He had not mentioned the duchess or anything else that had occurred that night at the Charost Palais. He was willing to ignore almost anything if it meant getting what he wanted. Her parents weren't much better. Since she'd announced that she would marry Felix after all, they'd both pretended the visit from Cora had never occurred.

In truth, she could barely remember what had happened that night. Once Cora had informed her that she had no intention of staying in Paris, that her plans didn't include her, Manuela had mentally fallen apart. It had not been easy to face the reality that, when it came down to it, for Cora—like her parents, like Felix—Manuela was nothing but the means to an end.

Cora wanted Manuela, may have even loved her, but her business came first. She'd once again been nothing more than a pretty accessory. If she was going to be that, she may as well do some good in the process. The women in the collective would, in their own way, fulfil her abuela's dream in a way she never would.

"Manuela, please think this through," Aurora pleaded as the organist began to play. "Your happiness still matters. Your parents don't deserve you sacrificing yourself like this."

She didn't want to think about her happiness. She didn't want to think at all.

"I know that Cora hurt you, but you can't throw yourself away like this." The desperation, the urgency in her friend's voice barely registered. Aurora didn't understand that Manuela's heart was frozen now. "There is still time."

She didn't need time. She needed to get this over with.

Aurora's words rang in her ears as Manuela's father approached her. She couldn't even resent him, hate him for the way his weaknesses had trapped her. How in the end she'd been the one to pay for his shortcomings.

"I am proud of you, Manuelita," Don Prospero told her as he

wound her arm through his and they began making their way down the aisle. The mostly empty church seemed unbearably sad. Desolate, like the building itself sensed the wretchedness of the occasion.

She'd never truly dreamed of a wedding. It had been one of those fantasies that never quite fit the reality of what she thought was possible for her. But she'd always loved a celebration.

She thought of Cassandra's home, of the friends she gathered there, who had become each other's family. Of Cassandra and Frede and the other couples she'd met, who seemed bonded in a much more lasting, loving way than many of the society marriages she knew. She thought of the women she'd met who had walked away from fates like the one she was throwing herself into. Because she *was* throwing herself away. Allowing her parents' selfishness and Cora's ruthlessness to rob her of hope. She was using their carelessness with her as an excuse to give up on herself. She looked up at her father, searching for even a glimpse of warmth, of sympathy, but she knew there was nothing there to find.

"What is it that you're so proud of, Father?" she asked, feeling fury and resentment surge in her. "Of my docility while you sell me off?" Her father was much too callous to bristle and only offered her one of those paternal smiles people perceived as loving but had only ever been used to manipulate and emotionally truss Manuela up.

"I'm proud of you for accepting your place, your purpose in this world. Look at that so-called duchess. Women who think they can curtail the ways of the world end up becoming heartless bitches." His mouth twisted in repulsion at the idea of a woman aspiring for the same rights he enjoyed. How had Manuela ever thought this man was worth sacrificing herself for? "Women can't ignore the rules of men. You have a function in our family, and you are fulfilling it." The heartlessness of his words managed to chip away at some of the ice around her heart.

Just because the society she'd been born to condemned her for who she was didn't mean she had to live her life as if she deserved their scorn. Cassandra, Frede, Patricia, Celestine—all of them were there as proof that leaving all this hate and judgment behind was not an end but a beginning, and Manuela deserved a life where she could be herself and be loved for it.

She wasn't dead inside. She was in pain, she was heartbroken. But pain meant healing could happen, that her spirit was still fighting to live.

As they made their way down the aisle, her blood pumped hot in her veins, her heart forcefully reminding her that there was life in her, that she still had choices, even if they were incredibly hard ones.

Cora did not want her. Cora had chosen her place in the world she detested over her own happiness. But Manuela didn't have to make the same choice.

The priest asked something of her father, and he answered, nudging her toward Felix, who took her gloved hand in his. He always looked at her like she was a very pretty curiosity in a museum. A rare, exotic artifact to keep on a shelf while he lived his own life however he chose.

"Estas bien?" he inquired, and she nodded numbly. Was she truly going to do this? Her pulse raced, as if her body was trying to make her do what her mind kept talking her out of.

Aurora reached for her then, and Manuela started, then realized her friend was waiting to be handed the posy of white hothouse orchids Manuela had in her hands.

By the time the priest's mouth began to move, Manuela could barely see as her mind reeled with the prospect of what she was about to commit to. Endless days of lonely misery, years and years of pretending.

But could she truly walk away? If she ended this, she would be disgraced. Her parents would almost certainly disown her. She could never return to Venezuela or the Dominican Republic without a shadow cast over her. She would be a pariah. Her name would be tainted, never spoken out loud in the decent homes of Caracas and Santo Domingo.

If she left Felix at the altar, the Manuela who had walked into this church would be dead. But wouldn't this marriage be another kind of death? And she knew she wouldn't be alone. Aurora and Luz would never abandon her. Then there was Cassandra and Claudine. She could live in Montmartre, teach at Pasquale's like he'd offered. She could sell her art. She could be free. Brokenhearted, alone, let down by the one she loved, but free.

She turned to Aurora, who looked miserable in the lavender dress Manuela's mother had insisted she wear. But the moment her eyes landed on her, her friend roused in alertness. Before she could talk herself out of it, Manuela mouthed the words *I can't.*

Felix squeezed her hands, aware something was wrong.

"I can't do this," she whispered to him and then said it louder so the priest could hear. "I can't marry you, Felix." She heard a cry from the pews and assumed her mother had realized what Manuela had done. But when she turned around, she saw Consuelo was facing away from the altar, her fingers pointing at the person who had just burst through the doors of the church.

Manuela heard who was causing her mother's agitation before she saw her.

"Manuela, you can't marry him," Cora shouted, before she began to make her way up the aisle. Manuela began shaking so hard her legs could barely hold her up. But before she could collapse, Aurora was there, whispering in her ear that everything would be all right, offering her an arm to lean on. On her other side was Apollo, who kept his attention focused on Felix, who was now hurrying down the aisle to confront Cora.

"What is the meaning of this?" Felix demanded, while the guests milled around her mother, who had fainted in her pew.

"You can't have her," Cora shouted, standing to her full

height. "She doesn't love you." She was shorter than Felix by a few inches, but somehow she seemed to tower over him.

"I don't care how she feels," Felix countered, finally showing his true colors. "I paid for this wedding, and by God, I will see it happen."

Cora lunged forward, her hands fisted at her sides. Her eyes burning with menace, like she intended to strike him down. The controlled duchess Manuela had gotten to know in the last month was now this unraveled, desperate woman. "You will marry her over my dead body," Cora shot back.

"I beg to differ," Felix retorted coolly. "She cost me a fortune, and I plan to recoup my investment." That was when Manuela had enough. She wasn't a rag doll to be fought over.

"Cora, what are you doing here?" she asked, stepping around Felix, who stared at her with disdain.

She expected to be confronted with defiance, for the Duchess of Sundridge to demand her wishes be listened to. But this Cora was not the imposing duchess who had shown her Paris or the sophisticated lover who had made her body throb with pleasure. This disheveled woman with haunted eyes and trembling hands was as far from any of that as anyone could be.

"He doesn't deserve you," Cora said, taking Manuela's hand.

The words made her angry. Because even now, Cora chose control over simply admitting her feelings. She'd come here not to tell Manuela she loved her but to convince her this was for her own good. This was what it would always be with Cora. Manipulating any situation to make herself appear stronger. Even when she looked utterly done in, when she was making a scene, she was still trying to deflect that her own feelings were involved. The Duchess of Sundridge could never act out of passion—she was only doing her duty.

Manuela was done with duty. She would not sacrifice herself for it, and she would not accept it in place of love. "You don't deserve me either, Duchess." She made sure she held Cora's gaze as she spoke, and she held back nothing. No more hiding her pain behind sultry smiles. Cora had broken her heart, and she would damn well have to see it.

A hand clamped her arm, wrenching her backward.

"I paid for you," Felix seethed. "You will not make a fool out of me."

Cora took a menacing step forward, but Manuela was done being talked about like she was an object, of being treated like one.

"Get your hands off me, Felix," she protested, digging her nails into her would-be groom's wrists, then stomping on his foot hard enough to make the man wail in pain. He lunged at her, his face twisted with fury, but before he could touch her Cora leaped onto his back, screaming like a banshee, all semblance of respectability lost as she tried her best to rip every strand of hair from Felix's scalp.

"Don't you lay your hands on her, cabrón," the duchess yelled, her face screwed with rage as she tugged on the man's head hard enough to tear it clear off his shoulders while Manuela stared slack-jawed.

"Easy there, Your Grace," Apollo bellowed as he struggled to unlatch Cora from Felix. Once he managed that, he made quick work of placing Felix in a headlock. Manuela's mother was still prostrate, and her father was slumped on the pew next to her. The few guests were craning their necks to witness the spectacle.

She might not be able to return to South America at all after this.

"If you don't stop thrashing I'll knock your head against the flagstone," Apollo threatened a whimpering Felix before turning to Manuela. "You need me to do something about her?" He arched an eyebrow toward Cora who looked a proper mess, with her face full of scratches and her chest heaving from leaping onto a man's back like damned spider.

"No," Manu said, with a shake of her head. "I'll talk to her.

"You ruined my wedding," Manuela rebuked Cora, hardening herself at the raw pain etched all over the duchess's face.

"Go in there," Aurora whispered behind her. Her finger pointed toward a door behind the altar. "I will deal with things here."

"Why are you here, Cora?" Manuela demanded the moment she closed the door behind them.

"I couldn't let you go through with it without telling you how I feel." Cora's voice cracked, and Manuela willed herself to not let a few pained words to weaken her resolve.

"Your feelings were stated quite illustriously when you attempted to buy off my parents."

Cora flinched, but to her credit she didn't look away. "I just wanted to get you away from him."

"You wanted your land and a clean exit from our arrangement." This time Cora did turn away, but not before Manuela saw the tears in her eyes.

"I love you." Her voice was so clogged, Manuela barely understood her, but then she said it again, stronger, louder. "I love you. And it terrifies me." The words came out in a rush, but again Cora turned something that should've been glorious into a disappointment. It broke her heart all over again that this woman who did so many kindnesses for others, could not do the same for herself.

"I don't want you to love me in spite of your common sense, Cora. I want you to love me because nothing else in the world could stop you." Each word out of her mouth seeped into Manuela's bones. "I want to be loved because the idea of a life with me is enough to change everything, not something you do against your better judgment." Her voice broke then, and she wished she could conjure the old Manuela, the one who could pretend nothing ever affected her. The one Luz and Aurora thought of as fearless.

"Manuela." Cora's voice was choked with tears, but Manuela moved away. If they touched, she'd falter, and she wasn't done yet.

Manuela could feel the tears streaming down her face, but she was tired of pretending that her parents' neglect and manipulation hadn't wounded her. That no one seeing how alone she felt didn't devastate her. Mostly she was done putting on a brave face for Cora. This woman had wounded her to the heart, and Manuela didn't feel like sparing her that truth.

"You hurt me, Cora." She laughed, a broken, hollow sound, while she looked around the airless dark room they were in. Her dress that had cost a fortune was now streaked with dust. "In a way I should thank you, because loving you has finally taught me there are worse things in life than not having money for pretty dresses. You taught me there is always more to lose."

"Manuela. I will do anything."

It was not easy to resist the yearning in those violet eyes, but she knew if she gave in now, Cora would go back to that life of machinations, secrets, power and greed. Manuela wanted no part of that. If she was to burn down her life to be free, it wouldn't be to allow Cora to drag her back into that mire.

"You don't want me, Cora," Manuela retorted, tiredly. "You just can't stand the idea of Felix having me."

"No," Cora denied the words, head shaking stubbornly. "I love you. Look at me. I made a spectacle of myself." The unsaid *for you* hung in the air between then like venom.

It was right there: the resentment. Cora still holding herself to the rules of a society that barely tolerated her. Of people who saw their love as despicable.

"You know the irony of all this?" Manuela spoke into the miserable silence between them. "It was you who opened my eyes to this. It was knowing you, your world," Manuela continued, even when her voice was barely audible through her tears. "*Loving you* made me see I deserved more than the crumbs I was allowed to have. It's not enough that you don't deny who you are, Cora. I want you to love yourself, and me, enough to be different. To value your own happiness above the validation from people that hate what we are."

"It's not that simple, Manuela," Cora protested, shaking her head again.

"Why can't you walk away?"

"Why do I have to walk away to have you? Men can have it all, why can't we?" Cora demanded. Just weeks ago, Manuela wouldn't have had an answer. Had it not been for the world she'd found through Cora, had she not seen the light, the fearlessness in the eyes of those women she'd met, Manuela would've had nothing to counter with. But she knew now. Cora had shown her.

"Men only have it all by being willing to take from others. To ruin lives, to oppress. For you to have it all, you'd have to do the same. If you continue to lean into the fantasy that you can prove yourself as their equal, you will destroy yourself."

"But how will I protect us? How I will I protect you?" Cora sounded lost, and Manuela wanted more than anything to go to her, but this was much too important to leave anything unsaid.

"I don't need protection from the opinions of morally bankrupt people. Not from the men willing to ravage anything in their path to feed their greed, and not from the women who turn a blind eye to it to protect themselves." Suddenly everything that had always felt so nebulous for Manuela, about her life, her purpose, seemed to come into perfect clarity. "I was going to be one of those women. My mother has been one for so long she can't see she's bartered herself away in the process. But that is not what I want. We don't have to be pawns in this game anymore, Cora."

"I am not a pawn," Cora said bristling, her old defenses coming back to the surface. "I play to win. Always."

"But it is not your game, my love." Manuela was not letting

either one of them escape the truth of what they faced. "The only reason you are allowed to play is because they can use you. Admitting you are their equal would mean having to share their power, and they will never do that," she pushed, expecting Cora to deny her words, but she didn't. She only stood there. "You've told me yourself they only let you in the room because you make them money. Why do you measure yourself against a ruler that was built to strike you down, Corazón?"

"I've spent ten years building this, Manuela. I can't just walk away from it." Tears were streaming down Cora's face now. She'd wondered what the implacable Duchess of Sundridge would look like when she cried. She'd imagined it to be a dignified, muted thing. A single tear rolling down her cheek, a slight reddening of the eyes, but this was soul-wrenching despair. A woman at her breaking point yet still desperately holding on to her old life.

She should've walked away then, left Cora to her misery, but instead she reached for her, clasped her shoulders and kissed her with the full force of her love and her frustration, until they both cried out in pain. A bruising, punishing thing that hurt as much as it breathed life into her. Agony sliced through her chest as her lover's hands clutched the bridal lace of Manuela's dress. Manuela licked into the mouth that she craved more than water. Inhaled the scent of bergamot and sorrow clinging to skin that she'd learned like a treasure map. *Mine. Mine. Mine.*

"I love you. I think I will always love you, but I won't be with you if you can't give up this world that makes you miserable," Manuela said, breathless, misery almost tumbling her to the ground.

"I don't want to lose you," Cora begged, anguish brimming in every word. Manuela sobbed, even as she moved in to bite Cora's bottom lip. She let her hands roam over Cora, shoulders, breasts, hips, and she pressed a palm to that triangle between her thighs that Manuela could draw from memory.

You belong to me. Fight for us, she wanted to say. But instead she kissed Cora again. Held her tight until the other woman whimpered. I love you, she thought, almost more than I love myself.

You are now so deeply etched into the bone and muscle that hold me up, I don't know how I will stand, how I will walk, without you.

She wanted to rage at Cora, at her parents, at Felix, at the men who made this world so wretched, so cruel. So devoid of compassion. A world that made Cora believe the only way to live was to hoard power. To play games that only reaped destruction. But she knew it was useless. She couldn't make Cora close the door on that world. She had to do it herself.

With excruciating effort she made herself pull away and left the room even as Cora's fingers tried to hold on to her.

"Are you all right?" Aurora asked as Manuela stepped out into the hallway. Her friend who never quite understood her but was still there to pick up the pieces. Tears streamed down her face as a strong arm came around her waist. "Where do you want to go, Leona?"

"Anywhere but here."

Twenty-Five

Cora was still standing outside the church, somewhat dazed, and not in the mood for conversation. She recognized the Earl of Darnick, who had been, as far as she could tell, assisting Manuela and her friend Aurora with their departure.

"This was not what I expected when I arrived this morning, but I am pleased to see that South Americans are just as melodramatic on foreign soil as they are in their motherlands." For all the mockery in his tone, she saw the worry in his eyes. The tightness around his mouth as he took in her state, which she could not imagine was any better than the disastrous one she'd started the day in.

"What do you want, Darnick? To ridicule me?" she asked, then made the mistake of looking down at herself, and a hysterical laugh escaped her lips. "I've done that quite well myself, as you can see, and clearly for nothing." She would not cry in front of him, but it was beyond her to appear anything other than wrecked.

"Why don't I take you home?" The gentle tone he used stung worse than if he had continued to mock her. "I used your carriage to send Miss Caceres Galvan's parents home. As you may imagine, they were not quite themselves."

She just stared at him. She didn't care about her carriage. She cared about where Manuela had gone but knew the answer she'd likely get. "I heard him making threats," Cora said, feeling the blood come back to her veins if only enough to battle the man Manuela almost married.

"She and Aurora are going somewhere safe for now. I've made that little shitbag aware of how poorly things will go for him if he goes anywhere near either of them," Apollo assured her, his face tight with fury.

"I need to make sure that man can't touch her." All she'd done was make things worse. "He's going to want his money back, and I won't let him come after her for it. This is all my fault."

"I won't disagree that Felix will likely make himself a nuisance if he's not taken care of swiftly." Apollo gave Cora a funny look but nodded in agreement. "But none of that will be resolved in front of this church."

"I need to settle whatever he thinks he's owed," Cora told him, remembering the man's words at the altar. "It's the least I can do, after what I did today." And the one thing she could do for Manuela. Make sure she could start her future with a clean slate. Cora covered her face with her hands and swallowed her tears.

"It is an unholy mess," Apollo said, then grimaced and quickly added, "No offense intended." He looked like he expected a priest to jump out of the shadows with holy water. "The good news is that we're rich and can at least solve some of the trouble we make for ourselves with our money."

"Manuela doesn't want my money," Cora told him, numb and hollow. "She doesn't want anything from me."

"That was abundantly clear to me when she left without you, Your Grace."

"I don't like you," Cora said, sniffling as she ran the back of her hand under her nose. If Blanchet and the others could see her now.

"I am an acquired taste," Apollo conceded before pointing to a carriage down the road. "I do have a proposition for you," he offered, as he ushered her to the conveyance. "Why don't I take you home, and we can discuss possible ways in which you can at least partially get yourself out of this mess." He threw up his hands when she cut him a look. "Not your romantic troubles. Those you will have to solve yourself, and likely on your knees."

"She's right, about everything," Cora admitted once they were in the carriage, and Apollo had stopped amusing himself with the double entendre. Everything Manuela had said was true. She had opened herself to Cora, unafraid, brave and beautiful, and she'd destroyed her.

"I can't say that I've seen any evidence to the contrary," Apollo confirmed after a moment. The man was a nuisance, but it was almost a comfort to be with someone who had no interest in coddling her.

"What is that you want with me?" Cora finally said.

"I have a solution for your conundrum with the railway," he told her succinctly as Cora reared her head back in surprise.

"What are you talking about?"

Darnick lifted a shoulder, as if they were not discussing a transaction that amounted to millions of francs. "From what I could gather from Doctora Montalban, who is wonderfully loquacious when she is worried, it seems that if you are to walk away into the sunset with the gregarious Miss Caceres Galvan, you will have to begin to reduce your involvement in your many business interests."

"That doesn't explain how you know about my interests in the railway."

The bastard actually lifted his hands in applause. "Very good, Your Grace. Sharp even when you are clearly not at your full capacities."

329

"It's a miracle no one has shot you yet," Cora groused, and the idiot winked at her.

"Who says they haven't?" His humor evaporated in the next second, and his face was all business. "I've known about your railway since you began sniffing around for land in Venezuela and Colombia. I suspected, like the canal, it would go nowhere." He lifted a shoulder at the unfriendly look she sent him. "Given Monsieur de Lesseps's unfortunate departure from my homeland, I find myself wanting a stake in your enterprise."

"This is purely out of self-interest, then."

"Naturally." Cora had never met anyone more shameless. It was so brazen, she almost respected it. "But I am also attempting to garner some good will with Doctora Montalban, and she is very invested in her friend's well-being," he informed her, a little too casually, as he picked a thread off his shirt. "And it seems Miss Caceres Galvan's future happily-ever-after is intimately tied to you."

"She doesn't want anything to do with me. You saw her send me away."

"This self-pity is getting quite tiresome." He had the gall to send her a disapproving look. "I have not heard this much lamentation since the last time I had to endure a dinner at a gentlemen's club." Apollo sighed, as if he found her despair exceedingly irritating. "You're a woman," he explained to her with a roll of his eyes. "I thought these matters were easier to discern for you. For God's sake, it's as if I've come to this continent solely to help aristocrats sort out their love lives."

"*You're* an aristocrat." It would do a world of good for her soul to punch the man in the face, and she would've but for his offer to get her out of one of the many issues she'd have to quickly resolve if she was to get Manuela back.

"A very reluctant one," he muttered, and for a moment Cora saw a glint of something that looked like discomfort. At any other time she would've squirreled that away to pursue at a later moment. But for now Apollo seemed to be one of the few allies she had.

"I assume divesting me of some railway shares won't be your only request today."

"Oh no, I want *all* your shares. And to take the helm in your stead."

At his words, Cora saw it all as it would play out. They would know the reason she stepped down. She might buy herself a few weeks, but eventually the rumors would spread, and soon the rumblings that she could no longer be trusted in a business venture would start. They could tolerate her as long as they never had to think about her personal life, but after this, they had the excuse they needed to close the door on her forever. There would be no triumphant return to London with Alfie. So many years of pulling strings, of brokering little pieces of power, gone in a matter of weeks.

She waited for the despair to set in, the rage, the fury of losing everything she'd worked for. It didn't come. She didn't care. All she wanted was Manuela, happy, safe, with her.

Benedict, I hope you are proud of me, she said in a silent prayer and turned to the Earl of Darnick.

"Half my shares."

Apollo's mouth flattened at her counteroffer, those keen eyes sizing her up. Whoever assumed this man's good humor was an inkling to a lack of intelligence made a grave mistake. Cora held up a hand when he opened his mouth. "Not for me," she told him. The idea coming to her faster than she could relay it to the man. "To put into a trust."

"A trust?" Apollo said, clearly doubting her sincerity.

"For a—" She had to look away from him then, before he saw the tears that were blurring her vision. Even if she had destroyed everything, she could at least make sure this happened. "For a women's collective," she said vaguely. She didn't know the man well enough, and women organizing were not exactly regarded favorably by powerful men. "There is a meeting in the morning to decide on the bonds issue. You should be there." She did feel a bit of satisfaction at the thought of the stuffy gentlemen of the consortium dealing with the Earl of Darnick.

"Now that the news about de Lesseps is out, everyone will want to invest in the railway," Apollo said, approval in his voice.

"Yes." It had been her grand idea. This would be the moment she'd typically make him aware it had been her idea, but suddenly the regard of this man or any of the others seemed to have lost its appeal. When the carriage stopped she opened the door. "I will have my man take you home, my lord. You will have the papers signing over my shares in the morning."

"Will you be at the meeting?"

She shook her head as she descended to the street and looked up at her bedroom window where Manuela's easel was still erected, waiting for her return. "I will not."

"Not a single *I told you so* yet, Aurora. You must be worried," Manuela quipped as her friend helped her out of her now-ruined wedding dress. She knew she was being horrid, lashing out at the one person in Paris who was not judging her. But her misery was absolute.

"If you think I'm falling at your novice attempts at cruelty, you are just confirming what I knew all along," her friend retorted, seemingly unmoved. "Neither you nor Luz Alana have ever listened to a word I've said about what I was put through in medical school." For some reason Aurora's loving rebuke seemed to take the last bit of wind out of her sails, and Manuela artlessly dropped onto a settee, still half-dressed, and began to sob. Aurora let out a long-suffering sigh.

"I really wish Luz Alana was here, because I really am desperately bad at the comforting bits." That was said as she attempted to pull off Manuela's petticoats and remaining layers even with Manuela sitting down. "Just lift up your nalgas, Manuela, por

Dios!" her friend grunted, making quick work of her clothes. Once she was down to her chemise, Aurora quietly passed her a dressing gown, which she seemed to have produced out of thin air.

"You are impressively strong," Manuela sniffled, as she tied the sash of the silk robe and tried not to think of Cora's luxurious collection of them. That way lay madness, and she had much to consider for the next few hours, for the next few days—months, really. How long did it take to completely remake one's life? She recoiled at the mere thought of trying to answer that question in her current state and decided to turn her attention to solving more tenable mysteries.

"Where are we?" Aurora made a face at the question, then busied herself with pouring tea into one of the cups from a tray a maid had brought them earlier. They'd left the church in such a daze that she'd had no clue where the carriage had taken them.

"Apollo's apartment. I can only assume this is where he stashes the women he's sleeping with." Manuela sipped the tea and distracted herself with Aurora's obvious intense feelings about Luz Alana's brother-in-law. They had a view of the Champs-élysées. The apartment wasn't very large, but it was very well-appointed. Aurora was quite resourceful, but finding a luxurious hideout on such short notice was impressive even for her.

"I think he likes you." There was no more effective way to detonate Aurora's temper than to imply there was any kind of romantic entanglement in her life.

"*I* think he's a cabrón who uses a criminal amount of cologne and has an oversize sense of his own importance," Aurora fumed, even as she waved a hand as if the Earl of Darnick were nothing more than a bothersome gnat. "But his incredibly infuriating person is not important right now, you are." Her friend's eyes softened as she took Manuela's hand in hers. "And although I am delirious with happiness that you extracted yourself from the clutches of that insipid buffoon and that you did so in quite a spectacularly public way…" they both cringed at the mention of the debacle at the church "…we need to talk about what you're going to do, Manuela."

"At least I remain consistent in always making a Greek tragedy out of things when a simple *yes* or *no* would do," she joked feebly, then closed her eyes and let herself feel the strength in her friend. She didn't feel strong herself, but maybe she didn't have to. "I need to talk to Felix. He will be furious with me."

"Apollo said he advised—"

"Or threatened," Manuela interjected, to which Aurora nodded in agreement.

"Quite, but in any case, he will not bother you for now, so you can at least get your thoughts in order." For all that Aurora detested Apollo, she seemed to have a lot of trust in him. After a long pause, she added, "The duchess also seemed intent on having words with him."

"Cora has nothing to do with this," Manuela protested, unsettled just by the mention of her name. Aurora, perennially undaunted by her fits of pique, waved the outburst away.

"Manuela, now you are speaking for the sake of it. Cora has everything to do with why you are not currently enjoying a life-depleting wedding breakfast with your so-called guests at Le Café Anglais. She is the reason you could not marry Felix. She is the reason you have finally taken a step to be free of your parents' hold on you," Aurora declared with a very satisfied tone in her voice. Manuela in turn clamped her lips together, knowing any protest would just encourage more ranting. "I can't say I love her methods, or yours, but I appreciate that she was willing to go to extreme measures to tell you how she felt."

It was not as if she wasn't telling the truth. Cora might not be the only reason she stopped the wedding, but she had been the catalyst for everything that led Manuela to this moment.

"*After* she attempted to bribe my parents to break the engagement." Aurora winced at the reminder and without a word stood up from her chair and plucked a decanter of amber liquid from the sideboard. Without asking Manuela if she wanted any, she poured a generous portion into each of their tea cups, before taking a very long sip. Manuela followed her excellent example and drained her own in one gulp. While she coughed, Aurora spoke again.

"This is why I don't toil with emotions," she declared and poured more into Manuela's cup. "Since your parents only associate with gossips, the news of what happened at the wedding will likely spread to every Spanish-speaking person in Paris before sundown."

"This is not making me feel any better."

Aurora threw her hands up in exasperation. "This is why we need Luz Alana. She is much better at coddling than I am." She lifted the cup to her mouth, then thought better of it and picked up a glass of lemonade. "But what I am very good at is stopping the bleeding." That was said pointedly, which meant her friend had devised a plan of attack. "You are in love with Cora. Cora is in love with you. And given both of your willingness to publicly humiliate yourselves for each other, my assumption is that this isn't over."

"It is over," Manuela insisted, serving herself more rum. "It was over when she tried to *buy* me. Not because she wanted me, but because she couldn't stand Felix having me. I'm not a piece of furniture or a painting." Aurora made a face at that, but Manuela knew her friend better than to think she was giving up.

"That was a tactical error, yes, and if it was me I'd put her through an extensive groveling period, but in a way I understand her." That surprised Manuela. Aurora was not one to tolerate high-handedness, which was, of course, one of Cora's biggest defects. "When you have had to make your way among men who pick apart your vulnerabilities, who leverage your own emotions against you, you can become caustic. The constant slights, the constant need to prove yourself, create this instinct to be on the offensive all the time. What she did was not right, but that woman was utterly undone today."

And that was the trouble, wasn't it?

Aurora shook her head, sending Manuela a pitying look. "I've seen her look at you, Leona. You make that woman light up inside." Her friend sighed impatiently at Manuela's frown. "I'm serious. That duchess is the most impassive woman I have seen in my life, but when her eyes are on you, she unlocks. You are far from her punishment. You set her free."

Manuela wished that a little warm ember of hope didn't flutter to life in her chest at her friend's words. There was no question she loved Cora, but she never again wanted to be in a position where she had to depend on someone else for her security. For her to have any future with Cora, she first had to secure one for herself, independently.

"I never thought I'd say this, but you were right about everything." She grinned when Aurora pretended to slide off the couch in shock. "Well, almost everything! You were wrong about my decision to sell the land to Cora." Aurora rolled her eyes but conceded the point with a nod. "It is true that there were likely simpler ways to get into Cora's bed, but the temptation of getting some leverage for once was hard to resist. It also turned out to be what I needed to finally realize that I deserved more than settling for a life that would make me desperately unhappy. That it was wrong and wasteful to throw myself away only to keep my parents, and myself, in luxuries that we were not entitled to."

It was so clear to see it all now. Her grandmother had given her the means to seek her own path, and she'd almost thrown it away. But in the end, it had been the key to her finding a place for herself. Baluarte had opened doors, and now it was her choice to walk through them.

She heard a sniffling next to her and turned around to find her stoic friend's eyes brimming with tears.

"Are you about to cry, Aurora Montalban?" she asked, amused even as her own eyes filled with tears.

"I am most certainly not. It was all that rum," Aurora lied, even as she wiped her eyes. "I loathe that things had to come to this, but I am glad for you. I've always known you were capable of this, of stepping out on your own."

"I think I believe it now too," Manuela said, despite the flutter of unease in her belly. She was scared, but for the first time, every decision she made from now on would be about what served *her* life. Not the whims of others.

"You can stay with me at the Place des Vosges until I go back to Mexico in November," Aurora told her, as if reading her mind. Manu gripped the rough, dry skin of her friend's hands, calloused from the harsh chemicals she used to ensure the safety of her patients. The evidence of dedication, of hard work, etched into her skin. Manuela smiled at her own fingers, which always had a few smudges of paint. Her own palms perennially chapped from dealing with turpentine. It was not the same, of course. Aurora saved lives and Manuela made art and Luz Alana made rum, but each of them found joy and passion in their work. They'd been reared to be ladies, but they had found purpose beyond society's expectations. Manuela could no longer let her life be dictated by others. Not even by the woman who owned her heart.

"Thank you, Leona," she said, grateful but determined to do this on her own. "But if I am going to make a life here in Paris, if I am to have any chance at happiness, I have to begin betting on myself." Despite all that had been broken, saying those words made her hope that new things could be built in their place. She silently wished that somewhere in Paris the woman she adored was also thinking of her own future, and that it included love.

"You don't have to do it alone, and you don't have to do it all at once," Aurora reminded her, and though Manuela already knew that to be true, hearing it from her friend began to repair some of what had been badly broken in the past few days.

"I have to start somewhere," she said, fortified by the thought of making some decisions of her own. Making that deal with Cora had been the first time she'd truly chosen a path for herself. And though it didn't end quite as she would've wished, it had been worth it. "I think selling my wardrobe alone should get me enough coin to get settled somewhere," she suggested.

"Your dresses! Truly, Manuela?" Aurora gasped in real horror, making Manuela laugh.

"I never thought you'd be the one to come to the defense of what you once called my *bloated collection of outrageously priced rags*," Manuela teased.

"I may have been a mite harsh," her friend said in apology, and for some reason Manuela found Aurora's contrition absurdly humorous. They were both laughing heartily when there was a loud knock on the door to the small apartment.

"Who is that?" Manuela clutched the front of her gown, while Aurora stood, suddenly very alert.

"It's the cavalry." She reached for the doorknob, turning it without even asking who it was.

The cavalry? It could not be Luz Alana: she and Evan had sent a telegram that morning saying they'd arrive in Paris the next day, and Antonio had gone to Berlin for the rest of the summer.

She didn't have to wonder for long.

In the next moment all her questions were answered when Cassandra, Pasquale and Claudine strode into the room.

"Ah, querida, we came as soon as we could," Cassandra exclaimed as she entered the room with a basket of what looked like champagne bottles and cheese. Manuela stood in surprise, realizing she was absolutely not dressed for company. "No, don't move," the Brasileira said, gently pushing her back down on the settee. "We are here to ply you with champagne and devise a plan of attack for your new life in Paris."

"Don't worry about anything, chérie. We will take care of everything," Claudine assured her as she bussed Manuela's cheeks.

"I thought you'd be with Cora," she said in a low voice, fighting tears...again. "I thought you'd all be so mad at me for what I did to your friend."

"*You're* our friend too," Pasquale declared, already working on uncorking one of the bottles from Cassandra's basket.

"You are our *dear* friend," Cassandra echoed, handing out coupes to everyone. "And what were you supposed to do? I love Cora like a sister, but she has no sense of theatrical timing. Did she truly burst into the church like an avenging angel?"

Claudine clucked her tongue as if the whole thing was utterly hopeless, then pulled something out of the basket, which had to have a very deep bottom.

"Have some cheese. We will discuss our plan," the older woman declared. In that moment Manuela began counting her blessings to have found friends who not only came to the rescue but who knew there was no problem in life one could not tackle armed with good cheese and champagne.

"Thank you for being here, but—" she said, washing down a delicious bite of Mimolette "—I would like to be clear that I have no intention of patching things up with Cora unless—"

Cassie threw her hand up. "Darling, we are here for *you*. We don't need to discuss my extremely stubborn friend at all, if you prefer."

Despite how furious she'd been with Cora, she immediately felt bad that her friends had come to be with Manuela. She had to be suffering just as much. "She's not alone, is she?" she couldn't help but ask. Cassandra's lips turned up at the question, and she turned to Pasquale with a hand cupping the side of her mouth as if she intended to share a secret. "They are much more well-matched in temperament, no?"

Pasquale's kind face shone with affectionate approval. "They are a perfect match," he said and patted Manuela on one knee while she tried her hardest not to sob. "Don't worry about our dear duchess. Her son and tante are with her." A wave of relief crashed over her at Pasquale's words. Neither of them had to be alone today.

Cassandra pulled a small piece of paper out of her pocket. When she looked up her eyes were cautious. "And I do have something from Corazón." Manuela's own fingers prickled with the urge to snatch it from her. "I will respect your wishes if you don't want to read it, but she asked me to deliver it." Feeling unsure, she looked over at Aurora, who was standing by the door, observing the scene.

Her friend rolled her eyes in exaggerated annoyance. "Please, as if you have the self-control not to read it!"

"All right," Manuela practically yelled, holding out her hand. She opened it with trembling fingers, her eyes ravenously scanning her beloved's neat handwriting. And just from the first two words, she regretted not going somewhere more private to read it.

Manuela,

It was a sorry case indeed that merely seeing the woman's loopy calligraphy was enough to set off butterflies in her stomach.

I have no right to ask you for anything, but I am begging you to give me time. You were right in everything you said.

Her vision blurred, and soon a teardrop stained the paper.

I've lost myself in a quest that no one asked me to embark on, but you have set a trail for me to find my way back. Back to a life with you. I will come to you wherever you decide to go, but I hope that you stay here in this place that I think will allow you to spread those magnificent wings of yours. I pray that I get to see it, my love.

A sob escaped as she read the few lines again and again. When she finished, she folded the tear-stained paper and put it back in her pocket. When she finally looked up, four expectant faces were staring back at her, their eyes bright with questions.

"You are staying in Paris, non?" Claudine asked, eagerly.

Was she staying here? Life would be very different than when she'd arrived. Except that was not quite true. She was still an artist, she still had her friends, friends that today had been more than family to her. More than her own family had ever been, other than her abuela.

The Manuela who made the deal with Cora was so desperate to have one last taste of freedom that she had been willing to exchange the last thing she owned to get it. That Manuela didn't believe she was strong enough to stand on her own. This Manuela knew she could.

"Yes," she told her friends, her oldest one, and the new ones who had come here to hold her up. "I'm staying in Paris."

"Magnifique!" exclaimed Claudine, before immediately launching into making plans. "I have a small apartment in my building that you can take." To Manuela's surprise it was Aurora's eyes who welled with tears, the expression on her face one that said *I told you, you are not alone.*

"I need to find work first." She turned to Cassandra, who was smiling wide across from her. "I'd also like for us to formally begin working on the collective. I believe that we could create something lasting and powerful if we work as a unit."

"The exiled artists of Paris collective," Cassandra declared, her eyes focused on something far away.

"The *working* exiled artists of Paris collective," Manuela amended, then laughed when Aurora made a face. "We can work on the name," she appeased her friend.

"You already have a job," Pasquale reminded her of the invitation he'd made her to be one of his instructors. "I also know there was an offer for your pieces at the exposition." Manuela frowned at that piece of news.

"What?"

"Yes. I heard yours was one of about ten which were of interest to a few heads of state."

Heads of state? "Please don't toy with me, Pasquale," she began, and her friend grinned.

"I promise, I am not joking. I know because four of the pieces are from artists at the academy. I told the broker that you were also one of my instructors. I hope I was not being presumptuous." Again Manuela found herself laughing on what should've been the worst day of her life. Bruised as she was, she knew that someday she would look back on this moment and think of it as one of the greatest in her story. She was full to the brim with gratitude that she was fortunate enough to have choices. She silently vowed to do everything she could to pass forward that blessing to others.

"Thank you," she said to no one in particular, to everyone there. Even to Cora, who had shattered everything but left her enough pieces to build something new.

"We're in Paris, and we drink champagne when we laugh and when we cry," announced Claudine, pulling another bottle from her very large handbag, and soon they were toasting once again. Not exactly the kind of toast she'd envisioned on her wedding night, but it was a fitting way to walk away from a life that had always felt like a cage.

With a trembling hand Manuela lifted her own glass and let the tears for what she'd lost and what she'd gained roll down her face, unashamed. "Tonight we grieve," she told the new friends she'd made and her sister, her Leona, who was by her side. "Tomorrow, I start building a life that is all my own."

Twenty-Six

It took two months. One in which she had decided, among other things, to regretfully retract her decision to donate the funds from Baluarte's sale to the collective and instead use it to settle matters with her parents and Felix. In typical Duchess of Sundridge fashion, Cora sent a message via Cassandra, offering to help with those obligations. Manuela, using her newfound skills in asserting herself, refused, and Cora, in turn, reciprocated by exhibiting her nascent restraint in high-handedness and accepted Manuela's wishes.

The news of the disastrous end to her engagement had quickly spread to nearly every South American family in Paris and the rest of the continent, but in the world where she now lived, that kind of notoriety was not exactly unheard of. Well, that wasn't quite true. Cora stopping her wedding in such dramatic fashion had been quite a scandal—it still was. But her friends had not abandoned her, and she no longer had any use for the opinions of the Doña Amaditas of the world.

The meeting with her parents had been excruciating. Her mother could not forgive her, and her father refused to even see her. Still she felt obliged to at least see them settled. The exorbitant payment she'd extracted from Cora at that fateful luncheon had been enough to repay Felix for the debts he'd settled for her father—not the clothes or the trips, he could swallow that loss—and to set them up with an allowance. They'd been back in Venezuela for over a month, and in that time Manuela had gone about constructing a small but gloriously full existence for herself in Paris.

She'd refused any offers from Cora to assist her financially—even the tertiary ones like when Pasquale suddenly suggested giving her a raise after only working for him a week—and in the end she hadn't needed it. She'd returned most of the trousseau and whatever else she'd purchased for her marriage and sent every cent back to Felix, who the day after the fiasco had boarded a train to London and, from what she heard, took his mistress back with him to Caracas. The dresses she could not return she'd given to Bernadette to sell for her. In the end, between the sale of her paintings—to an American banker, of all people—and the money she got from the sale of the gowns, she'd had enough to set herself up in a small apartment in Cassandra and Frede's neighborhood. Luz Alana and Aurora, despite her protests, had insisted on gifting her the furnishings and all the necessary implements one needed to set up a house.

But it had been not only her Leonas who'd come to her aid. It turned out she'd found a mighty pride in Paris too, and they had shown her again and again she was exactly where she belonged.

"There you are!" Pasquale's happy tenor alerted Manuela to the fact that she was not the last person in the academy.

"Bonsoir," Manuela said happily, as she greeted her employer. "I was just tidying up the studio," she told him, pointing to the couple dozen brushes soaking in a mix of water and vinegar.

"How is the botanical class going?" he asked, taking a seat on one of the artists' stools.

"It's been wonderful," she told him, sincerely. "We're working on creating some samples they can show to book publishers or periodicals. It's very exciting." From that first conversation about implementing classes for artists looking to do commercial work, they'd launched an exciting variety of classes led by Cassandra and Manuela. They now offered four different courses, in botanical, fashion, medical and architectural illustration, but the interest had been so great they planned to open four more for the coming term.

"I knew you'd be a wonderful teacher," he told her, and she felt her face warm. Pasquale had become not only her boss but her mentor. The father figure she'd never had. He was protective—generous with his time and advice. In the moments when she'd felt the weight of her decisions bearing down on her, he reminded her gently, but firmly, that the path to freedom was never easy, but always worth it.

"I received the advance for that commission," she told him, feeling the now familiar flush of pride.

"Ah, très bien, Manu." She grinned at the nickname for her he'd adopted and his clear excitement for her.

"You were the one who found the work. I should be giving you a share." He immediately looked cross, his cheeks bulging in outrage, which made her laugh. She'd been asked to paint four pieces for a new hotel that would be opening the following year. "I said *should*," she pointed out, with a finger in the air, "not that I would. These funds are going toward getting a small space for the collective," she told him, with satisfaction. There had been many moments just like this one in the last two months. Moments of satisfaction in seeing her dedication and passion yielding fruits. This was a new—and not always comfortable—feeling, granting herself permission to feel gratified in her achievements. One of the many things polite young ladies could never do, but lesbians who lived on their own terms certainly did.

She'd discovered a new passion while working with her community of artists and their budding collective, finally understood what it meant to strive with purpose. She had lofty plans, they all did, to secure not only a meeting space but eventually find something large enough to serve as a communal studio for those who could not afford one. They'd even discussed the possibility of hiring solicitors on retainer in the future to help them with contracts as well as brokers to help them procure new work. Their plans were ambitious, and it would take time and effort, but she believed in their talent and their potential. They were a small but mighty group, and every day there was more demand for the work of artists like them. The world was changing, and the women of their collective were actively working to meet the moment.

In truth, her life had gained such meaning that it would be almost perfect, if it wasn't for the glaring hole in her heart Cora had left. Cora, who had sent her that note, and a few others regarding business, but had yet to come see her. She had not set eyes on the duchess since that morning at the church, and there were days when she thought she'd lose her mind with longing, with the need to touch her.

Manuela missed her. She *loved* her.

And she was grateful that Cora had heeded her request for time. She'd needed to find her way in Paris. To stand on her own two feet. So far she'd done it. She wasn't Prospero and Consuelo's daughter, or Felix Kingsley's fiancée, or even Cora Kemp Bristol's lover. She was Manuela Caceres Galvan: artist, teacher, organizer. She was her own person. A woman who had broken with everything in her past and brick by brick erected a new life for herself. That woman would only accept a lover who was strong enough to do the same, but now, two months on, she wondered if Cora had reconsidered what she was willing to give up for Manuela's sake.

"Have you heard from Cora?" she very casually asked Pasquale, as she busied herself with wiping down the table the students used for mixing the paints. She was facing away from her friend, too embarrassed to look him in the eye while she asked. He didn't answer right away or give her the usual, apologetic *not yet*. She tried not to let her imagination get the better of her and start creating scenarios in which he'd come here just to tell her Cora had fallen in love with someone else or decided she wasn't worth the trouble.

There was a rustling behind her, and then he cleared his throat. "I have, actually," he told her, and she turned so fast a pile of palettes tumbled to the ground. He laughed sympathetically, that kind smile she'd learned to trust completely tipping up his lips. "She asked me to give you this." There was an envelope in his hands, and Manuela had to hold on to the table not to join the scattered utensils on the ground.

"What is that?" There was no quieting the anticipation in her voice.

"I have not opened it, chérie," he said chuckling, extending his hand so she'd take it. She sucked in a breath as she reached for the white paper and began to shake when she saw the *CKB* seal stamped on the back. The prudent, respectable thing would probably be to wait until she got home to open it. To read it in private, but Manuela had never been very good at patience.

Princesa,

A sound between a whimper and sob escaped her lips, and a moment later Pasquale was pressing a handkerchief into her hand.

> *I know how hard you've worked the past couple of months to carve a path for yourself in the world, and my deepest hope is that you've left a place for me to walk with you wherever you choose to go from now on.*
> *If you have, if you want to… I will see you soon.*

There was a time and place below her signature.

"That's tonight," Manuela exclaimed, when she looked at the date. Immediately she began to move, and though there was a very tiny voice inside her—which sounded a lot like Aurora—telling her to not run off before she knew what to expect, she could not stop. She was halfway to the door when she remembered Pasquale was there with her. "Pasquale, my apologies—"

He shook his head and came to help her with her coat. "Please," he waved a hand at her, his eyes bright with mirth. "I already have a fiacre waiting for you outside."

"You do?" she asked, surprised. She wondered if he'd known what Cora had been doing and didn't tell her, then decided she was much too happy to care.

"I suspected whatever was in that letter, you'd likely want to go somewhere else after you read it." He winked at her as she buttoned up her coat. "I assume it is good news."

She felt the smile splitting her face. "I think so," she said, with caution. "I hope so. I will tell you in the morning."

It was what her heart wanted, still. Since she'd walked away from the life she'd almost lost herself to, she'd harnessed her strength. For the first time she'd acted as if *her* actions and her desires mattered. But still, in this newfound place where she could make choices, there was only one thing she wanted.

"Pasquale told me an American banker had purchased them," said the woman standing with her back ramrod-straight in the foyer of 82 Boulevard St. Germain. It was torture, but Cora made herself approach slowly, as if she were coming upon a doe in the forest. Her blood rushed all at once to her head, urging her to get close enough to touch. She answered Manuela instead.

"He did," she admitted. "It took some convincing for him to part with them." And an ungodly amount of money. "But I was determined to have these here."

Manuela didn't move or even acknowledge Cora's admission, keeping her attention on the art on the wall for a moment that seemed to stretch out forever. When she turned, her eyes shimmered with emotion. Cora could barely contain herself. This woman could always humble her, remind her she was a mere mortal and there were still things that could bring her to her knees.

"I wonder how your gentlemen's club clientele will feel about my Eurydice." She smiled then. It was easy and slightly impish, and it filled Cora's lungs with oxygen for what felt like the first time in months.

It felt like years, like a lifetime. She had come here to implore, beg, whatever it took. But her negotiation skills were never very sharp when it came to this woman. Cora had spent more hours than she could count conjuring up this face, this body in her mind. Remembering every detail, every inch of Manuela, and yet none of it could hold a candle to what she had in front of her. Her dress, a simple walking suit, was still done in one of those vivid colors Manuela loved. This woman was not the seductive siren from Le Bureau or the brash heiress from that fateful luncheon. There was a certainty in her now, in the way she stood tall, that made Cora's heart thump in her chest.

It's time, Cora, she's here.

It was barely eight in the evening, and like so many other days in the past few months, it felt as though she'd lived a lifetime since she'd woken up that morning. The difference was that today she'd cut the final string tying her to her previous life. It had taken weeks to dissolve her interests. To extricate herself from all the ventures and schemes that over the years had become her fuel. In just a month Manuela had transformed all those things that seemed all-important into hindrances.

The heiress who had made a mockery of the Duchess of Sundridge's so-called achievements, standing silently, waiting for her. Cora, who had always been too bold for her own good, took a step toward her. Her eyes eager for the face, the eyes, the lips, the riot of dark lush hair that had bewitched her since the moment this angel had landed in her arms at Le Bureau.

"There won't be any gentlemen admiring these paintings, not unless you deem it so," she finally said.

"Cora, I can't play these games anymore," Manuela said tiredly, confused. "What say could I possibly have about who comes into your gentleman's club?" She sounded so peevish, but her eyes were wary. Like she thought that Cora had come here to hurt her again. God, what a mess she'd made of everything.

"You would have a say," she began, risking yet another step closer, "because as of this morning this building, along with all my remaining shares in the South American Railways, have been passed to your artists' collective."

Manuela's eyes widened comically, round as saucers, but she didn't say a word. She examined Cora, her eyes darting over her as if looking for clues about what this all meant. The Manuela from before would've exploded in cries of delight, showered Cora with kisses at the gesture, but this one was more careful.

From this close under the light of the chandelier she could see shadows under her lover's eyes. A tightness around her mouth that hadn't been there before. The carefree wild girl was gone, and in its place was a woman who took up space differently. Tempered in the fire of what she'd given up.

"Why would you do that?" she asked at length, fierce brown eyes flashing, not giving Cora an inch. There were no easy smiles forthcoming—every single one would have to be earned with truth and courage.

"Because there is nothing I can think of doing with my life that matters more than spending it with you," she breathed out, not caring that her voice broke. Not caring that her shoulders were not perfectly straight. She watched as Manuela's face softened, her eyes widening with something like tenderness and Cora hoped, prayed it was so.

"But your companies, your work is everything to you," Manuela hedged, cautious, reluctant to believe. Cora remembered the words she'd said the morning of the wedding. What Cora had done to her had taught her to fear. And she saw it now, the wariness. The apprehension. She'd put those shadows there and she would do whatever it took to replace them with light.

"*You* are the most important thing in my life." Manuela inhaled sharply, her eyes glistening with unshed tears. "I know I need to earn your faith in me, my love," her voice trembled, her eyes blurred, but she carried on. "But if you let me—" She took Manuela's hands. Smiled through tears as she rubbed her finger over a smudge of paint on the edge of her glove. Pressed her lips to an open palm. "If you let me, I will love you without fear, in the open air, with my loudest voice, for as long as I live."

"Cora…" Manuela whispered, and the longing in it echoed the one in her own heart. But after a moment, the steel returned to those brown eyes. "You will get bored after three months, and you'll resent me."

She shook her head in denial, needing to make her see that everything had changed. "I have plenty to keep me occupied. It's my priorities that have changed."

The night of the wedding, after she'd broken everything, she'd gone home and begun making a plan with Alfie and Tia Osiris by her side. They had been delighted by the news that she'd finally found a reason to slow down, to shift her priorities to doing things that would make her happy. It turned out that within the web of businesses and investments she'd taken on over the years, she'd amassed a respectable amount of philanthropic interests that she was merely supporting financially but now looked forward to being actively involved in.

Apollo had remained true to his word and had smoothly taken over her interests in the railway, and in a matter of a few telegrams, the construction of the last portion of track-laying was underway. Not one of her associates in the consortium had sent her a message expressing their regrets that she was no longer involved. As Tia Osiris and Manuela had told her, they never cared about her presence, just the money she made for them.

"This building was the last of my business interests to be dissolved. I will be taking over the philanthropic efforts Alfie oversaw, since he is now occupying his place in the House of Lords." Manuela's eyes widened, her fingers tightening around Cora's.

"How is Alfred?"

"Giving all those old windbags in Parliament hell and raising some of his own." That rewarded her with a smile.

"He learned from the best." Cora could not quite tell if it was a compliment or not, but so far she had not been sent packing, and that had to mean something. "I appreciate the help for the collective, but I hope you didn't put any of that money or this building in my name. I do not need it," Manuela admitted, humble and magnificently dignified all at once. "I am faring well enough," she assured Cora.

"I heard you were thriving."

A blush of pink settled on those gorgeous round cheeks, and something that had been wild and restless for weeks settled in Cora, seeing that her princess still bloomed like a flower under her praise. It was just a different kind of validation Manuela was after now.

"I have my work at Pasquale's, where I am compensated well, and I've secured a few commissions that pay handsomely." A rueful smile appeared on her lips. "I won't be ordering gowns at Worth's anytime soon, but I don't exactly have much use for them these days."

Cora recalled the night Manuela told her she'd marry Felix because she liked pretty things and didn't care enough about pride to deny herself those luxuries. That woman was gone now, and the one in her place could probably teach Cora a lesson or two in fortitude.

"Are you truly ready to leave your old life behind, Cora?"

She let the question hang in the air for a moment as she considered what to say. She could confess her love and be done with it. Throw herself to her knees and beg, like she had once before. But that didn't seem enough.

"The first day we met, I came to you with an offer, and you countered with one that changed my life," she said, her voice tight with emotion. "I have a new offer for you."

Manuela let out a long exhale, her eyes still guarded, but her body thawing somewhat. "I don't want balls at pleasure palaces. I don't want baubles," she said still skittish but standing a little closer now. "I let the shine of pretty things smother my own light for too long. I don't want to be anyone's trophy. I won't be the pretty, silly thing on anyone's arm."

Of all the regrets she had with Manuela, allowing her even one second to think that was all she'd been worth to Cora was one of the biggest.

"What you started here with Cassandra and the other women...that's the kind of legacy that matters. You were right about my priorities. I thought that if I leaned into ambition, if I pushed myself into the rooms where women were not allowed, my presence would be enough for these powerful men to recognize that we all belong there. But the truth is that I was selfish. The moment I pushed my way inside, I spent all my energy devising ways to stay, not in helping others get in." She'd been such a fool, blinded by arrogance. "The truth is we win by seeing each other thrive. Settling with the crumbs of the power they're willing to part with is admitting defeat. I want more than crumbs."

"I want to believe this is real. I want you to be really mine." One of Manuela's hands tightened on Cora's back, as she voiced the words Cora wanted more than anything to hear.

"I did bring one more thing to try to convince you," she said, as she pulled the last weapon in her arsenal out of her pocket. For a moment Manuela looked confused, but then she opened the small folder paper, her face scrunched in concentration as she examined it in the low light of the room. Cora held her breath as she waited, wondering if Manuela would be unamused by the gesture, but then a miracle happened. The radiant smile that Cora had desperately missed appeared on Manuela's lips. How could she have lived thirty-five years without this light? How could she ever think even for a moment that she could go back to the shadows?

"This is absolutely terrible, Corazón," her princesa griped as she held the paper in her hands.

"Absolutely horrific," Cora echoed, while hope began to bubble up, small but mighty, in her chest.

"Is this what you brought to win me over?" Manuela was now grinning too wide for there to be any doubt that she was thawing just a bit.

In Manuela's hand was a very poorly hand-drawn picture of two stick figures standing on a giant lily pad, holding hands. One was taller and had very straight black hair falling down her shoulders, the other plumper and shorter, with a riot of curls that floated around her like seafoam.

"Everything I need to be happy is in that picture," Cora said, gasping when she lost her voice.

"Are you going to be content with just me?"

"With just you?" Cora exclaimed, genuinely flabbergasted at the implication that life with Manuela could ever be boring. "You are enough of a handful to keep an army occupied just picking up stray charcoal pieces and getting smudges off the mirrors." That earned her another smile and she was granted a few more inches of closeness.

"I am done measuring my success with a ruler that was made to strike me down." Merely repeating the words Manuela had said to her that morning made her feel lighter, more powerful than she'd ever felt. And she knew she had the woman in front of her to thank for it. "I was waging a pointless war. You forced me to look at myself, to find a purpose beyond this thirst for power. All I ask is that you give me a chance to be by your side as you make the world more beautiful and give those who want to do the same a chance at doing it with dignity." The words felt like a vow, her chest was full, her mind brimming with images of their future. "The only legacy I want to be known for is that of a woman who, when the time came, was brave enough to change the course of her life for love."

Hands pulled her tight, and their lips met, and life shot into Cora forcefully. Her limbs straightening, alive again. She held on as the woman she loved slid back under her skin, filled her to the marrow of her bones. The mingled breath of their kiss rushing through her veins, strong, vital, an undeniable reminder of what she'd almost lost.

"I love you," Cora said, her forehead pressed to Manuela's, and their smiles molded into each other. "I hope someday you can believe it."

"I believe," Manuela said a little breathlessly, as Cora squeezed her tight. "People will talk when they hear the Duchess of Sundridge has gifted a building to her sapphist lover's cause. This place will be crawling with opinionated women in trousers. It will be quite the scandal," she said defiantly, even as she tipped her head to look at the vaulted ceiling and the vast space that now belonged to her. "Will you be able to live with a building attached to you being a hotbed of rabblerousers?"

This Cora could do, she was being tested, and she'd always excelled at those. Especially when the stakes were high.

They'd never been higher than at this moment.

"Only if you let me build a men's entrance in the back of the building," she countered, and watched in wonder as her lover's lips tipped up, just a little vicious, and absolutely perfect.

"Your Grace," she cried out with feigned shock, then bent down to lick into Cora's mouth. "If you continue to talk like this, I might begin to think you are trying to get me caught up in another scandal."

Dios, but she loved this woman. Her mere presence filled her with happiness. "Scandal *is* one of our greatest talents," Cora said, before taking her lover's lush bottom lip between her teeth.

The news of her involvement with Manuela had been the talk of Paris for weeks. It seemed every day there was another more outrageous account of how Cora had stopped the wedding. That she'd turned up at the church with a sword in hand, that she'd shot Felix, that she'd shot the priest.

Her greatest fear had come to pass, the gossip hounds once again had a field day at her expense, but this time she had more important things to worry about than parlors and drawing rooms. No, she would not be receiving invitations to society balls any time soon, but from now on, she'd only be dancing in places her lady was welcome. If her lady would have her.

"You'll have to remind me what our other talents are." Manuela shifted and pressed her heat right into Cora. She took that overture as an invitation and hastily found a place to better reacquaint herself with this treasure in her hands. Within seconds she was sitting on an armchair with Manuela astride on her lap, kissing hungrily, that rump moving like the tide. "Mm, we are still quite good at this one." That low, throaty purr. Cora would spend the rest of her life coaxing it out of this woman at every opportunity.

"I mean to spend a long time going over each one," Cora promised, sliding a hand under Manuela's skirt.

"And then what?" her princess asked, her hands cupping Cora's face before placing a sweet kiss on her mouth. "What happens after that, Corazón?"

"We live happily ever after, princesa," she answered instantly, her heart full of this wild, untamable love, and she believed every word.

★ ★ ★ ★ ★

Author Note

Reader, we are back in Paris, and this time, it's about the party, and the art. In *A Caribbean Heiress* in Paris I focused on the role of commerce and trade at the Exposition Universelle and explored, as much as I could, women's contributions to distilling. For *An Island Princess Starts a Scandal* my goal was to render, to the best of my abilities, life for women artists and Paris's queer community.

Women who loved women had a flourishing queer community during the Belle Époque. Paris was a wild place in 1889—people from almost every corner of the world were present in the city at that time, and many were enjoying themselves in Pigalle and Montmartre. Montmartre, since those days, has come to be known for its artistic scene and the bohemian lifestyle of its residents. There were a few well-known establishments at the time that catered specially to women looking to meet other women. Clubs like Le Rat Mort (which was the inspiration for Le Chat Tordu), Chez Palmyre and Le Souris were widely regarded as bars where women of all walks of life came to find romance. Because sex between women wasn't illegal, they were able to more openly socialize than men (that didn't mean that gay men were sitting at home though…not in the least). Many also lived openly with their partners, and quite a few of these ladies were artists.

Not everything was, of course, champagne and sexcapades.

For example, as noted in the book, women who wanted to wear trousers in Paris could do so only if they obtained an expensive permit from the city (this ordinance was put into place in 1799, after the French Revolution, and remained on the books until 2013). This meant only women of a certain class could have those freedoms, and that went for many other areas of life as well. Then there was also the sometimes-violent backlash from the male population for "the liberties" women did take. The attack on Le Chat Tordu mentioned in the book is based on a real incident that occurred at Chez Palymre in 1892. Still, Paris was in many ways one of the few places where women and people of color could enjoy certain freedoms which were denied to them in most of Europe.

One of my absolute favorite things to discover in my research was how much the art world, the lesbian community and the Exposition Universelle overlapped. From what I could find digging around, almost a dozen women who were openly accouplé to other women presented at the Exposition Universelle. One of them was Rosa Bonheur. Rosa was a self-proclaimed freewoman, wore trousers and was lauded for her majestic depictions of wildlife in her work. Rosa was also a lesbian and lived openly with her partner, the American artist Anna Elizabeth Klumpke.

As far as Latin American history is concerned, there is some of that in the book too. Although Cora's railroad is not real, the debacle around the Panama Canal certainly was. De Lesseps, who was a hero after the construction of the Suez Canal—and was the man who delivered the Statue of Liberty in France's name—died in disgrace due to the failure to build his canal in Panama and an embarrassing embezzlement scandal.

Because it is moi, along the way and as I wrote Manuela's story I discovered another thread: women in exile. The 19th century for many of the countries colonized by Spain, France and Portugal was one of liberation, set off by the most successful slave revolt in history, the Haitian Revolution. Haiti's world-changing example launched decades of struggle for freedom throughout the Americas, which resulted in hundreds of thousands of people having to seek refuge in other countries while theirs were in conflict. Manuela's family was one of those, and in some ways Cora's story is one of exile too.

I wanted to write this series to highlight Latine history and culture. To see us centered and celebrated, but along the way I've discovered so many amazing stories of our people being daring, bold and ferociously brave that make me infinitely proud to be a thread in the tapestry of Latin America, of being an Afro-Caribbean adventurer, of being a Dominican storyteller.

Once again, I am eternally grateful to Jhensen Ortiz, the librarian at the Dominican Studies Institute at the City College of New York, who is a wizard and who I was able to meet in person this time around when I visited the institute to look at some archives containing a wealth of information about Dominicans exiles in Venezuela in the 19th century, among other things. The French National Archives also came in clutch again, with an absolute treasure trove of information about the artists that presented in the Exposition. For those who want to read further, below is a list of some of my sources.

- *Public City/Public Sex: Homosexuality, Prostitution, and Urban Culture in Nineteenth-Century Paris*, Andrew Israel Ross (2019)
- *Homosexuals in the City*, Journal of Homosexuality, Leslie Choquette 41:3-4, 149-167 (2002)
- *Lesbian Decadence: Representation in Art and Literature of Fin de Siecle France*, Nicole G Albert (2016)
- *Beyond the Myth of Lesbian Montmartre: The Case of Chez Palmyre* Leslie Choquette Historical Reflections / Réflexions Historiques, Summer 2016, Vol. 42, No. 2, 75-9 (2016)
- *Livre D'or de L'exposition*, Lucien Huard (1889)

- *Manual* de Historia Dominicana, 16th Edition, Frank Moya Pons (2018)
- *Women Through Women's Eyes: Latin American Women in 19th Century Travel Accounts*, edited by June E Hanher (2005)
- *Juan Pablo Duarte En La Venezuela Del Siglo XIX: Historia y Leyenda*. Santo Domingo República Dominicana: Banco Central de la República Dominicana, Cecilia Ayala Lafée-Wilbert, Wilbert Werner, and Ariany Calles (2014)
- *La Mujer En El Arte Dominicano (1844-2000)*, Santo Domingo Republica Dominicana: Banco Dominicano del Progreso, Jeannette Miller (2005)

A final theme that emerged in this book was that of an artists' union. Historical romance has long highlighted the many women in Europe that fought for labor rights, reproductive justice and suffrage during the 19th century. Latina women were very much doing the same in their part of the world. The French-Peruvian feminist Flora Tristan y Moscoso (who was incidentally Paul Gaugin's grandmother) who I mention in the book wrote the essay that birthed a movement in the French labor classes. Flora was one among many Latina activists of the time. By 1899, when this book is set, women in Mexico, Argentina and other parts of Latin America were staging strikes to demand better work conditions. By the end of the 19th century almost every Latin country had one or more fairly radical feminist periodicals like *La Voz de la Mujer n Argentina*, which was first published in 1896, and like *Femina* in the Dominican Republic, which ran until 1939. But those stories will be for Aurora's book to tell.

Acknowledgments

Getting a book written is its very own endurance test…and this one felt like the biggest one yet for me. It fought me until the very end. I think Manuela and Cora wanted to make sure I did their love story justice.

Writing can be such a lonely job—you are in your head so long and so often, trying to extract the story out of yourself. That solitude is a necessary part of the process, but with this book I was more grateful than ever for my writing community.

Zoraida Cordova, Tracey Livesay and Alexis Daria are the ride or dies every author needs. They managed to keep me writing—and revising—when I was ready to chuck the whole thing into the Long Island Sound. My pal Sarah MacLean who, despite what I put her through for the past year and a half, still picks up the phone when I call her trying to untangle the mess I've made of a manuscript. All truly the absolute greatest support team in all romance.

To my editor Kerri Buckley, who talked me through a million different pivots and remained cool, calm and collected—even with all the extension requests—and as always, stewarded this book for and with me like the pro she is.

My agent Taylor Haggerty, the most steadfast human I have ever met and one I am deeply grateful to have on team.

To my husband and child who dealt with me for the last year as I wrote this love story. They cheered me on a lot, and occasionally came to my office with nourishment when things got real dicey!

To write historical romance, you've got to love the research… but it can get tricky when you don't have much to go by as reference texts. One can go into the weeds very easily trying to render histories, places, people that romance hasn't really allowed in the ballroom before, so to speak. I am eternally grateful to the wonderful, amazing, phenomenal Jhensen Ortiz and Sarah Aponte at the Dominican Studies Institute for the support they've given me as I work on this series.

This book started as a way for me to bring to life the wonderfully vibrant lesbian community of the Paris Belle Époque, and in the process it became much more. It is also a story of exile, of resilient women, and it's a story about the kind of feminist ideals I'd like to see more of in the world. It's a story of Latinas stepping into their power and finding community. I am so grateful I got to write this story.

And as always, this is for my readers, those who come to these pages for resonance, for a mirror.